THE MISSING PROFESSOR

BY ANDREA INSTONE
TRANSLATED BY RACHEL REYNOLDS

THE MISSING PROFESSOR

Originally published independently in Germany under the title "Der Verschwundene Professor," in 2013.

Published in the United States in 2024 by Auguste Crime, an imprint of

Clevo Books
530 Euclid Ave #45
Cleveland, Oh 44115
www.clevobooks.com

©2017 Andrea Instone

English translation copyright ©2024 Clevo Books

All rights reserved. No part of this publication may be reproduced or transmitted in any form or by any means, electronic or mechanical, including photocopy, recording, or any information storage and retrieval system, without permission in writing from the publisher.

Library of Congress Control Number: 2024934454
ISBN: 978-1-68577-013-6
eBook ISBN: 978-1-68577-014-3

Printed in the USA

Translator: Rachel Reynolds
Interior and cover design: Ron Kretsch

First American Edition

AUGUST 1926

Heinrich August Schumacher, professor emeritus of Egyptology at the University of Bonn, continued to pace across his study; he'd already covered several miles that evening. He ran his fingers through his gray mane over and over, highlighting his resemblance to Beethoven. If a stranger had seen him, they might even have mistaken him for Bonn's most famous son, struggling over the final fanfare for his latest symphony.

But Professor Schumacher had other worries. Without even trying, he'd somehow gotten entangled in a dangerous situation. If his conscience would allow it, he'd simply ignore it. Maybe he should truly keep his mouth shut? Would that be enough? Would they leave him alone after that? He'd promised them a thousand times that he wouldn't make even the slightest move. But could these hooligans and thugs trust him? He wasn't even sure he believed it himself. Why had this devil and his hellions singled him out? Him of all people? Someone who'd always been honest and sincere. Someone people considered upright and good. And yet it was him! They'd approached him and then calmly presented a plan in which he'd be playing an important role. They were so sure that he'd go along with it.

No, they wouldn't leave him alone. He was absolutely sure about that. So he was going to see the police first thing in the morning, before their next meeting. He needed his peace and quiet and wanted to resume his research without interruptions and to be in touch with Howard Carter finally. He didn't want to waste time on such intrigues. What had that scumbag said? Forget it, don't even think about it, stay out of his way. Or else!

Was that supposed to be a threat? Ridiculous! Absolutely ridiculous! He, Professor Schumacher, was an expert in his field. His word carried weight, dammit! What could a creep like that do to him? And yet the professor felt uneasy. He kept picturing him— his oily elegance, affected gestures and facial expressions like an actor in a movie. He looked silly, but the other gentleman... Ha!

Gentleman! Crooks! Real crooks, if ever he'd seen one! The way they'd stood guard at the door without taking their eyes off him, their grim mugs...

This new era! It made the professor feel old. Sure, this new world brought hope and freedom. But that didn't change the fact that he was now part of a dying breed: a real gentleman, someone true to their word and honorable. He sighed. He'd made up his mind.

Pull yourself together, ol' boy, finish up your work and write to Emma.

Then he thought of his daughter and smiled. She would be in Bonn soon, visiting him to celebrate her birthday. This whole affair had to be settled by then! The professor sat at his desk littered with papyri, books and pamphlets, statuettes, jewelry, and stone fragments. He opened his diary and jotted down some data on the artifacts that he'd been examining and authenticating for the past few days.

Egypt continued to amaze him, not just its treasures and riches, but its knowledge. It could help shape the future, he thought. The Egyptians were innovative and creative. They had zest for life that found expression in everything they did. The ancient Egyptians, at any rate. It remained to be seen whether the same held true for Egyptians today. The British had recently granted the country a degree of independence. Time would tell in which direction Egypt would head. He was eager to visit the excavation sites and examine what they'd found there. But even more than that: he wanted to pay respect to this country and to witness the dawn of the new kingdom.

If only the Dean would hurry up and approve his trip and the budget for it! He's too old! He's supposed to be in retirement by now and to behave accordingly! Rubbish! What an outrage! Burning with rage, he wrote the Dean what amounted to an epistle in which he made his opinion and his anger clear, listed his demands, and suggested that the man to whom he was writing was an ass.

Now for the letter to Emma. If only this nasty business could be settled...

He jumped to his feet, hurried across the room, and snatched his coat from the hook. The little package that this crook had handed him! He'd absentmindedly tucked it in his pocket when their conversation got tense. Such a piece of evidence spared him from showing up at the police station empty handed. Where was it now? His coat pockets were empty. No, of course it wasn't there! He'd been wearing the dark jacket, not this grey one. Oh well, he was about to go home anyway. He just wanted to finish the letter to Emma and stick it in the porter's box. He wrote quickly, asking about relatives and her health, about what she'd been up to, and promised to send another letter soon in which he'd fill her in on the details of their reunion in October. With a kiss and a greeting, he concluded the letter and sealed it with old-fashioned sealing wax.

On his way out, he dropped the letters in the mailbox, then opened the heavy castle gate and stepped out. He wanted to walk home; the night enveloped him in its pleasant warmth. You couldn't feel even a trace of the humidity from earlier. He turned to the left and was treading lightly for a few yards when he heard hurried footsteps behind him. Before he could even turn around, someone touched his shoulder. Then he felt something soft cover his face and darkness overwhelmed him.

A YOUNG LADY IN CORNWALL

"Emma dear, dear, please stop the plonking! Always Bach!"

"Beethoven, Aunt Sybil, I'm plonking away at Beethoven."

"Bach! Beethoven! It's all the same. Play something merry, if you must." Emma merely sat down at the piano when her aunt rushed into the small parlor.

As she always did whenever this occurred, Emma reacted by removing her hands from the keys. She turned toward Sybil, who had thrown herself onto the chaise longue and was leafing through a magazine with meticulously manicured nails. She then tossed it aside and turned to gaze out the window with a dramatic sigh.

Emma stood up. "I'm going to town. I'm sure my yarn has arrived. Do you need anything, Aunt Sybil?"

"Emma dear, please stop calling me 'aunt' before it slips out in front of other people. Do try to remember that. You probably have too much nonsense floating around in that little head of yours, which is why you keep forgetting."

Just then the thought occurred in that "little head" that her aunt's thoughts were quite a bit simpler than her own.

"But if you do go to town, please pick up copies of *Vogue* and *Tatler* for me."

And as usual, she doesn't have her purse handy, Emma thought.

Indeed, Sybil nonchalantly asked Emma to cover the cost; surely her niece could spare a few shillings. Perhaps she could bring a chocolate—or better yet a small box of chocolates!—to go with them? And could Emma take her letters to the post office too? Sybil would do it herself, but Mother was bound to wake up soon and she was expecting a call from London as well. Oh, the absence of good society out here was appalling, and this place... Before Sybil could get so worked up that she'd require comfort and consolation from her niece, Emma hurried into the hall, grabbing a basket, money, and a key, and as she'd promised, the bundle of letters too and then dashed out of the cottage.

Below her stretched the cove with the small harbor around which Polperro was nestled. Narrow granite houses—some rough and dark, others whitewashed—formed tight lanes that extended from the water high up to the cliff's edge. No breeze was blowing from the sea. August had brought with it sunshine and an oppressive heat rare for Cornwall. Emma was already dreading her later walk back up to the cottage, but this was preferable to listening to Sybil's complaints all day. She descended the steep streets with long strides, stopping now and again to enjoy the view and her freedom.

Polperro's streets were overflowing with summer visitors. Many of them were searching for that one special artist that they could show off in London, thereby adding to their cultural, if not real, capital. And the painters, sculptors, and potters put themselves on display for all to see. They set up their easels on every corner, opened their studios, and pretended to be loners who eschewed money; they lived for art and art alone. Emma wound her way through the crowded alleys, dodging a stick here, an elbow there, all the while wishing she was already back up high on the cliffs in the little garden. Crowds made her uncomfortable, and she breathed a sigh of relief when she reached the dockside shop.

Mrs. Bunbury, a plump middle-aged woman, businesslike and affable, gave her a perfunctory greeting. Busy selling souvenirs as well as haberdashery, candy, magazines, and tobacco, she rarely had time for a chat. Just then she was setting out various shell-covered boxes for an elderly lady and her granddaughter, who were clearly taking great care with their selection. With a smile in Emma's direction, she nodded toward the back of the store where she had packed the yarn in a box. The invoice was pinned to the lid along with a free set of knitting instructions for the latest sweater from Paris.

Remembering Aunt Sybil's whimsical desires, Emma turned to the magazines. She failed to locate a copy of Tatler but found the current issues of Vogue and a London gossip magazine that offered the much-needed information essential to Sybil's hunt for husband number three. Meanwhile, the two other customers in the shop were now busying themselves with choosing an appropriate postcard, while Mrs. Bunbury packed up their shell-covered box. Emma gestured to indicate that she was leaving the money for her purchases on the counter.

She reluctantly left the coolness of the store to once again fight her way through the heat and the people. Halfway home, she remembered her aunt's letters and stopped abruptly. That set off the woman walking behind her, who gave her a shove and some harsh words before pushing past her with one final shake of her head. Emma burned with embarrassment, as she always did after such incidents, so she tried her best to steer clear of everyone else on the sidewalks.

Arriving at the post office, she was pleased to find no one there but the clerk, who glanced up with obvious disinterest. Emma took it as evidence that she was fated to be nothing but a source of trouble to other people. And the letters had, of course, gotten jumbled up with her purchases, which she had to unload one by one onto the counter, much to the clerk's dismay. One ball of yarn promptly rolled off the counter, followed by a second, as the Vogue sailed to the floor. Emma tried frantically to catch them, but as she did so, she brushed against the basket, causing it to topple over and scatter the letters all over the room.

"Oh, pardon me, I ... Oh, I'm sorry. Perhaps if you could hand me the yarn ... Oh, thank you." With her head down, Emma gathered everything up, feeling small and hot. She couldn't help wondering what kind of sight she presented with her cheeks flushing pink beneath her red curls. If only just once she could remain confident and aloof like Aunt Sybil. She had a knack for making everyone feel as though they alone were to blame for her mishaps. How incredible that must be!

As she stood up and brushed her hair out of her eyes, she caught sight of the clerk's hands reaching out to her, though not to help her. The right hand was waiting impatiently for the appropriate amount of postage—"Two shillings, Miss!"—while the left one held out a bundle of letters for her to take: "These just arrived. Take them with you, so Tommy won't have to cycle up to your place."

"Yes, of course, gladly. Thank you and sorry again." Without even glancing at the letters, Emma stuffed them into her basket, wedged the second ball of yarn that was waiting for her at the door on top of them, and fled.

The way home was long and arduous, the heat oppressive, and the basket heavy; it was a more exhausting climb than she had feared an hour ago.

Finally, she stood panting in the garden in front of the cottage, looking for her key. She thought she'd taken it with her, but it was nowhere to be found. Grandmother was hopefully done with her afternoon nap; Lady Milford valued routine, and if anyone interrupted her she looked stricken with disappointment.

Emma hesitated. Instead of knocking, she could go around the house, climb over the little wall into the kitchen garden, and get Ada to open the window over the sink. Not the most convenient way inside, but to escape Grandmother's silent disapproval, she would gladly accept any inconvenience. She was about to sneak through the garden when the front door swung open and Ada let her in. "I was standing upstairs and could see from there that you were out of breath. Come on in. Milady and Miss Sybil are already sitting down to tea."

Flushed with heat, Emma stepped into the living room with the basket still on her arm. Only two of Ada's scones remained on the cake stand. Tomorrow Sybil would stand in front of her mirror and complain about how difficult it was for a woman in her mid-thirties to maintain her slim figure. It would be a lot easier to maintain were she to let others have a bigger share of the afternoon delicacies.

"Emma dear, did you get it all done? I'm craving chocolates and some witty conversation. You brought the magazines?"

"No *Tatler*, I'm afraid, and no chocolates. Mrs. Bunbury was busy, and I didn't want to disturb her."

Sybil's spirits could only be lifted by another scone, which she spread with a generous portion of cream and strawberry jam.

Emma sat down quickly so that she could get at least the last crumbs of the afternoon tea. "Is it alright with you, Grandmother, if I take the last scone? Or would you like it?"

"Go ahead, sweetheart, go ahead. You should eat more as it is. You are so skinny I can see right through you." Lady Milford pulled the basket toward her, held the olive-green yarn up to Emma's face, found it tasteful after scrutinizing it for a moment, and then distributed the letters. "Darling, please make your father understand that he shouldn't address his mail to you with "Fräulein Schumacher." It sounds so German, practically Jewish even. You are my granddaughter here and, as such, should be addressed as Miss Milford. I'm coming to think he does this on purpose."

"I will explain to him again, Grandmother, but he is so absorbed in his work, he forgets. You know he doesn't have a malicious bone in his body." Emma would like to have added that it was rather a lot to ask of her father, especially at his advanced age, to stop addressing his own daughter by her given name. However, quiet and shy by nature, Emma didn't wish to contradict her grandmother, although this silence was becoming harder to maintain with each passing year.

After her mother's death and the subsequent end of the war, Papa had capitulated to his mother-in-law's urging and placed Emma in her care. That way the child could refine her English and receive a good education, and he wouldn't have to worry about not raising her properly. Besides, his research consumed all of his time, and potential trips to Alexandria and Cairo would be out of the question for the delicate creature, whom he didn't want to expose to any dangers following the loss of his wife.

Seven years had passed since Emma had moved into Lady Milford's household, shuttling back and forth between London, Edinburgh, and various coastal towns. Eleven months ago, Sybil had moved in with them. Following the death of her second husband, she had sold their townhouse for a stately sum but was nevertheless reluctant to spend her money. Who knew, after all, if she would be able to find a wealthy husband a third time around? Whether it was due to Sybil's presence or whether Emma, soon to be twenty, had simply had enough of being the child in the household, obstinacy and a growing self-confidence had recently started awakening within her. She had begun to observe people more attentively, more closely, and her judgment wasn't always mild. Her harshest critiques she reserved for her aunt.

Like just now. Emma glanced silently over at her aunt, only to flinch a moment later when Sybil addressed her. "Emma dear, the hem of my blue coat is drooping—you are so handy with a needle. You wouldn't mind mending it, would you?"

"Put it in the sewing basket. Maybe I'll get to it in the morning. Right now, I want to read Papa's letter. You'll excuse me?" Emma slipped the letter into her dress pocket where she found the house key, which made her feel like an idiot again. She poured herself another cup of tea, nodded farewell, and walked down the hall to the kitchen: "Ada, do you have a sandwich or any cookies for me? I'm so hungry."

Ada reached behind her and handed Emma a blue plate with two scones on it. "I figured that would probably happen. That there'd be nothing left for you."

Emma thanked her from the bottom of her heart and rushed upstairs to her bedroom.

In front of a window overlooking the bay, there was an upholstered armchair covered in an English-floral pattern. Emma sat down and enjoyed her snack before opening the envelope. Two sheets dropped out: a larger one folded crosswise and a smaller one showing a pen-and-ink drawing of a Bastet figurine. The feline goddess sat there, calm and collected, her head cocked slightly upward, her eyes attentive and wide. Across the pedestal a row of hieroglyphics, only two or three of which Emma actually recognized. Her father had carefully noted all the details: size, weight, material, condition, and presumed period of creation. In the lower right corner, her father had jotted down a question mark and underlined it twice. Like her father, Emma was fascinated by everything that came from the Old Kingdom on the Nile, and she especially loved Bastet. She joyfully unfolded the letter and read:

August 11, 1926, Bonn am Rhein

My dear Emma,

I hope with all my heart that you are well and enjoying your stay in Polperro. How are your studies going? How is your piano playing? Do you go for walks in the nearby countryside? Cornwall is rich in history and picturesque places. Perhaps you could send me sketches of what you see or, better yet, bring them with you when we see each other again in a few weeks.

Please forgive me for not giving you exact dates and details about connections for your visit in this letter. I am busy with all sorts of big and little matters, which is why—this will not come as a surprise to you—I continue to be at odds with the Dean, who sees no need whatsoever for us as renowned institution to get more involved in Egyptian research. This is astonishing considering that there are sufficient funds available for the mathematicians and the botanists and whoever else hopes for such generosity. They are all linked with each other through their faith in the future, but the past is the only thing that can really teach us anything. Considering their limited technological capabilities, the Egyptians were far ahead of us, but does anyone care about that? Does anyone recognize their significance? Every day, I make a renewed effort to get hold of the Dean. Does he think I don't see him trying to avoid me? But enough of that. I do not want to spoil your vacation with my troubles.

Your Tante Tinni, who sends you her warmest greetings as always, has begun the preparations for your visit. Your bedroom has new curtains, and Tinni has collected some books and magazines for your enjoyment. She is already planning the meals, which are becoming increasingly Provençal in flavor—the affair with the French lieutenant no longer seems so insignificant. He was discharged in January but has decided to stay here a little longer. Your aunt seems to have played a role in this development, although Monsieur Barbier is talking with increasing frequency about wanting to see his Toulouse again. She is not easy to deal with at the moment. Every harmless joke I allow myself sets her off. But at over fifty years old, the two of them cannot be seriously thinking about getting married? I don't mind the old girl having a bit of fun with her Frenchman but beyond that? If you think I am being selfish, you are absolutely right—but as you well know, I would miss her support greatly. Anyway, she left yesterday to visit her friend in Cologne, where she plans to stay for the week. This is merely a spontaneous trip, but just think how much worse it would be for me if she went to France and stayed there forever! Feel free to give me a good scolding when we see each other, and then talk your aunt out of this nonsense.

I will soon have a lot to do, including a new project. Among other things, I am going to have a telephone installed and will be meeting with a young Englishman who is connected to Carter's excavation crew. I am hoping for a lot from this contact and will report back to you. And one more thing! Tomorrow morning, for the first time ever, I will be facing a police inspector in the flesh. I feel like an excited old man, almost as if I were a little boy again and had been allowed to help a boilerman with his work. Now I am old and sometimes even wise, but I am still a child at heart, to whom everything new seems exciting and scary at the same time. Do not worry about this. It is nothing of importance. I just had all this on my mind, and you know how I do not like to waste paper, so I ramble on and on without aim or reason just to satisfy my sense of order.

There is just enough space left here to include my greetings and an affectionate kiss, and to remind you that your Aunt Sybil has always been a most silly person, even when she was a teenager. She will probably never change—do not take her chatter to heart!

Loving greetings from your old Papa,
Heinrich August Schumacher

Emma smiled, although the brevity of the letter disappointed her. Her father usually lost himself in detailed descriptions of hounding his Dean and verbally jousting with the Rector. He would regale her with tales of how he had inundated the booster club with requests, pleas, and reproaches, and describe to her artifacts of extraordinary beauty and rarity. He often trailed off into reminiscences and crafted amusing stories about his sister, to whom he clung with loving affection.

The brevity of this particular letter didn't deter Emma from immediately sitting down at the dressing table to compose a reply. She laid out her paper and fountain pen, and considered what she could report. Her days passed with marked uniformity, especially now that Grandmother was no longer steady on her feet and Sybil could only muster enough energy for dances and outings with her posh acquaintances.

A few months earlier, Emma had enrolled in a stenography school in London. Who knew where the world was headed? And for what something like stenography might one day come in handy? She had explained this all to Grandmother, who though probably a bit taken aback by this explanation, nonetheless generously paid for the course. Apart from the stenography course, in Edinburgh, Emma had helped the vicar's wife with her parish duties. Her life offered nothing more exciting than this, and so she pondered before writing each letter to Papa what she could say that would entertain him. Her hand hovered indecisively over the paper.

Glancing up, she studied her reflection in the mirror. Freckles blossomed on her delicate skin like daisies in a meadow. Her mouth was nicely shaped, though too large. Pale and inconspicuous—that was Emma's opinion of herself. Too thin too. The only feature she regarded with benevolence was her red curls, which she had inherited from her mother. She sighed, took one more look down at the bay and the darkening sky, and set about answering:

August 19, 1926, Polperro, Cornwall

My dear Papa,

I am doing very well and am enjoying the warm weeks here by the sea. I haven't seen much of the area yet, but after receiving your letter, I think I will take some day trips and promise to send you drawings to prove it.

Did I already tell you that I completed my stenography training with distinction? According to Grandmother, looking for a job is out of the question. I waver between disappointment and relief: so many hours for nothing. But the idea of having to apply at a personnel office scares me a lot, so I'm maintaining the status quo for now.

Did I mention that Aunt Sybil is looking for another husband? She may be silly, but she is also striking and has no shortage of suitors, at least in London. Here, on the other hand, the options are limited to staid family men and artists who don't have a shilling to their names. You can imagine her mood. However, there is a vague hope that she will return to London soon, and I will be back to being on my own with Grandmother.

You see I have nothing to report, and so I have a series of questions for you instead:

Have you thought about my suggestion of trying to find some private funders? Even here the newspapers are full of articles about mummies and sphinxes. Surely the interest in Bonn is equally great?

And how did the Dean react? Did you really waylay him during your Sunday afternoon walk? I can imagine you jumping at him from the side, all worked up as you often are, and him leaping in terror into the Rhine rather than talking with you.

And can you really not bring yourself to offer a word of encouragement to Tante Tinni? If she has an admirer who appreciates her, you shouldn't stand in her way. I will certainly scold you in person and do not count on me to talk her out of anything! If things are as serious as you think they are, we will find a new housekeeper for you, and then we will travel together once a year to Toulouse, which rivals Cornwall in terms of beauty and history. You can't object to that.

By the way, your letter didn't include a detailed description of the papyri whose arrival recently excited you so much. I also hope very much that you will write to me quite soon and fill me in on your encounter with that Englishman, although I have no idea why I should support your travel plans when you refuse to take me with you. I might look fragile, but I am not. On the contrary, I am quite tough and tenacious. Desert sand and sun wouldn't bother me much, I assure you. At least not as long as I wrapped several veils around my nose to keep from burning, and yes, I know, by this point, you are banging on the table and shouting loudly that I am simply daydreaming and refuse to acknowledge reality. Let me reply: I have inherited this from you and you alone!

Please write to me again soon, so that the days until October don't feel so long to me. A few short lines would suffice. Please also reconsider my request to stay with you until the new year this time. I am no longer a baby and quite capable of keeping myself busy.

Hugs from your loving daughter,
Emma Charlotte

Post script:
Grandmother has asked me to remind you once more that you should address your letters to me as "Miss Milford"!

In the weeks that followed, Emma surprised Lady Milford and Sybil with her adventurousness. Soon she was bicycling daily along the coast or having Mr. Bunbury take her to Liskeard Station in his milk wagon. As promised, she sketched views for her father and spent evenings coloring them or planning her next excursions. While Grandmother listened with polite interest to Emma's reports, Sybil's mood visibly deteriorated. Although her niece's freckles multiplied and Ada's scones fell to her unchallenged, she missed Emma's willingness to take on everyday chores.

Sybil got nowhere whenever she tried her luck with Ada by waving sagging stockings or torn hems in her direction. Ada had made quite clear that she truly had enough to handle considering the bedrooms, the garden, and the numerous meals that some people consumed. When Ada slammed her mop bucket down on the floor during their final altercation, Sybil fled and decided that the sewing could wait on her London maid. The girl would cost her enough in the coming season as it was, an unavoidable expense if Sybil didn't wish to lose standing in her friends' eyes. And thus, Sybil fired little barbs in Emma's direction morning and evening, which her niece hardly noticed. Sybil was quickly souring on her stay in this wretched fishing village.

Emma, on the other hand, was bubbly and boisterous, and found herself more frequently on the verge of firing back occasional rebuttals. This was the first holiday in which she was feeling an air of confidence and a zest for life. Even if her excursions were minor ones, she felt as if she were traveling the world.

September started off gray and gloomy, and for a week, storms chased each other all over England. Emma thought it was the end of the wonderfully carefree summer days, but summer returned for one last hurrah. Every morning, the fog surrendered to a hazy heat that gave Emma's grandmother migraines.

Instead of leaving Polperro as hoped, Sybil invited a friend for a visit whose London apartment hadn't withstood the recent floods. Sibyl naturally expected Emma to vacate her bedroom and share Ada's maid's quarters, but the girl refused. A victory without spoils, however. After a mere twenty-nine hours and seventeen minutes, it turned out that Sybil and her bosom friend Nancy weren't quite as inseparable as they had thought they were. Sybil's room was too small for the two of them, as was the bed and the closet. The living conditions were unbearable! As if that weren't enough, Nancy lamented at length about her faithless husband, whose affair with a dancer she refused to get over as long as he dared to stay upset about her "perfectly harmless acquaintance" with an actor. Likewise, this heartless person had the gall to berate her tennis instructor. And as for her flirtation in Zermatt ... What could she, a desirable woman, do about all this?

As things would have it, Nancy was also hunting for a new spouse, which alarmed Sybil since her dearest friend was showing too much interest in Sybil's potential suitors. Sybil would have gladly sent the "snake" packing, but then Nancy would have driven back to London and spread all sorts of malicious gossip. And since Nancy, despite her cramped quarters and foul mood, preferred to live with Sybil than in a London emergency shelter, the two friends were stuck with each other, which meant that everyone was forced to suffer.

Due to the explosive atmosphere at the cottage, Emma set off early every morning, defying the fog. Her destination these days was Fowey, where she had met a woman her own age on one of her outings. They had literally run into each other at the harbor. Emma had apologized repeatedly while Daphne had remained cool and taciturn. Their paths would have parted had Emma not stumbled as she left and pulled the other woman down with her. They had both dissolved into laughter. And when they couldn't stop laughing, they had decided to go have tea together.

Emma felt comfortable in Daphne's company, although she couldn't quite figure her out. Despite her coolness, Daphne was intensely attentive; it was as if she were studying Emma in depth. She was interested in Emma's views, in her previous life, and in her family. She asked question after question, wanting to hear everything. On the other hand, Daphne divulged very little about herself. She was spending the summer alone at her family's home. Her father was a fairly well-known actor, although Emma had never heard of him, and Daphne had ambitions to make a name for herself as a writer. Emma suspected Daphne's interest in her lay in her authorial aspirations, but it didn't bother her, and so she spent increasingly longer days with her new acquaintance. Often Daphne would ask questions that began with "What would you do if...?" before diving into stories and dramas about things that took place among the upper crust. Daphne's commentary was always so ironic and compelling that Emma couldn't help but listen with fascination. Whenever Sybil talked about the very same people, she could never suppress a yawn.

When Emma returned home in the evenings, she was usually greeted by a bad mood, empty plates, and an exhausted grandmother. A slight break in the routine came one Thursday when she returned to find another letter from her father.

"Emma, I beg you. You must convince your father to use Miss Milford and not Fräulein Schumacher," Lady Milford declared as she handed Emma the envelope. Even after all these years of Papa forgetting "Miss Milford" and writing "Fräulein Schumacher" instead, Grandmother refused to give up.

Emma noticed the crossed-out address. "The letter was forwarded from London, Grandmother. Why do you think that was?"

After another day of migraines, arguments, and griping, Lady Milford couldn't have cared less. "Your father is not getting any younger, my girl. We old folks cannot concentrate when the noise around us will not stop!"

Grandmother had uttered the last words with an uncharacteristically loud and biting tone, casting a glance under raised eyebrows at Sybil who had just entered the room. Sybil sighed, dropped onto the sofa, and launched into another of her dramatic lamentations. Emma immediately jumped up, wished her relatives a good night, and retreated to her room to read her letter in peace.

Why had Papa sent it to the London address? Well, Grandmother was probably right; he had forgotten. The envelope contained only one half-sheet of paper:

Bonn, August 15, 1926

My beloved daughter,

I hope you are well and that you are being a good granddaughter to your grandmother. I hear it is exceptionally warm in England and especially in London. I presume you are spending your days by the water? Just don't forget your studies! We can see all around us how important an excellent education is nowadays, even for women. Since the Great War, there has been an unfortunate shortage of potential husbands, and thus, you may need to provide for yourself one day.

I myself am well and am dashing off these lines to you in order to sign off for the next few weeks. Do not be surprised if you hear nothing further from me for a while. I am heading off on a lecture trip in a few days to various museums of antiquity, and I am not sure when I will find time to write to you again.

Please give my regards to your beloved grandmother and feel embraced by your father.

Emma turned the letter over three or four times, then reached for the envelope and scanned the inside: no drawing, no picture, nothing. She skimmed the few lines once more. They seemed brusque, almost imperious, and strange. Or was she just imagining it?

She approached her bed and opened the nearby dresser drawer where she kept her sparse correspondence. She took out Papa's last letter and compared the two of them. What on earth had happened? Had Papa finally fallen out completely with the Rector and the Dean? Had there been a fight between him and Tante Tinni? Was his savings that he had worked so hard to set aside during the phase of massive inflation already gone? Or was Papa ill, and had old age and the late nights spent working finally taken their toll?

She shook herself and rubbed her temples. Why was she worrying? What was bothering her? She reread both letters, then picked up a pen and marked the differences, comparing the letters over and over again. Well past midnight, silence reigned in the cottage. She finally put everything aside, telling herself that she was exhausted and that a plausible explanation was bound to present itself in the morning. After a quick wash, she sank into her bed, listening to the sound of the sea drifting softly up through the open window, and finally fell asleep.

Emma probably had dreams filled with dangerous adventures because the next morning when she looked in the mirror, she was greeted by puffy eyes and flush-red cheeks. She splashed icy water on her face until it tingled but still felt exhausted and strangely restless. Papa's letter, of course! She gazed out of the window at the sun beaming down on her. She quickly pulled a simple summer dress over her head and dashed downstairs with the letters, still barefoot. Grandmother usually got up early and today was no exception. Unfortunately, Sybil and Nancy were also seated at the table, their perfectly made-up faces unable to mask their mutual disdain. Only shared malicious amusement could still unite them. Glancing at Emma's feet, Sybil asked if Cinderella had lost both her shoes the night before.

Nancy chuckled, whispering loudly and clearly: "But isn't it delightful how she fits in here, so natural and simple? You should just move here permanently. London is no place for the three of you—an invalid, a Cinderella, and a mature widow."

"A tart is certainly better suited to certain parts of London!" hissed Sybil.

Grandmother looked up and drummed her fingers on the table.

Sybil and Nancy were still seething with jealousy, but their upbringing and convention dictated that they behave. The bosom friends declared an unofficial truce, referred to each other as "dearest" and "best," affirmed that they didn't wish to offend the other, and turned their attention to their breakfasts. Lady Milford sighed with a roll of her eyes and asked her granddaughter to pour her a cup of coffee and sit down beside her.

Emma handed her grandmother the cup, then put both letters in front of her and asked her to read them. Didn't the last one seem strange to her?

No, she could not say that it did, Lady Milford declared.

"You can't tell any difference, Grandmother? Just look, the salutation, the date, and the tone ..."

Grandmother wasn't in a position to judge. She hardly knew Emma's father from the few times they had met, and her German was really not very good. And after all, he was German and therefore—well ...

Lady Milford was at a loss. To this day, she couldn't understand what her daughter had seen in the much older German scholar. She believed that everything Heinrich August Schumacher said and did was the result of his Teutonic nature. For Lady Milford, that was explanation enough.

Emma laughed. "I assure you that Papa isn't some medieval Germanic knight, who rides roughshod over reason."

"My dear Emma, you misunderstand me. I merely meant that he just cannot be measured against the decorum of a British gentleman. And as I told you yesterday, he's not getting any younger either. In his previous letter, he wrote that he has a lot of things to do, and obviously running around like a man possessed. Don't you think he might have overextended himself? It's certainly no less hot in Bonn than it is here, and who knows what the heat may have done to him. Well, now, dear girl, do not look so distraught. Surely, it's nothing bad, and in a few days, you will receive a letter like you usually do. Don't worry. Eat something, will you?"

Emma loved her grandmother. Sometimes, though, she wished her grandmother were more spirited, or at least more curious, and more interested in her. In any case, Lady Milford rarely denied Emma her wishes, which were always reasonable and modest.

Grandmother also secretly often thought that Emma lacked a bit of vim and vigor. Outwardly she resembled Charlotte so much: her face, her unruly curls, her figure. But Charlotte had been very determined, even at an early age. She had proved how truly stubborn and obstinate she could be when she married Heinrich.

And so they both sat, old and young, lost in thought at the breakfast table until Sybil asked what the fuss all was about. Emma was worried about her father? Well, he was a full-grown man, and if Emma had to worry about something, it should be about her complexion, which was on the verge of sinking into a sea of freckles.

For the moment, the friendship between Sybil and Nancy was knitted back together, and they let their wit run wild.

A short time later, Emma lay in the mid-morning sun with a newspaper on her lap which had informed her that this was the hottest September since the turn of the century. She looked at her legs. All of her biking and walking had rounded her calves, and by now she was covering the distance up to the cottage as quickly as the way down.

Emma decided that after lunch—Ada's kitchen was already wafting the scents of freshly baked bread and mint—she would go to Daphne's house and show her Papa's letters, too. If Daphne dismissed her fears as ridiculous and mere speculation, she would wait patiently for her father's next missive. Until then, however, her thoughts wouldn't stop circling incessantly, so she picked up the newspaper again and read from the first page to the last. Half an hour later, she knew that only Sunlight Soap could wash her hair shiny and Persil would make her workload easier. A new film with Lilian Gish would be out soon. The world was hoping for a better future and hailing Germany's entry into the League of Nations but fear of the Russian Soviets was also growing. It also seemed impossible to find good staff, to maintain silk stockings, and to distinguish literature from trash. But matters of neither triviality nor seriousness managed to distract Emma from her unease.

Ada leaned out the window, "Do you want to eat out there or come inside?"

"Has Aunt Sybil gone out?"

"She's sitting at the dining room table, Miss."

"I'd rather stay out here a bit longer. The weather's far too nice to be indoors."

"Certainly, Miss. You just sit tight, and I'll bring you something out here."

Ada appeared a moment later with a tray, which she placed on Emma's lap: two slices of bread along with a little tub of butter, salt and pepper, tomatoes, cheese, cucumbers, and an egg on the side.

A slice of apple pie and mint lemonade were also balanced on the tray. "Today the kitchen stays cold. Miss Sybil and her friend had me hauling and pushing furniture around. And guess what, their bedroom didn't get one bit larger!"

"Oh, Ada. I'm sure we'll be all on our own again soon."

The maid sighed and hurried back into the house. Disappointment was soon reverberating throughout the house. "Dry bread and eggs? Not even real sandwiches? Or a light soup? Ada, we worked hard all morning to improve our cramped conditions, and this is what you serve us?"

By a little after two, Emma was ready to leave. She packed sandwiches, bathing clothes, and the letters before pedaling off. Daphne received her graciously, eyeing her up and down. "What's the matter, my dear? Has something happened?"

"I don't know. It's possible that I'm just imagining things. At least my grandmother thinks so."

Daphne led her through the house and out into the garden where she had spread a cheerful blanket on the lawn and placed cool drinks in the shade. "Go ahead and change so you can work on your tan or on your charming freckles. Champagne? It makes it so much easier to talk."

Daphne filled their glasses with a generous pour. Emma was self-conscious about getting into her bathing suit in front of her friend, but Daphne disrobed and slipped into her suit with such unhurried nonchalance that Emma dared not go inside the house to change. She preferred being embarrassed to appearing prudish.

As they lay on their stomachs side by side, she spread out all the letters she had received from her father over the past few weeks. Daphne read one after another, often laughing out loud and seeming oblivious to Emma's presence unless she needed help reading the German. "Your father writes beautifully, and you seem very close. I understand why you would like to spend more time with him. But why am I reading these?"

"I received another letter yesterday."

"And?"

"Read it."

Daphne skimmed the lines, "Strange. This is his handwriting, isn't it?"

"Yes. What do you think?"

"Why is he so curt? And why doesn't he mention your upcoming visit? Is your father usually inclined to such impromptu ventures? A tour like this would require fairly significant preparations."

A tear trickled down Emma's cheek, followed by another. Something must have happened to Papa. She wished that Daphne had just laughed and dismissed her worries as irrational and hysterical.

"Oh, dear, please don't cry. You really are worried! What do you think happened?"

Emma struggled to put her vague suspicions into words. "It's Papa's handwriting, yes. The paper and envelope are the usual ones too, and he even used his seal. But look at the address—Papa knows I'm in Polperro... And he's never forgotten my birthday. It's a special day for him because—" she faltered, "—it's also the anniversary of my mother's death. Whatever else may be going on, my father is always in Bonn on that day. With me!"

Daphne gave her friend a sympathetic hug. Emma took a breath, glanced up at the sky, and spoke quickly, all in a rush. "It was my twelfth birthday. I was sick for a long time. Mama went out to get ingredients for a 'get well soon' birthday cake. She didn't come back though. It was horrible. For many days we didn't know what had happened, where she was, or if she would return. I was weak, and I remember praying with Aunt Tinni, firmly believing that despite my fears, Mama would come back. Papa, however, gave up hope before I did. He suspected the truth."

Emma gulped as she ran out of words. After all these years, she was still grieving for the cheerful woman who had been her mother. And now she was afraid for her father, although she doubted that this fear was either logical or justified.

Daphne urged her to let the rest of the story go for now and pressed the still-full glass of champagne into her hand. "Drink up, it will do you good."

Emma sipped and grimaced.

Daphne smiled. "What an expression! There is more to life than tea and cookies."

While Emma drank, choked, and spluttered, Daphne turned her attention back to the letters. "You know, I really think there's a secret behind this one," she declared, fanning herself with the last letter. "Let me think... what could it be?" She flipped herself over onto her back and circled her right foot gracefully in the air, her face set in dramatic concentration. Daphne was doing all she could to cheer up her friend.

Emma sat cross-legged in front of her and wondered a little about the waves that seemed to be rippling across the meadow. Could the champagne be to blame? She quickly stuffed a piece of bread in her mouth. Sybil had once mentioned that the only way she could get through the dance-filled nights overflowing with bubbly was by eating a snack every couple of hours. Hmm, Sybil. Why had Sybil come to mind? And how funny Daphne's toes looked—painted red-orange and circling incessantly like fat bumblebees, lots of fat bumblebees. Oh, she was being silly—she really should stick to tea and lemonade from now on.

Emma kept nibbling as she pulled herself together and focused on Daphne, who now sat up.

"This is what I think! Your father is surrounded by all that Egyptian hocus pocus. Couldn't it be that—well, I don't know—there might be some magical device behind all this? Or better yet, a mummy has risen from the dead and, in righteous anger, has made your father his obedient slave. Emma, please don't look so incredulous, and don't you dare laugh at me. Look at what's happening to all the men who found that golden pharaoh. They're dropping like flies, aren't they?"

Emma started to chuckle. "Daphne, you can't be serious? In that case, shouldn't the person who discovered the tomb have been carried off first? Do you think my father has been turned into an unwilling slave to a mummy who has ordered him on a lecture tour?"

"Well, as a fantasy story, it wouldn't be all that bad. Something could be done with it. But for real, what about all those old men at the university? After all, your father doesn't seem to be very diplomatic. Maybe there was a big fight?"

"I thought of that but does that explain his change in behavior toward me?"

"Unlikely. You're right. Your aunt! She must know more about it. Your father couldn't have vanished without taking a single pair of socks. Write to her or send her a telegram, and you might get more information in the next few days."

She hadn't thought of her aunt. Of course, she would know more! "Oh, that's what I'll do!"

They spent the rest of the afternoon swimming and dozing,

indulging in silliness and spooky stories. That night Emma tumbled into her pillows, pleasantly exhausted, and slept deeply until late the following morning.

AN ADVENTURE BEGINS

"I'm really very sorry, but it has to be in German. My aunt doesn't speak English!"

"Just write her a letter, Miss. This is an *English* post office, and you're holding up traffic!"

Emma glanced around. No one else was in the room except for her and the postal clerk. A few caustic remarks floated through her mind, but as usual she held her tongue. It didn't occur to her that had her eyes met those of a more sympathetic person she wouldn't have been so reticent. As it stood, the young woman in front of her had been refusing to help her for the past fifteen minutes, and for every solution Emma offered, she had an excuse. The clerk wouldn't allow Emma to write down the text for her, nor could Emma dictate the words for her to write down herself.

Emma was beginning to wonder whether she might have more success in Liskeard or Fowey and was about to admit defeat, when the door opened and Mrs. Bunbury bustled in, her arms full of parcels and packages.

"Oh, good morning, Miss Milford. Phoebe." While Emma got a smile, the clerk received only a curt nod.

Phoebe remained silent, scowling at the vast number of boxes she carried, then sighed loudly and waved Mrs. Bunbury over as she whipped the telegram form out of sight.

"Well, I don't suppose Miss Milford's finished yet, is she? Is there a problem, Phoebe?"

The clerk groaned and left Emma to describe the incident. However, Mrs. Bunbury's reaction was far from the patriotic outrage Phoebe had expected and Emma had feared. Mrs. Bunbury was furious. Loud and eloquent, she threatened to box the ears of the disgruntled young clerk and to report her to her mother, which made Phoebe move like the wind to fetch another form and write out the telegram—laboriously, but legibly—according to Emma's dictation. Mumbling under her breath, she cursed her fate, and declared that she would spend the rest of the day wondering who had actually lost the war. Them or the bloody Germans?

Emma, grateful and ever polite, helped Mrs. Bunbury sort her parcels. With her perennial offers to post souvenirs to the homes of the tourists who came in her shop, hardly anyone slipped through her fingers with the excuse that their suitcases were too full. After handing over the boxes and cartons to Phoebe, they left the post office together, and Mrs. Bunbury took the opportunity for a few words of stiff encouragement: "Miss Milford, really! You mustn't put up with everything, especially from that lazy hussy. Stand up for yourself. You're a smart girl after all!"

Over the next few days, Emma waited for a response from her aunt. The hours dragged on and on, especially since Daphne had gone up to London for a while. It had turned noticeably cooler and wetter, and Emma was stuck at home for the most part. By now Ada was threatening to quit, Grandmother was losing her patience, and Sybil and Nancy were straining to maintain the vestiges of their sisterly friendship.

The final straw was the visit paid by a young gentleman named George, who tried to persuade Sybil to return to London with him. Ada, Emma, and Lady Milford were all secretly rooting for his success. Nancy, on the other hand, did everything she could to prevent this hopeful outcome. Right under everyone's nose, she flirted with him until, bewildered, he abandoned Sybil, the original object of his desire. It was to Nancy he now turned, praising her as a goddess and imagining himself as her future husband.

And with that, Nancy had achieved her ultimate goal: George on a leash and Sybil throwing a fit. Ada refused to serve anything but dry bread for lunch, as well as dinner. Grandmother—who called Nancy a *hussy*—was considering how to arrange a timely fall off the cliff for her. And Emma? Emma preferred wandering for hours through rain and wind to lingering one second longer than was absolutely necessary in the cottage.

Meanwhile, Polperro was quieting down. The summer visitors were leaving, abandoning the lanes and squares to the locals. The artists shuttered their studios and counted their earnings. Many an artist had made his fortune, whether due to his art or to the infatuation of a patroness with his wildly romantic appearance. Who could say?

As Emma walked past the post office on Monday, Phoebe called out to her with exceeding politeness to inform her that she had just received a telegram from Germany. Did Miss Milford want to take it with her, or should she have Tommy bring it up?

It's amazing what a few clear words can do, Emma thought as she gratefully accepted the message. For a moment, she remained still. Why wasn't she opening the envelope if she believed everything was all right and Tante Tinni's reply would offer reassurance? Of course, everything is just fine, she told herself. She tore open the envelope, pulled out the telegram, and read:

Miss Emma Milford, Seaview/ Polperro – Cornwall / England

Have no idea what is going on—very worried—chaos and work here— will write again when there is news— hugs, Tinni

All Emma's vague fears and anxieties came crashing down on her. Unable to form a clear thought, she ran up the streets and steps, on and on, until she was standing in front of the cottage, panting, her hands pressed into her aching sides. Papa, what had happened to Papa? This one thought filled her mind, blocking out everything else. She pounded on the door, harder, stronger, and more times than was necessary. She continued knocking even after Ada had opened the door. Standing perplexed in front of her, Ada finally seized her hands and turned Emma toward her. "Miss, Miss, listen to me! Emma! What on earth is the matter? Has somebody done something to you? Emma, look at me, please! What's going on?"

Emma threw herself into Ada's arms, gasping and crying and trembling, searching for support. And Ada held her, patted her hair, and murmured that everything would be all right.

Lady Milford descended the staircase. She had assumed that nothing less than wild Mongol hordes were demanding admittance, and was startled to find Emma weeping in Ada's arms. "Emma, dear girl, whatever is the matter? Ada, what has happened, what has she told you? You are so horribly upset, my child."

Somewhat awkwardly she stroked her granddaughter's back and brushed the curls from her damp face. "Dear Emma, come inside, I beg you. Don't stand in the open door. Ada will make you a good cup of tea, won't you, Ada?"

"Certainly, M'lady, there's not much a good cuppa can't fix. If you'll let go of me, Miss, I'll bring you one straight away."

Emma had enough English blood in her veins to trust tea. She let Grandmother guide her to the chaise longue, and wrapped in a blanket, she found herself sipping a strong infusion mere moments later. Lady Milford pulled up a small stool and sat close to Emma, patting her head gently.

It was strange how easy it suddenly was for her to embrace and touch her granddaughter. When Emma had first come to live with her all those years ago, she couldn't look at this quiet, serious girl for long without being overcome with grief for her deceased daughter. It had taken all of Lady Milford's self-discipline to hide her feelings. A lady never lost her composure. That thought had been drilled into her. She'd made sure Emma wanted for nothing, taking the time to read books with her, play games, and follow her progress in school. But except for a kiss on the forehead at dinnertime, there was no tenderness between them. The upbringing of the one and the shyness of the other stood in their way. But now here she was, years later, sitting next to a sobbing Emma, not knowing what might have happened, and it was as natural to her as anything else to hold her beloved granddaughter.

It took a good half hour and two cups of very sweet tea before Emma could tell her grandmother about her fear that something had happened to Papa. As before, Lady Milford believed the girl was unnecessarily stoking her own fears; her granddaughter, despite her reticence, had a colorful imagination which expressed itself in her sketches and drawings. The older woman understood Emma's fears that what had befallen her mother might also occur to her father, but was all this truly based on one single letter? So far, Emma had never been inclined toward hysteria, but how else to account for this dramatic behavior?

All right, so the professor had left without informing his sister or making any arrangements, but was that truly inconceivable? Lady Milford recalled Charlotte once telling her about overcooked dinners and guests left waiting as a result of Heinrich having lost track of time while studying his dusty artifacts. Had Emma really forgotten these incidents? Hadn't her father once gotten off the train in Hanover instead of in Düsseldorf because of being engrossed in an argument with a fellow passenger over an Egyptian princess? And now Heinrich had forgotten his sister, but he had at least notified his daughter ahead of time. Lady Milford thought his behavior was quite plausible. Emma would have liked to have agreed with her, but she couldn't. At this moment, emotions triumphed over reason.

"Look, my child, it's late. I will give you some of my medicine, and then you will sleep everything off peacefully, won't you? I promise you that, in the morning, we will figure something out."

Lady Milford helped her granddaughter up to her feet, and the young woman allowed herself to be led to her room, weak and teary-eyed. She took the medicine indifferently and placidly, and soon fell asleep with Grandmother's cool hand on her forehead.

Her night's rest, however, didn't last long. Around four o'clock in the morning, Lady Milford's voice drowned out an argument that had been raging outside the front door for some time already and had invaded Emma's dreams. "Now that's enough! Why are you bickering out here like two fishmongers' wives? Compose yourselves immediately! Not another word!"

Only with difficulty did Emma find her way out of her restless sleep. Slamming doors, footsteps, and indistinct murmurs from every corner of the cottage confused her. She heaved herself out of bed and rubbing her eyes, stepped into the hallway. The door to Sybil's bedroom was open, light pouring out of it. She peered inside and saw her aunt standing next to a wardrobe trunk amid countless clothes and shoes scattered across the floor, bed, and end table. "Aunt Sybil, what are you doing?"

"Packing! I've got to get out of here, out! I had my suspicions! That low-down hussy! I tell you, London, no—England!—England's not big enough for the both of us!"

"Are you talking about your friend?"

Sybil howled, "My friend? My friend? Ha!"

Lady Milford came in. "Sybil, what in the world are you doing?"

"I will tell you, Mother. I am going on a trip. Today. To Paris or Nice or Wiesbaden, it doesn't matter. But one thing I know for sure! Before that harpy gets divorced, I'll be married again. And she'll still be surveying the options! She can just go ahead and sink her hooks into those little fellows, silly goose that she is. I can easily find a more distinguished, wealthier man!"

"Pull yourself together, Sybil, and watch your language! Such conduct from my daughter!"

"Oh, Mother, we don't live in the Middle Ages anymore; just take a look around for once! And we can't all be sheep, like Emma!" Sybil had started to stuff her suitcase rather haphazardly, and it was already overflowing, although most of her wardrobe was still strewn about the room.

"And what do you intend to do with your friend Nancy, who is downstairs on my sofa?"

"She's perfectly capable of taking care of herself for once!"

"Sybil!"

"Kick her out, set her out on the doorstep, I don't care what you do. Appeal to your higher morals, Mother. You can't very well tolerate an adulteress under your roof, can you?"

Emma had trouble following what was going on. The effects of Grandmother's medicine resembled those of Daphne's champagne.

Over the next few minutes, Sybil provided an embellished version of the tale that George would be spreading around London only a few hours from now. Although neither she nor Nancy had any real interest in the young gentleman, neither could bear to lose his attention to the other. George had been more than flattered by this unusual amount of attention from two such sophisticated ladies. Since he never doubted in the least his superior masculinity, he found the competition over him quite justified, and when Nancy suggested a trip to Torquay to dine in "elegant company" once more, he had agreed enthusiastically, provided that Sybil came along. The latter had no intention of leaving George and Nancy alone anyway. George had imagined himself entering the ballroom with the two beauties on his arms and all the ladies fainting at his feet before the evening was out, while their gentleman companions would be begging him to consider their business propositions and membership in their clubs.

These reveries came to an abrupt end when the two women began accusing each other of deceitful behavior while still at the café. At first, George tried to calm them down with his charm, impersonating a debonair, man of the world. When that failed to have its intended effect, he gave up, and suggested they all go home. But Nancy and Sybil dragged him from one locale to the next, flirting unabashedly with every—literally every—man in sight. When George tried one last time to reconcile the two of them, magnanimously forgiving them for the way they had fallen out because of him, they laughed in his face and called him a "silly monkey" and a "painted rooster."

He then gave them the choice of letting him drive them home immediately or "staying the hell away from him."

After dropping them off in Polperro, he hit the gas and drove off without a word of farewell, while the two women continued their bickering without so much as noticing his departure. And now Sybil was packing her bags in order to continue her hunt for a rich man on the continent, so she could return to London victorious.

"I'm coming with you!" Emma jumped up. "Aunt Sybil, take me with you, please. Bonn isn't far from Wiesbaden, and I really must go there. Please!"

"Emma!"

"Grandmother, please, I have to go to Tante Tinni. I need to be there when Papa comes home. I can't stop wondering what might have happened, and I keep doubting my sanity. I was going to leave for Germany in a few days anyway."

"Emma, I don't understand you. You have become so wrapped up in this fantasy. I don't recognize you like this ..."

"I don't know this me, either. I don't understand it all, but I know I need to go home right away."

"Home, Emma? Home? Isn't your home with me?"

"Oh, Grandmother, of course, and it will stay that way. But Bonn—it's my home, too, and... yes, I beg you. Please."

Sybil stepped between them and pressed a pair of shoes and a jewelry box into Emma's arms, declaring that if no one was going to ask her if she even wanted to drag her niece along, the least the girl could do was make herself useful and help her aunt pack.

"Will you come back, my dear girl?"

Emma threw herself at her grandmother for the first time in both their lives. "Grandmother, I don't know. I've wanted to spend more time in Bonn for so long, and I'd like to travel with Papa someday, I want to help him. I don't know what comes next, but—dear, dear Grandmother—I... I love you very much, and maybe I can come back soon. Please let me go with Aunt Sybil."

Lady Milford nodded and asked for the rest of the discussions to be postponed until breakfast. With that, she withdrew.

After Sybil's suitcase was packed, Emma hurried to her bedroom and packed for herself as well. Then she sat down at her desk and dashed off a few lines to Daphne, explaining her departure and hoping her friend would write to her in Bonn. She handed the letter to Ada and asked her to forward it to Miss du Maurier, Ferryside, Fowey.

Although a light drizzle was falling from a gray sky, no sound penetrated the house. Emma, Sybil, and Grandmother were sitting silently at the breakfast table. Nancy, who had spent the night on the sofa, had left the cottage without saying a word to anyone. Mr. Bunbury carried her off in his milk cart, and Sybil ordered a cab to arrive at ten o'clock to take her and Emma to Liskeard, from where the train for Brighton departed.

Half an hour more and they would be on their way. Emma went up to her bedroom one last time, checked to see if she had forgotten anything, smoothed out her bed, adjusted the stool, and suddenly felt strangely lost. Should she really be leaving? She was almost tempted to cancel the trip when Lady Milford called for her.

Grandmother was perched upright on her bedroom recliner, a small box on her lap. Emma took a seat on the edge of her bed.

"You know I am not as rich a woman as I once was, so I ask you to use this," she handed Emma a checkbook, "carefully and thoughtfully. I have signed the blank checks, and you understand what that means. I know I can depend on you. No, please, don't interrupt me. I don't want you to diminish your savings or forgo necessary expenses. Emma, no, please hold your tongue and listen to me. I know that Sybil, for all her faults and silliness, will see to your safe arrival. But we also know that she will boss you around in exchange for it... You are not her chambermaid. You are her niece, and you should remember that. Furthermore, it might be awkward for you to let her know about this little book. Feel free to let Sybil pay for your trip. She can afford it."

The checkbook still clutched in her hands, Emma vowed not to take advantage of Grandmother's gift. She would only use it in extreme emergencies.

"It saddens me greatly to let you go without knowing when you will return. Please write to me regularly, I beg you."

Emma promised that too. Lady Milford then reached into the little box. She pulled out of it a small, hinged case, about the size of her hand, covered with dark blue velvet, and placed it in Emma's lap. "I have wanted to give this to you for a very long time but had difficulty parting with it. However, our farewell—it feels very... oh, open it, you will understand."

In the velvet box was a silver chain—gossamer-chased, interlocking links punctuated at small intervals by tiny rosebuds. The real treasure, however, was the pendant: a portrait of a child set in silver who resembled Emma herself. The girl must have been about eight or nine, her red curls curling across her forehead and cheeks. The painter had depicted her as curious and alert. "It's Mama, isn't it?"

Lady Milford nodded. Her husband had refused to have their two daughters photographed or even painted—they were just children, as everyone in the world had once been a child, and thus, no reason for the sentimental waste of money. Later, when their daughters reached marital age and were prettier to look at—and photographs were cheaper to acquire—Lord Milford had had them photographed regularly and handed the pictures out generously among his circle of acquaintances. You never knew whether some lord or another might fall in love and a favorable arrangement could be made. For Sybil, this haggling had paid off. Financially, at least.

This particular portrait, however, had been paid for by Lady Milford out of a small inheritance her husband had generously granted her access to, and it meant a great deal to her. In Charlotte, she had found everything she kept in check inside of herself. Charlotte laughed and cried when the mood struck, and no amount of fussing could quiet her. She had been both a tomboy and a cuddly little thing, climbing trees, running across meadows, and sliding across the parquet floor, and Lady Milford had wished a world of adventure for her spitfire daughter. Sybil, on the other hand, the latecomer, had taken after her father.

"I can't accept this, Grandmother. And I'll be back."

Grandmother ignored her, reaching for the piece of jewelry and scrutinizing the portrait. Then she put the necklace around Emma's neck, checked that the clasp was secure, and kissed her granddaughter on the forehead, as had long been her custom.

Sybil called out, "Emma, hurry up! The cab is here!"

"Go on, my girl. I'll stay up here. My daughter won't mind if I don't say goodbye to her in person."

PARIS

In the center of the room, on a pedestal covered with dark red velvet, sat a wooden box. Long, dark, narrow, weathered: a foreign object in the midst of an atmosphere of pomp and splendor. Alphonse Meridot walked toward it. He cared only about the object and not about the undoubtedly prominent and wealthy members of society that surrounded him.

Before he reached the dais, the host, Monsieur Jérôme Alexandre LeDaudet, intercepted him. His spongy face contorted into a smile, he reached for Meridot's right hand, pulled it toward him, and engulfed it in both of his hands. Meridot was eager to slip away from LeDaudet's warm, sweaty palms. "So very glad you could make it, Meridot. In a moment, my staff will serve the caviar, and then we will open the chest. It's going to be spectacular!"

Meridot nodded. He would have gladly expelled everyone from the room, but he smiled, a little pained perhaps, as he glanced around. High society? Was there even one among them with a modicum of intellect and education? Even one who had the slightest interest in the past? Back against one of the columns stood a journalist who regularly published articles on various historical topics. Next to him, a writer who worked in motion pictures. Everyone else seemed to be here to have a good time, to set their nerves on edge, to have a pleasantly creepy experience. Nothing more. He felt disgusted by it all.

On the other hand, LeDaudet was often generous. He would enthusiastically buy antiques, show them off at a soirée, and then donate them to the Louvre or some other museum to great public acclaim. All this helped him to maintain a reputation as a wealthy patron, a connoisseur, and a host of distinction. In Meridot's eyes, he was nothing more than a man lacking in culture or taste.

Half an hour later, LeDaudet positioned himself beside the low dais before calling for silence and attention. The chandelier above him provided the only light in the room; the rest of the hall was in darkness. Whispering and laughing excitedly, the visitors gathered around their host. Meridot pushed his way to the front row and watched every move of the summoned servants, who used two crowbars to pry open the lid. Meridot groaned. On the sides of the box, he could make out faded hieroglyphics. He stood there, helplessly forced to witness the destruction of what was presumably an ancient archaeological find in order to secure further donations for the Louvre.

The lid crashed to the floor, breaking into three pieces. Dust and a musty smell rose into the air. The audience murmured and pressed closer. The assistants pried off the front side of the sarcophagus, and a collective sigh echoed through the room. A figure, wrapped in yellowed strips of linen, a gold amulet edged with turquoise around its neck, lay before their eyes.

LeDaudet laughed, called once more for silence, and asked the audience for a wager: What might be revealed beneath the layers of yellowed cloth? A man or a woman? He rubbed his hands together, urging the crowd on. Meridot wished he could make him stop speaking. Where was the respect for the dead? He kept silent but clenched his hands into fists.

Within minutes, piles of banknotes rested beside the coffin, the host himself acting as bookie. The crowd pushed even closer. An assistant took a narrow knife and cut the bandages with marked indifference. The audience gasped, urging him to work faster, faster. Both assistants now tugged the cloth covering aside with rough fingers. Dust, scraps of cloth, and possibly human skin tumbled across the dais. A few women cringed theatrically, giggling fatuously, while several men cracked crude jokes or took the opportunity to draw a nearby lady closer to their sides.

A dark, withered body lay before them.

"I won, it's a man!" someone shouted from the front row. Someone else shot back that it was more likely a dwarf, otherwise he would have had more to offer. Everyone laughed. "Just look at that hair. Magnificent, that shine!"

Meridot waited until the excitement subsided, and everyone returned to their tables spilling over with food and spirits. He then strode over to the dead man, crossed himself, and bent over him. That hair: too full, too shiny, too nicely groomed. He glanced around; no one was watching. The highlight of the evening was already long forgotten. He whispered an apology to the dead man, then ran his fingers lightly across the body, on top of the head, and through the hair. He hoped his search would be in vain, but then he felt something. A small hole right above the ear. Meridot continued his search on the opposite side of the head. A second hole of the same size.

The coffin and the amulet might have been ancient, but the mummy definitely was not.

September 28, 1926, Montmartre

Dear Daphne,

I have been sitting here in Paris for three days now. Aunt Sybil insisted on making a stop here because she knows so many people here and she wants to have a little fun before getting down to work. Do you know what she means by that? She is traveling to Wiesbaden, where the fashionable crowd gathers around the gaming tables, and it is there that she plans to catch a suitable husband. That is her work! I am naive, of course, but why should she get married if she expects neither fun nor joy from marriage? Yes, yes, the financial support, but my aunt is wealthy and has very little good to say about her first two husbands.

I walk the streets during the day, visit the markets, work on my French, and try very hard to enjoy it. Tomorrow afternoon, we will take the night train to Cologne and will reach our destination Friday morning, and from there we will take a car home to Bonn. I hope very much that Papa will be there and that all my worries will turn out to be silly and blown out of proportion.

But what is going on with you? How was London? Have you started your novel? Sorry I'm such a lousy letter writer. My mind seems to be everywhere at once: sometimes here, sometimes there. By the way, Parisian women really are as elegant as Sybil's magazines say they are. Have you noticed how the skirts are getting longer again? Sybil rushed into one of the ateliers as soon as we arrived, just to be à la mode. She gave me three of her older dresses, one in a wonderful sage green that she said made her look too pale but which would probably suit me just fine. And I love it! It flows and flutters around me so lightly that I always feel like jumping around in it, which isn't very ladylike of course. Dear Daphne, as you can see, I'm just writing nonsense at this point; blame it on my restlessness. As soon as I get to Bonn, I'll write again.

Affectionately yours,
Emma

BACK IN BONN

"Just as you'd expect. In Bonn, it's either raining, or the crossing arms are down."

With that, the driver bid farewell to Emma and Sybil after unloading their suitcases, bags and boxes, and depositing them at the top of the steps beside the front door of Arndtstraße 13a. The two women couldn't see from here whether the railroad gates had been lowered, but it was raining, steady and heavy. And now, despite all their knocking and ringing, the front door remained unanswered.

"Emma dear, I asked you to notify them of our arrival. Why isn't anyone here? One second longer in this deluge, and my shoes will be ruined."

Emma was silent. She had sent a telegram from Paris, and as for Aunt Sybil's shoes, what sensible woman wore silk shoes on a day like this? Emma sighed, as she had done with some frequency on this trip, and knocked again, more vigorously this time. No response. She leaned down to the mailbox, lifted the flap and tried to peer inside but saw only darkness. From the brim of her hat, raindrops dribbled incessantly down her neck as puddles formed in her shoes. Each step she took made a gurgling sound, and her hands were freezing. She could hardly blame Sybil for being in a foul mood.

Emma looked up and down Arndtstraße, wondering if any of the neighbors she had once known were still around. Most had been either pensioners or the widows of privy councilors—all had been of an advanced age. There was Fräulein von Veith from across the street and the professors in the houses to the left and right, that Papa met sometimes for a glass of wine or to play chess. Oh, they really should have asked the taxicab to wait! Then they could have been sitting in one of Bonn's many coffee houses right now instead of soaking up the rain.

Sybil shifted from one foot to the other, holding a hatbox over her head and shooting Emma glowering looks.

"Is that Fräulein Schumacher? What are you doing standing there in the rain?"

"Herr Bachmann, how are you? Do you know where my aunt is?"
"Oh, that I don't know, but why don't you come into my house?"

Two minutes later, Sybil and Emma were sitting in Herr Bachmann's parlor while he, armed with several umbrellas, ran to 13a to prop them over the suitcases to prevent them from getting too wet.

The maid was bringing in several towels when he returned. "These are the finest towels there are. We have just started offering them in the store, and if you ever want to come by..."

After that, there was silence. Emma overcame her shyness and inquired about Herr Bachmann's health and his business—the two were inseparable—and then asked when he had last seen her father and her aunt.

Well, he couldn't say exactly when he had last seen the professor hurrying through the streets. It must have been a few weeks ago, but he had just chatted with Fräulein Feuerhahn yesterday.

Again, everyone fell silent, which Emma found fairly unpleasant, though she kept that to herself. Sybil, on the other hand, had no problem displaying the full extent of her annoyance. Herr Bachmann was leaning forward in his chair, studying the foreign lady from her delicate ankles all the way up to her haughty face, obviously enjoying himself immensely.

The doorbell rang. Emma first heard the girl open the door and then Tante Tinni asking if her niece had sought shelter here.

Emma jumped right up and ran to meet her aunt. "Yes, yes, here we are, Tante Tinni! Herr Bachmann was very kind to rescue us, and—oh, I'm so glad to see you at last!"

Despite how reserved Emma was toward Lady Milford, she kissed and hugged the small, round-faced woman in front of her as naturally as could be. Her aunt returned the kisses and hugs warmly, and then turned to Sybil and Herr Bachmann, who had trailed Emma into the hallway. Tinni thanked Herr Bachmann for his hospitality and extended her hand to Sybil, declaring they would say their proper hellos in just a moment.

Back at 13a, the three women hauled the luggage into the foyer. "Take up only what you need right now. Jean can carry the rest of the bags upstairs tonight. Mrs. Mallaby, you may have your sister's room. Will you be staying longer with us in Bonn?"

Even though Sybil's German was quite good, Tante Tinni had switched from her Rhenish singsong into French, which suited her understanding of fairness. She herself didn't speak English, and if Sybil was forced to speak a foreign language, she could do the same.

Sybil was astonished. This Fräulein Feuerhahn had struck her as a rather simple woman with no pretensions to elegance, but her French was flawless. "Thank you, Mademoiselle Feuerhahn. I think I shall stay for a few days, if that is all right with you. Bonn seems like it must be a beautiful city, if the rain would just stop."

"Bonn is indeed, Mrs. Mallaby."

Emma giggled.

The two older women looked at her in astonishment.

"You are both my aunts. Aren't you being just a little too formal with each other?"

"Emma dear, Mademoiselle Feuerhahn may call me Sybil, of course. As my elder, she should decide how we address each other."

"I don't want that to be up to me. I'm Christel."

"So why does Emma call you Tinni?"

"Oh, when she was little, she couldn't pronounce my name. Heinrich and your sister Charlotte thought it was cute, and so now I'm just Aunt Tinni."

"Charming. Well, do you suppose there's any chance of a hot bath, dear Christel?"

"Emma, show Sybil the bathroom. Remember to kick the boiler, or it won't heat. And you should rest for a while before we talk. You must be hungry. Lunch will be in an hour."

And before Emma could delay Tante Tinni any longer, she disappeared into the kitchen, where the clattering of pots and oven doors could be heard. It wasn't long before Emma heard Sybil warbling the latest popular songs from the bathroom. She was probably planning a longer stay in Bonn to make up for the travel expenses she had covered for Emma. Well, she could do that. Aunt Sybil had been quite generous during the trip.

Although lunch—fried potatoes and eggs with a salad—was more rustic than luxurious in Sybil's opinion, she enjoyed seconds and showered her hostess with compliments, which the cook accepted with satisfaction. Christel loved to cook and was proud of her talent to turn the simplest meal into a delicacy. Unfortunately, her brother took her cooking for granted and rarely praised it. To make up for that, whenever they ate out, the professor delighted in griping about the chef's lumpy sauces, mushy potatoes, and bland desserts.

He would wrap up his tirades by informing the waiter that he was used to better culinary creations. And Christel Feuerhahn had been content with that, until Jean-Baptiste Barbier entered her life and her kitchen. His expert compliments, along with his brown eyes, contributed more than a little to his success when he set about convincing this Rhenish woman of the advisability of marrying a Toulouse innkeeper. It was Jean-Baptiste, too, who was now sitting between Emma and Christel, spouting good humor, inspiring even Sybil into a fit of laughter lasting several seconds.

Emma watched him and Tante Tinni. She didn't understand much about these kinds of matters, but she could tell that they were sincerely very fond of each other, and she realized that her aunt would probably leave Bonn at some point in the next year. *Papa will be so sad*, she thought.

Papa. The jolly mood at the lunch table had almost made her forget her concerns about him. After all, she had come here because of him! "Tante Tinni, don't you think it's time that we talk?" she asked.

Her aunt and Jean-Baptiste exchanged a glance, then invited her into the professor's study.

Heinrich August Schumacher's private study hadn't always been so private; this was where he had held seminars for his students, and even today the room was home to two worn sofas and several armchairs. Emma recalled the hustle and bustle of the students, and Papa's thunderous voice calling on them to quiet down. Dark bookshelves crammed to bursting reached the ceiling, giving way only to the hallway door and the glazed double doors to the garden. A long table, one end of which the professor used as a desk, stood in front of these French doors, and was covered in periodicals, books, correspondence, and small artifacts, in addition to drawings and all kinds of pens.

"Where is Papa? Have you heard from him?"

"I don't know, Emma. And yes, he's been in touch."

"Oh, thank goodness! How is he? What is he doing, when will he be back?"

"I don't know. It's strange. Look." Tante Tinni opened one of the table drawers and handed Emma four cards. "I've received these over the past few weeks."

Emma found herself holding ordinary postcards, the kind vacationers send to their loved ones back home: views of the town on the front, and just enough space on the back to jot down some trivial greeting. Two cards had come from Koblenz and one each from Frankfurt and Mainz, sent at five- or six-day intervals. The last one had been sent the previous weekend. This was all simply too peculiar. Papa didn't even like postcards. He always called them commonplace, and everywhere he went he took the time to write actual letters.

There was no salutation—only the message that he was well, that the lectures well received, and then a terse farewell. The cards themselves hardly differed one from the other. No mention of next stops, no witty commentaries, no greetings to his daughter.

"Wait a minute, Tante Tinni!" Emma ran up to her room, grabbed her bag, and within a minute was sitting next to Tinni on the sofa. She handed the letters she had received to her aunt. "Read them, please. Does this sound like Papa? Has he changed lately?"

Christel read, sniffing loudly from time to time—probably annoyed at some of the lines pertaining to herself and Jean-Baptiste. Then, she put the letters aside, but paused before speaking. "Has he been different lately? Well, your father seemed more forgetful than usual, and he was losing his temper more quickly about all sorts of things. There was all that fuss at the university, of course. And occasionally one of the students was tardy, which got him really angry. He would accuse them of taking advantage of his good nature and shout that he would no longer help the lazy lot of them with their studies. After all, they had their regular professors for that. He could really work himself up into a serious fit of rage these past few weeks. The other day, he made a scene with the mailman because some package had gone missing. It turned out later that it hadn't even been sent yet. He was a bit distracted and unfocused, but just up and going without leaving me a message—no, Emma, I can't believe that. And he didn't pack anything—not a single thing. Heinrich didn't even take his toothbrush."

"Grandmother thought that maybe he was just getting old."

"He hasn't gotten any younger, that's for sure, but—well, in a nutshell, I'm worried. And that's why I went to the police station a few days ago and..."

"Yes, and? What's happening now?"

"Nothing at all! I was informed that your father is a grown man who doesn't have to let his womenfolk walk all over him, and I should be glad that he contacts me at all. That's what the officer told me! If Jean hadn't dragged me out right then, I would have slapped him, let me tell you!"

"Then you'd be behind bars."

"It would have been worth it!"

Despite her worry, Emma had to laugh. How much she had missed this aunt and her Rhenish singsong dialect! But what should they do now? Papa was out there somewhere without a suitcase, without a forwarding address, sending kitschy postcards instead of his wonderful letters.

Tante Tinni admitted that although she was concerned, she hadn't done anything except go to the police station. She had been visiting Amelie in Cologne for a few days, and when she'd returned, half the world had descended on her, so she hadn't had the time or energy to devote much thought to her absent brother's whereabouts. Gas and water fitters had been in and out of the house at all hours, in addition to someone who insisted that he was there to connect a telephone to the house—something she had known nothing about. When all was said and done, she had been allowed to clean up the mess they'd made, wasn't that nice? Then there were all the boys whom Heinrich helped with their studies. They dropped by every few days, asking for him in increasing desperation. And the Berlin publisher had also been calling—yes, Heinrich had wanted to write a book about the Egyptian pantheon—and the devil knew who else had wanted to talk to him. Inquiries kept coming in from the university. Where was this or that book? Otherwise, they were probably pleased to finally be left in peace by Heinrich. Last but not least, Christel confessed that she had been out with Monsieur Barbier with some frequency. And that was how five weeks had sped by since the disappearance of Heinrich August Schumacher.

"So let's think this through: Papa took no clothes, no bag, nothing at all. Did he at least take some money with him?"

"He always has his wallet and checkbook with him," Christel explained.

"We should check with the bank to see if he has cashed any checks."

"And what would that tell us? Remember, your father always carries a large amount of cash on him. He isn't dependent on his checks."

"So he could have just left spontaneously, and bought himself suitcases and clothes in Koblenz... But someone must have put the lecture trip together for him, right? The train tickets, lodging, food, and drink. Papa couldn't have gone to the university one morning and left that evening without having planned everything. Maybe we can find a letter with the invitation and dates? Have you looked through his records?"

Tante Tinni gestured at the cluttered table and messy shelves, and asked her niece if she was serious. "Does this look like I'm allowed to touch anything in here? And what am I supposed to find in this mess?"

Emma pondered this. She knew enough about Egypt to organize things in here: drawings on the left, correspondence on the right, pens in the drawer, books on the shelf, Old Kingdom on the top, New Kingdom on the bottom. Surely, she would be able to find something in all this to explain Papa's absence.

She sorted through his things until late in the night. From time to time, Tante Tinni and Jean-Baptiste appeared in the study to hand her a piece of cake and later a vegetable tart. Emma was so absorbed, however, that she hardly registered what she was eating. After several hours, everything around her was in good order, but nothing had turned up to help her. An empty photo album had fallen into her hands along with a box of old pictures. She lovingly pasted photographs into the album that were mostly of her mother, though some were of Emma too. Papa's sketches now sat in a large stack. Many were of the same Bastet statuette that had appeared in the drawing she had received in his next-to-last letter. The drawings showed the figure from all sides. What was missing, though, was the object itself. To all the other prints she had been able to assign either the artifacts themselves or notes about the object's current location. But Papa had failed to mention the Bastet in any of his notes.

There was his office at the university, though, which he had refused to give up after his retirement. It was a tiny room, but nobody would grant him regular access to a lecture hall. He had argued that he would need to use his private home for his seminars, and the Rector had agreed to the arrangement in the hope that this would keep him quiet, a hope that had never been fulfilled. Well, Emma would take care of the other office tomorrow. Now she wanted nothing more than sleep.

Every morning, at 10:15 a.m. on the dot, Anton Wagenknecht stepped into the porter's room, poured himself a malt coffee, and ate his breakfast while making plans for the evening. He was a strikingly handsome young man, who had managed to graduate from high school more by luck than effort. And whatever effort was involved came from other people, that is, from his father, a Cologne merchant with political ambitions who expected just two things from his only son: to do great things and to stay far away.

Anton didn't trouble himself overly much with his old man's expectations. He had, nonetheless, done him the favor of hanging around Bonn instead of Cologne, which his father supported with periodic gifts of money. Now and again the merchant would urge Anton to achieve great things. But most of the time, he merely wished that his son would finally settle on a field of study and stick to it. Far from sticking to any one course of study, Anton had worked his way through various majors. In the end, he learned that he cared more about enjoying the company of his fellow students than he did about his professors' lectures. And that was why instead of relying on his father's generosity, he was now stuck with the porter, working as his errand boy and assistant. Nonetheless, Anton trusted in his father's money, assuming that fate would smile on him, and hand him a well-paid job when the time came.

He had just devoured his cheese sandwich when he heard a knock at the door. The knock caught him off guard. Most people dispensed with such formalities and simply rushed inside. Thus when he opened the door to a young woman that he'd never seen before, he was dumbstruck and fumbled to take possession of his usual charm. Under normal circumstances, he fancied himself quite skillful with the ladies, and here stood a young woman who seemed to possess a few charms of her own. Perhaps a little too skinny for his taste, but with a little color in her face, she wouldn't look half bad. "Come in, come in, gorgeous. How may I be of service to you?"

Emma fell back two steps and blushed. *Drat!* she thought as she apologized to Anton for intruding.

"But, my lovely girl, how could you ever intrude?" Anton took Emma by the arm and pulled her inside.

What a strange person, Emma thought. "I would like to see the porter. Does he happen to be here?"

"Well, he isn't really necessary since I'm sure that I can help you. What did you want to ask him?" Anton's voice betrayed only the slighted hint of a Rhenish lilt and possible origins from somewhere other than Bonn.

"My father asked me to fetch something from his office, but the key must be here. Could you please let me in?"

"Your father, then. His name?"

"Professor Schumacher, he has an office next to the library. Perhaps you could..."

"He's your father? Who would have thought it?! Well, come along with me, beautiful." With his left hand, he removed a bunch of keys from the peg board next to the door, before slipping his arm around Emma's waist and guiding her down the hall to her father's office.

Emma found his behavior too aggressive but didn't know how to escape. When he came to a stop in a doorway but didn't leave, she hurried to declare, "I don't want to keep you. You can see what a mess my father left. It will take me a while to find what I'm looking for."

Anton announced that he had plenty of time and could wait. Or if she would only tell him exactly what she was looking for, maybe he could help. Was her father ill?

She nodded. What else could she tell him? She opened several drawers indecisively, then gathered her courage and asked if Anton wouldn't mind leaving so she could search alone.

He grinned, calmly scanning her from head to toe. "Well, I'll leave Fräulein Schumacher to her own devices. I can lock up later, so just pull the door shut. And don't let anything get away."

He saluted with a smile and finally disappeared. Emma closed the door and put a chair under the handle, even if she thought it was perhaps a silly thing to do. Nonetheless, she left it there and got down to work. Over two hours later, she had accomplished nothing more than to bring order to the office. She'd packed up some of the documents, drawings, and art objects that she wanted to take home in a box, but she hadn't discovered even the slightest clue as to her father's whereabouts.

Just as she was about to leave the building, Anton jumped out to open the outer door and offered to carry the heavy box home for her. For such a delicate young woman, she was hauling quite a bit back to her father, he remarked. Before Emma could refuse, he grabbed the box and peered inside. "Well, your father seems to be a slave driver just like my old man is. He sent you out to get all this stuff for him? I haven't seen the professor in a long time, but if he's so sick, why has he asked you to drag all that clutter home?"

"Oh, my father—he's not sick. He's traveling. And I can carry that box just fine by myself, if you'll just give it back to me, please."

Anton ignored Emma's request and marched ahead. "Which way? Come on, don't make such a fuss. You can't possibly carry this all by yourself. That's where I come in. I'm a gentleman, always in the right place at the right time." He studied her closely. "Where did he go, your father? Did he finally make it to the desert? I can tell you, the professor kept this place on its toes. Egypt this, Egypt that and he *stepped* on a lot of toes too."

Emma followed him. What else could she do? And this young man seemed to know quite a bit about the goings-on at the university, and he knew Papa. "What's your name?"

He stopped, "Allow me. Wagenknecht, Anton Wagenknecht." And with that, he resumed his brisk pace. Emma struggled to keep up. "My father isn't in Egypt, as far as I know. He might be on a lecture tour?"

That's right, he'd heard something about that, Anton replied. One of the professors had mentioned it, or had one of the students? Either way, it was much quieter without her father around. Anton declared that all fathers were exhausting, and that he could tell her a thing or two about that.

And that was exactly what he did until they arrived at Emma's doorstep. Not waiting to be invited in, he simply stepped through the front door and would have followed her into the house if Tante Tinni hadn't intervened. She gave him a stern look, silently letting him know that he better behave himself and stay outside. He got the message and moved back onto the sidewalk. But Anton wouldn't have been Anton if all this hadn't made Emma seem even more appealing to him than before. Whistling, he made his way to the nearest wine cellar.

By dinner time, Emma had put the contents of the box away in Papa's study. The records seemed to be complete with nothing missing, and they stretched all the way back to July. However, the little Bastet statue was nowhere to be found. As a rule, Papa kept the artifacts he examined for a few months, then noted to which collection the piece belonged and the dates it had been in his possession. Why was this notation missing?

Sybil fluttered in, an undergarment draped over her arm and Emma's needlework basket in her right hand. "Emma dear, look at this strap. The lace is hanging on by a single thread. Would you be a dear? After all, it's only two little stitches."

52

While Emma mended the strap, Sybil sat down beside her and told her about her latest acquaintance: a delightful Russian, good-looking, distinguished, and elegant. He was taking her to the Zehrgarten restaurant tonight and then out dancing. It was a shame that he had only been able to save his title of nobility from his barbaric country and not his fortune. But until she departed for Wiesbaden, she could enjoy herself a little, couldn't she? If he dances even half as good as he looks, she'd wouldn't be home until breakfast—at the earliest. Would Christel mind much? Considering that she herself had that Frenchman on a string? Sybil chatted on and on, bouncing her foot up and down and occasionally twirling a strand of hair around her fingers. Emma had never seen her aunt look so pretty or so cheerful. She didn't know that Sibyl could be this lively. Emma was even more amazed by Sybil's effusive thank-you when she swooped out of her bedroom.

The rest of the evening passed pleasantly enough. Jean-Baptiste was invited to dinner, and afterwards they played a game which the Frenchman lost gracefully. They didn't talk about Papa.

Emma spent the first weekend of October in the house. Rain poured steadily from the clouds that towered ever darker and more threatening in the sky. A violent storm ripped the leaves from the trees and hurled brown mud against sidewalks and house walls. Tante Tinni heated the small coal stoves in the bedrooms, and Emma felt extremely cozy in her room. She settled herself with pillows and a knitted blanket on her wide window seat, glancing up occasionally from her books and magazines to look at the garden. She was very glad not to have to go outside and instead wrote letters to Grandmother and Daphne, telling them about her arrival and the autumn weather, without mentioning Papa. She also knitted diligently on the sweater she had begun in Polperro.

Despite the weather, Aunt Sybil was rarely at home. She had borrowed overshoes and a weatherproof cape from Christel. If she wasn't sitting in a coffee house with her Russian duke or attending a tea dance with him, they were strolling along the Rhine or exploring the Botanical Garden. Alexei flattered her: he had never met a woman who was both cosmopolitan and interested in nature. Sybil enjoyed the walks as much as the evenings spent dancing, a realization that surprised her. She decided to postpone indefinitely her plans to continue on to Wiesbaden.

Unlike the Russian duke, Jean-Baptiste had little interest in high society or refined tastes or even nature for that matter. He put more stock in simple pleasures: domesticity, good food, and enjoying the company of people with a down-to-earth sense of humor. He spent every weekend hour, except for the nights—Fräulein Feuerhahn would not consider such a thing!—at Arndtstraße, cooking and frying and baking, while Christel sat next to him, chopping vegetables and sewing her niece a skirt to match her new sweater.

Emma thoroughly enjoyed the meals in the kitchen, in the warm glow of the wicker lamp. She forbade herself to think about Papa or the future, laughed at Jean-Baptiste's teasing, nibbled on Tante Tinni's cookies, and talked about Cornwall, stenography school, and Sybil's quarrel with Nancy. In short, she reveled in being at home and in being able to relax and be herself. With Grandmother, she felt burdened by the weight of gratitude, unable to be at ease. With Tante Tinni, however, she acted and spoke as she saw fit without worrying about saying or doing the wrong thing.

Monday morning dawned clear and sunny; Emma was almost disappointed. Beautiful weather, she thought, was a duty: it forced you outside, to visit a coffee house terrace or to go on a long walk. On a rainy day, you could justify staying indoors and whiling away your time. But not when the sun was shining. Especially not on a golden October day. Resigned, she wondered what she should undertake.

The bell rang. She heard Tante Tinni thank the mailman.

Even before the door had swung shut, Christel was hurrying up the stairs and calling to Emma: "Your father has written, dear! A postcard from Würzburg!"

Am now in Würzburg for a few days before traveling on. A little rest would do me good. The lectures are exhausting. Look after everything at home. I will let you know when I am returning.

Emma stared at her aunt. What was wrong with Papa? Why this reserve? Why no salutations or greetings to her? "Tante Tinni, I don't understand, and I refuse to accept it. I don't believe that Papa would write something like this to you and forget me so completely."

"But, my dear, your father doesn't even know you're back in Bonn. I'm sure he has written to you in England."

"I'll find out! We have a telephone in the house now, don't we? And Grandmother is back in London." Still in her nightgown, Emma hurried into Papa's study, dialed the exchange number noted on the dial, and asked the telephone operator to connect her to London. It would take a few minutes, she was told. Emma sank into one of the armchairs and waited, drumming her fingers on the backrest until the phone started ringing.

It was Ada's voice that she heard through the hiss and gurgle of the line. Lady Milford was still asleep and didn't wish to be disturbed.

That was fine, Emma declared. Had any letters from her father arrived in London?

Alas, no, was Ada's reply.

Emma thanked her and told her to please say hello to Grandmother for her before hanging up . She began to pace the room, from window to door, from door to window. So, what did things look like at this point? In four weeks' it would be the anniversary of her mother's death, which was her own birthday as well. Yet, her father hadn't mentioned that date at all. He hadn't mentioned anything to her or his sister about his plans, nor provided even a clue about why he had agreed to take this trip in the first place. Emma went through Papa's notes, address book, and calendars again to see if she had perhaps missed something. But she found nothing of note.

Then the doorbell rang again, and again Tinni answered the door.

"Good morning, madam, I'm sorry to disturb you so early, but may I have a quick word with the honorable Fräulein Schumacher?"

Emma peered out into the hallway. Oh, that young man! Shouldn't he be at work? She was about to close the door when Anton noticed her. Disregarding Tante Tinni's indignation, he walked past her and dragged Emma into the hallway, where he eyed her with apparent amusement. She looked down at herself: barefoot and in an elegant nightgown that she'd inherited from Sybil. Of all the people on this earth, he's the last person she'd want to catch her half-dressed!

"Young man, get out of here! I've never seen such impudence! Out with you at once!" Tinni wrapped Emma in a coat and tried to drag Anton to the door.

"Don't be like that, good woman. We weren't all born yesterday!" shouted Anton, tearing himself free. "Here, I found this note. It was wedged in the back of the mailbox. I'm sure your father didn't see it." Anton handed Emma an envelope before Tinni could push him out the door.

The unopened letter was addressed to Professor Schumacher and had come from a Herr Wilhelm Joseph Meerbusch of Koblenz.

Koblenz Egyptological Collection Wilhelm Joseph Meerbusch

Koblenz, July 17, 1926

Dear Professor Schumacher,

You may have already heard about our collection, which is modest but has some very exceptional pieces that we hope to present to the public soon. One difficulty we currently face is that we are all amateurs in the field. Enthusiastic and eager to learn, but more dilettantes than true experts.

In the past few months, we have been offered various artifacts for sale that have aroused our suspicion. Among all the experts who have made a name for themselves, you are certainly the one who knows best how to evaluate our works and—in mentioning this I do not mean to belittle your worth—you also live in Bonn, which is not too far from our collection.

And therefore I am approaching you about two matters. Would you be willing to take a look at several pieces whose authenticity we would like to have verified? And secondly, would you be interested in ennobling our institute with a lecture to precede the opening of our collection? You have a reputation as an engaging speaker, and we thus think that a lecture from you would arouse considerable interest in the collection. We would, of course, offer you an appropriate honorarium.

Furthermore, I am in contact with several other museums and institutes that also have Egyptian art treasures in their holdings. In our conversations, the directors of these collections have expressed similar interest in hosting lectures for the general public.

Waiting for your reply, I remain with best wishes,
Wilhelm Joseph Meerbusch

THE SEARCH BEGINS

"What are you up to? You can't possibly think that I will actually agree to this." Tante Tinni was wiping the dining table for the fourth or fifth time. Not that it could get any cleaner than it already was. But whenever she became agitated, she cleaned and scrubbed everything she could get her hands on.

After reading the letter, Emma had retired to her bedroom and dressed with more care than usual. She then packed a small suitcase. Her grandmother had taught her; a lady should always be prepared for whatever may happen. Koblenz was less than two hours away by train, and this Herr Meerbusch had to be the reason for Papa's departure. She wanted answers from him, since there was a chance that he knew where Papa was staying. She had a plan. "Tante Tinni, I beg you. I'll be twenty soon! Other women my age have a job and an apartment, and travel around the globe. I just want to go as far as Koblenz."

"Don't talk to me about other women, my dear. They didn't grow up as sheltered as you did. And what do you want to do there? You don't even know if anyone has time to meet with you!"

Tinni scrubbed the table vigorously until Emma snatched the sponge from her hand, pushed her onto a chair, and asked her to take a deep breath.

"Emma, your father never even received that letter. So how should this Meerbaum—or Meerbusch, or whatever—how should this gentleman know where your Papa is?"

"Perhaps he contacted him again when he didn't receive a response. It would be a very strange coincidence if this invitation had nothing to do with Papa's disappearance, wouldn't it?"

"Disappearance! Emma, your father has not disappeared. He just left in a hurry. That's all."

"If you think there's nothing to worry about, why did you go to the police?"

Well, Tinni admitted, of course she was worried about her brother. Why make her worry that Emma might vanish into thin air too? Young women were exposed to dangers everywhere these days, Tinni continued, and her niece was a little lamb to boot. She started playing with the sponge again and was about to give the table another thrashing when Jean-Baptiste appeared.

"Jean will tell you just how dangerous it is out there, right? Emma wants to go to Koblenz. All by herself!" Tinni described the potential dangers in detail, not letting the Frenchman or Emma get a word in edgewise.

With a slight bow, Jean-Baptiste turned toward the young woman: "Then may I take the liberty of accompanying Mademoiselle? I have no doubt you would manage wonderfully on your own, but in conversations with strange gentlemen, a male companion can often be useful. And your aunt would feel better about it. Wouldn't you, Christèle?"

Christel grumbled but had nothing further to say about the plan.

"You know, when I marched into Germany with the army, I was sure I wouldn't find anything nice here, and I despised the people. And in the first few years after the war, I went through all the places where I was stationed with a closed heart and blind eyes. Then I was sent here on the Rhine." Jean-Baptiste pointed at the river flowing by their compartment window. "That was three years ago already. I had been promoted and was working in the military administration in the city center. For the first time, I saw not only how hard the war had hit me and my country, but how it was still weighing all of us down. All the poverty, the hardship…" He glanced at Emma, who sat quietly across from him, before clearing his throat. "I love your aunt very much. We might not be twenty anymore, and perhaps we accepted long ago that we were meant to go through life alone. The fact that we have found each other, at our age, from different countries, in this era of all eras—that means something, don't you think? A Frenchman and a German: might that not be the way forward?"

Emma smiled. "But Monsieur Barbier, it isn't all that unusual. You know that my grandmother was from the Alsace and considered herself more French than German?"

"So you have no objections? You will encourage your aunt? Believe me, she will be just fine with me in Toulouse—ah, she will love it! A city so full of beauty and light, and the surrounding countryside. Perfect for Christèle! And you will always be welcome there."

"You must miss your home country very much."

"Oh, I could live here on the Rhine. Still…"

"When will you move back? Have you two come to an agreement?"

"Oh, there's no rush. And as for getting married—well, Christèle wants your father's blessing, which is why I am very anxious to find him too. If it were up to me, she would have been my wife a long time ago."

At the train station, they rented a locker for their luggage, hoping to be back in Bonn by evening. They fortified themselves with a bite to eat from the station buffet before hailing a cab to take them to the Egyptological Collection. Once there, Emma hesitated, but Jean-Baptiste climbed the steps and yanked the bell pull. It took a while before the door opened. A man in a dark suit looked at them skeptically.

"Allow me to introduce myself. My name is Barbier, and this is my niece, Fräulein Schumacher. We have an urgent matter to discuss with Herr Meerbusch. Is he in?" Jean-Baptiste made his request coolly, and stepping into the foyer, he made it clear he would not be put off.

The other man reluctantly stepped aside, declared that he would go check, and disappeared down a hallway.

Emma looked around the reception area. Paintings of scowling gentlemen in powdered wigs adorned the walls, and low display cases stood underneath them on dainty rococo feet. She stepped closer. "Look, Monsieur Barbier. Here are several scarabs from the Old Kingdom. And these buckles and crucibles are probably from the tomb of some noblewoman." Emma grasped Jean-Baptiste by the cuff of his sleeve and pulled him to the nearest vitrine, where various papyri lay spread out.

"You know your way around quite well, Mademoiselle, don't you?"

Emma blushed. "Not really, I'm afraid. But Papa taught me a lot of things. Just imagine how many millennia these objects have seen. I think it's exciting. Oh, look how gracefully this crane is drawn and how vibrant the colors still are after all this time!"

Light footsteps echoed behind them. "The gracious Fräulein has exquisite taste. If I may introduce myself, my name is Meerbusch. I am the director of this modest collection. How may I help you?"

Herr Meerbusch, a man in his forties with a melodious voice, bowed slightly to Emma, nodded to Jean-Baptiste, and asked them both to follow him into his office. "May I offer you some refreshment? Tea perhaps, or lemonade? Herr Friedhelm, please be so kind."

His office was spacious and furnished with modern pieces. A glass door led to a terrace, which also featured elegant furniture.

"Perhaps we should enjoy this lovely weather we are having," he suggested, opening the door and letting Emma go first. He pulled out a chair for her before taking a seat himself. "How may I be of service to you?" he asked Jean-Baptiste directly.

The latter nodded toward Emma; she should tell him what she was after. Emma provided an account, at first haltingly but then with increasing assurance, of her surprise over the professor's sudden trip. She didn't mention her anxiety or the significance of their annual meeting on October 31. She suspected her fragile self-confidence would dissolve into tears if she should so much as mention that special day.

"In fact, I wrote to your father a second time, as I was very anxious for his cooperation." Mr. Meerbusch stubbed out his cigarette and leaned back, crossing his legs.

Jean-Baptiste sat at Emma's side, spine straight, as if he were her military attaché and she his queen. He ignored Herr Meerbusch's attempts to carry on the conversation with him, instead of the young woman.

The director of the Egyptological Collection didn't usually speak with women as equals; he flirted with them. But Emma hardly noticed his effort to impress her with his charm and attentiveness. Herr Meerbusch sighed. "Your father responded to me personally, to my great delight. He came by and viewed our collection, which he found interesting, and returned a fortnight later. During that interim, I made appointments for him to visit other collections, and had my secretary, Herr Friedhelm, arrange for the lodging and tickets."

"My father gave a lecture here?"

"Not yet, dear Fräulein. You see, our institute will not open its doors until early November, and that is when Professor Schumacher will give a speech as guest of honor. His previous visit—that was, just a moment—yes, was on August twenty-first. If I remember correctly, your father then traveled on to Frankfurt on Sunday, the twenty-ninth."

Emma hesitated, then asked if Mr. Meerbusch thought her father had seemed confused.

Herr Meerbusch didn't usually work with the mentally ill, was his indignant reply.

Emma fell silent, and for the first time, Jean-Baptiste intervened: "It would be helpful if you could provide us with the professor's itinerary." Not a question, not a request, but a declaration. Jean-Baptiste's statement reflected not even the slightest doubt that Herr Meerbusch would accommodate them on this matter.

Indeed, the latter beckoned to his secretary, who had been lingering in the background throughout the conversation and asked him to take down all the information for their kind visitors. With a glance at his watch, Mr. Meerbusch rose to his feet, explained that he had an appointment, bowed once more to Emma, squeezed Jean-Baptiste's hand, and excused himself.

It was a good quarter of an hour before Herr Friedhelm returned, a sheet of paper in hand: "I have written down for you the institutions and hotels I arranged for the Professor's tour. Right now, his itinerary ends at Munich, from where we will then plan the rest of his tour. I have jotted down for you the places where he will be stopping along the way." He handed the sheet to Jean-Baptiste. "If I may escort the lady and gentleman to the door? My dear lady, your bag!"

Emma turned, grabbed her bag, which she had left hanging on the chair, and stumbled a little as she crossed the threshold. Jean-Baptiste caught her, but not before she had a chance to notice Herr Friedhelm's sneer.

It was three o'clock in the afternoon by the time they left the institute. Jean-Baptiste hailed a cab and helped Emma inside. First things first, a piece of cake and a cup of coffee would do wonders for him, he remarked. Could he interest Emma in joining him? This would give them an opportunity to consider how they might want to proceed from there.

Ten minutes later, as they took their seats in a coffee shop, Emma reached for his hand: "Thank you very much for your help, Monsieur Barbier."

"It's my pleasure as well as my honor. And since I have already introduced you as my niece, wouldn't you like to call me by my first name?"

She agreed and received a kiss on her left and right cheeks in thanks. A stylish serving girl took their order and returned quite promptly with the requested coffee and fragrant puff pastries.

Emma sighed. How wonderful life could sometimes be! She wondered if Papa had thought the same thing as he set off on his trip. Was he perhaps sitting in Würzburg this very moment, enjoying his life, peace, and freedom? No, absolutely not! Her father reveled in his quarrels, whether with colleagues or students. He loved his sister, his daughter, and his comfortable home, and was completely devoted to his work. Yes, he sometimes lost track of time and where he was, he might be growing old and forgetful—but he would never just disappear without a good reason.

Emma took a bite of her pastry. "What are we going to do next? We have this list, but to be honest, I don't really know what to do with it."

Jean-Baptiste pulled out the notes and skimmed them before replying. "Some of the boarding houses are connected to the telephone network. We can inquire if your father has been staying at them. With any luck, you will reach him personally."

He waved to the serving girl, settled the bill, and asked for the nearest post office. It was only a few hundred meters away, well within walking distance, the clerk replied, smiling over the generous tip.

Although the post office was quite crowded, the clerk greeted them cheerfully. Emma and Jean-Baptiste showed him their list and asked to be connected to the boarding house in Würzburg first. They left their list with the clerk so that he could also put them through to the other hotels, one after the other. The clerk sent them to cubicle three, assuring them that the connection would be coming in shortly.

It was a challenge for the two of them to squeeze into the phone booth together, but with a little pushing and stomach tightening (Jean-Baptiste's, that is; there was nothing for Emma to pull in), they made it.

The phone rang. A woman's hearty *Grüss Gott* rustled through the line. Emma introduced herself and asked a little awkwardly about her father, who had apparently rented a room from the landlady.

Yes, the professor had been her guest, that was correct.

"Oh, he's gone already? We're quite worried about him, because we don't know where he is and—excuse me, but what impression did he make on you?"

Yes, well, the professor appeared quite spry and had been out a lot. Würzburg was nothing if not a beautiful city, with many attractions, good food and fine wine. That must have done the professor a world of good, and perhaps his daughter would also like to visit one day and avail herself of one of the finest guest rooms in the city. Before the solicitous landlady could enumerate the other advantages of her boarding house and the surrounding area, Emma thanked her and hung up.

She asked for the next connection with a wave, and it took a few minutes before the phone started ringing again. Emma introduced herself once more and asked the gentleman on the other end about her father.

"The professor—just a moment—yes, his reservation was for the day before yesterday, but he never showed up. We are accustomed to our guests notifying us when they need to cancel a reservation, but unfortunately, Professor Schumacher neglected to do so. We have, therefore, sent an invoice to his home address—Excuse me?—Yes, of course with pleasure. We will give him your message should he still arrive. However, his room will be unavailable after tomorrow. With pleasure, Madam, goodbye."

Only five minutes ago, Emma had thought that her worries had all been for nothing. that she just didn't know her father as well as she had supposed, and that her naïve fears had gotten everyone—from Daphne to Jean-Baptiste—upset for no reason at all. Her father was old, had worked far too much all his life, and had outlived two wives. Was it so inconceivable that he might leave everything behind for a while? To be honest, yes, it was improbable, and she needed to stop constantly wavering between this and that. Her intuition was telling her that something was wrong, and she needed to rely on those feelings, starting now.

Emma pulled open the door and asked the gentleman at the counter to connect her with the Würzburg Museum. She waited. Finally, the bell rang, and Emma answered. She repeated her same line of questioning for a fourth time that day. Calmly, clearly, and firmly. Jean-Baptiste cocked an eyebrow: this clarity suited her perfectly. Emma listened, frowned, and asked, "But my father was invited to speak there, wasn't he? He wouldn't have traveled all that way if he hadn't received an invitation."

"It was like this: we received an offer to be included in your father's speaking tour. We gladly accepted and prepared one of our lecture halls for it. We were set to discuss the next steps with your father as soon as he arrived, which Professor Schumacher did a few days ago. He introduced himself briefly and inspected our exhibit spaces. Afterwards he refused to give a lecture in our museum, claiming that there was not enough interesting material available for him here. We accepted this decision with regret and—if I may say so—displeasure. Your father is highly respected, not only as an Egyptologist but also as an appraiser of antiquities, and I am sure that he is very well-informed about the extent and quality of all German collections. His refusal was therefore taken as an insult by some people here."

Emma listened in dismay. Who or what had driven Papa to such behavior? He was direct, sometimes brutally honest, and quick-tempered, but never hurtful. He rarely behaved diplomatically, but he usually tried to be cordial with others. What had brought about this change? "I thank you very much for your frankness. If I may ask you one more thing: Do you know if he ended up giving his lectures at the other museums?"

"I apologize, but I don't know anything about that. Is that all you needed? My wife's expecting me for supper."

Outside the post office, Jean-Baptiste glanced at his watch and realized it was already half past five. Emma shivered. A chill was rising with the onset of twilight.

"It isn't far to the station, and I think a brisk walk would do us good," Jean-Baptiste said, taking Emma's arm; she felt drained and lost. "It's been a busy day for you."

Once at the station, they reclaimed their luggage and studied the departure board for the next train bound for Bonn. Emma's gaze lingered on one word: Frankfurt, the first stop on Papa's journey. Four hours away. The next train there was leaving in a few minutes. She pointed at the connection and shot Jean-Baptiste a questioning glance.

"You want to go to Frankfurt now? Does that make sense? We can call the hotel and museum from Bonn."

"It's a hunch, nothing more. I'm sure you're right about calling being enough, but still..."

The train to Frankfurt was practically empty, and nobody else was in their compartment. Emma and Jean-Baptiste chatted about the day and what'd they'd learned so far, about books and films, about the promised bright future. Jean-Baptiste was impressed at the confidence with which women made decisions these days, how they both worked and enjoyed themselves. If he'd had a daughter, he'd be glad for her sake that society was changing to make more room for these "new women." What was Emma planning to do with her life?

Emma pondered this question. Did she even count as one of the "new" women? All these years, she had sat protected in her nest. Life simply eddied and flowed around her, remaining largely theoretical. She had attended balls with Grandmother—pompous and stilted affairs that had changed rather little since Lady Milford's youth. They were marketplaces for marriage, and Emma had danced shyly and self-consciously with more than one downy-cheeked young man without getting a word in edgewise. At least not a meaningful one. Sometimes she'd get annoyed, observing in silence their antics, wondering what right these snot-nosed idiots had to impose on her. The perfect bride should be lively, bubbly, the center of any social gathering; beautiful and elegant but also modest and domestic, and eager to add sweetness to her husband's life. She could do some of the thinking, but the laurels were to be left to him.

Without really meaning to, Emma uttered these thoughts aloud, working herself into a rage about the injustice of the world, which mainly affected the female sex. In the eyes of most men, women still seemed to be nothing more than decorative dolls, and although they denied that women had any brains, these men nevertheless expected thrift, support and, when called upon, hard work from those same dolls. She was just fine with her limited experience with men, just fine, thank you very much.

Jean-Baptiste chuckled, and Emma fell silent. Had she actually said all that out loud? In front of Jean-Baptiste of all people, who had been steadfast in his support throughout this whole ordeal? Hadn't Grandmother admonished her more than once to behave like a lady? She blushed. If she could at least stop doing that!

"Emma, you are nothing if not unexpected! Who would have thought you would argue so passionately for the cause of women? No, no, I promise I'm not laughing at you, not at all. I only ask you not to judge all men by those who have stepped on your toes. They were stupid boys, self-absorbed and narcissistic. Don't measure all men against them! The world is changing, and men are changing with it. The women, yes, they have seized the change with both hands! But someone will come along someday whom you will like, and I'm sure he will be a smart and modern man who does not want a doll by his side, but a smart and modern woman. Don't let the traditionalists scare you. Stand up to them and laugh them down."

"You give me too much credit. I don't know anything about the world."

"That will come, that will come. But right now, you look exhausted. Close your eyes and get some rest. I'll wake you up when we reach Frankfurt."

Once at the hotel, Jean-Baptiste requested a room for himself and his niece. The receptionist eyed Emma, winked at Jean-Baptiste, and offered him a discreetly located double room.

"I asked for a room for myself and one for my niece, and it's reasonable for me to expect that you will not misinterpret my request. Am I mistaken in my assumption that this is a respectable establishment?" Without waiting for an answer, he turned to Emma. "And this is the downside of our new world: lewdness and disrespect toward women. Obviously, some people imagine in others what they wish for themselves."

The young man behind the reception desk had the decency to look abashed. He then added, as if in passing, that breakfast would of course be on the house, and with that he wished his honorable guests a restful night.

Jean-Baptiste had already had breakfast and was sitting at the table with the Frankfurt newspaper and a cup of coffee when Emma entered the dining room. He set the paper aside, stood up, and held her chair for her. She wasn't used to such attention and smiled sheepishly at him.

"Did you sleep well, Emma?" he asked, handing her the breadbasket.

She had, Emma replied, before selecting a raisin roll and spreading it with butter and jam. She ordered tea and an omelet from the waiter, feeling hungrier than ever. She was still concerned about her father, but her anxiety was now overshadowed by an excitement that was foreign to her. Sitting in the hotel restaurant, surrounded by new faces in a city to which she'd never been before, she felt eager to travel somewhere else and talk with people she didn't know. She kept telling herself that this little trip with Jean-Baptiste was merely to appease her worries about her father's inexplicable disappearance and behavior. But were she to be honest with herself, she would have to admit that she was enjoying this taste of real life. She was almost grateful to her father. If he hadn't disappeared, she would still be sitting in Polperro: knitting, drawing, writing, and counting the days until her departure. Ada would have accompanied her to Paris, where she would have been met by her father. She would have stayed in Bonn for three or four weeks—doing more knitting, drawing, and writing—before Tante Tinni would have accompanied her to Paris, where Ada would have been waiting to take her to Edinburgh. There, presumably, John McGivern would have eventually asked her to be his wife, and the rest of her life would have been spent tending to prayer books and church flower arrangements. John would have praised her food and sketches in the evenings and sought to make his little wife as happy as a parish minister could.

Not that he had ever kissed her or even so much as flirted with her. Nonetheless, she had noticed how hard the pastor and his wife had been trying to pair up the quiet and helpful Emma with the equally quiet and helpful vicar. John seemed to have been content with this effort, and he had presumably planned to ask her to marry him at Christmas, because by February he would be in charge of his first very own parish, high up in the north. His conventionality demanded an absolutely faithful, caring, and self-sacrificing wife.

Emma shuddered, for she doubted whether she could have escaped that future. But now, at this very moment, she decided she would not return to England. She would visit Grandmother in London in the spring, but from now on she would take her life into her own hands. She set down her teacup with such a loud clatter that everyone in the room looked up, startled. She blushed. Again. Well, she would work on that too.

She jumped to her feet and caught her chair just as it was about to tip over. The teapot wasn't so fortunate. Her elbow brushed against it, spilling its contents all over the immaculate white tablecloth. The other guests looked up as the waiter hurried over. Jean-Baptiste rescued his morning paper, while Emma's blush deepened. With the Frenchman at her side, she hurried out of the room and into the street.

Jean-Baptiste, who had asked the porter for a map of the city, suggested they first go to the Zum Blauen Bock Hotel, which was only a few blocks away.

The innkeeper there welcomed them warmly, until he realized that the visitors didn't want a room but to steal his precious time. He listened impatiently to Emma and grumbled something unintelligible. He nevertheless accommodated their wish that he look through his guest book. Yes, a Professor Schumacher had stayed here from August 29th to September 5th. No, he couldn't remember him specifically; after all, that had been more than a month ago, and new guests arrived every day. And no, even if the young lady continued to ask, he knew nothing, absolutely nothing about this professor. He really had better things to do than to spy on his guests and be interrogated by women.

What a nasty old codger, Emma thought, and she thanked him curtly.

"That's your Rhenish temperament, isn't it?" asked Jean-Baptiste as she followed him out of the boarding house. She didn't understand his question and shot him a quizzical look. He smiled. "Your aunt also tends to—well, she can be quite direct, can't she? Ah, now please don't look at me like that; I mean no harm. I appreciate this quality in both of you."

"We're not alike at all! She doesn't put up with anything, but I, on the other hand..."

"Hmm, maybe you don't realize how you put that poor innkeeper in his place, with that brusque thank you," he said with a chuckle. "Surely, you've had an admirer observe that you make a formidable impression. It's like you've fallen out of the past and are planning to lead the Celtic army against the Caesars tomorrow." When she stopped in the middle of the sidewalk, dumbfounded, he urged her to keep moving and asked her not to take him too seriously; sometimes his Provençal fancy for invention got the better of him.

Half an hour later, they reached their destination: a private bank whose principal owner collected ancient Mediterranean artifacts. Emma was impressed by the building, whose wide marble staircase led up to double doors that opened onto a lobby of regal proportions. To the right of the entrance was a long reception desk, behind which sat three young women who would have caused a sensation even in Hollywood. Emma could hardly tear her eyes away from these beautiful women.

The one in the middle beckoned to them and asked how she could be of assistance. She didn't bat an eye when Jean-Baptiste inquired about the collection instead of an investment advisor. These days, you never knew if someone who walked through the front doors today as a poor wretch might not return tomorrow as a millionaire; every bank employee took this as fact. It would a be source of great annoyance were the bank to lose a potential customer through arrogance and false pride. The road from riches to rags, could be just as swift, a fact unappreciated by many bank customers.

The receptionist asked them to take a seat for a moment and pointed toward the opposite wall. There, ready and waiting, sat a row of armchairs intended to make anyone who sat in them feel like they were in the right hands. The young woman placed a phone call, and a young man appeared, balancing a tray with refreshments. Tea, coffee, or lemonade?

Emma recalled her mishap at breakfast, felt the unsettling nature of the grandeur around her, and declined, as did Jean-Baptiste.

The young man moved away, and soon a gentleman of imposing stature strode toward them. Despite his bulk, he bowed to Emma with elegance and offered his hand to the Frenchman. He introduced himself as Dr. Meinhardt, curator, and asked them to follow him. He led them down a corridor, past countless doors and into the annex that housed the collection. Once a month it was opened to the public for a not-insignificant fee.

The curator's office resembled Papa's. It was brighter and more modern than her father's, but there were the same wooden boxes in the corners, the same shelves groaning under the weight of encyclopedias, folios, and art volumes, and the same display case crowded with all kinds of figurines and trinkets. Letters, books, and brochures were scattered in piles across the desk, and in their midst stood a framed photograph of a woman and a girl.

Emma smiled; the pompous lobby might have intimidated her, but she felt right at home in this clutter. Dr. Meinhardt pushed a stack of magazines off the couch and asked his guests to take a seat. He himself sat down in the armchair opposite. "My dear young woman, what can I do for you?" he began the conversation.

By now Emma was well versed in her line of inquiry about her father and thus repeated it with ease.

Dr. Meinhardt sighed, glanced at the photograph of his family, and appeared to hesitate. He seemed like a genuinely polite person who disliked giving bad news to others. After a second sigh, he replied, "Where do I begin? Your father, of course, is well-known to me through his work and his writings. I, myself, am an expert on the Etruscans and the Romans, but of course there are sufficient points of commonality with Egyptian antiquity. We have some very nicely preserved artifacts from the New Kingdom, and so Herr Meerbusch offered me—I'm not sure if you know him—aha, wonderful, you do! Anyway, he suggested that we, um, invite your esteemed father to deliver a lecture. I must say, it was a surprising proposal, and at very short notice. Usually, we plan such events several months in advance. Nevertheless, we didn't want to miss the opportunity to have your father as our guest. Two gentlemen from the board and I met with him on Sunday, right after his arrival. We showed him around the gallery and agreed that he should give his first lecture to our Board of Trustees on Monday afternoon and another on Tuesday evening for invited guests. For that second event, he would present his subject matter for a lay audience."

He once more exhaled loudly, fiddled with his tie, and shifted some books back and forth. "So, well—your father arrived late the following afternoon, which—I assure you—was taken with good humor. I mean, we expect that sort of thing from a distracted professor, after all. Your father stepped up to the lectern and began his lecture, which was—well, how shall I put it?—was not quite up to snuff for the audience. Although there were no Egyptologists among us, there were some historians and connoisseurs of antiquities who are not entirely without prior knowledge. I explained to your father that the more general laymen's lecture was the one planned for the following day... however—well, your father was not pleased and declared in—I am very sorry, Fräulein—in very unvarnished words that his knowledge was superior to ours in every way possible, and he was merely adapting his speech to our pitifully low level. I am afraid his manner of expression was rather inappropriate, and I regret to admit that some of our gentlemen were quite indignant. I made every effort to reconcile the gentlemen and your father, and you might say a kind of cease fire was achieved. We decided it must all have been the result of a misunderstanding, and your father apologized. Well, since he was to give the lecture the next day, we thought it would be a good idea if we showed him some of the exhibits that we were especially proud of. Well..." Dr. Meinhardt's next sigh was deeper than before. "Well, we showed him a small figurine, which in all probability represents Ramses II, and which is our pride and joy. Your father, well, he examined it briefly and claimed it was more junk than a Ramses, and if it did represent a pharaoh, it was surely some justly forgotten descendant of the great ruler. We showed him our expert evaluations, pointed out the fine design, the whiteness of the marble and the gold inlay, but I must say the mood was, well, less than amicable. Your father laughed at some of the gentlemen and insulted everyone present in the most egregious manner. I'm very sorry to have to share this with you. After this scandal, I inquired at other collections about whether your father was known for such performances, but everywhere I asked I was emphatically assured of his good humor and affability. He could get excited and a little angry sometimes, but as a passionate connoisseur, this was within acceptable bounds."

Emma remained quiet for a moment, trying to process what she had just heard. She then asked Dr. Meinhardt to believe her when she assured him that such behavior was absolutely unheard of, and that she knew her father to be passionate and quarrelsome but always within the limits of decorum. "May I ask you if my father showed any signs of exhaustion or confusion? Was he perhaps ill?"

Unfortunately, Dr. Meinhardt didn't know the professor well enough to be able to judge that. However, the professor had appeared quite clear-headed and had targeted his insults well. But sadly, that wasn't all—there was still one other point to mention. He exhaled loudly. "The little statue—Ramses II—well, it's been missing from our collection since the day of this incident..."

CAIRO

Zahi Saddik, director of the Egyptian Museum in Cairo, and police officer Hasan al-Aziz, met for a late dinner on the terrace of Shepheard's Hotel. They sat off to the side, close to the band, which belted out the season's most popular tunes with more enthusiasm than skill. Eavesdropping on their conversation would have been practically impossible, almost as difficult at resolving that issue that had brought them together. Ever since Howard Carter had discovered the tomb of the historically insignificant child king four years ago, the entire world had been clamoring for Egyptian artifacts. An appetite that could hardly be satisfied, at least not legally.

But small antiquities weren't the only things that were finding their way abroad. Mummies were also highly desired by world-weary Europeans and Americans for whom money was no factor. Mummies that were thousands of years old were presented at parties, festooned with flowers, used as tabletops. They were even unwrapped by party guests who tore open their "gifts" with the zeal of children before playing with their contents for a few minutes and then discarding them in the corner. And this was done by adults who prided themselves on being cultured and knowledgeable. These individuals apparently couldn't care less about the fact that they were destroying priceless treasures, or about the amount they spent for this fleeting entertainment. Nor did they care about where the mummies came from. People kept disappearing from the shacks on the outskirts of Cairo, and resourceful, ruthless gangs had long since set up workshops specializing in the production of counterfeit mummies. And business was booming. Not only did the mummies themselves generate money, but in these turbulent times there were more than enough individuals out there eager to pay for a corpse. Any corpse.

"So, did the lead pan out?" asked Zahi Saddik.

The police officer nodded. "It did, but we got there too late. The workshop had been burned down, and two of my men had disappeared. I assume the worst. The sarcophagi have been outside the country for a while already. We only caught a few of the underlings, who don't know much at all about the overall operations. Besides that, I have personally received threats: They know where my daughter goes to school..."

Saddik tapped out his pipe; he had received similar warnings. As long as they were only against himself, he wasn't afraid. But against his family? "Where do we go from here?" he wanted to know.

"I don't see many options moving forward."

"We have, of course, sent statements to various museums around the world, particularly those with Egyptian antiquities collections. I took special care to draw attention to the mummy trade. Many of the museums have promised to carefully examine all incoming offers and to notify us of any irregularities, but how reliable is that? In most cases, the buyers are private citizens, not museums or institutes."

Al-Aziz nodded again. "We have increased our presence at the ports, but so far, not much has turned up. These smugglers are completely ruthless—a human life is worth nothing to them. Anyone who gets in their way is eliminated, and too many of my officers are intimidated. I can hardly blame them."

Saddik threw his hands up in resignation. For now, there was nothing more they could do.

GODDESSES & MEN

"Yes, we have no bananas. We have-a no bananas today. We've string beans and onions...!" the chorus to the latest popular tune imported from America echoed through Arndtstraße 13a early Wednesday morning, Sybil's soprano soaring to ever greater heights as she splashed in the bathtub.

Emma pressed her pillow over her ears. Oh, please! She wanted sleep! Some peace and quiet! She tossed the pillow across her room and grabbed the alarm clock: seven o'clock. The sun wasn't even up yet. Still exhausted from the previous day, she got up and dragged herself to the bathroom. In the meantime, Sybil had moved on from the bananas and was now begging an unknown man to visit her in Hawaii, since her "little heart" was now free. "What's wrong with you, Aunt Sybil? I wanted to sleep in today!"

"Emma dear, what's stopping you? But more to the point, who in the world wants to sleep until noon when there's so much amazing beauty around us? Don't look so glum; you'll just spoil my mood." Sybil continued to splash around in the sudsy water with a sponge, her face covered with therapeutic clay and her hair wrapped in a towel.

"You're behaving quite strangely, Aunt Sybil."

"Will you stop calling me *Aunt*! It makes me feel old, and what I feel is young!" Sybil giggled and switched gears from popular songs to opera, "Reach out to me, my life, and come to my castle—"

"Go to your castle, I beg you, but be quiet!"

"Emma! Why would you use that tone with your aunt?"

"Ah, which is it? Aunt or no aunt?"

"Emma! Are you feeling sick? What's the matter with you?"

"What's the matter with *you*?"

Sybil laughed and smiled so broadly that her clay mask crumbled. She looked like a mummy, a very happy mummy, Emma observed.

"Emma dear, I'm in love! In love! Oh, it's quite wonderful. No, he is! He's quite wonderful. Charming and obliging, handsome and melancholy, sad, genteel, soulful—oh, he's..." Sybil's face suddenly lost its radiance. "And he's destitute, of course! But I tell you, I'll worry about that tomorrow. Today—"

"Do you want him to give you some bananas first?"

A dripping wet sponge whizzed past Emma, just missing her head.

Over breakfast, Emma reported what she and Jean-Baptiste had learned on their trip. They had arrived back in Bonn late, and Christel had sent her niece to bed without asking any questions. Now she was sitting across the table from her, shaking her head; none of this sounded like her brother at all. "Do you think your father hurt his head? He's acting like he's not all there." She reached for Emma's hand. "But whatever happened to the little figurine? There is no way your father had anything to do with that. One of those fat cats must have thought he could make a little money on the sly. They can't be trusted with anything!"

"I'm honestly quite sick of everything right now. Look, Papa left Würzburg, but he didn't go to Augsburg. And that makes sense! If he didn't feel like giving a lecture in Würzburg, why would he continue his tour?"

"Yes, but where is he then, child? He hasn't come back here."

"I've thought about that. Maybe he went to Lake Constance. To Lindau. Perhaps he just needs a rest? Wouldn't he maybe go to the place he used to visit with Mama?"

"Perhaps. But you don't want to go to Bavaria now too, do you?"

"Oh, I'm done with traveling on the train for the time being. I think we'll just wait a few days. I'm sure he'll write soon, or he might already be on his way here. Where else could he go?"

The morning dragged on with Emma not quite knowing what to do with herself. It was raining nonstop: sometimes drizzling, sometimes pouring. Christel and Jean-Baptiste sat in the living room, listening to Schumann and enjoying just being together. Sybil retired to her bedroom to make up for the missing night hours spent dancing, singing, and canoodling.

Emma threw one book after another into the stack of books next to her window seat. She found them all boring and pointless. The magazines weren't much better. They never had anything new to say. Rudolph Valentino's death overshadowed every other newsworthy topic; increasingly absurd theories were circulating about how the world's most handsome lover could have passed away at such a young age. Nothing else had changed either: the Russians were still evil, the Italians lazy, and the French unscrupulous seducers. The human race was either teetering on the brink of the abyss or facing the brightest future imaginable. She threw the magazines on the floor next to the books.

Emma stood up and faced her closet mirror: Jean-Baptiste had called her impressive. John McGivern, in a rare show of interest, had once declared that it was amazing how striking her appearance was compared to her demeanor. It wasn't her reserve that bothered him, he had confessed; he was embarrassed by her fiery hair and full lips.

She pivoted to the left, to the right, not knowing where to put her hands and feet, but unable to tear herself away from her reflection. She then reached up to the nape of her neck and loosened the combs and clips she used to pin up her curls. Titian red was the term Grandmother used to describe her hair color; Tante Tinni simply called it fussich. The dark curls contrasted with the pallor of her face and seemed much too heavy for her delicate frame. Had she been alive fifty years ago, she would have made a wonderful model for the Pre-Raphaelites. But today? She looked old-fashioned even to herself. She thought of the receptionists at the bank, how sophisticated they looked, even in their uniforms. She gazed down at herself. She had never paid much attention to her clothes; not that she was indifferent, though. No, she thought, she merely lacked the elegance and grace of other women. After all, what woman could possibly exude grace in a tweed skirt, solid shoes, and a practical sweater? In the past, Grandmother, along with the dressmaker, had decided what would suit Emma best; she had never gone shopping on her own. And that was exactly what would distract her now from her languid thoughts and boredom. Let Papa go off somewhere else and ruin his reputation! The rain had stopped for now. She pinned her hair back up, grabbed her bag and umbrella, and left the house.

Emma adored Bonn: its bourgeois respectability, its lingering signs of historic wealth and proud nobility. Bonn had been destroyed numerous times, but the traces of all those who had lived and ruled there were still evident. Romans, Frenchmen, Wittelsbachs, and Prussians. They had all left their mark on the city and had themselves been charmed by Bonn's picturesque location on the Rhine and the warmth of its people. Over the centuries, the city's residents had learned to deal with their foreign masters without losing their identity. The French names that were sprinkled throughout many a family tree reflected how close the cultures sometimes came. It wasn't uncommon to find a Marguerite Müller or an Alphonse Schmitz in a genealogy—*hony soit qui mal y pense...* "Shamed be whoever thinks evil of it."

Emma strolled across Münsterplatz, entered the Basilica to offer a brief Hail Mary to safeguard her father, and then stepped into the Louis Berg department store, which by its own evaluation was "the largest and cheapest specialty department store for footwear." A saleswoman greeted her the moment she entered, before graciously presenting one pair of shoes after another, and praising Emma's fine ankles and noble instep. Armed with two pairs of elegant pumps, the salesclerk then led her to the checkout counter and urged her to return soon.

Her spirits now perking up, Emma moved on to the Blömer fashion house. Here, too, one of the employees took her under her wing, escorted her to a dressing room, and pulled out a tape measure. *If the lady could be kind enough to take off her coat and dress, the salesclerk could note down her measurements and bring her any items she might wish to try on.* After a moment's hesitation, Emma recalled Daphne and her carefree attitude, and valiantly stripped down to her undergarments.

"What a pity that fitted waists are out of fashion, considering you possess such a slender one. Anyway, I'll find you something flattering. Do you need some everyday dresses?" In quick succession, one of the best employees of the house dressed and undressed Emma, discarding one garment before setting another aside for further consideration. This continued until they had selected four models which could get Emma through the day, from morning to night, in a simple but elegant manner. And these dresses also showed off her figure and delicate complexion to their best advantage. How could Emma say no?

Once this was accomplished, there was one more thing that Emma wanted, which Blömer did not carry: a dance dress—one that exuded exuberance, a rosy future and joy. She had no idea why she wanted a dress like this, to be honest. The desire had probably been growing ever since Mama had read Cinderella to her. She asked the saleswoman where she could go to find such a dress, and she recommended the Atelier Albert Dézière on Friedrichstraße.

The store was a dream in black and white, and the director, a Frau von Zanitz, struck Emma as the epitome of elegance. She invited Emma to a seating area and asked her what she was looking for. After listening, she smiled. "I think our atelier has just the thing"—she turned—"Gertrud, will you please bring me *Venezia* and *Irish Waltz?*"

Emma found herself standing in her underwear again, this time in a fitting room whose mirrors stretched from floor to ceiling. The decor was completed by standing screens, low armchairs, and an open cupboard that held the dresses to be tried on. Frau von Zanitz helped her into the first dress, made of dark green silk, with long, tight sleeves and a high neckline. The wide-sweeping skirt sat low on her hips; however, the bodice didn't drape loosely across her torso like most dresses did, but instead clung tightly to Emma's body. A complete stranger gazed back at Emma from the mirror, one who seemed bolder and more interesting than the real Emma.

"It suits you exquisitely. But let's try the second model."

Venezia was a dress like the ones Emma had admired in the magazines. The peachy hue looked delicate and innocent, but the cut suggested pride and confidence. Sleeveless and low-cut, the top joined a skirt that seemed to be composed of large petals. These gossamer flounces and cascades flowed one on top of the other, revealing glimpses of the wearer's legs as she moved. Emma stood still and speechless before her reflection. So this was what dresses could do! Was this why Sybil kept running from one dressmaker to the next? Cautiously, she spun around.

"You don't have to worry about anything slipping. We place great value on excellent fits. We can shorten the straps a touch. That would make you feel more comfortable."

"Do I look ridiculous though? These are beautiful dresses, but they're certainly better suited to a woman with—oh, I don't know..." Emma gazed steadily into the mirror. She didn't really think she looked ridiculous, but maybe it would be apparent to people who saw her that she lacked self-confidence?

Frau von Zanitz smiled. She had a sixth sense about what was special about every woman, and she was never wrong. Emma might become a loyal customer who would do honor to Dezière. "You look lovely in both gowns, though I would recommend *Irish Waltz*. *Venezia* is a bold design, and it looks marvelous on you, but it lacks that something special, something out of the ordinary." She helped

Emma back into the dark green dress, and now when Emma stood in front of the mirror, she saw the Emma that she had always hoped to one day become.

Emma's stomach rumbled, loud and unladylike, as she crossed the square. No wonder; the clock on the town hall said half past four, and she hadn't eaten anything since breakfast. The Behrendt Bookstore was her last stop, and then she would hurry home.

She had just entered the store when someone tapped her on the shoulder from behind. Anton Wagenknecht, of all people! Grinning, he stood in front of her, obviously pleased to see her. "Well, this is a surprise! There I was locking up my office, and who do I see strolling by but Fräulein Schumacher, loaded down like a pack mule. Of course, as an honorable gentleman, I rushed over to help." Without waiting for her response, he reached for her purchases.

Emma wondered if she would ever be allowed to hold anything that he wouldn't try to snatch from her. Nevertheless, the bags were getting heavier and heavier, and if he really wanted to be useful, then he could go ahead and help her. Plus, it was a way to keep his hands occupied with something other than her. She turned and asked the bookseller for a recommendation; she wanted something lighthearted and cheerful to read.

The clerk mulled this over for a moment. Something cheerful, something unlike most of the books out these days, tomes exploring the depths of the human soul or politics or glorifying the German past. The bookshelves were teeming with madmen, criminals, and melancholy duchesses. "Oh, what about this one? It's an English translation, *Enchanted April* by Elizabeth von Arnim. A light, summer story but not without depth."

Emma examined the cover and realized that she'd read some of von Arnim's other books before and had enjoyed them. She decided to buy it . But how could she escape Herr Wagenknecht? In short, she couldn't; it would have required something a lot more direct than her politely phrased request that he please return her bags to her as she didn't want to detain him further. He refused and instead of vanishing, as she wished he would, he stubbornly planted himself right next to her. She sighed and gave up, trusting that she could count on Tante Tinni and her assertiveness to deal with him.

"Are you feeling unwell, Fräulein Schumacher?" asked Anton quite sympathetically. "Are you worried? Is your father still on the road?"

Her father was still traveling, yes.

"I can't tell you how much I wish my old man would come up with such a fabulous idea. All he ever does is work, work, work!"

Emma replied that yes, she did have a sense of that situation, since he had droned on about his father during their walk from the university to her home.

"If you only knew how much I regret that! Really, I'm downright ashamed. What an impression I must have made on you. Yes, just admit it—a hooligan, a drunkard, an ungrateful son—that's how I must have appeared to you. That was a particularly bad day for me. I was so depressed that I could barely see straight." He gazed at her sincerely, from head to toe the very picture of remorse. "And then you ran into me, and I completely lost my head. Please forgive me, but you must be used to this sort of thing? We men can't help but be drawn to women like you, who possess something special or unique. Oh, you see, there I go on and on again. It's all your fault, Fräulein Schumacher!"

Emma had no idea where to turn her face. How did someone behave in such a situation?

The heavens intervened. Already as they were leaving the bookstore, heavy winds had begun to pick up and clouds were chasing across the sky, blocking the sun. Then just as they were turning down Kaiserstraße, a storm broke out, making any reply to Anton's questions irrelevant. Within seconds, torrential rain soaked every inch of fabric on their bodies. They looked like two wet cats.

"I think this is an excellent moment for a cup of coffee, Miss Schumacher!" exclaimed Anton, pointing at the Rittershaus Bakery.

Within a few moments, they were sitting in the coffeehouse's conservatory, watching the rain not only drum against the windows, but turn the street into a rushing torrent. The serving girl handed them towels and draped newspapers across their chairs before they sat down. More and more passers-by crowded into the café. The heaters were running at full blast, causing the windows to fog up. It was almost cozy, sitting there with their coffee and cake, bathed in warmth. Emma glanced over at Anton and felt a quiet disappointment. Why did her first time sitting alone with a young gentleman in a café have to be with Wagenknecht? At least today he wasn't behaving like a complete pest as he had before. He looked up and caught her eye. Inquisitive, without his usual grin. *He has nice eyes*, Emma thought in surprise.

"You're blushing, Fräulein Schumacher," he declared sincerely. "I think it's delightful. You have no idea the kinds of things that can be said to some women, and all they do is shrug, as if they've already experienced everything, seen everything—yes, yes, I know I'm not exactly innocent in all this. Why would I say such things to any woman? But you know, you're hanging around, visiting the Kerze bar and all the other snazzy dives, out with a few guys, dancing with loose women and having a good time, and all of a sudden, you're a completely different person. My father's right: I'm wasting my life, and I should start something. Work, a family, whatever. But if you don't meet someone who is worth taking that step for..."

Emma was in uncharted waters. She didn't really feel completely comfortable in his presence, but what Anton Wagenknecht was saying from his chair across from hers, so calm and level-headed, didn't sound all that different from John McGivern's declarations about his plans for the future, about good timing and the right partner. But while John had gazed off into the distance, barely noticing Emma, Anton only had eyes for her.

"Look, the rain has stopped. Let's get you home quickly so you can warm up properly and not catch a cold." He waved to the serving girl, paid their bill, and asked Emma to hold the door for him, for on no account was he going to allow her to carry even one of her bags.

Jean-Baptiste opened the front door as Tante Tinni stepped out of the kitchen. Before she could send Herr Wagenknecht packing, Emma thanked him politely, while Jean-Baptiste took her purchases off his hands and carried them to her room.

Christel studied the completely drenched Anton. It didn't seem right to send him out into the roaring wind, soaking wet. And even if she had mistrusted him previously, she didn't want to be blamed for his untimely demise. Plus, he had, after all, accompanied Emma and kept her safe from the rain. Christel asked Emma to look in the coat closet for one of her father's overcoats, which would keep Herr Wagenknecht warm and protect him from the elements. She would appreciate it if he could drop it back by their house in the next few days.

While Christel returned to the kitchen—a hearty pot-au-feu was simmering on the stove—Emma searched the closet until she found one of her father's dark coats among Sybil's colorful and Tinni's stolid ones. She took it off the hanger and was about to hand it to

Anton, who would surely be swallowed up by it, when she noticed how heavy the coat was. The right pocket was bulging strangely. She reached in and wrapped her fingers around a medium-sized object, loosely wrapped in several layers of thick wrapping paper. She handed Anton the coat before unrolling the item.

In her hands, she held Bastet, the cat goddess whose tilted head was gazing at her intently.

It was late at night, but Emma was wide awake. She was sitting cross-legged on her bed, a cardigan over her nightgown. Spread out around her were the drawings Papa had made of Bastet. His notebooks were piled up on the nightstand, and the cat goddess herself lay in her lap.

Emma was trying in vain to follow a single train of thought: something bothered her about this figure and the drawings. This wasn't the first time she had held a millennia-old artifact. As a little girl, she had often been perched on the table while Papa showed her all the wonderful treasures the Bonn collection held. If a piece seemed sturdy enough, he would gently place it in Emma's hands or let her lightly run her fingers over it. He had enjoyed drawing her attention to the smoothness of an object or the roughness of its weathering, pointing out traces of paint and explaining to her how the object had been created eons ago and what purpose it might have served. Whenever Mama had attended the theater or an evening women's club event without him, Papa would put his little girl to bed and read to her. Instead of the fairy tales of the Brothers Grimm, he would read accounts of archaeological excavations or stories from ancient Egypt. Emma had adored these nights; her father was the safest fortress against disaster she could imagine, and when the greatest misfortune of all had struck, she'd found solace only in the company of her Papa and Tante Tinni.

She understood why he had sent her to live with Lady Milford, and she felt grateful both to him and Grandmother for everything. If she had remained here—well, she might have been less well-read and might have lost her English skills, and her general education would have been more superficial. But she would have learned everything Papa knew about Egypt. And instead of being stuck with only vague hunches and speculations, she would have been on more solid ground. She would also have made sure that her father hadn't made a fool of himself. But then again... Emma thought of all the books and novels she had read under Grandmother's tutelage and of the quiet security she had felt with her, as well as of Ada's affection. She felt a little ashamed.

Emma listened into the night, only now becoming aware of the howling storm that was sweeping over Bonn. Her hands were icy cold, and her legs tingled with numbness. She stood up a little stiffly, stretched and yawned, then carefully placed the small statue wrapped in a piece of cloth in her nightstand drawer and set the drawings aside. A few minutes later she fell asleep, dreaming of high priests chasing her through Frankfurt and Egyptian goddesses dressed in dark green dance dresses hurling fireballs at her.

Emma was surprised to find Alexei at the breakfast table. If she had been honest with herself, *shocked* would have been a better choice of words.

Shortly after Emma had sent Anton off with Papa's coat, Sybil had returned home accompanied by her Russian nobleman and had asked dear Christel to invite Alexei to dinner. Jean-Baptiste, who was happy to have male company, had immediately opened a bottle of red wine and warmly welcomed the young man.

Alexei was about ten years younger than Sybil, with dark blond hair that fell in waves across his forehead. He was skinny enough to cause everyone to suspect this wasn't a voluntary state. And after Christel had told him to forget his genteel restraint and just dig in, he had eaten with pleasure and a relish that warmed the cook's heart. After each bite, he had praised the stew, the fresh bread and wine, and had been grateful for the cheese. Later that evening, Christel had decided to cut into the cake she had prepared for a friend's birthday.

Within the hour, Alexei had won everyone's affection. He was rather quiet, which is why Emma had felt like she had found a kindred spirit, and indeed he seemed to share her thoughts. But Alexei was also eloquent, sprinkling well-timed bon mots throughout the conversation. He exchanged memories of southern France with Jean-Baptiste, describing his struggles there. He hadn't wanted to be the caricature of an exiled Russian driving a cab in Paris, and so he had ended up in Toulouse—driving a cab.

They had all been taken with the way he talked about his fate, without bitterness or self-pity. It was what it was, he had explained. He had saved himself, and that was more than some others had done. He had been able to take his mother with him, and she now lived in Denmark with one of her sisters. He spoke of his own sister with admiration, a woman of convictions. She had broken with her family at an early age to marry an artist and was now a committed Communist. At the time of Alexei's departure, his father was already old and infirm, and fleeing would have been unthinkable. Thus, he had done what any old-school officer would have done in such a situation, he stayed behind. But even if he, Alexei, carried grief in his heart, all that had been a long time ago, and he now wanted to enjoy this evening among his new friends.

And here he was, sitting next to Emma at the breakfast table, biting with delight into Jean-Baptiste's croissants. All at once, he glanced over at Sybil, and there was such warmth in his gaze that everyone felt it. Sybil held his hand, tousled his hair, and was charming, cheerful, and kind. Emma watched Tante Tinni and her Frenchman, who showed no sign of disapproval over Alexei's presence. If Jean-Baptiste approved of that, then why didn't he make such allowances for himself? Why did he insist on sleeping at his own house every night? If he were worried about Tante Tinni's reputation, well, Emma was now living here and could serve as a chaperone. No sooner did this thought occur to her than she uttered it aloud.

"Emma dear," Sybil chimed in, "you Grandmother would be appalled at your loose morals. Here you are sitting next to your aunt and her intended, and instead of registering your disapproval, you propose a similar arrangement for your other aunt!"

Alexei slipped his arm around Sybil's shoulder and asked her not to mock her niece, but to be glad that she welcomed him with open arms. Sybil apologized, begged Emma's pardon, and asked her not to be angry with her. She then turned to Christel: "But the question is justified, dear Christel. You and Monsieur Barbier are engaged to be married. Naked people dance on the stages of every city in Europe, and what used to be a scandal is these days no more than a side note. So why go to all this trouble?"

"That may be true in some places, but especially here on this street people still value manners and appearances. Why should I make life unnecessarily difficult for myself?"

Later Emma sat upstairs in her room. Christel and Jean-Baptiste were off shopping. Sybil and Alexei had gone to the Victoria Swimming Hall. Emma had stayed behind and had retreated to her bedroom when Frau Vianden, who had been the Schumachers' housekeeper for decades, had driven her out of the living room. For the thousandth time, she looked through Papa's papers while the cat goddess stood next to her on the table, her slanted eyes staring fixedly at the young woman, almost as if she wanted Emma to force her to divulge her secret.

Emma gently stroked the feline's cool head. She examined Bastet from every angle, comparing her to the drawings Papa had made of her. Something was different; she just couldn't quite figure out what it was. The Bastet in her hand was less vivid and luminous than the one in his drawings. The contrast bothered her because Papa's drawings were always very detailed and accurate; he never embellished them. It didn't make sense that the figure and his drawings should differ so greatly.

She sighed. Was she driving herself batty over nothing? Shouldn't she be searching for Papa, calling all the boarding houses and hotels? Her father had spent a whole week in Koblenz before setting off on his lecture tour. According to Herr Meerbusch, he had planned to use the trip to relax, and had suggested that he might be interested in visiting various castles and hiking trails along the way. Like all historians, her father was fundamentally interested in the past, and whenever they had stayed at Lake Constance he had enjoyed hiking as much as he could. So why was she having such a hard time believing her father was taking a hiking tour from castle to castle along the Rhine and Moselle?

She stood up, opened the windows, and took a deep breath. It was drizzling lightly, and fresh air flowed pleasantly into the room. What nonsense she had cobbled together, without any common threads or unifying ideas! Her thoughts were in constant flux, jumping hither and thither between anxiety and reassurance, fear and reason. Exasperated, she gave herself a shake and resolutely stashed the statue, drawings, and notebooks into the far corner of her closet. If she stared at the goddess any longer, she would go insane and start imagining that Bastet was talking to her.

Frau Vianden was now sweeping the hallway with serious intent. She could have used the vacuum cleaner that Professor Schumacher had purchased in his enthusiasm for technical innovations. She found it unsuitable for thorough work, however, and slightly disturbing. "Nothing good," she would say, "could come from a noisy monster called 'Vampy'." And yet Frau Vianden herself made a real racket with her broom and mop, reasoning that it didn't hurt if her employers noticed how hard she was working to get rid of the dirt in their homes.

By now, Emma had relocated to Papa's desk to write two lists that bore the titles "Things I've Accomplished" and "Things I Really Need to Learn." Her shorthand teacher had repeatedly stressed the importance of well-organized work and had required her students to make lists for everything. Perhaps she was right, and thus Emma Charlotte Schumacher was now setting about making plans for her future.

Her aunts would still be gone for a while. Sybil would certainly want to visit a hairdresser and a pastry shop after splashing around at the pool, and Jean-Baptiste had suggested to Christel that they go see a motion picture after finishing up their shopping. Emma couldn't help laughing to herself as she imagined the two of them sitting in a theater, surrounded by baskets of flour, leeks, and coffee beans. Then she continued writing.

So far, her list of things looked rather modest: she spoke fluent German, English, and French—skills that would most likely convince someone to hire her, especially now that the world was once again interested in trade relations with Germany and foreign languages were gaining importance. Shorthand, typewriting, and dictation, of course, but these skills weren't particularly unique. She could draw quite well and knew her way around literature. She added knitting and sewing to the list. And dancing, of course.

It was now time to start on list number two: she absolutely needed to learn how to cook, because the only thing she knew how to prepare at this point were sandwiches. She wrote down that it would be good to learn how to manage a household budget. After years of saving her allowance money and weighing every potential expense, she had been a little startled at the ease with which she had spent money the day before. "Never blush again!" was also added to the paper, and because she couldn't think of anything else, she concluded her list with: "Stay indoors when it rains."

She studied both lists and was astonished to see that the credit side looked better than the debit, but since she didn't have any clear idea of what skills she lacked, the result was of limited benefit. She wondered what job her talents might fit; she had yet to see a job posting looking for a typist for a yarn-selling literary café that hosted evening dances. Emma doubted the usefulness of her list-writing exercise and tore both sheets to shreds. Tonight, she would ask Tante Tinni to give her cooking lessons, and then, between selling yarn, dancing the tango, and taking dictation, she could mix mayonnaise for her guests.

"Fräulein Schumacher, there is a young man here who would like to speak to the professor. Shall I send him on his way?"

"I'm coming, thank you, Frau Vianden."

Emma stepped into the slippery, freshly waxed hallway, and her feet started to slide out from under her. But instead of landing on the floor, someone caught her by the upper arm and held her upright. Her feet refused to stay planted on the floor, though, and she suddenly found herself in the arms of a gentleman of whom she could see no more than his chin and tweed jacket. *Oh, forget the blasted cooking*, she thought. The issue with excessive blushing seemed like a more urgent concern at the moment.

The gentleman gently steadied her and bowed slightly after taking a step back. From his knickers to his flat cap, from his elegant shoes to his rolled-up umbrella, he was the epitome of the sporty Englishman. Just as he was about to introduce himself, Emma asked, "You're English, aren't you?"

He was a little taken aback by this, having assumed that after months away from home he must somehow appear more continental. On the other hand, he had apparently and unexpectedly met a compatriot, and a quite lovely one at that. "You're right, I am—James Stuart Beresford, at your service. And you are?"

"Emma Charlotte Schumacher. You're here to see my father?"

"Oh, the professor is your father? No, really?—Your English is quite excellent, I never would've taken you for a German. Oh! Not that I hold anything against the Germans, not at all. Well, the war, that was—sure, it wasn't nice, I... I..."

To Emma's surprise, he began to blush. She never knew that men blushed too! Mr. Beresford's stammering was clearly embarrassing to him, so Emma quickly cut in. "My mother was English, and for the last few years, I've been living with my grandmother in England. But you came to speak with my father, is that right? May I perhaps ask you to join me in the living room?"

Emma set off to lead the way, having already forgotten about the floor wax. James reached for her, but she was already sailing to the floor, dragging him along. *I really need to work on my technique for meeting people*, she thought as she scrambled to her feet with James' help. They both inched forward carefully until they reached the living room.

Once inside, James finally got around to answering her. "I had an appointment with the professor about six weeks ago, but unfortunately he didn't keep our meeting. Anyway, I thought I'd try again on my way back through Bonn. Is he at home, or may I drop by again tonight?"

"I'm sorry, but my father isn't in Bonn at the moment. May I ask what reason you had to meet with him? Would you like to study for your comprehensive exams with him?"

"Oh no, I finished up my studies some time ago. I met your father at an event at the university, and he told me about his desire to travel to Egypt. I mentioned that I had, well, connections with Howard Carter. Not very close, but I went to Cairo once at his invitation. Unfortunately, not because of my brilliance as a scholar—before you start thinking I'm something special. Well, not that I think you think I'm special... Anyway, as it so happens, my mother's sister is friends with the wife of the brother-in-law of one of the diggers—or was she the brother-in-law's girlfriend? But I guess the wife wouldn't have liked that... if he was married that is. Or was it my aunt's friend's sister-in-law? It doesn't matter—I received an invitation and traveled there, only to realize that I'm not suited for hands-on work. I'm more of a desk man myself. Well, now I'm looking for the right desk, so I've been hanging around all kinds of receptions. I explained this to your father, who asked me to speak with him again because he absolutely has to go to Cairo. And now I've told you half my life story. Normally, I don't talk so much or spout so much nonsense."

"Oh, I see! You're *the Englishman*!" exclaimed Emma.

"Well, we've already established that, remember?"

"No, no, that's not what I meant. My father mentioned you in a letter."

"That's very flattering. When do you expect the professor to return, then?"

"I can't tell you, I—he—" Emma broke off. She had told the story of her father's unexpected departure so many times that she practically knew it by heart. She looked at the young man sitting across from her. He was quite tall and slim. His face was striking and a little crooked, which was emphasized by his dark, carefully coiffed hair. He noticed her observing him and he gazed back at her. She lowered her eyes, feeling caught.

James wondered what was going on in Fräulein Schumacher's mind. Just a moment ago, she had seemed chipper, but now she looked as if she were about to burst into tears. Women were the most complicated creatures, weren't they? Had he said something wrong? He glanced at her legs. Very elegant, very elegant indeed. He quickly returned his gaze in the upward direction. An altogether delightful person, he thought. Should he offer her comfort? Or a handkerchief? Was she truly crying? Romantic and given to flights of fancy, he imagined himself as a knight offering her protection and assistance. He was dazzled by the vibrant image of her sinking into his arms.

There's no way you're going to start crying now, Emma chided herself, no way! She was considering how to inconspicuously wipe away a tear when James tossed a huge, colorful plaid handkerchief onto her lap. Dumbfounded, she looked up to see a blushing Mr. Beresford, his eyes roaming the room to avoid making eye contact at all costs. This tickled her for some reason, and Emma broke into peals of laughter, as the living room door swung open. Jean-Baptiste and Christel stepped over the threshold and were astonished to find a red-faced stranger and a chuckling niece sitting in the living room.

James was about to flee from the house—he was sometimes a bit touchy—but Jean-Baptiste blocked his way. Emma reached for his hand and apologized to him. However, it was her blushing face, not her words, that made him stay.

MARITAL BLISS

She smoothed her dress again, adjusted the fit of her stockings, and fiddled with her hair. Should she put on lipstick? She was supposed to make herself look elegant, but also respectable and modest. She dabbed on the color carefully and then wiped it off until only a hint was left behind. That was all she could allow herself.

She hurried down the stairs to the dining room. She counted the glasses, checked the distances and angles of the cutlery to the dishes, and rearranged the bouquet of chrysanthemums, roses, and gerberas for the third time that evening. In the adjacent room, she surveyed the serving arrangement, felt to see if the chafing dishes were keeping the food warm, and burned her index finger. Tears welled in her eyes, which she hastily wiped away. There was no way she was going to look teary-eyed or distracted.

"Mama, Father's coming. He's at the corner!" shouted Mareike. The twelve-year-old was watching the street from the upper bay window.

"How does he look?"

"He's laughing."

The girl's mother shivered. At home, her husband never laughed. He rarely smiled. He saved all his cheerfulness and charm for his business associates. The only guests they ever had in their home were the men to whom he wanted to sell things. There were never any friends, any acquaintances, any confidantes. She took a deep breath, forced herself to calm down, and donned a smile the same way she had put on the precious necklace—it belonged to him, not to her.

He entered along with four other men. Beaming, he moved toward her, embraced her, kissed her cheek. *You look wonderful, your new dress suits you perfectly,* and *I hope you have cooked something delicious for the gentlemen and me.* Turning to his visitors, he jokingly apologized for his indecorous behavior, declaring that his sweet little wife was the apple of his eye, and he wasn't ashamed to admit it. The gentlemen, older than him and sentimentally recalling their own youth, nodded, smiling, and hurrying to kiss the "little wife's" hand and congratulate the husband on his choice. They hoped the delightful housewife hadn't gone to too much trouble on their behalf.

"Where is Mareike?" asked the husband, ever the proud father. The daughter appeared instantaneously on the stairs, wearing a gossamer batiste dress that made her childlike figure seem even more delicate. Jumping down the last steps, she threw her arms joyfully around her father's neck, who patted her head and asked her about her day, before slipping her a bar of chocolate. Loudly enough for the others to hear, he whispered that she shouldn't tell Mama and chuckled. The gentlemen joined in the laughter, wagging their index fingers and asking about how well she must be doing at school, which Mareike answered courteously and shyly. The husband hugged his wife once more, telling her not to be angry with him for spoiling his beloved daughter. But after all, he had also brought his dear wife a little something too. She smiled, obediently closed her eyes, and held out her hand, in which he placed a small package.

"Unwrap it, Elisabeth. You've slaved away for us all day, and now here's your payment!"

He shouldn't have, she demurred, before unwrapping the gift and discovering a pendant of amber with a tiny bud trapped inside. *As the stone carries this bud, so I carry you in my heart,* he said. The gentlemen smiled. Their host now invited them to his table and seated himself at the head of it.

"Would you like to bring out the food for us, darling, or would you prefer that we serve ourselves?" he asked in high spirits. The gentlemen jumped up hurriedly, but the housewife forbade them to move and carried the plates one by one to the table, while Mareike poured the drinks and curtsied at each thank you.

"The flowers are a bit unusual today, aren't they, my dear?"

The woman, still in the next room, flinched, almost dropping the plate she was carrying. She gulped and replied that the florist had assured her that the floral arrangement was elegant and unique. Her husband nodded. She had exquisite taste, that's what he loved about her. As he loved everything about her. The guests reached for their cutlery, drank heartily of the Rhine and Moselle wines, toasted the lovely lady of the house, and enjoyed the evening. The next morning, they would happily conclude their business, having finally found a man who deserved their trust. Anyone so attached to his family was beyond reproach.

Intoxicated on good cheer and wine, the guests took their leave late in the evening, the husband waving after them until they turned the corner. He then closed the door, quietly and deliberately before turning around. "Mareike, to your room. Now!"

The daughter dashed upstairs and jumped into her bed, the covers pulled over her head, her arms wrapped around her knees.

"It went well, didn't it?" whispered the wife.

He didn't dignify her with a reply.

The first blow struck her face. He always hit her face only once, with the flat of his hand, careful to leave no marks behind. He dragged her into the dining room and knocked the vase to the floor. "Elegant flowers, I told you. Elegant, not colorful daisies."

He then yanked her into the next room and hurled a bowl from the table to the floor before flinging his wife after it. He kicked her, as she apologized and wept, pleaded, and begged. Kick after kick, blow after blow. Not in a rage, cool and deliberate. He carefully selected where to hit her until he eventually tired of it. He sat down in a chair and gazed at her with disgust, as she cowered next to the spilled sauce and whimpered. He calmly explained what he saw in her, how she disgusted him with her stupidity.

With that, he stood up, drew the curtains, removed his clothes, and went to her. She wasn't allowed to say a word but was expected to remain silent and perform her wifely duties. She held her tongue, as she always did.

THE SUFFERINGS OF YOUNG EMMA

Tante Tinni and Jean-Baptiste will end up running one of the most popular restaurants in Toulouse, Emma reflected over dinner. It won't only be for the cooking either; it will also be for their hospitality. They had not only managed to gather around the table several Germans, an Englishman, a Frenchman, and a Russian. They had also got them talking and laughing, and acting as if they had all known each other since childhood.

"Tell me, James," Alexei asked, "that Opel at the front door—is it yours, perchance?"

"Yes, it is! My pride and joy. It makes a good seventy kilometers an hour."

"And it can fit six people?"

"Well, yes, if they're people who like each other. Otherwise, it does get awfully cramped."

"James, what are your plans for tomorrow?"

"I should be looking for a job, so my father doesn't take the car away from me. What did you have in mind?"

"The GeSoLei!"

"You mean the Loreley?"

Alexei explained that he really wanted to visit the Great Healthcare, Social Welfare and Physical Exercise Expo in Düsseldorf before it closed its doors in a few days. Hadn't anyone else at the table heard of it? It was a fair, where people could ride through the human organism on little trains, attend sports demonstrations, and learn about healthy living. That was where they should all spend the day together! Searches for jobs, fathers, and old, unpleasant spouses—he shot Sybil a disapproving look—could be tackled any time after that.

"You young people should go," Tinni declared, reaching for Jean-Baptiste's hand, "and we'll have a quiet day all to ourselves."

Early the next morning, James reappeared at the door, and two hours later they were strolling through the Düsseldorf Fair. Sybil declared that it was her treat—old, unpleasant spouses were useful for something after all!—and refused to tolerate any protests.

They rode through esophaguses and lungs, marveled at girls doing gymnastics in Rhön Wheels, attended a lecture on the importance of leisure for the modern man, and feasted their way through various menus. Sybil and Alexei walked along hand in hand, and James offered Emma his arm. She glanced around from time to time to see if anyone had noticed her excitement or was staring at her with disapproval, but no one seemed to mind. On the contrary, here and there she saw couples holding each other closely. She even caught sight of a couple kissing in the middle of the crowds. She immediately looked away and turned toward James. He, too, had seen the couple, and Emma saw him quickly lower his gaze.

Sybil laughed, "You two are both beet red! May I introduce you to the year 1926? This is the world of today, so you'd better get used to it."

On the drive back, Sybil and Alexei snuggled arm in arm in the back seat, absorbed in each other and a little tired. It felt to Emma as if she were riding alone in the car with James. Throughout the day they had joked with each other, read to each other from various brochures, and marveled together at all the wonderful things they saw. Now, all of a sudden, she felt tongue-tied. This twilight drive home seemed too intimate. Or not intimate enough?

Over an hour's journey still lay ahead of them, and she was searching for words. "Your father gave you this car as a gift?"

"*Gift* isn't quite the right word, I'd say. It was more like: *Boy, see that you get a decent job, or you'll join the company.* My father considers himself a fair man, so he bought me the car and is financing me for this one year so I can find a job through which I can make a name for myself."

"That sounds quite fair."

"It probably is. However, he made it very clear that he didn't believe I would succeed and that the only reason he was paying for my nonsense was because he himself has done well in the world. That dimmed my gratitude considerably."

"What does your father do?"

"This and that, a little of everything. Real estate, financial transactions, company shares. He also continues to manage his grandfather's publishing house. Novels, penny dreadfuls, newspapers, all that sort of thing. He is constantly expanding his professional umbrella, and each of his ideas is a hit. I can't tell you how much that annoys me. I don't begrudge him his success, but he's so bloody smug, blasé almost, that I want to scream at the top of my lungs."

"And when are you joining the publishing company?"

"Oh, thank you very much, Emma. So, you don't think I'll get anywhere on my own either, eh? My father would call you a clever girl and give you a big hug. He loves anyone who thinks I'm a washout."

Emma gazed at him, aghast, and fell silent. James stared fixedly at the road, his lips pressed together into a thin line. A few minutes later, he inhaled loudly, glanced over at her, and apologized. She continued to be silent.

"I'm supposed to start work there after New Year's if I haven't found anything suitable by then. And basically, it's a fair offer. I'm twenty-six years old, have been spoiled my entire life, and even got to study what I wanted to in college, despite the fact my father thinks archaeology is a useless field. If I join the publishing house, my father will pay me a decent wage and make sure that I learn the business inside and out so I can eventually take over for him some day. And it's not that books don't interest me. They really do! It's more that I think I should be setting off on my own at this point."

"Wouldn't you have to give up this car and the luxuries you're used to, like spending a year hunting for the right position?"

"Of course, of course. I'm well aware of that. But it's complicated. I'm no longer even sure if I would make much of a mark as an archaeologist and historian, or as a scholar at all. I don't even know if I would have gone down this path if my father hadn't been so convinced of its futility. There's no way I want to grovel before him now."

"Isn't that kind of silly?"

James regarded her out of the corner of his eye. He had thought she was shy but instead of pitying him, she looked amused. "You think so?"

"Your father seems like a generous man, and I don't see why you shouldn't indulge him a little. Would you really take up a profession you don't even like, just to spite your father?"

Perhaps it would be best if they didn't discuss his father anymore, he suggested. What about Emma's Papa?

What was her father like? Well...

Emma talked and talked. About the bedtime stories, the arguments with colleagues, his work. She described how he could be at turns kind and eccentric. Finally, she admitted in almost a whisper that she was afraid she might lose her father, just as she'd already lost her mother.

By the time they arrived back at Arndtstraße, it was pitch-black outside. Sybil and Alexei climbed out of the back seat, and Emma was already swinging her legs out of the car when James grabbed her hand: "It's late, and you're tired. I beg you, please don't worry about your father anymore today. May I pick you up tomorrow morning for a walk around the city? You can show me the sights, I'll take you to lunch, and then you can tell me more about why you're so worried. Would you like to do that?"

Emma moaned and groaned. For the past half hour, she had been dressing and undressing, but nothing pleased or suited her. She'd bought all these clothes and shoes that were supposed to make her everyday life easier and more beautiful, and instead she was wasting a lifetime wondering what to wear.

"Wear the plaid one with the suede shoes, and I'll let you borrow my green coat."

Emma wheeled around as Sybil detached herself from the doorframe and stepped inside. "I'll help you. When's he coming?"

"Who?"

"Emma dear, don't play coy with me. James, of course. Stop wiggling, or I won't be able to close the hook. I'll put your hair up. It doesn't always have to be in that roll, you know. If you don't want to cut it, make something special out of all those wild curls. Wait a minute, I'll be right back." She hurried out and returned with all sorts of little bags and cloths. "Now, let me do this.—Sit still, Emma!—See, now you look like Clara Bow—Hold still, dear, hold still," Sybil admonished, as she held Emma's face, "Eyes closed... yes, that's better... look up. Like this." She finally let go, pleased with her handiwork.

Emma didn't dare look in the mirror.

"Now take a look at yourself. Go on!"

Emma turned and was astonished. "How pretty, Aunt Sybil! Thank you. I don't think I'll be able to manage it myself though."

"Oh, I won't be going anywhere for a while, so I can show you again. Do you like it? What did Nancy call you? A Cinderella? Well, she's the one who caught the prince, after all. Anyway, you look very nice."

But Emma was already running out of patience. She glanced at her watch; James would be ringing the bell any moment now. Instead of that though, she now heard hurried footsteps on the stairs, and suddenly Tante Tinni appeared in the room, wheezing, and pressed a letter into her niece's hands. Emma swiftly broke the seal and pulled the sheet of stationery from the envelope. She read the letter out loud:

> Augsburg, October 5, 1926
>
> My beloved daughter,
>
> I was astonished to learn of your arrival in Bonn. I am confused as to why you undertook such a long journey, considering that I had informed you that I will be traveling for some time.
> Of course, I understand that you would want to see your aunt again, and so I hope that the two of you will spend some pleasant days together without me. Treat yourselves to little day trips to the Drachenfels or to Cologne, whenever the weather is nice, and don't worry about me. I am quite well, despite the toll that every lecture takes on me at my age. I am enjoying every minute of this trip and will be back in touch as soon as I find the time.
>
> Give my regards to your aunt.
> Your Father

Christel groaned. "I'll tell you, Heinrich had a head injury. He doesn't know his left from his right anymore!"

Sybil had only peripherally registered Emma's worries, having been too occupied with Alexei and their joint undertakings. She was shocked to see how pale and mute the girl now was, the letter crumpled in her cramped hand. She asked Christel for clarification, and the latter promised to fill her in on the situation over a cup of coffee. "Emma, come downstairs with us. The coffee will do you good."

No sooner were they sitting at the kitchen table than the doorbell rang.

"That will be James, Emma dear. Now put that letter aside and have a nice morning," Sybil said as Christel hurried to the door.

But it wasn't James who entered, but a neatly groomed Anton, the professor's coat over his arm. He was also carrying two small boxes and a bouquet of flowers, which were in no way inferior in splendor to the flora of the Botanical Garden, a fact that was anything but coincidental. He deposited one of the packages into Christel's hands, "Madam, may I take the liberty of presenting you with these chocolates?"

He stepped into the foyer, put down the flowers and the other present, and asked, "I would like, if I may, to take Fräulein Schumacher out. A stroll through the city. That would be acceptable, wouldn't it, Fräulein Feuerhahn?"

Before Christel could answer, James appeared in the still-open front door. He hadn't come empty-handed. He was balancing a pastry box in his right hand and a bouquet of roses in his left. With mild surprise, he looked first at Christel's package, then at the bouquet Anton held.

The latter eyed him with a mocking grin and pointed at his flowers. "Nice little blooms you have there. I'm afraid Mrs. Mallaby is used to more splendid ones, though."

James breathed a sigh of relief. It was Sybil the boy wanted. "I'm sure yours will satisfy Mrs. Mallaby, my good sir."

"That isn't my intention." Anton turned to Christel, "Isn't Fräulein Schumacher at home?"

James stepped forward. "Fräulein Schumacher has a date with me," he explained, striving for suave grandeur. A hint like this would suffice among gentlemen, and he expected to see the other suitor leave gracefully.

But alas, Anton Wagenknecht was only a gentleman when it suited him, which wasn't the case just then. He remained where he was standing.

"I'll go fetch my niece," Christel declared before vanishing into the kitchen. "Emma, James is here. And so is Herr Wagenknecht."

Sybil tried to suppress her laughter, unfortunately without success. She'd never seen her niece provoke even the slightest interest from men before, and now she had to deal with two prospects at once.

Emma looked as if she was considering staying in the kitchen, but Tante Tinni resolutely pushed her into the hallway and closed the door behind her, on the other side of which Emma could hear peals of laughter. Shouldn't aunts behave with a little more decorum? She didn't have a chance to finish the thought, however, as Anton and

James rushed up to her, pressing flowers and gifts into her arms as they tried to talk over each other. For the first time, John McGivern's polite disinterest seemed appealing to her.

"Emma, if you will kindly inform this gentleman"—James eyed Anton with contempt—"that we have a date? He doesn't seem to have understood me."

"Fräulein Schumacher, please forgive my appearance. I merely wanted to return the coat I borrowed and to ask if you would do me the honor of accompanying me on a stroll through town. You see, I work hard during the week, and Sunday belongs to my father, with whom I want to reconcile, as you so sternly advised. If I had guessed that you were otherwise engaged..."

"Well, you will just need to schedule an appointment with Fräulein Schumacher for next Saturday. It isn't very polite to put a lady under such distress. An Englishman would never do such a thing!"

Anton snorted. "You're right about that: I'm no Englishman. Real blood flows through my veins, not lukewarm beer! I'm not ashamed of my feelings for this young lady here, and I won't mince words about it!" He nodded at Emma, "Forgive my outburst. It's simply that I had thought the day was so nice, but little did I know that I would come at such an inopportune time. If it's all right with you, I'll return next week. What I have to report to you can wait until then."

He turned to leave, but before he reached the door, Emma called him back, "To report? You mean about Papa?"

"I asked around at the college a bit, but I didn't learn anything of much importance. We can talk about it next time. Enjoy your weekend." He again turned to go.

Emma glanced over at James, "Wouldn't it be a little silly if we walked around town, while Herr Wagenknecht was doing the same? We'd be bound to run into each other all the time, but together we could...?"

James saw the matter differently, as his face clearly indicated. However, now that he had acted like an old school gentleman, he had no choice but to agree to his lady's wishes. While Emma dashed back to the kitchen to entrust the flowers and goodies to her aunts, he hissed at Anton that he was only taking part in this silly game for Fräulein Schumacher's sake and that he would be keeping an eye on him.

Anton smirked back. Fräulein Schumacher now seemed more interesting to him than ever, and as he had suspected, with a little color in her face, she was more than acceptable. She wasn't as stylish and overtly alluring as the women he usually went for, but she was undeniably cultivated and elegant. And his father would certainly like her. As far as his rival was concerned, even if Tommy Boy took some effort to compensate for his crooked face and the stiff shirts, it wouldn't do him any good.

The three of them sat in Em Höttche, Bonn's oldest restaurant. Emma and the two gentlemen were in agreement that its ambience would have been much improved were there one male guest fewer at their table.

From time to time, Emma glanced over at a lady who was dining alone at the center of the room and who seemed quite comfortable with herself. Emma felt, contrary to her good nature, a pang of envy. For the past three hours, she and her companions had wandered through the city, from Beethoven's birthplace to Schumann's grave, taking in every site of interest. Anton and James had exchanged only a few words, and these had been marked by such exaggerated politeness that occasionally bystanders had glanced back at them suspiciously. Emma could have overlooked this, but unfortunately the two men had outdone themselves in trying to please her. They competed to see who would open a door for her or pay for admission, who would lead her across a street or stand protectively in front of her at the tracks of the Rheinuferbahn tram.

Around noon, Emma had nearly reached her breaking point. With a sigh of exhaustion, she hadn't suggested but insisted that they go to a restaurant. The men had practically punched each other for the honor of helping her out of her coat and adjusting her chair. And now they were talking at her, recommending food and wine. She was fed up with their childish behavior. She informed them, in a tone sharper than she had intended, that she could read and that she didn't eat red meat, thank you very much. James and Anton responded with dismayed silence, crestfallen faces, and wounded sighs.

Never again, she swore, would she make such a fuss as she had getting dressed that morning, just to please some man!

When the waiter appeared, she ordered potato pancakes with apple sauce, while the gentlemen requested whatever dish was at the top of the menu.

Jeez, Anton thought, *the Fräulein has more of a temper than I thought.* He looked at James. Well, Tommy certainly couldn't cope with that.

The way he looked—so fussy. Anton wouldn't have to worry about him much longer.

He glanced over at Emma with a smile on his face: "I apologize a thousand times over. You already know that I can let my Rhenish temper get the better of me. Don't be angry with me, please?" He turned to James, held out his hand, and unexpectedly offered to use first names. That was the only decent way to end this stupid feud.

James was annoyed. If he refused, Emma would see him as stiff and unforgiving. If he did accept and shake hands, this pretty boy might think he didn't see through his game. Reluctantly, he took Anton's hand. His grip was firm and painful, his smile overly friendly. James struggled to hide his dismay, wishing that he could slap Anton instead. However, this annoying twit might be able to best to him in a physical competition. He sighed, then glanced at Emma. Damn, he liked her a lot. He smiled at her and kept silent while Anton continued to crush his hand.

Emma didn't imagine that either of them felt even the slightest bit of respect for each other; she was just glad to be able to eat in peace. And now that she had fulfilled her duty—and that is what she felt the morning had been so far—to both of them, she wanted to know what Anton had discovered.

He cleared his throat dramatically as James rolled his eyes. Anton grinned, then leaned closer to Emma. "Well, I asked around among the students and talked to Professor Neumann—you know, your father's successor—and I also went to see the Dean. I wanted to know if anyone had heard anything about this lecture tour. And lo and behold, one of the boys who is studying with your father said right away that he had talked about it a few times. Professor Neumann didn't know anything concrete, but he seemed to be a little jealous. I don't think he would admit it even if he did know more about it. Yes, and the Dean also said that an extensive trip would certainly do the professor good, because he is an old gentleman who obviously needs more rest than he gets at home. He seems to think it very likely that the whole thing is more a pleasure than a work trip."

"What else?" asked Emma.

"What else? Well, that's all I know," replied Anton. "I told you this morning that what I'd found out wasn't all that important."

Yes, he had indeed said that; however, he had acted in such a way that Emma had assumed the opposite. Just as she was about to rebuke him, he stared deeply into her eyes: "You have known for some time now that I am more interested in you than in your dear father. So you shouldn't scold me when I take the opportunity to spend a few pleasant hours in the best of company." He grinned and pointed at James. "I'm sure my friend here can understand that."

James winced but nodded with a wry smile.

"Well, that might be true, but I care about my father, and I don't care about anything else today." Emma hesitated. For a person who considered herself shy and withdrawn, she had already told a good many people about her worries. Jean-Baptiste had actively supported her. Tante Tinni cared as much about her father as she did, but like Sybil she was preoccupied with the changes happening in her own life. Emma often felt alone with her anxiety. She studied both men closely.

Anton was courting her with exaggerated attentiveness, but he had indicated that his parents placed great value on good manners. And he had asked around at the university in an attempt to ease her worries.

And James? It was strange, but she felt oddly comfortable with him. And he had met Papa in person, if only briefly.

Surely, she could trust them both, couldn't she? She decided to tell them everything from the beginning: from the first letter, which had struck her as strange, to the one that had arrived today, in which her father expressed surprise at her visit to Bonn, as if he had completely forgotten the special day in both of their lives. She went on to describe the travel plans that had begun with Herr Meerbusch, the scandalous behavior in Frankfurt and Würzburg, and Doctor Meinhardt's suspicion that the professor might be involved in the disappearance of an artifact.

Emma talked without pause, posed every question that came to mind, and realized that she was gaining clarity with each successive sentence. Wasn't it strange that her father had written about how exhausting his lectures were even though he was hardly giving any? What could have happened to make him forget the anniversary of his wife's death? Why was he insulting colleagues when he was usually overjoyed with anyone who showed even a glimmer of interest in Egypt? Why did people at the university know about his trip but not Tante Tinni? How could he travel without clothes and shaving gear? Why had he promised her a letter that had never arrived? And why had he sent a letter to London when he knew she was staying in Cornwall?

At some point she paused, thirsty and hoarse. Anton immediately ordered a lemonade for her, which elicited a scowl from James. This fellow was really getting on his nerves.

Anton coughed. "I'm sorry to interrupt, dear Fräulein Schumacher, but I promised my old man that I would accompany him and my mother to a gala tonight, and the train to Cologne won't wait for me. Or should I stay here with you? I'd do that in an instant if you wanted!"

Emma glanced at her wristwatch: three o'clock already! James waved to the waiter and asked for the check, because of course, he and Emma would escort dear Anton to the station. Anton beamed and strode ahead to open the door, rattling on about the unexpected friendships one sometimes made in this world. He would probably have maintained his effusive rambling all the way to the platform if someone hadn't interrupted him.

No sooner did the three start to cross the market square when three drunken fellows pounced on Anton, embraced him, and tried to pull him along with them. James saw Emma recoil from these noisy young men and wrinkle her nose, which wasn't surprising since they didn't exactly smell like roses and carnations. He felt a little ashamed of his gloating, but the feeling only increased as Anton tried to extricate himself from the drunkards. James took Emma by the arm and led her a few steps away from the pack, but they could still hear, loud and clear, how the trio bombarded Anton with indiscreet questions about the "yummy dish" and about where he had been the past few nights. Why was he now acting all hoity-toity and stuff?

Anton answered coolly, with a gaze of indifference, and then flashed a grimace of embarrassment in Emma's direction.

"Anton, Tony boy, don't make such a fuss! We're on our way to see Rosie. She's waiting at the city wall as usual. You're not going to miss that, are you?—Ooooohhhhh, now you're acting posh, aren't you? It must be that dish's fault that you're letting your chums down like that. First Hannes up and disappears, and now you're going to waste. Yeah, it's all right, do what you want…" the drunken members of the future elite shouted in confusion, until they finally staggered away in search of Rosie.

Anton bowed with unusual formality to Emma and pounded James on the shoulder so vigorously that James only narrowly escaped falling down by taking an elegant step backward. Then Anton asked the two of them not to bother accompanying him any farther than this point. He would find his way to the station on his own and trusted his friend James to escort Fräulein Schumacher safely home. He apologized for this embarrassing incident and hurried away.

This is how a Saturday afternoon should be, James reflected a little while later. How relaxed they were, sitting here together, talking and laughing. His mind drifted to his mother's tea parties, where he'd had to present himself as a well-bred son who was supposedly interested in the various daughters of her friends! At the Schumachers' living room table, however, no one seemed to be concerned about his suitability as a husband. Yet this time such concerns wouldn't have bothered him. He examined Emma's profile: her delicate nose, full mouth, long eyelashes. He liked her a great deal, and almost subconsciously he began to count her freckles. He had only met this young lady on Thursday, and yet it seemed like he had never been closer to anyone, which was ridiculous, of course. But did Emma like him at all? Twenty-one freckles adorned her left cheek. He gave himself a shake. What was wrong with him? He tore his eyes away and caught Alexei studying him.

The Russian winked at him, nodded slightly in Emma's direction, and raised his eyebrows as he reached for Sybil's hand before bringing it to his lips and kissing it.

James blushed, which only increased his embarrassment.

Emma, on the other hand, was watching her Aunt Sybil as she snuggled up to Alexei. "By the way," she asked, "what about your plans to go to Wiesbaden?"

Immediately, Alexei's face darkened. "Yes, kitten, what about your plans?"

Sybil frowned and helped herself to another piece of cake. Emma felt instantly ashamed. Why had she started blurting out everything that came to mind lately? She hadn't meant to upset anyone.

Fifteen minutes later, the displeasure seemed to be forgotten; everyone was chattering and laughing as before. Emma was the only one who remained silent, wrapped in her thoughts. She hadn't told James about Bastet. She leaned toward him and asked how well he, as an archaeologist, knew Egypt?

Sufficiently well, James replied, because although his area of expertise was the high Middle Ages, he was fascinated by the country on the Nile. That was why he had traveled to Cairo.

"There's one thing I haven't told you yet. Would you mind following me up to the study?"

He rose immediately to his feet.

Emma lit the table lamp, asked him to take a seat, and disappeared. She soon returned to set the wrapped Bastet statuette in his hand and the drawings on the table. What could James tell her about these?

Looking at the figurine, James suddenly seemed like a stranger. He struck her as serious, confident, and focused. Cautiously, he turned the goddess in all directions, examined every detail, and then compared it to the drawings. "Why are you showing me this sculpture?"

She explained to him how her father worked, where she had found the statuette, and how she vaguely felt something was wrong with it.

"You're right," he said, handing her the figurine. "What do you feel when you touch it?"

"It's smooth, cool, and heavy."

"Exactly. The sculpture in your hands is made of marble. Take a look at the drawings. How does this figurine appear to you?"

Emma picked up two of the pictures, though by now she could have traced every detail in her sleep. "It seems more alive, warmer, gentler somehow. I can't describe it any better than that."

"In fact, that describes it quite nicely. Look here, on this sheet your father noted the material: alabaster. The figure in your hand and the one on this sheet are not identical. Alabaster is often compared to marble, which seems unfair to me because alabaster can only lose in such a comparison. Alabaster is easy to work with and feels warm to the touch, while marble is cold and hard, but unlike alabaster, it's weather resistant. Emperors built their palaces from marble, which was considered a material befitting wealth, power, and pomp. But objects made of alabaster have a shimmer that makes them special; they seem to glow warmly. And that's what your father captured in his drawings. He's a true artist, Emma."

She once again compared the statue and its likenesses. Now that she knew she wasn't imagining the difference, she more fully appreciated her father's talent. The cat in the painting was characterized by a warmth, a luminous transparency, that the sculpture before her lacked. But what did all this mean? Did it mean anything at all? And if the figure in her hands wasn't the one in the drawing, where had it come from, and where was the alabaster cat?

James sat down on the sofa and extended his long legs. "Let's think. I'm truly not an expert in this field, but after thousands of years, it's rare to find two specimens of the same shape and in the exact same state of preservation, made of different materials to boot. What is found quite often are items that were placed in pairs or even by the dozens in temples or tombs, but these were usually made of the same material and typically differed just slightly from each other. After all these millennia, under rubble and sand, details like arms, noses and ears break off, but rarely in exactly the same spot. Some figures may even have been damaged during placement or when a tomb was relocated. Even if the objects were identical when they first started out, time is likely to have changed that."

Emma listened intently, then asked if he had considered the possibility of a forgery.

"I may be wrong, but it strikes me as odd—assuming we believe the drawings to be accurate—that we would have in our hands two cats, absolutely identical in their details, made of such similarly fine materials. If I recall correctly, Bastet was a very popular goddess, whose sphere of action was considered—let's say—domestic in scope." James blushed a little, because Bastet had served as the patron goddess of lovers and pregnant women, among other things. "Be that as it may, smaller figurines are frequently found, made of basalt, bronze or even alabaster. Probably to symbolize the different colors of fur, but I don't know that for sure. Some scholars think that the word alabaster comes directly from this goddess. Just the material alone conveys a lovely warmth to the figures. As you can see, there are various reasons why I don't really understand why the same sculpture also exists in this exact marble copy. It's too small to have stood outdoors, despite the fact that durability is the one great advantages of marble. The pure material value is higher with marble, but the artistic one? If the alabaster figure is as well-preserved as this, despite its delicacy, then it is many times more valuable. I'm talking in circles, pardon me, but just as you had a bad feeling when you saw the drawings, I feel the same way about the idea of this marble figure. From an artistic standpoint, there was no reason to use marble. And look at the left front paw. See? A tiny piece of the paw is missing there. On both of the figures!"

"I see. Papa has certainly examined fakes in the past. Do you think this is one?"

James shrugged; he wasn't knowledgeable enough to know for sure. They sat side by side in silence for a moment, then he asked when exactly her father had left.

It must have been at some point between August tenth and eighteenth, although she didn't know exactly since Tante Tinni had spent a few nights at a friend's in Cologne at that time and had only noticed her brother's absence once she'd gotten home.

"But that's most peculiar—" James started to say as Alexei stepped into the room to ask if the two of them wanted to go out dancing.

As he said this, Alexei's eyes fell on the cat figurine, and he immediately drew closer. "Oh, I love cats. My mother always had them. One day, I'll breed cats. The most adorable and lovable cats on the planet! Ah, a beautiful dream, don't you think? May I see her a moment? Is she very old? She's gorgeous." Alexei could hardly tear his eyes away from the figure. "Well, what do you think? Are you coming? Starting tomorrow, I'll be carrying food on a tray every night. Today I'd like to have some fun with you."

FEAR!

Over the foot of her bed hung her dress, stockings, and coat. On the floor in front of it, lay her shoes. Behind Emma herself: the most exciting night of her life. At four in the morning, she sat at her window seat, snuggled in a crocheted blanket, massaging her sore feet. She wouldn't take a single step downstairs today—no, make that not even tomorrow. Neither the sun nor an entire cavalry of horses could make her leave her room. She would possibly make an exception for James, though. James Stuart Beresford. Beresford, such a melodious name. Emma Charlotte Beresford. *Oh, stop it, silly,* Emma scolded herself, *you hardly know him.*

She massaged her feet more vigorously until her toes tingled. It must be because of all the newly-in-love couples around her that she was imagining feelings for the first man who crossed her path. Actually, Anton Wagenknecht had been the first one. Emma Wagenknecht. She dissolved into giggles.

Although...? Why did she find the very idea that she might like Anton so ridiculous? He was courting her, not with finesse and subtlety, but at least openly and sincerely. And he was a man who could turn heads, much better looking than James. But what about James? Did he see anything more in her than someone he'd meet by chance, who could make his stay in Bonn a little more pleasant? Oh, her head was full of nonsense! *But there is sense in nonsense, isn't there? Sensible, nonsensical,* she let her thoughts drift. She might have made a good philosopher, sensual, and sensible. Everything made sense. Or maybe she was just tipsy? She giggled and then laughed heartily. Tipsy. Her! Ha! At Haus Daufenbach they had drunk wine, one glass after the other, while at the Schauburg, it had been champagne. And afterwards, they had danced their way through every pub and hotel that would let them in. And she had danced not only with James and Alexei—oh, and Alexei danced divinely!—no, other gentlemen had also asked her to dance. Some had even asked to see her again, but Emma had just laughed and moved on to the next partner. She had bubbled over with esprit and charm. It must have been the magic of the dress. Or perhaps the alcohol...?

When she awoke around noon the room was rotating around her. That made her suspect that alcohol might have played the greater role in her transformation. She blinked. How bright it was! A torment to her half-opened eyes! She climbed out of bed carefully, staggered to the window, drew the curtains, and dragged herself back to her pillows. How could such a lovely evening have led to such a headache? Yesterday she had been disappointed to learn that James would be spending three days in Düsseldorf, where a college friend was staying on his honeymoon. Now she felt grateful to this unknown friend and his bride; James shouldn't see her like this.

Emma curled up, her knees drawn up to her chin, so she could bear the swaying of the bed, the constant up and down, up and down, up and...

She began to snore quietly.

Emma bolted awake. A door banged somewhere downstairs, footsteps echoed from the hallway, then the front door was slammed loudly. It was pitch dark. Emma felt around for the alarm clock. Half past eight. Morning or evening? It was dark, so it must be evening, then. Sunday, probably. Someone was crying, and she could hear Jean-Baptiste's bass humming something incomprehensible. Another door closed, quietly this time.

Emma lay still for a few minutes longer before flicking on the lamp and tentatively lifting her head. She stood up, swayed only briefly, and reached for her glass of water. She felt better, although her thoughts still seemed kind of hazy and her feet complained when she slid them into her slippers. Carefully, she plodded down the stairs and listened before entering the living room. She saw a tearful Sybil, sobbing in Tante Tinni's arms. Jean-Baptiste was handing out tissues from a small stack on the table in front of him.

I wonder if Jean is ever unprepared, Emma reflected. *He seems ready for anything.* She blinked, forcing herself to concentrate: this is about Sybil. She isn't well. She's crying. Do something. Comfort her.

Emma staggered over and knelt beside her, reaching for her hand. Only then did the three of them notice her. Jean-Baptiste stood up, took her by the arm, and guided her to where he had been sitting next to Sybil. Tante Tinni nodded at her.

"Aunt Sybil, what's the matter? Don't cry, please."

Sybil turned and collapsed against her niece's shoulder. Emma held her aunt tightly, stroking her cheek and murmuring over and over that everything would be all right, everything would be all right.

Tante Tinni explained what had happened. Alexei had left the house after a quarrel. They had been sitting at dinner when he dropped by on his way to work. He'd had a small box with him and had been excited and happy. He had then asked Sybil to come out into the hallway, but just a few moments later, she had stormed back into the living room, angry and upset, slamming the door. Alexei had followed her, shouting something like, 'Then you don't deserve any better!" before also hurrying away and slamming the front door. Sybil had raged and shouted, but only briefly. She had been crying ever since.

"Aunt Sybil, why were you fighting? What did Alexei want?"

Sybil gasped and whispered, "He wants to marry me. The stupid boy. Marry me..." as she burst into tears again. It wasn't until late in the night that she allowed herself to be sent to bed. Emma, who could hardly fall asleep after such a tumultuous, hungover day, could hear her sobs through the wall. She got up two or three times but never screwed up enough courage to venture into her aunt's room. What comfort could she offer after all? She couldn't figure out the why or wherefore of this particular argument. Shouldn't Sybil be happy that Alexei loved her?

Emma woke up early, no sound piercing the dark house. She switched on the light and read a few lines in *Enchanted April*, whose characters also seemed to be suffering because of love and marriage. She put the novel aside and got out of bed. In the kitchen, she set the table and waited for the others to wake up. She basked in the warmth of the stove's fire, crackling and cracking, and thought about nothing and about everything in a swirling chaos with no beginning and no end.

Jean-Baptiste arrived at six-thirty; Emma hadn't been aware that he had his own house key.

"Are your aunts still asleep?"

"I suppose so. We were up late."

He nodded, then tied on an apron and set to work. Like Christel, he believed that food, though it couldn't solve every problem, was comforting. What could be more suitable for a lovesick woman than crêpes for breakfast?

Sibyl ate her breakfast dutifully. Silent, hoarse, and exhausted from weeping, she was now sitting hunched on the kitchen bench. They had been talking for an hour—about Alexei, his poverty, his age, his proposal, about the brevity of their acquaintance, Sybil's previous marriages, and her conviction that she must marry a wealthy man, about her age, her acquaintances, and her general state of uncertainty.

Then suddenly Christel slammed her hand on the tabletop, causing the dishes to clink and the tea to slosh out of the cups. "And now we're done with the long faces and the dressing gown. Go put something nice on. Don't argue, make yourself pretty. Jean and I are taking you to Cologne with us," she declared in her best effort at High German.

Not daring to contradict her, Sibyl traipsed to the bathroom and dug deep into her little makeup jars.

An hour later they departed, but Emma stayed behind. She strolled through the house, putting away plates here, pillows there, shaking out the beds, drawing back the curtains, airing rooms, and at eleven o'clock, opening the door for Frau Vianden, who came as she did every Monday and Thursday "for the deep cleaning." The maid preferred to work undisturbed. Her employers were allowed to hear her, but to see her fingers grow raw from scrubbing? That was forbidden!

Emma fled from room to room, wishing she had gone with the others to Cologne. She really had no idea what to do with herself. Listless and bored, she picked up her knitting only to discard it again after only a few rows. In the garden, she tried her hand at pulling weeds around the flower beds but was soon doubtful whether the removed stalks were truly weeds. Abandoning this, she swept up the loose leaves on the terrace until a spider scurried across her feet, inspiring her to leave the garden to its own devices. She checked the coal boxes for the stoves and refilled them with briquettes she fetched from the cellar with the scuttle. Before too long, Emma ran out of things to tidy and clear.

She sighed. When her aunts and Jean-Baptiste drove off, she had been looking forward to the day ahead. She now had several useful little chores behind her, which was laudable though not exactly enjoyable. Time to take a break and think through a few things. If she ever got married, these chores would make up her life's work:

organizing, washing, cleaning, cooking... What if she wasn't cut out for all this?

"All done, Fräulein Schumacher, unless there's somethin' else?" Frau Vianden stood in the doorway, her coat and gloves already on. Emma would never have dreamed of stopping her. She bid a cheerful goodbye to the housekeeper and accompanied her to the door, sending a silent, joyful thanks heavenward. Now that peace and quiet had returned, she could finish her novel. Or, since she was hungry, she could eat something. Armed with a cookbook, she ventured to the stove. An hour in the kitchen reinforced her fear that she wasn't born for the domestic world. Once she cut off the blackened edges, her roasted potatoes were definitely, well... roasted. A thick slice of rye bread with butter and salt completed her meal.

I could go for a walk, Emma considered. However, she left it at that because her toes were still covered in red blisters, and a walk inevitably meant having to fasten shoes over those sores. Bored, she threw herself into an armchair. The day and the house were at her disposal, and what was she doing with them? Nothing. How dull!

A bath! That would be just the thing! From her aunt's bedroom, she collected bubble bath, oil, and a jar of almond cream, and a few minutes later she climbed into the fragrant water, her face covered with at least an inch of pale-yellow cream.

This is how you get through things, she decided as she sank into foam up to her chin. Dense steam filled the small bathroom, drifting around her in gentle swirls. The golden pattern on the blue-green tiles seemed to sway gently, and she imagined herself in a Turkish bath, dreaming herself into distant worlds and times. Could she find donkey milk and coconut oil to replicate Cleopatra's beauty regimen? She imagined herself surrounded by servants who anointed her before she paid homage to the gods and greeted her people, her eyes fixed on the Sphinx. For a moment she thought she could feel the warm sand beneath her feet and hear the sound of the Nile...

Papa!!! Emma bolted upright. She had completely forgotten about her father amidst the dancing and drinking and daydreaming. What had James said about alabaster and marble? He, too, suspected something mysterious behind this pair of cats. One of them might be a fake, but how was this connected with Papa's peculiar journey? She was done splashing in the tub, so she jumped out, covered in foam.

Finally dry and warm in her robe, Emma brewed a cup of tea and padded over to Papa's desk, spreading the drawings and the Bastet figure in front of her. Under the bright light of the desk lamp, she took measurements of the figure and compared them with her father's measurements; they all matched perfectly. She went on to examine every notch and detail, convinced, like James, that it was impossible to find two absolutely identical statuettes in the world.

She stood up and pulled several encyclopedias and reference works on Egyptian art from the shelf. Many theories existed as to how an artist thousands of years ago could have created perfectly symmetrical faces and towering statues with ideal proportions, and all without any significant technical equipment. Many scholars had described the roles played by the grids and rectangular blocks, the traditions and catalogues of forms that craftsmen utilized.

Emma was a talented draftswoman, though freer, more imaginative in execution than her father. She now forced herself to be precise and to sketch the marble figure with accuracy. She was so absorbed in her work that she failed to notice the falling dusk. No light burned in the house other than the small desk lamp with its red glass shade. It illuminated only a limited area, causing the bookshelves to vanish into the darkness. Emma drew, erased, and made comparisons. At some point, she pulled her bare feet up onto her chair to protect them from the evening chill that had begun to spread. But she continued to sketch, ignoring her own shivers. She registered nothing but the paper and pencil and Bastet.

Then she suddenly lifted her head, glanced around, and listened. Had the garden gate just squeaked? Were the other three back already? She waited but heard nothing else—no voices, no footsteps. It had probably been the wind. She continued to draw, though less focused than before.

There! Again, she thought she heard something. She pushed back her chair and walked to the center of the room.

The sound of the doorbell echoed through the house, and Emma winced. How shrill and piercing that bell was! Only then did Emma notice the silence and the blackness that surrounded her. Her sudden feeling of being profoundly alone was heightened by finding herself unexpectedly torn from her concentration and enveloped in the cold and—yes!—loneliness. She was freezing and shivering, but that didn't explain why she wasn't stepping out of the study to turn on the hall light to see who this late caller was. Why was she rooted to where she stood, fighting a fear that must be unfounded? She could barely breathe as she listened to what was going on outside.

The doorbell was followed by a knock, energetic and loud. Emma flinched but remained motionless. Then she heard the squeak of the garden gate. Whoever had rung the bell had given up and left. She was about to laugh away her fear when she heard footsteps. Footsteps that climbed the steps once more. No ringing this time, no knocking. And suddenly she realized why she was afraid: Papa's students, the mailman, the cleaning lady—none of them would come at this time. Who else could be at the door? Tante Tinni and Jean-Baptiste had keys. James was staying in Düsseldorf, and Alexei was waiting tables tonight. If it were Anton he would call out loudly for her. But would any of them ring the bell at a darkened house? From the street, it had to look deserted this early evening.

Emma still didn't move. She hardly dared to breathe for fear of missing some new sound. She listened intently. A scratch, a soft clang, a rattle—whatever those sounds meant, they increased her fear immeasurably. There was no time to think, so she hurried to the table, switched off the light, opened the patio door, and stepped outside. She quietly and carefully pulled the glass door shut behind her, and then dashed barefoot across the damp lawn to the end of the long, narrow garden. There a shed had stood for ages, tiny, shabby, and surely full of spiders and bugs. She tugged at the door, which was stuck on its long-rusted hinges.

Please, please, open, please!!! Desperately, Emma looked over her shoulder back at the house, still engulfed in darkness. Had she imagined everything? But then she saw a glimmer inside the house, a moving beam of light. Someone must have opened the door to the study. At any moment, he might notice the not-quite-shut patio door and follow her. She pulled and tugged at the shed door, tears of terror running down her cheeks, and at last—*at last!*—it jerked open a little. The creaking sound startled Emma. Please don't let anyone hear her! She glanced back once more, but the light remained motionless.

She yanked on the rusty doorknob once more, and now the door opened a hand's breadth wider, enough for her to squeeze through. Splinters gouged into her arm, and she felt her robe rip. Although her shoulder now ached, she had made it. She groped her way to the farthest corner of the room, struggling against disgust and nausea. The musty stench inside the shed took her breath away as she tried to ignore the cobwebs in her face, the slimy dirt floor under her feet with its sharp stones, and the unseen creatures she suspected were in there. However, her fear of the unknown inside the house forced her to stay calm. Through the crack of the door, she watched the light to see where it wandered. Would the intruder find her out here? Were they looking for her, or did they think the house was empty?

She quickly scanned the shed walls. Before the war, the gardener had kept his tools in here, and she managed to find something useful, even if was only a spade. Firmly clutching the handle, she was now ready to lash out should someone come in. Her eyes, tearful and damp, stared fixedly at the windows of her home. Papa's office was dark once more, the light had vanished.

But then it flared brightly and briefly, a flicker only. Whoever was in the house was now looking around on the second floor. In her room! For a few minutes, the cone of light shone there, then it disappeared and reappeared in Sybil's room.

Something crawled up Emma's left calf, and she almost screamed. Instead, she slapped her free hand against her leg in panic, then wiped it on her robe. She glanced back at the house. It now looked black and still. She waited—an eternity, it seemed to her. But no light shone again, no one entered the garden. She lost all sense of time, as well as all feeling in her limbs. She was shivering, as much from fear as from cold, but didn't dare to leave the shed. Gripping the spade tightly, she leaned against the wall and let herself weep quietly. After several minutes, she slowly slid down to the ground, her legs no longer able to support her. And there she sat, not knowing what she was waiting for. She didn't care; she felt numb inside and out.

"Emma! Child, where are you? *Emma!!!* Are you here?"

"Emma dear, please answer!"

Her aunts. Emma scrambled to her feet, balancing laboriously on her wobbly legs as she called out repeatedly, "Here! I'm in here!" Then a crash, a splintering crack, and Jean-Baptiste was there, pulling the old wooden door out of its frame. It took only two strides for him to reach her, and then he was carrying her out, through the garden and into the warmth. The last thing Emma registered was Sybil gingerly loosening her fingers from around the spade's handle.

"I wish you had notified us sooner," Assistant Inspector Siegfried Mertens repeated for the umpteenth time. "If you had, we might have been able to find more clues." He took a seat at the professor's desk, opened his notebook, and proceeded to write down:

>Date: Tuesday, October 12, 1926
>Location: Arndtstraße 13a
>Offense: Burglary and theft by unknown assailant
>
>Owner:
>Heinrich August Schumacher, born July 18, 1849, in Bonn, widowed, retired professor. At the time of the crime, traveling, destination unknown.
>
>Witnesses:
>Christine Maria Feuerhahn, born May 12, 1870, in Cologne, unmarried, seamstress. Since 1906, housekeeper in the home of her half-brother. At the time of the crime, on her way back from Cologne to Bonn, accompanied by M. Barbier and Mrs. Mallaby.
>Emma Charlotte Schumacher, born on October 31, 1906, in Bonn, daughter of H. A. Schumacher. Was alone in the house at the time of the crime.
>Jean-Baptiste Barbier, born on March 3, 1865, in Toulouse, France, former lieutenant, innkeeper. Engaged to the aforementioned Fräulein Feuerhahn.
>Sybil Alexandra Mallaby, née Milford, born on December 22, 1890, in London, England, widowed, aunt of the aforementioned Fräulein Schumacher. Is visiting.
>
>Sequence of Events:
>At about six o'clock in the evening, Fräulein Schumacher heard a knocking. Not expecting any visitors, she did not open the door, but hid in the tool shed. When questioned, Fräulein Schumacher made a frightened and overwhelmed impression, which may suffice as an explanation for her behavior.
>She observed the glow of a light from where she was hiding, which, in her opinion, could have come from a flashlight. This glow traveled through the house. Fräulein Schumacher remained in the shed until her relatives returned home from a visit to Cologne at around eight o'clock in the evening.

According to Barbier, Feuerhahn, and Mallaby, the front door was closed, but the window above the door handle was broken, the house was dark, and Fräulein Schumacher could not be found in the house. Only by shouting did they discover her in said shed. Fräulein Schumacher was put to bed by the witnesses since she was barely responsive as well as severely hypothermic.

An examination of all the rooms by the witnesses revealed that an unknown person must have searched cupboards, tables, etc., at which time no object was reported missing except a pearl necklace belonging to Mrs. Mallaby, which was not without value (an exact estimate is being obtained).

Since the concern for Fräulein Schumacher had been quite urgent, the police were not immediately notified, in part because the women feared that the unknown assailant might attempt to re-enter the house; thus M. Barbier kept watch in the entrance hall overnight. No one thought to call in a message to the police station, since the device was only recently installed in the house.

At half past eight this morning, M. Barbier appeared at the Königstraße police station to file a complaint.

I followed him to the scene and took the witness statements with the result listed above. Fräulein Schumacher then also searched all the rooms and discovered the loss of some drawings that she herself and her father had made of a work of art from Egypt, as well as the theft of a similar figure. It is a representation of a sitting cat, about fifteen centimeters in height, made of marble, whose value must still be ascertained.

Jean-Baptiste thought he embodied the ideal German officer, full of ambition and efficiency; the three women thought he was merely a thoroughly capable and trustworthy individual. He had introduced himself with exceeding politeness as Siegfried Mertens, and they couldn't think of a more suitable first name than that of the legendary dragon-slaying prince.

Sybil leaned back, relaxed, a little bored almost. If this encounter had occurred two weeks ago, she would have flirted with him just to see if she could conquer this cool giant. Today, however, no man stood a chance against Alexei's noble delicacy and grace, and her thoughts drifted.

Christel, on the other hand, pondered what might be hiding behind the inspector's smooth facade. She recalled a long-lost childhood love and what had led to the termination of their engagement. Jean—shorter, darker, rounder—might not be an incarnation of male beauty, but he embodied everything she had ever wanted.

Siegfried Mertens was a young man who left an impression on those he met, and Emma was no exception. She felt smaller, more insignificant, and more unimpressive with each minute she spent answering his questions. She could hardly string together a coherent sentence and kept mumbling and whispering her words until Herr Mertens eventually had to bend down to her in order to understand her. The more encouraging and indulgent his gaze, the more shy her responses became.

Emma wondered if she liked him or if she felt fearful of him. She came to no conclusions except for one: men were all so different, and she herself was different in their presence. Why did she seem confident with James? Why was she never sure what she really thought of Anton, vacillating between annoyance and curiosity? And why did she feel helpless and fragile when Herr Mertens looked at her? Did all women behave differently depending on which man was facing them?

She looked at Tante Tinni: she had always been a warm-hearted woman, direct, honest, and spirited. Whether she was scolding Anton Wagenknecht or mothering Alexei, talking to James or laughing with Jean-Baptiste, she was always the same woman.

It seemed to be different with Sybil. In the past, she had flattered men who could be of use to her, and they had all rushed to fulfill her wishes. However, with Alexei a new Sybil had emerged, a woman who laughed unreservedly and seemed to honestly be enjoying life.

"Fräulien Schumacher, did you hear me?"

Caught off guard, Emma glanced up at the detective who was standing before her, awaiting an answer.

"If it's all right with you, I would like to have another chat with you in private, without your relatives. Do you feel comfortable enough to do that?"

She nodded and asked her relatives to leave the room. Now the two of them were sitting by themselves, facing each other across the long table: Emma with her arms folded, her legs crossed, and her head lowered; Herr Mertens leaning forward in concentration, his left arm resting on his thigh, his right on the tabletop. After studying her for a moment, Mertens exhaled loudly, and drummed his fingers lightly on the table for a moment. "Let's forget about all these Egyptian cats for the time being. You must be wondering why I'm here, aren't you?"

Emma looked up. What was he talking about?

Siegfried Mertens sighed. "Well, I'm no ordinary police officer, I'm an Assistant Inspector. Minor crimes like burglary and theft are not usually part of my duties," he explained. "The major crimes squad works with capital crimes."

"You mean you deal with money?" asked Emma, who tended to skip over the articles about murder and manslaughter in the daily newspapers.

Siegfried looked at her speechless, taken aback. Normally, when he said he was an Assistant Inspector, people responded with respect and admiration. Barely a year ago, he had risen from rookie to assistant, and he already envisioned himself as a full detective, if not a chief inspector. Siegfried had joined the police force after completing his military service, during which he'd risen to sergeant. Before the military he'd studied accounting, but he abandoned that pursuit when he developed a fascination for the latest developments in forensics, a passion that had not abated. In his free time, Siegfried read anything he could get his hands on about forensics, fingerprints, crime scene photography, and body measurements; he meticulously studied every crime that he could. He was convinced that everything that took place was somehow connected, linked by secrets and conspiracies. He dreamed of making a name for himself, as his idol Ernst Gennat had managed to do. "No, not *that* kind of capital. My department handles particularly serious crimes, like murder and manslaughter."

Emma's head flew up, her eyes wide. "Oh, but—I don't understand. Who's been murdered? Was I supposed to…?"

"No, no," Siegfried exclaimed soothingly. "It's—let's say—my intuition that has led me here. Your father…"

"Papa? What about Papa? Is he…" Emma's voice faltered.

"Oh no, for goodness sakes, Fräulein Schumacher, please stay calm. That's not what I meant… I…" Herr Merten's sense of superiority was beginning to waver. He needed to act carefully, because his superior, Chief Inspector Simon Wertheim, didn't even know that he was investigating on his own—but how else was he supposed to show his competence? He had been on his way home and was only supposed to drop off a file at the District II police station, but as soon as he'd heard the name Schumacher there, he'd offered to step in for the officer in charge. The latter was on his own at the station and had gratefully accepted the suggestion.

"That's not it at all. You see, I came across your father's name yesterday afternoon in connection with another case, and when I was at the Königstraße station this morning and Monsieur Barbier came in, I thought I'd take the opportunity to follow up on this lead."

Emma wasn't fully following his train of thought.

"Well, *lead* is perhaps too grand a word. I don't suppose you've read today's *General Gazette*, have you? Early yesterday morning, a young man jumped off the Rhine Bridge, and only a few hours later, we received word from Wesseling that his body had been found there, caught between some boats. This boy had been studying at the University of Bonn and was a student of Egyptology under Professor Neumann, to be exact. And he also studied under your father's supervision. I'm sure you can see why this connection struck me as interesting, don't you?"

Emma shook her head. No, she couldn't quite see the link between this unfortunate young man and the theft, or even with her father. And if she could be honest, she didn't particularly want to hear about such horrible events.

Siegfried Mertens ignored Emma's request. "We're still at the very beginning of our investigation, and I can't draw any definite conclusions yet. Where is your father at the moment?"

"I don't know."

"Is your father in the habit of not telling you where he's going or how long he'll be away?"

"No," Emma whispered. She wondered if she should tell Herr Mertens about her trip to Koblenz and Frankfurt.

As if he could read her thoughts, he reached to pat her hand and asked bluntly if she was worried. If she would tell him everything, regardless of how insignificant it seemed to her, he would do his best to help her.

"But, Herr Mertens, it might make more sense if you spoke to my aunt. After all, I don't live in Bonn, and I only see my father once a year."

"I'm going to have a long talk with your aunt too, but it seems to me that you and your father are very close. The way you described the drawings... there's more to it than that, isn't there?" Once again, he looked into her eyes as if he wanted to explore her every thought.

Emma withdrew her hand, turned her head, and gazed out into the garden. She hesitated only briefly, then spoke. She felt as if all she did these days was tell everyone about Papa's letters, his squabbles with professors and administrators, and Dr. Meinhardt's suspicions.

When she reached that point in her story, the policeman interrupted. "Has this theft been reported to the police?"

"It might've been by now, but I don't know for sure. Dr. Meinhardt hoped that the perpetrator would see reason, and he asked me to encourage Papa to return the item if I happened to learn anything. He doesn't want to harm my father's reputation as long as he has no proof. However, his patience won't last forever; he told me as much."

"And do you consider your father capable of theft?"

Emma would have liked to have answered in the negative, but how could she explain the marble figure in her father's pocket? Papa wasn't in the habit of carelessly pocketing borrowed artifacts or wrapping them in brown paper. Had he secretly stolen the figurine?

"Fräulein Schumacher, please don't hold anything back. I can tell that you haven't shared everything with me."

Emma obliged him, explaining how the day before she had drawn the marble cat, which had been stolen along with the sketches. She then showed him all the letters and postcards she had and shared with him her theories and worries. Siegfried Mertens asked for clarification about certain points, asked a few questions, and finally noted the names of all the people who had knowledge of the stolen artifact.

Seeing Alexei, Anton and James on this list bothered Emma, since it almost felt as if she were betraying these young men.

"You seem to run a very international house," the assistant inspector remarked. "I think we have both come to a standstill for the moment. Could you please ask your aunt to come in? If it's all right with you, I will call on you again tomorrow morning."

Even though she couldn't imagine why he would want to speak to her again so soon, Emma nodded and left the room, somewhat confused and weary. She headed to the kitchen, where Tinni and Jean-Baptiste were chopping vegetables and potatoes in quantities sufficient to feed an entire battalion.

"Tante Tinni, could you join Herr Mertens in the living room?"

Reluctantly, her aunt headed off, still in her apron. Herr Mertens wouldn't be keeping her out of the kitchen for long.

"Are we expecting visitors?"

Jean-Baptiste nodded. Amelie was coming with her husband from Cologne, and since they'd had an extra visitor for supper every night last week, there was no harm in being prepared. Whatever food was left over would taste twice as delicious at tomorrow's lunch.

Jean-Baptiste declined Emma's offer to help, probably because of the charred potatoes he had discovered in the garbage that morning. She should rest, preferably wrapped up warmly in her bed.

She nodded as her eyes fell on the *General Gazette*, which lay unread on the kitchen table. A few minutes ago, she had been reluctant to hear anything about the dead student, but her conversation with Herr Mertens had sparked her curiosity. She carried the newspaper with her upstairs.

In her room, she opened the windows wide and leaned on the windowsill. Hardly a cloud in the sky, the city below bathed in soft light, the air cool. She took a deep breath of the crisp air, as if it might drive the previous night from her mind, and then snuggled into her bed, burrowing cozily into the fluffed pillows. The wind whisked several bright leaves into the room, where they danced and swirled across the floor for a moment.

Emma immersed herself in the newspaper, reading about the storm surge danger on the East Frisian coast, and about the trapped steel workers whose odds of being recovered alive were dwindling. She blushed at the mention of the first international congress for sex research in Berlin, but then found the news she was looking for:

Bonn Student Jumps to his Death

Yesterday morning, several people witnessed a sad incident. Johannes Schmitz, 24, was on the Rhine Bridge near the Bonn riverbank, apparently showing signs of great confusion and distress. However, he could not be calmed down by the surrounding passers-by, so they were forced to watch as the young man plunged into the river. He was immediately caught up by the current and dragged under. Despite the efforts of some passing boatmen, he could not be saved. By late after- noon, the river had already released him.

Johannes Schmitz was an Egyptology student who had been living alone in Bonn since the deaths of his parents. His landlady and the university administration are dismayed by this event, as the young man was considered hard-working and friendly. The police are now investigating potential motives for this desperate act.

Emma set the newspaper aside. How desperate would someone have to be to give up their life in exchange for eternal nothingness?

Sliding down deeper into her bed and pulling her eiderdown up to her chin, Emma was ready to make up for the sleep she had missed over the past few days. After twelve days in Bonn, her previously well-ordered daily routine was little more than a memory; Grandmother would have been horrified if she knew the times of night her granddaughter had been awake and how she could now sleep away her days. But Grandmother was enjoying her lunch far away, and so Emma lay nestled in her bed on an ordinary Tuesday afternoon, feeling outrageously decadent.

She slept only an hour. The sky had darkened, yet Emma's alarm clock indicated that it was only a little past two-thirty. More and more leaves were being blown into the room by the gathering storm; the curtains fluttered and blew, as if they wanted to tear themselves loose, and the first raindrops were already drumming against the windowsill and wooden floor. Emma hastily swung her feet out of bed and collected the dancing leaves. With childlike joy, she tossed the colorful pieces of wonder into the wild wind and closed the window. Not knowing what to do with the vibrant energy that was now surging through her, she jumped up and down in place a few times, stretching left, right, and forward, unable to reach her toes, and firmly resolved to do physical exercises every day from now on. Done with that, she sank into her chair and gazed into the closet mirror, from which a tousled Emma stared back. She vigorously brushed her red curls, pinned them up, and applied face powder, which promptly went up her nose and made her sneeze. Oh well, she could get prettied up later. She had more important things to do right now.

She located Tante Tinni in the laundry room. If there was one activity Emma hated more than anything, it was doing laundry. The steam, the stuffy air, the soapy water that made her hands raw, the rubbing and agitating, and the washtub that was always hard to operate. Grandmother sent the laundry out to be done, but in Bonn Tinni had been doing this work for years without complaint. Emma felt obligated to help her, so she rolled up her sleeves and, following her aunt's instructions, moved the clothes from the lye tub to the tub filled with clear water. She twisted and stirred the clothes until they were free of soap. A couple of hours soon passed without the two of them exchanging a single word, but finally all the bath towels, tablecloths, bodices, and stockings were hanging on the line.

"Dear, you haven't eaten anything yet, have you? Come on, that's enough for today. Let's go put our feet up now. I'm sure Jean will make us hot cocoa if we ask him nicely."

They didn't have to ask too nicely, though. Exhausted, they stretched out in the armchairs and enjoyed their warm drinks. The living room was in semi-darkness, the coal fire crackling, and Emma thought that now was a good time to ask Tante Tinni the question on her mind: "That student who killed himself—did Herr Mertens also tell you that he was one of Papa's students?"

"Yes, he did. He wanted to know if that seemed suspicious to me! Well, I gave him a piece of my mind. What could your Papa possibly have had to do with his death? I think Mertens reads too many detective novels; he talked on and on about clues and intuition and suspicious coincidences, you should have heard him, my dear." Tante Tinni snorted.

Emma, on the other hand, wasn't so sure. "Do you remember him?"

"Who?"

"The young man. His name was—wait, it was in the General Gazette, what was it?—Josef Schmitz."

"No, not Josef, you mean Johannes. Johannes Schmitz. Yes, he visited us once a week, starting last fall. What was he like? Calm, a bit quiet and inconspicuous, he never said much. I only saw him when he came to the door and when he left. And those times your father invited everyone for dinner after a long afternoon, I also sat at the table. Johannes Schmitz always thanked me very politely. He also helped clear the table and held the doors for me—not like a few of the others who marched in and out of here, hooting and hollering. There were some spoiled brats among them, I can tell you that. But Johannes had no one else, so your Papa gave him things every now and then—sometimes a loaf of bread, or a scarf, whatever he just happened to have at hand. You know how your father is when he wants to help someone. He was supposedly a smart fellow, sharp as a tack but poor as a church mouse," Tinni said. "When I think about it, I can see how everything might have become too much for him. When your father disappeared, he stopped by every day for two weeks, asking for him; he seemed really desperate. I sometimes gave him a piece of cake or a small roll, but you can't save someone like that... if I'd known... no, he was a fine fellow, but weak and much too sensitive. He must've taken everything too much to heart."

"Did you tell this to Herr Mertens?"

"Yes, but not in such detail. That wouldn't have seemed right to me. This Mertens is surely one of those people who's got no sympathy for things like that. I just told him that Hannes had been a student here and that I could imagine that he simply gave up at some point."

"It's all so sad." Emma pushed a damp strand of hair off her forehead. Something was bothering her, something that seemed strange, but the more she tried to figure out what it was, the more it eluded her. Her thoughts had been clearer, more straightforward, more tangible earlier. At least, that was how she remembered them.

Earlier—that had been just two months ago. Until then, she had lived quietly and without excitement with Grandmother. Had gotten up in the mornings, had breakfast, read and chatted, painted, embroidered, or written letters to Papa. She'd eaten lunch, accompanied the pastor's wife on her rounds or helped her prepare for parties and charity meetings, drank tea, read or knitted, had eaten dinner, played bridge, and had gone to bed. She'd slept soundly and had awoken refreshed, and the next day had always passed like the day before. Her greatest adventure had been her three months of training in London, during which she had regarded her classmates with wonder. She would have liked to have made a friend among them, but from the start she had been on her own during the breaks. It wasn't that the others disliked her, but their morning greetings and remarks about the weather had never developed into deeper conversations. Emma had been unable to determine whether the others were keeping away from her or whether she was separating herself from them. Her upbringing, her family, her speech—everything about her shouted that her life was different from the ones her classmates were leading. In Edinburgh she'd experienced something similar: everyone thought she was different, whether in the ballroom or in the poor quarters of town. Here in Bonn, however, she was more self-confident. From Papa and Tante Tinni she had never held back her real thoughts and feelings, the ones she hadn't even known she possessed in England.

But what about now? She seemed to be constantly vacillating between being worried and carefree, anxious and exuberant. She slept badly and irregularly, was confused, happy, discontent, curious, and usually everything at the same time. No wonder she couldn't keep a straight thought; she was all twisted up inside.

Tante Tinni watched her niece, how she was leaning back in the cushions, a relaxed and motionless figure, while all sorts of ideas seemed to flit across her face. She put her hand on Emma's, who glanced up in surprise, as if she had forgotten about her aunt. "My dear, what's going on with you? It's all been a bit much, what with the break-in and your Papa, and all that stuff in the paper. This is not how we imagined your stay in Bonn would be. But you know, our street has a break-in every now and then, so eventually it was going to be our turn. And Hannes—he was a nice boy, for sure, but he didn't have it easy either, and you didn't even know him. Your father, well..." Tante Tinni fell silent, then she squeezed her niece's hand. "He's been through a lot, and who knows what life does to people. Our mother—in her old age, she grew quite strange. She became forgetful, often left the house and couldn't find her way back, cried a lot and believed that everyone was out to do her harm. I've thought quite a bit about her lately, ever since Heinrich just up and left."

"Herr Mertens wants to come by again tomorrow morning. Shouldn't we ask him to search for Papa? We have to do something! In any case, I don't want to just keep waiting for the next letter."

Tante Tinni nodded. They chatted for a few more minutes about this and that, until the grandfather clock chimed five o'clock, and they both glanced down at their clothes, startled: this wasn't how they wanted to receive their guests: wrinkled, worn out, and in an apron.

"Hop along, sweetheart, and make yourself pretty. I want to show you off to Amelie. Her daughter takes after her father, and if that isn't a curse, I don't know what is!"

"Tante Tinni!" Emma exclaimed with a laugh.

"Kindness and nobility always come with a pinch of malice," her aunt declared.

MUNICH

"Herr Huber, have you seen the professor? He forgot his umbrella here."

"Yes, he just left. If you hurry, you can still catch him!" the museum guard exclaimed, pointing at the exit.

Herr Stadlmeir dashed past him and down the stairs and glanced around. He took off again when he caught sight of the unmistakable gray lion's head. "Professor Schumacher, stop, please stop!" he shouted. At last, he caught up with him and handed him the umbrella. Out of breath, he doubled over, wheezing.

"I thank you, young man, but you should definitely take better care of your physical health. At your age, you shouldn't be gasping after just a few steps."

What an incredibly rude person! He behaved so arrogantly and rudely that it made you want to throttle him. Well, that was just the way it was with highly-educated Prussians. Herr Stadlmeir watched as he strolled down the street, swinging his umbrella.

The Prussian in question couldn't have cared less about the thoughts that were trailing him. As he arrived at his boarding house, the landlady handed him a folded note. He read it, sighed, and crumpled up the paper. Of course, it was about time to call in again and ask for news. Munich was supposed to be his last destination for the time being. Should he extend the tour, though? Down to St. Gallen perhaps, or back north via Stuttgart? That might be worthwhile...

He left the guesthouse again. At a post office, he placed a telephone call before speaking agitatedly into the phone. After a few minutes, he slammed down the receiver and hurried out of the building back to his lodgings. He asked the landlady for his bill; he had to leave tonight, and could she please call him a cab. Exactly forty-eight minutes later, he boarded a train.

Herr Stadlmeir returned to the conference room where his supervisor, Dr. Brandl, had presented several artifacts to the professor. The fine professor had refused to hear anything more about giving a lecture; he was only available for written evaluations at this point in his tour. And so, they served him coffee and cake followed by a Gentian schnapps, but the only result of this attempt to butter up the professor was that he, Stadlmeir, was now tasked with cleaning up the mess. He nibbled on the leftover cake, folded up the documents, and reached for the glass vitrine in which the gold jewelry lay nestled on a soft base. They were exquisite pieces, found in the tomb of an Old Kingdom princess. The box usually held a crane, a scarab, a palm leaf, and a representation of the goddess Hathor. The crane, scarab and palm leaf were resting on the silk.

Herr Stadlmeir remained calm as he tidied up the dishes and the stacks of papers, looked beneath the glass case, and checked under the silk cloth. He moved the chairs away from the table, searched the floor on his hands and knees, and felt in his jacket and trouser pockets. At this point, considerably less calm, he hurried into the exhibition hall; perhaps his colleague had mistakenly packed the goddess up somewhere else, though he knew how unlikely that was. In a panic, he scanned all the display cases. Nothing! Loosening his tie as he ran and taking two steps at a time, he raced up the stairs, along the corridor, and into Dr. Brandl's office.

The latter was just putting on his hat and reaching for his briefcase when Stadlmeir appeared before him, beet red and upset. The director looked up, astonished.

"Hathor! Did you put the Hathor somewhere?"

Dr. Brandl joked that his wife wouldn't tolerate any other goddesses in his life beside her, but the young man interrupted him, "Do you have her? No? She's gone, just gone. I can't find her anywhere!"

AMBITION REKINDLED

Emma got dressed with particular care. If Tante Tinni thought she could one-up her schoolmate with her pretty niece, then Emma wouldn't deprive her of that pleasure. Sybil would certainly have turned her into a stunning beauty, but she was satisfied with what she had achieved on her own. Where was Sybil anyway? She had left the house that morning, despite the weather. The rain was still splattering against the windows, and over the Venusberg a raging thunderstorm was rapidly approaching. Truly not the right time for a walk. Or had she long since returned home?

She knocked on Sybil's door, but no one answered. Emma opened the door anyway. She wanted to steal a few drops of Shalimar perfume. But as soon as she entered, she stopped in astonishment. Her aunt was used to the help of chambermaids and personal maids, but the chaos in here exceeded her usual carelessness many times over. Had the thief ransacked this room with particular fury? Shoes, clothes, linens—everything was dangling from cupboards and chairs. Books and magazines lay scattered across the floor, while the bed was rumpled and the armchair overturned.

Perplexed, Emma stood in the midst of the mess and then began to pick up the books. She shook out the bed, drew the bedspread over it, set the armchair upright again, and toiled away until the room looked homey again. Just as she was about to leave her handiwork, Sybil stepped through the door, looking radiant, exhilarated even, but above all, drenched. She stared in amazement. "Emma dear, you picked up in here? How sweet of you!"

She hugged her niece, who quickly disengaged herself. "Aunt Sybil, you're soaking wet! Where have you been?"

"Oh." Surprised, Sybil stared down at her shoes, ran her hands through her damp hair, and then hurriedly peeled off her wet clothes.

Emma handed Sybil her dressing gown and repeated her last question.

"With Alexei, of course!"

"You've made up? Shouldn't he be at work by now?"

"Yes, we made up. And no, he won't be playing the servant at that dreadful inn anymore. I won't allow it! We'll find something more suitable."

"And then you took a romantic stroll and watched the downpour?"

"I didn't even notice the rain, so it can't be all that bad. I just wanted to get home to the rest of you," Sybil replied.

"You were going home? Did you start fighting again?"

"Emma dear, don't be silly. I've never been the sort of woman to quarrel. Don't choke, dear, and don't gape at me so stupidly. Why would I quarrel with Alexei?"

"Perhaps because you don't want to marry him?"

"Marry! Emma dear, who's talking about getting married?"

Emma began to doubt her aunt's sanity, "Alexei? You remember that, don't you? He proposed to you on Sunday, and you refused because you're too old for him."

"Emma!"

"Oh please, Aunt Sybil, will you tell me what happened?"

Sybil sighed, playing with the sash on her dressing gown as if it were of the greatest interest. "If you must know, I've been thinking about things, and around noon today I decided to go see Alexei at his lodgings. You have no idea what a wretched dump he lives in! Disgraceful, I tell you, absolutely disgraceful! And his landlady charges him a fortune for it. A horrible woman! I thought I was going to be nauseous when she led me up to his room. Poverty may be a hard fate, but my goodness, a little soap and water can go a long way. To let herself go like that..." Sybil shuddered.

Eager to stop her aunt from carrying on about the insufficient hygiene of certain women, Emma urged her to forget about the landlady and to talk about Alexei.

"Oh, Alexei smells wonderful, even though he's poor—proof that it's quite possible to maintain good hygiene—all right, don't make that face, Emma dear. You'll get wrinkles! I explained to him that we haven't known each other long enough to talk seriously about the future, but that under no circumstances would I let our time together be derailed by trivialities."

"And then?"

"We had a long talk. Do you know why he lives in that dump? So he can save as much as possible from his pittance as a waiter to impress me and give me presents."

"And to keep from starving, I bet."

"That too, I'm sure. I don't understand why you pick on him so much. I thought you liked him."

"Yes, I do, very much. I'm sorry."

"Anyway, he recently borrowed some money from a friend so he could present himself more properly and thereby find a better position. He would like to change his situation for my sake, since he wants to earn enough money to convince me once and for all to marry him and not some fat old money bags."

"So... you do want to marry him?"

"Emma dear, what is it with you and marriage?"

Emma felt like screaming. This was love? The subject of every popular tune? Nothing but complete confusion and utter nonsense? And with what job could Alexei—who, by his own admission, had limited marketable skills—bring in sufficient income to be able to afford Sybil, of all people? And if Sybil wanted to live with Alexei, did it necessarily have to be the husband who earned the money? Regardless, the guests might arrive at any moment, so she shouldn't start a fight with Sybil right now. "Tante Tinni is expecting a school friend for supper. You'll be coming down, right?"

"Of course, let me just tidy myself up quickly. Alexei will be over soon too. Is James still in Düsseldorf?"

Emma shrugged and hurried out. She didn't want Aunt Sybil to see how red she had turned at the mere sound of his name.

The evening began civilized enough, apart from a few friendly jibes exchanged between the two former schoolmates. Amelie and Christel teased each other with delight; they outdid each other in recounting memories of their school days. With each glass of wine, they grew increasingly fanciful in their descriptions of the pranks they used to play on each other. During dinner, Jean-Baptiste and Frederick, Amelie's devoted husband, had sat at the dining table, half hidden by the huge bouquet of roses that Alexei had presented to Sybil. The ladies eventually relocated to the sofa from where their boisterous laughter reverberated throughout the room. Only Emma remained silent, smiling. After her first glass of wine, she had switched to lemonade and hadn't touched the brandy, which Amelie herself had distilled. Regardless, the bottle was soon drained, and the mood of the schoolmates was even bubblier than before. Their companions were also enjoying themselves. Frederick, in particular, was taking note of more than a few of the details divulged by his wife; they might come in handy should Amelie again accuse him of spending too much time with his "useless" drinking buddies.

For his part, Alexei was leaning back in the armchair next to Emma. After a few minutes, he declared that once he was Sybil's husband, he would do his best to keep her away from any home brew, since she would probably share a few too many things he would prefer to keep private. He also observed that while he found it flattering to be considered a devoted lover, his devotion sometimes led to less-than-comfortable moments, like the one he had just witnessed. Namely, Amelie had staggered over to him and settled her not inconsiderable weight down on his lap, and demanded to know what he had just heard her say. Frederick intervened manfully, though he was secretly quite satisfied with the development; he could now excuse his occasional flirting with their pretty neighbor with a reference to this evening.

Around midnight, Jean-Baptiste served onion soup and jet-black coffee, so that the ladies could start getting their merriment back under wraps. This succeeded to such an extent that Frederick was ultimately able to lead his wife through the empty streets to the train station at about two o'clock in the morning without being confronted by angry, awakened residents armed with the contents of their chamber pots. Fortunately for them, Tante Tinni and Sybil's walk home was considerably shorter, although they were rather perplexed by the steepness of the staircase. Arm in arm, they struggled up, step by step, sinking down onto the staircase no less than three times. Laughing and giggling, they called their niece a Philistine of the first order just because she had made the upstairs journey effortlessly. They also bestowed unusual terms of endearment on Jean-Baptiste and Alexei, but this didn't prevent the good gentlemen from actively supporting their sweethearts' endeavors to get to bed, before retiring to the study to make their nightly camp.

Until the glazier could repair the door the next day, Jean-Baptiste refused to leave the women alone in the house, and so he offered Alexei pillows and blankets for the night. Although Alexei had noticed the door's broken window, he hadn't asked about it and only now learned about what had happened the night before. He questioned Jean-Baptiste for a good hour before the Frenchman's eyes finally closed and a snore was provided in lieu of an answer.

The young Russian then rose cautiously and slipped quietly up the stairs.

The next morning dawned just as gray as the day before had ended, and it was likely due to the pouring rain that neither Christel nor Sybil exuded much charm as they crept into the kitchen. Or perhaps, Jean-Baptiste suggested, could it have been the liquor? The two ladies groaned and snatched the proffered coffee from his hands without so much as a thank-you. Instead, he received a light slap from Christel, in addition to an order to wipe that smirk off his face.

Emma asked him if it was her aunt's temper that appealed to him so much. Hadn't he mentioned something to that extent once? They laughed together, while Tante Tinni shot them accusatory glances.

"Where's Alexei?" asked Sybil after the coffee had taken effect and she had somewhat gathered her wits about her.

Jean-Baptiste raised his eyebrows, stepped out into the hallway, and called for him in a bass voice. No one answered or appeared. It seemed a little strange to the Frenchman, since he had assumed that Alexei had snuck up to Sybil's room the night before. Jean-Baptiste's search was interrupted by the glazier, who cheerfully wished him good morning through the missing pane and asked if he could go ahead and get to work. The craftsman recommended investing a little more money in the repair and, instead of the simple pane, putting in one reinforced with wire mesh to prevent another incident of this kind.

He could do as he saw fit, Jean-Baptiste told him, as long as he didn't get too fancy with the billing. The glazier, whose name was Patt, promised to do his best. He then promptly shooed his apprentice to the Lubig Bakery around the corner to fetch some rye rolls for them.

The boy scampered off like a weasel through the rain and arrived back at the garden gate with the rolls just as James was climbing out of his car, holding a newspaper over his head. "Great ride you got there! It's a 4/16, isn't it? Sedan, four-seater, 80 mph—right?"

"That's right, my boy. You'll have to sell a few more rolls before you can afford one of these."

"Come on! I don't sell rolls, I'm a glazier!"

"Emil, hurry up and get to work! Otherwise, you can forget about your prospects in the glazing profession! Now let the gentleman pass!" the master craftsman interrupted.

Emil immediately hurried up the wet stairs and handed the bag of rolls to his supervisor. Herr Patt, however, sent him back outside to kick off his wet shoes.

James, following Emil's example, also retreated two steps and rubbed his soles extra dry on the doormat while the younger man grinned at him. "I bet your mother scolds you all the time too, doesn't she?"

His boss slapped him on the back of the head and apologized to James for his cheeky apprentice.

James nodded and hung his damp coat up on the coat rack. "The family's at home, aren't they?" he asked.

Stepping out of the kitchen, Jean-Baptiste greeted him with delight. With a nod at Herr Patt, James asked what had happened.

"I'm sure Emma would rather tell you herself. You've come to see her, haven't you?"

James blushed. "Is it that obvious?"

Jean-Baptiste declared he wasn't in a position to say for sure, but as a Frenchman, he always suspected an affair of the heart to be behind everything.

"Ah. Isn't that a bit of a silly cliché?"

Clichés are always silly, the Frenchman replied, but he wasn't wrong, was he?

James' blush deepened; at any moment, Emma might appear, and he didn't want her to catch him in the midst of any embarrassing confessions. This was why he had deliberately come without flowers and a day after his return to the city. He didn't wish to reveal his heart before he was sure of his feelings—and, more importantly, hers—but here was her future uncle questioning him about his intentions at the door in front of attentive eavesdroppers.

Jean-Baptiste dropped his line of inquiry. Just in time too, since Emma had suddenly appeared and was hurrying down the stairs. When she saw James, she stopped abruptly and probably would have fallen had both gentlemen not rushed over to catch her and set her back on her feet.

Now the two young people stood facing each other, flushed and eager to discover each other's feelings without betraying their own. They formally shook hands and exchanged polite greetings without making direct eye contact.

Emma started firing off one question after another: How had he liked Düsseldorf? Was the bride pretty and the groom happy?

When had he returned to Bonn, and what were his plans for the next few days? Would he be staying here for some time, or would he be heading off again soon? How was his job search going? Emma sputtered out this last question and then fell silent.

James was silent too, which was due to his marked inability to make small talk about things that weren't foremost in his mind. And what was actually on his mind were things he didn't want to discuss at all—not here, not now. How would it look if he pulled Emma into his arms, and told her how delightful and sweet she was and that he knew exactly how many freckles she had and that he had never seen more graceful hands or more elegant legs and that he was captivated by her? It would look completely silly, and he would make a fool of himself by whispering sweet nothings into a young woman's ear after only knowing her for a week. That might have worked for his grandfather, seventy years ago, but nowadays...

He looked into Emma's inquiring eyes and fretted. Yes, it was much better to stand silently before her like a fool and make a stern expression. Heavens, couldn't he have been born a Frenchman, or better yet, a Russian? Sybil's attachment to Alexei was the result of only one day's effort! But he remained silent.

Emma's impatience grew. Why did he refuse to answer her while he kept sighing and looking so grim? What must he think of her? He was bound to see her as little more than a schoolgirl who was embarrassing him with her obvious crush. Crush? Had the word crush just crossed her mind? How silly, how exceedingly silly!

The two of them probably would have just stood in front of each other, blushing in silence, until late in the evening had the next visitor not arrived. Assistant Inspector Mertens tapped Emil on the shoulder. "Could you gentlemen please let me pass?"

With an exaggerated and obliging eagerness that Mertens deliberately ignored, Herr Patt and his apprentice jumped aside. Nothing should distract him from his mission. With an outstretched hand, he stepped toward Emma and gave a slight bow before turning to James. As they shook hands, Mertens clicked his heels together. "Allow me. My name is Mertens, Siegfried Mertens, Assistant Inspector."

James flinched and glanced down at Mr. Mertens' heels, then at his face. Surely that clicking had to hurt, but the other man's face reflected nothing untoward. Instead, he wanted to know who this new visitor was. "My name's James Beresford."

"Well, that's an excellent coincidence! If I recall correctly, my colleagues tried in vain to reach you at your hotel yesterday. It would be best if we get straight to the point." He turned to Emma, who suggested they use her father's study, and strode off. James and Emma trailed along behind him like obedient pupils.

With the greatest of ease, Herr Mertens pulled up the professor's armchair and asked them both to take a seat on the sofa. Emma started to object, but before she could say anything, Herr Mertens began to question Mr. Beresford, asking him whether he could describe the figure of the cat goddess, what value he attached to it as an expert, whom had he told about the artifact, and what his alibi was.

James was about to rise indignantly, but under Mertens' cool gaze, this impulse seemed rather too theatrical. And so he remained seated, naming his friend and the boarding house as alibi references.

Then the detective asked about Mr. Beresford's relationship with the Schumacher family, causing James to blush again. "I didn't mean your relationship with Fräulein Schumacher, but with her father," the inspector clarified. "But if the two of you are in a relationship and not mere acquaintances, you should inform me. At this point, it's important to paint a complete picture."

James cleared his throat, "Excuse me, but you are asking me all these questions, and I don't even know what's happened. May I get some clarification?"

Siegfried stumbled to a stop, then summarized the events as he understood them.

Emma was a little annoyed. She would have liked to tell James herself about her terrible evening. In Herr Mertens' report, she sounded like an idiot who couldn't put two and two together!

James was also irritated. If he were currently in this room with Emma, alone and undisturbed, and she had told him about her experience, possibly in tears and trembling at her remembered fear, how easy it would have been for him to comfort her and tell her all the silly little things he hadn't wanted her to suspect a quarter of an hour ago; the situation would have been completely different. He resolutely pushed these musings aside and concentrated on what Herr Mertens was reporting. Then he understood: "So you're not here about the burglary, but about that suicide? What could Professor Schumacher have had to do with it? He's been traveling for weeks. That strikes me as a little far-fetched."

Siegfried Mertens had spent the night alone on guard duty in the town hall, reading the thin file on Johannes Schmitz. He had done this in secret, because on the one hand his colleagues believed he had committed suicide and on the other hand they didn't take Siegfried seriously; his duties were officially limited to tending the station at night, sorting files, and making coffee. Inspector Wertheim used to say that even on the major crimes squad, years of learning weren't the same as years of mastery. The fact that his colleagues weren't investigating this case any further but had closed the file and assigned him to the night shift for the next two weeks, suited Siegfried just fine. He would work the case independently during the day without anyone noticing. He, Siegfried Mertens, wanted to single-handedly solve a case that no one else had recognized as such.

And so he passionately defended his theory to James and Emma: "If you study the great criminal cases, you find that it's the details that lead to the solution. There's no room for coincidence. And when we look at what happened around the professor, the connections mean something!" Siegfried could no longer sit still, so he jumped up and started pacing in front of his audience, gesturing and speaking urgently to them. "Your father has been traveling since mid-August. That's eight weeks. Eight weeks in which you have received messages that have seemed remarkably strange to you. Eight weeks in which he was supposed to be lecturing, but instead became embroiled in disputes and was even suspected of having stolen a valuable figurine. Eight weeks in which he hasn't needed his clothes or his notebooks and calendars. Your father has saved his pension, his house, and his family's modest fortune throughout these years of inflation. Does it seem plausible to you, Fräulein Schumacher, that he bought himself an entirely new wardrobe for this trip? I took a look in his closet yesterday and found clothes that were, without exception, tailor-made goods, albeit somewhat threadbare. And now he's decided, at this point in his life, that he's a fan of off-the-rack clothes? Possibly plaid jackets, straw boaters, and knee breeches, to go along with his new hobby of flirting with questionable operetta singers?"

Siegfried came to a stop in front of Emma and looked at her sternly. "Has your father turned into a debauched Professor Garbage? You're shaking your head! You see, I don't believe he has either. Such things happen only in novels. Do you think that your father would spend his hard-earned money on a new wardrobe, that he would leave without a thought of you and his sister? You told me about the anniversary of your mother's death and about your fears. I don't want to frighten you, but I firmly believe that these fears are not groundless." Siegfried resumed his pacing, speaking louder and louder, exhilarated by his success in transforming Emma and James into a spellbound audience.

The two sat before him, silent and close together, so close that James could feel Emma's trembling and courageously grasped her hand.

Siegfried forged onward. "I don't know what may have happened to your father, whether he disappeared of his own free will, or had to flee, or was forced to do something against his will, but we will find out!"

"We?" asked Emma.

"Well, I—I'll look into everything. To do that, of course, I'll need your help and that of any other witnesses. Detective work is always the work of many with the same goal," he declared to the world at large. "But let's move on to the next point. To Johannes Schmitz. You see, people are fished out of rivers all over the world every day. Or someone hangs or shoots themselves or takes poison. We live in hard times and some people can't take it. Such a suicide isn't unusual, but the fact that one person disappeared and another died, and they both knew each other... well, there's a connection somewhere."

Siegfried stopped, pulled the recliner close to the sofa, and sat down; his knees touched Emma's though he didn't seem to notice. He resumed his monologue, though now at a whisper. "What I'm going to tell you now, please keep to yourselves. The witness testimonies—well, they are inconclusive. In my opinion, suicide is hardly more likely than murder is. The witnesses were all standing on the riverbank or had just stepped onto the bridge when Johannes Schmitz fell into the Rhine. It was still early in the morning, the sun had barely risen. All the witnesses could see were shadows, and the one who was closest to the scene thought he saw a second person trying to hold the student back. Everyone shouted and pleaded with him not to jump, but no one mentioned why they thought he was going to jump in the first place. Because he wasn't standing on the railing; he was standing behind it. Do you see why that matters?"

Emma and James shook their heads.

"What if the second figure wasn't trying to hold him back, but instead lifted him over the railing? Johannes Schmitz was rather slight, but he was muscular. He was a rower, which suggests he had strong arms, so he might have struggled. What was he looking for on the bridge to Beuel early that morning? He lived in Bonn and studied in Bonn, and his friends were in Bonn. So why was he on that bridge at seven o'clock? Did he want to meet someone? Was this someone hoping to push him quickly into the river before others appeared on the scene? Think about it: What would you do if you wanted to commit such a crime and your victim resisted more than you suspected and passers-by started to gather who could overhear everything? It's still foggy and dusky. You cannot let your victim go, or he would betray you. You don't know if someone has seen you. What would you do? No idea? I'll tell you what I'd do. I would call for help, I would ask my victim loudly not to hurt himself. Suddenly everyone joins in, everyone thinks they see what I've convinced them must be the reality. Even if someone notices me, they'll think I wanted to help. Without any inhibition, I can now approach the victim, grab him and, with one last lunge, hoist him over the railing. My adrenaline is pumping because I can now save myself from discovery by this act. I can act like I'm so upset I have to make off into the murky dawn, lose myself in the crowd, or flee onto a passing streetcar. It would probably be instinct, the moment that would determine what happened next! And if Johannes' death wasn't a suicide, but murder—then we have to wonder if your father and his disappearance are related!"

Emma stared at him. Was this man serious? How nonchalantly he talked about how a possible murder may have taken place, conjuring up a crime out of a rather pathetic story. All of it a product of his vivid imagination. She looked at James. He was following Mertens' words attentively, and she couldn't detect any doubt in his expression. Only now did she notice that her hand was in his, and she withdrew it. As much as she might wish to be close to him, now wasn't the time for that.

James glanced at her just briefly before turning back to Siegfried: "Yes, yes, that makes sense, of course. I've read about this sort of thing in detective stories, about a culprit hiding among the witnesses. But why would someone want to kill a poor student? Was he known to the police? What's the motive?"

Siegfried sighed and leaned back. James had hit on the weak spot in his framework. Motive is what shored up or destroyed every investigation. Yes, the motive was unclear, he admitted tersely, before quickly moving on. What had his colleagues found out so far? Johannes Schmitz had been a respectable young man, and he had lodged in a room in a professor's widow's home, which she had let him have rent-free in exchange for his help in the garden and the house. He had managed to get by like many others did and had never come into conflict with the law. When he lost his temporary job at the botanical garden, finances had grown tight, which was one possible reason he had jumped to his death. But Siegfried didn't want to simply accept this line of reasoning. Even if he had no solid evidence, his intuition told him he was on the right track. And he had built a convincing case for it.

James nodded while Emma folded her arms, leaned her head against the back of the sofa, and studied the policeman motionlessly. Siegfried jumped back up and tightly clutched the back of his chair, which vibrated with every word he spoke. "You aren't convinced, Fräulein Schumacher, I can see that. You probably don't want to hear all this and would prefer to imagine your father off on some serene vacation. And yes, you can hold the missing motive against me and tell me that your father wasn't the only person Johannes Schmitz knew. You would be right, of course. You are an intelligent person. But nonetheless I am not without experience, and my instincts have rarely deceived me. That's why I'm here, that's why I'm a detective. Because I make connections that are hidden from ordinary people."

He hit the back of the chair several times, and his face reflected a passion that unsettled Emma. Herr Mertens was a good-looking man; indeed, any heroic statue could have been realistically modeled after him. But it seemed to her that the intensity of his obsession had stripped him of every personal characteristic, every peculiarity.

She recalled the itinerant preacher who had fired up her and Grandmother's Edinburgh congregation some years ago. The preacher had thundered down from the pulpit the same way that Siegfried had spoken of his destiny and his gifts. He alone was in possession of truth and knowledge. He alone promised salvation and peace of mind. The pastor and his wife had been horrified by his sermon, but they had been even more shocked by the agreement expressed by many of their fellow parishioners. Emma had never felt more alone and isolated than she had in that whipped-up crowd that had willingly submitted to that Pied Piper. Not all of them, of course. The way some of them had glanced around, frightened and at a loss, the way they had sought support and reassurance among themselves, reaching across pews with silently formed sentences had left an impression on her to this day. How long had it taken until someone finally dared to open his mouth, to stand up to the self-described soul catcher? It had taken months to reunite the congregation, and for a long time, a certain discord had lingered, a distrust among each other that hadn't existed before that service.

Siegfried hesitated. He had let himself get carried away, had quoted books, talked about his war experiences, and completely forgotten why he was standing here. He caught Emma's gaze and chuckled to cover his embarrassment.

James felt torn. As Herr Mertens had presented the case, he had found every word the officer had said to be plausible; the connections, as the policeman described them, seemed clear to him. But he had also noticed his fanaticism. The expression *divine ecstasy* came to mind. He wondered if this ecstasy would have made him feel just as uncomfortable if Siegfried had been speaking of his passion for books or sports. Despite his uneasiness, James asked Siegfried to continue.

The latter gladly complied with the request: "Let's move on to the next event: the burglary at the professor's house, where Johannes Schmitz was also a regular guest. The items stolen: a pearl necklace and an antique treasure from Egypt—in other words, the country in which both the professor and the student were interested. The pearl necklace is not without value, but Mrs. Mallaby's jewelry box also contained a diamond brooch and other precious stones that the thief could easily have put in his pocket. Why didn't he? We know he wasn't disturbed during his search, but instead of more jewelry, he took the marble figurine of a cat. May we not assume that he was at least familiar enough with the field of antiquities to recognize the value of this rather inconspicuous figure? But even more astonishing to me is the fact that he took a bundle of drawings with him, however artistic their execution might be. Doesn't that look to you as if the theft of this figure was the real purpose of the burglary? The pearl necklace was nothing more than a red herring, or perhaps a spur-of-the-moment decision, but certainly not the purpose for which the stranger broke in here. Now do you see clearly how everything is coalescing around your father? A professor of Egyptology disappears, a student in the same field dies, an Egyptian statuette is stolen—do you still want to say all this is mere coincidence?"

Emma would have liked to disagree, but Herr Mertens' remarks reflected a certain logic, and she shared all too many of his thoughts. Had Papa really been traveling around for eight weeks? How had she let so much time pass without doing something about it? Sure, she had received the letter with his announcement late and had only been in Bonn for two weeks. But what had she learned so far? What had she done? Not much. The two men looked at her, expectantly, excitedly. She took a deep breath and exhaled loudly. "What do you think happened to my father?"

Siegfried sat down next to her. "I already told you, I don't know. But we should make every effort to find out."

James interjected, "Where do we start? What should we do next?"

Siegfried pondered this for a moment. Fräulein Schumacher, from what he could tell, was reliable and level-headed. Mr. Beresford, on the other hand—an Englishman who claimed to have met the professor only a few days before his disappearance and had recently sought acquaintance with his daughter, well... Was he hiding something? Could he be trusted? But the way they had both sat and listened to his flowery speech flattered Siegfried's ego immensely, which was why he felt little obligation at that moment to follow his superiors' rules. He stood up, swung his chair to face the table, motioned for Emma and James to join him, and opened his green notebook. "Let's look at your father's itinerary first," he said, asking Emma for the list she had received in Koblenz.

She pulled it out of one of the drawers, adding Papa's letters and the postcards to the pile as well, and laid it all on the table. Mr. Mertens noted each stop in his notebook, including the lodging and lecture locations. James looked over his shoulder. "Did you notice that three of the collections are private?"

"A good point, Mr. Beresford. Fräulein Schumacher, who does your father usually work with or for? Who commissions his appraisals?"

Emma reached back into the same drawer and pulled out one of her father's date books, opened it, and flipped through the pages. "His address book only lists the names of the universities and museums. I know he sometimes receives requests from private individuals who want an expert opinion from him, but Papa usually refuses those. He doesn't like seeing antiquities disappear behind vault doors, since he believes they should be available to the general public. If it were up to him that would be true of all of the Egyptian artifacts in Germany."

Siegfried jotted this down, as he did every detail, in his green book. Periodically, he would circle something or draw lines from one note to another, making connections and cross references between facts. Then he asked if she could possibly draw a picture of the stolen goddess for him.

"Not in much detail, but I should be able to produce a rough sketch for you," Emma replied. She set to work while James made a list of the features he remembered. Siegfried carefully tucked both the sketch and the list into his book.

The clock struck one, but the trio didn't hear it. Siegfried leaned against the table and read aloud what they had ascertained so far. "Can you think of anything else? No matter how insignificant?" he then asked.

"Yes, there's one more thing," James said. He had wanted to ask Emma this on Saturday night: how could it be that the college had been aware of Professor Schumacher's lecture tour, but the professor had nevertheless made an appointment with him, James, which he then failed to keep? In response to Herr Merten's prompting, he explained how he had met the professor on Tuesday, August tenth, at a luncheon of the Friends and Sponsors Association. He had been there looking for employment; since he was an archaeologist who didn't like to get dirty, he saw his future in academia and therefore took every opportunity to present himself at various universities.

Siegfried also wrote this down, which bothered James. Somewhat irritated, he continued to describe his meeting with Emma's father and their conversation about Howard Carter. The professor had been so enthusiastic that he had asked James to come by his house the following day so they could continue their conversation. James had agreed and arrived at the appointed time, but instead of Professor Schumacher, the only person he had encountered was the housekeeper. He stopped by Arndtstraße that evening again, but no one had been at home, and no light was on. The following day—Friday, the twelfth—he had stopped by one last time before resuming his journey, again without success. Since he had found the professor likeable and entertaining, and he'd also had hopes of finding a position in Bonn, he had returned to the city the previous week. Herr Mertens already knew everything else.

Siegfried looked satisfied. "You see, here we have another piece of the puzzle that could confirm our suspicions. Not only did Professor Schumacher leave without any preparations, but he also didn't even know he was going to travel a few days prior to his departure. Let's note August tenth through twelfth as possible departure days."

Emma interjected, "My aunt was in Bonn from the tenth to the eighteenth. It wouldn't have been especially odd if James had missed my father here during the day, especially if Frau Vianden had been left in charge. Besides, Papa might have eaten out that night. All we really know is that he wasn't here on August eighteenth when my aunt returned home, right? Wait, we know more. Give me the letters. Look here, he wrote to me on August fifteenth. *'Do not be surprised if you hear nothing further from me for a while. I am heading off on a lecture trip in a few days to various museums of antiquity, and I have no idea when I will find time to write to you again.'* Etcetera, etcetera. 'In a few days' would mean that he was still in Bonn on Sunday."

"But isn't that one of the letters that bothered you and seemed strange at the time?"

"Well—yes, but it's his handwriting, no doubt about it. And his seal too! Here on the envelope, look!" Emma handed him the letter, but then jumped to her feet and snatched the envelope back. How could she have been so stupid and blind? Why hadn't she noticed it before now? Or had this been the detail that had triggered her fears in Polperro?

Both men rose as well, standing to her left and right. Siegfried impatiently reclaimed the letter from her, while James asked her what was wrong.

In her excitement, she forgot all about her usual shyness: "Don't you see it? The seal! Who uses a seal these days? Hardly anyone, but Papa is attached to his. It's his quirk, his trademark, so to speak. He owns two sets of wooden boxes with stamps, knives, wax, and matches. Oh, don't look at me like that! Don't you get it?" She moved around to the narrow side of the table, to where her father used to write, and pulled out the drawer with such force that it fell out of her hands and onto the floor. She quickly bent down and reached for a dark box that was ornamented with rich carvings across its surface.

She rose, swaying a little, and leaned against the table. "This is the twin to the box he keeps at the university."

James didn't understand, but Siegfried excitedly reached for the box, cradled it in his hands, and nodded. "Of course, it's absurd, completely absurd."

James glanced from him to Emma, feeling left out and wondering what he had missed.

Emma turned to him. "If you had to leave in such a rush that you didn't say goodbye to your sister or pack a single pair of socks, would it occur to you to take along a seal set of all things, one too large to fit into your coat pocket?"

He slowly shook his head. No, he wouldn't. Then he looked anxiously at Emma, who had suddenly raised one hand to her head.

She was leaning heavily on the tabletop, feeling dizzy; her head was suddenly throbbing, and her throat was on fire. A tear trickled down her cheek.

Siegfried eyed her. "You look miserable," he said and promptly felt her forehead. "You're burning up. You probably caught a cold sitting in that cold shed for hours. Why didn't you tell us you were sick?"

James berated himself for overlooking Emma's condition; he wished it were him not Siegfried who were playing the role of hero. But then his concern for her won out over his perceived defeat. He led her to one of the armchairs, then hurried out to fetch Tante Tinni.

INVOLUNTARY STALEMATE

Emma sneezed. Once. Twice. Three times. She drummed on the bedspread with both hands and glanced out the open window. The sun was beaming down from a blue sky, and it was so warm it could almost be summer. But here she was in bed, wrapped up with a quilt, forcing down the latest cup of chamomile tea. It was coming to her by the pot. Tante Tinni kept bringing up more and made sure that she didn't leave a single drop. What a revolting brew! Everything was revolting: the stupid weather, her illness, Tinni's attention, Sybil's sunny mood—everything was terrible, awful, horrible!

Emma grumbled; even the most good-natured little lamb would have had enough by now. She had been locked up here for a week, swaddled in heavy blankets with compresses on her forehead and bed warmers at her feet. She was being stuffed full with soups and soufflés, puddings and purees, cocoa and crêpes at all hours of the day. Well, to be fair, eating Jean-Baptiste's crêpes wasn't the worst torture known to man, but imprisoning her in her room was completely different. What a drag!

She drained the last sip of tea, slammed the mug down on the nightstand, and reached for one of the books on the stack. This, at least, was the one aspect of the situation she didn't mind: everyone had sent flowers, chocolates, and books. A long letter had also arrived from Daphne, describing her encounters and plans, but also demanding news. Emma would answer her in the next few days. For now, she wanted to read, so she opened the novel. Novel, pah! The lovely damsel with golden curls sank sighing into the arms of the valiant hero every two or three pages. No, absolutely not! She was in no mood for that! Absolutely not! With a flourish, she hurled the book to the floor and was annoyed when it made nothing more than a soft thud upon landing. She had wanted to hear a bang, a crash, a thunderclap! She plucked the next book from the pile, ready to hurl it after the other one.

Oh, but who had put this here? It was Jane Austen's *Emma*, her mother's favorite book. The book contained an Emma so very different from the one in Bonn, whose time was being spent sniffling, bored, and cross. The other Emma could make snap judgements, was self-confident, and independent. Sure, she made mistakes, misinterpreted many things, and caused misunderstandings, but she possessed charm and vivacity:

> Emma Woodhouse, handsome, clever, and rich, with a comfortable home and happy disposition, seemed to unite some of the best blessings of existence and had lived nearly twenty-one years in the world with very little to distress or vex her.

For an hour, Emma read Emma. She was amazed to discover more similarities between herself and the protagonist than she had suspected. True, unlike Emma, she was neither beautiful nor rich, nor the center of attention, and she was more quiet than assertive. Plus, Emma Woodhouse had certain prejudices linked with her social status that this Emma found off-putting. These differences aside, their views of the world were, on the whole, quite similar. With each passing day, the Emma in Bonn was increasingly observant and critical of her surroundings, and she formed her own opinions—quietly, calmly, reservedly. Like Miss Woodhouse in the novel, she saw the humor in her fellow humans, and formed opinions quickly and probably with similar inaccuracy; the main difference was that she only thought what Emma Woodhouse said out loud. *I wonder if that's what Mama had wanted for her daughter. That she would say what she thought. That she wouldn't place great weight on convention. That she should find love where she didn't expect it.*

Someone knocked at the front door. Emma looked at the alarm clock; it was four-fifteen—so it had to be Anton. He had been visiting her every day at this time for a week now. He always brought chocolates or licorice or toffees, along with newspapers, cards, or other little things to relieve the boredom. Friday had been the first day he'd visited her, and that had been because he wished to scold Fräulein Schumacher. Why had she set that blond giant on him? Did she really think he had taken her cat goddess and wanted to scare her of all people? That he was a criminal? He wanted to ask her all this, but instead, Fräulein Feuerhahn had explained to him sternly that her niece had unfortunately fallen ill the night before and was lying in bed with a high fever. He wasn't allowed to see her because she was asleep and miserable. Nonetheless, he had refused to be turned away and ended up sitting with Emma's aunt in the living room, listening to her account of what had happened and growing indignant at Emma's opinion of him. He told Christel about his father and the nice weekend he had spent with him, as well as about how he had a lot of work at the university at the moment, which was why he hadn't come by earlier.

Christel had felt so bad for how offended Anton seemed that she offered him not only a cup of tea but also a strong sip of rum, which he had gladly accepted. He had then asked Emma's aunt, who no longer seemed so strict with him, to send Emma his best wishes for a speedy recovery. And would it be all right if he tried his luck here again tomorrow? Christel made no objections.

The next afternoon, Anton rang the bell at 4:15 p.m. on the dot at Arndtstraße 13a. Christel informed him that Emma was still a little feverish but awake and unbearably irritable—if that didn't scare him off? He stormed straight up the stairs, loaded down with goodies and reading material, knocked politely, and was ungraciously admitted.

The sick Emma differed considerably from the healthy one, he observed. She kept barking commands: asking him to open the windows and then close the windows, to hand her a scarf or her bottle of 4711, or to call down to her aunt for more lemonade or soup. She would ask him to just talk but would then brusquely interrupt him and demand silence, only to complain two minutes later that he was sitting around like a stuffed dummy.

Anton would smile, saying *yes* and *no* and *please* and *thank you* and *amen*, depending on what might appease the patient. He hastened to fulfill her every wish and did so cheerfully, causing Emma to apologize for her moodiness. He didn't want to hear a word of it, he assured her, and read to her from one of her novels until she fell asleep.

He was also available to help on Sunday, Monday, and Tuesday, staying longer and longer each day, chatting about this and that, reading or listening, and even once regaling her with anecdotes that the students had shared with him. Sometimes he would get a little too close, make puppy dog eyes at her, and hint at the fact he thought about her all the time, and that every one of his faux pas could be attributed to her charm and magic, which he was powerless to resist.

Emma was still bothered by his forthright expressions of affection, but she didn't think his openness was any reason for her to be upset with him. On Monday, she allowed him to exchange *Fräulein Schumacher* for *Emma*, although *Anton* still passed her lips with some difficulty. Her fever finally broke on Tuesday, and Tante Tinni allowed Anton to stay until supper, which he took along with Emma in her bedroom, or in his words, her *boudoir*.

Now it was Wednesday, and Emma's cold was on the wane, but she still wasn't allowed to get up. Tante Tinni had insisted that she had to hold out one more day or two until she was completely recovered. Emma received Anton as politely as she could despite her impatience.

"Well, you look sour, Emma! I guess I made a good selection with these," Anton teased, placing a small bag of candies in her hands.

Lemon drops! Very funny, indeed. Against her will, Emma had to laugh, and Anton joined in. "If you're sweet, tomorrow I'll bring you some salted Dutch licorice that'll open up your sinuses, then your aunt'll definitely let you get up," he promised.

"I'm fed up with being sweet!"

"Don't be crabby, Emma. Think about the wrinkles you'll get from making such a face!"

In defiance, Emma grimaced at him. Couldn't he just tell Tante Tinni that she was fit as a fiddle?

Anton cocked an eyebrow, reached for one of the books, and offered to read aloud.

She didn't want that; she was done with all of it.

"How's your sore throat?"

"Gone, disappeared, over and done with. I'm practically better."

"Then we can have a wonderful chat. Have you heard anything from James?"

Emma sighed and drummed her fingers on the bedspread again. She didn't want to hear from James. She wanted to drive with him across the countryside to look for Papa. Couldn't he have held out for these few days instead of dashing off without her? He obviously wanted to run around in a plaid coat and deerstalker hat, a pipe clenched between his teeth as he shouted for Watson. She couldn't forgive him for the fact that he had set off on Wednesday evening to plan the further course of action with Herr Mertens and had refused to take her with him. After all, it was her father who was missing, not his! He could never make up for that. Never!

Emma pulled a postcard written in English from her nightstand. "This came in the mail today. From Würzburg. As always, affectionate greetings, I should get well and not worry. He is now on his way to Munich," she translated for Anton. She would have liked to tear the card into smithereens, but instead she set it on her pile of books and continued her lament. "Still no word on what he's learned, or what he thinks, or if he even has a lead. He called last night, but of course I wasn't allowed to get out of bed. After all, I might catch another cold in the hallway! Jean-Baptiste laughed and chatted with James for over ten minutes, but when I wanted to know what had been so funny, what did he tell me? Nothing, nothing at all. James was doing well and had reached Munich. Why does he send these silly cards when they arrive too late anyway? And what could he possibly have to discuss with Jean-Baptiste?" Emma snorted as she struck the bedspread once more with her left hand.

"You're acting like a little kid who wants to unwrap her presents right away," Anton remarked, offering her a lemon drop.

"And you're acting like you don't like me today," Emma hissed back.

Anton stood up, bowed, and walked to the door; he could tell when he wasn't welcome.

She called him back and confessed that she was bored and out of sorts and angry and disappointed, as well as still—as he shouldn't forget—quite sick and worn out. She opened her eyes wide and feigned a pout. Anton grinned and sat back down, pointing out that she was just playing him. It wasn't her cold that was making her moody; it was more likely the boredom and disappointment. If he were in James' place, he never would have left Emma. Instead, he would have tried to pass the time until they could go together.

"Well, you've been doing that last part for days," Emma declared, acknowledging the hours he had spent with her. He was right; James' behavior was inexcusable. After all, she could have been seriously ill, could be hovering between life and death. She pictured him returning after his selfish car trip. He would ring the doorbell and expect her to gaze up at him with admiration and to hang on his every word. But instead Tante Tinni would open the door, dressed in black, pale, despondent, and emaciated, propped up by a broken Jean-Baptiste, and they would inform him that Emma had sunk into an early, chilly grave. Oh, how he would regret having torn himself away from her without confessing his love, and now she was gone forever! Never again would he feel joy, never again would he even notice another woman. He would wander through the world, eternally cursed, until he succumbed to madness and perished miserably in some desert. He would get his!

Emma sighed, comfortably and contentedly. Well, perhaps she had been leafing through Sybil's magazines full of kitschy romances too often in the past few days. She caught Anton's glance. He laughed as if he could read her mind, and Emma blushed. "I feel strange. I think my fever is rising again," she whispered, sinking back into her pillows.

"Lemon drop?"

Silly, Emma thought with a scowl. What was going on with Anton? The better she got to know him, the more the pushy, loud Anton faded into the background to make room for a more sensitive man, one who seemed to want nothing more than to sit by her side. He frequently handed her what she wanted before it even occurred to her to ask for it. Sometimes it seemed like he understood her better than she understood herself. He disagreed or agreed, laughed and wondered, and disapproved just as Emma hoped he would. In any case, he cared, while James—oh, James be blasted! Why was she thinking about him anyway? He was neither gentle like Alexei nor heroic like Siegfried Mertens nor attentive like Anton. And all three of them were more attractive than James with his crooked face. Were men even called attractive? And was James actually ugly? "Anton, I'm hungry! Will you please ask my aunt when there will be something to eat? Something proper? I can't handle any more soups and mashed vegetables. Please, please, beg her for some roasted potatoes, will you? Would you mind doing that for me before you go?"

Of course he wouldn't mind. With a deep look into Emma's eyes and a handshake full of warmth, Anton bid her farewell and hurried down to the kitchen, where the convalescent's wish was taken as a good sign. Saying goodbye until tomorrow, Anton left Arndtstraße in the very best of spirits.

Christel and her fiancé agreed that he was completely under their niece's thumb and that she was taking as much advantage of this as she could. While Christel felt concerned about this side of Emma, Jean-Baptiste declared that Anton simply shared the fate of all men in love.

And what exactly did that entail? his sweetheart wanted to know.

Love transforms men into meek lambs but women into ravenous lionesses, and it never behooved a lamb to contradict a lioness. And the fact that Christel was now threatening him with the soup ladle proved his statement was true.

The only reason Tante Tinni allowed her niece to go into the living room for lunch the next day was because Frau Vianden wanted to give the upstairs floor a deep cleaning. Propped up by pillows and blankets, and with a pot of chamomile tea on the side table, Emma vowed to never drink another cup of that poison again. However, Tinni believed otherwise and was sticking by her side to pour the brew herself. Above their heads, the maid was making a racket, while dance music was blaring from the study, accompanied by Sybil's lilting voice.

"What's Sybil doing?" asked Emma.

"If only I knew. Either she's out all hours of the night and day, or she's yodeling around the house with Alexei. But she won't explain what she's up to."

"Are they engaged now?"

Tante Tinni shrugged. Sybil cleverly dodged all her questions whenever she showed up on Arndtstraße at all. Most of the time, she came home loaded down with boxes. And the flowers in Emma's room and everywhere else in the house probably came from Alexei, at least one new bouquet for Sybil arrived every day—from the best florists in town at that. Neither aunt nor niece could figure out an explanation for this strange behavior.

After two hours, Frau Vianden stuck her head in the room: "Hello, Fräulein Feuerhahn, I'm done for the day."

Tante Tinni glanced up only briefly, declared that it was fine, and was preparing to shoo Emma back up to her bed when Herr Mertens' baritone sounded from the hallway.

"Herr Mertens, will you please come into the living room!" cried Emma, turning to her aunt and whispering, "Or shall I receive the good detective in my boudoir as well?"

"Cheeky girl," murmured Christel, who greeted Siegfried and then left the room. As usual, he reached for Emma's hand, bowed, and brushed a light kiss against it. He regarded her closely. "You're looking well. Are you feeling better?"

She answered in the affirmative. But her cold, she exclaimed, was less important than what he was about to share.

He awkwardly took a seat in an armchair and suddenly looked tired.

"How are you, Herr Mertens? Have you been ill as well?"

"I don't get sick. I don't let myself, but I admit I feel strained. There are too many tasks to be done, and I'm afraid I haven't made much progress in our cause." Siegfried was ashamed of this half-truth, but he was still reluctant to admit that he was secretly investigating on his own, and that the night and extra shifts of the past few days were getting to him. He was enjoying far too much the feeling of being considered an experienced police officer in Emma's eyes. "So, what did I find out? First of all, I went to the university on Friday and talked to some of Johannes Schmitz's fellow students. He was not unpopular; however, he had withdrawn from all his friends over the semester break. That could potentially be connected with your father's disappearance, since the chronology would fit."

"And what about my father's seal box? Is it still in the office?"

Siegfried thought about how he could get around the truth. He hadn't been able to demand access to the office without a police warrant, and so he had waited in the library and watched for an opportune moment during which he slipped into the room with a little help from a lockpick set. This activity wasn't exactly legal, strictly speaking. "Well, I searched the room, and our suspicions were correct. The set is no longer there."

Emma threw up her hands and looked at him—did she have to finagle every word out of him? She had pinned so many hopes and waited so long for his visit! She had expected great things from Siegfried's intervention, and now what? "Is that all? What about Papa, what about the theft? And the professors?"

"Well, I haven't discovered anything new yet." Again, he was only partially truthful. Siegfried would have liked to talk to the other professor of Egyptology about Schumacher, but the only way not to arouse the other man's suspicions was to limit his questions to ones about Schmitz, whom the professor remembered as quiet and unobtrusive. Siegfried had snuck in a question about whether the professor knew that Schmitz had also studied with Professor Schumacher, whereupon his counterpart had sighed deeply.

Yes, old Schumacher was an excellent scholar with extensive expertise and incomparable zeal. At the moment, the retired professor was apparently busy elsewhere. Siegfried inquired where old Schumacher might be, but the other Egyptologist was already hurrying to his next lecture, and Siegfried's investigations at the university came to a swift end.

"Have you at least heard from James?"

He hadn't but expected him back any day.

"And what about your contacts at the other police stations?"

Siegfried's ego suffered considerably under Emma's questions. A week ago, he had seen the next steps clearly in front of him, but by the very next day, he had realized how little he could accomplish without official authority. If he could verify his theory, he could convince Inspector Wertheim to reopen the case. "I'm afraid I'm still waiting for responses from them."

Emma threw herself into her pillows. A blind man would have recognized the disappointment in her face. "So now my father has been missing for eight weeks, and we haven't made any progress!"

"But Fräulein Schumacher, you've been ill. Don't be so hard on yourself, I beg you."

She didn't say anything, just looked at him with a shake of her head, a snarky reply on the tip of her tongue.

"I think you should rest a little longer. I have asked Mr. Beresford to let me know as soon as he returns. Until then, I continue to wish you a speedy recovery," Siegfried declared and took his leave.

Emma watched him go and blew a strand of hair off her forehead. Masculine energy wasn't all it was cracked up to be, she thought. One man was rushing around and forgetting about her, while the other was dragging his feet. She had really expected more from them. Much more!

DISCOVERIES

Emma pushed past Tante Tinni, who was standing in the doorway. "Mama always said colds take three days to build up, stay for three days, and take three days to leave. Just like this one did! I'm better, and I'm getting up! It's over."

Christel relented; after all, she could hardly drag her niece back to bed. Emma spent an hour in the bathroom, where she soaked in the tub, washed her long hair, applied cream and powder, and slowly started to feel like a human being again. When she reentered her bedroom, Sybil followed her. "Emma dear, let me fix you up. The tip of your nose is terribly pale."

"Are you bored, Aunt Sybil?"

"Be a dear and finally stop calling me Aunt! Aunts are old and gray and strict. Do I look like an aunt?"

"Does Tante Tinni look like an aunt?"

"Yes. Like a particularly delightful one though." Sybil began braiding Emma's hair. "You're still wearing it so long, when everyone else would have cut it off ages ago..."

"I'd love to have a bob like you. But—" Emma hesitated, "Mama's hair... I..."

Tears welled in her eyes as Sybil patted her cheek and, in a soft voice, launched into a story from her childhood. "You know, when I was a little girl, my mother was a young woman. Whenever her maid helped her dress up for a ball, I would curl up and watch from her bed. I admired her so much, and thought she was more beautiful than all the princesses in my fairy tale books. Even though we were very different, I loved her and still miss her a lot. Especially in the last few weeks. I wonder what she would tell me if she were here. What would she think of Alexei? Would she scold me or encourage me?"

Emma turned to her aunt, took the older woman's hands in hers, and replied that she knew without a doubt that Mama would have been just as fond of Alexei as everyone else was. Sybil looked at her niece for a long moment, bent down, and pressed a tender kiss on her forehead. Then she stood up and brushed a little more blush on her face. "Look how pretty you are, Emma dear."

For the first time, this salutation sounded affectionate, not merely mocking. "Thank you so much."

Sybil nodded. It was time for her to meet Alexei at the coffee house; in the next few days, they might have some news to announce. She stroked the top of Emma's head one last time, then left the room.

Sybil's cosmetic magic absolutely demanded one of the new dresses. Extremely pleased with her reflection, Emma skipped down the steps into the foyer just as the grandfather clock struck half past ten. She rushed into the living room, full of energy. Tante Tinni and Jean, who were quietly listening to their beloved Schumann, flinched in surprise.

"I want to do something, get some fresh air, get out of the house. What are we doing today?"

Somewhat morosely, Christel pointed at the window, and Emma looked out. It was storming once again, raining thick drops. This was what they called Golden October? She groaned and flopped into the armchair, stretching her arms and legs. She wanted to go out, out! Blast the rain; she wasn't made of sugar. She was steeling herself to brave the storm when it thundered—loud, crashing, deafening. A flash of lightning and another clap of thunder preceded the start of hail. Grumbling, Emma burrowed deeper into her armchair to sulk. Tomorrow... tomorrow nothing would keep her inside! But for the moment, she had to settle for Schumann.

Then the bell rang, again and again and again. She jumped up, ran to the door, and flung it open. James! There he stood, a bouquet of flowers in his hand, with flaming red cheeks and a grin that less well-meaning people would have called silly. Emma thought he was adorable! Until she remembered how upset she was with him. "Oh, you're still alive?" she greeted him, annoyed at her flippant tone. She had wanted to seem cool and superior, not like an offended ninny.

But her words bounced off James; he didn't even seem to hear them. He was too happy to see her again and to spend some time alone with her. He took her by the hand and pulled her along with him, stopping only briefly to press the flowers to her chest before maneuvering her into the study. There he released her hand and dropped into one of the armchairs only to hop back up and relocate to the sofa. Perplexed, Emma stood in the middle of the room with her flowers in her hands.

"Sit down, sit down," James urged, gesturing at the sofa. In his dreams, he was pulling her onto his lap; in reality, he didn't dare.

"Perhaps I should put the flowers in water first? And offer you some tea?" She returned to her haughty tone.

This time James noticed. "Are you angry with me?" he asked, pulling his face into such a droll smile that Emma had to laugh. This, too, annoyed her.

"Oh, you!" she hissed. "You go off and have adventures, leaving me sick at home. And now you're standing here with your silly flowers and... oh! I'll go get you some tea. After all, I'm a good hostess and happen to want a cup myself, not because you deserve it!" Emma felt her cheeks flushing and just wanted to escape, to get away from him. Why was she acting so beastly?

But James sprang up from his seat and strode over to block her way.

"Oh, just step aside!"

He took the bouquet from her hands but was unsure what to do with it, so he tossed it behind him on the couch. "But Emma, I didn't drive across the country for my own sake. I only did it for you, so you wouldn't have to worry any longer. You must know that, and I swear to you there wasn't much I enjoyed about my trip. Look at me, please. Shall I tell you what I did enjoy about it? Whenever I stopped at some particularly beautiful place, ate and drank something good, I would think how wonderful it would be if you were with me. Then I imagined the two of us roaring down the roads in my car, going to all the lovely places together. Sometime in the future..."

Emma stared at the floor, uncertain about what should come next. Was James trying to tell her something, or was she misunderstanding him? Did she even want him to talk about his feelings or discuss her own, which seemed strange and unreal to her? Could it be that one minute she wanted him to simply go away, while the next she was musing about the length of his dark eyelashes and the small scar on his right temple? And shouldn't she finally raise her eyes from the worn carpet at her feet?

She looked up. James' eyes were fixed on hers, and his cheeks were no less flushed than her own. Oh dear, their children would be doomed to having rosy cheeks forever... *Children?* What children? She shook her head to dispel that uninvited thought and cleared her throat sheepishly.

James beamed. He reached for her hands, surprisingly confident and assured. Somewhat hoarsely, he whispered, "Dear, sweet

Emma, I think of you all the time. Morning, noon, and night. I sugar my breakfast eggs and salt my coffee. I strap my watch around my calf and wrap my sock suspenders around my neck. Yesterday I even kissed the hand of a doorman when I told him goodbye. I'm constantly running into doors and lamp posts and fire hydrants. It's as if they sense my longing for you and want to play tricks on me. I've never experienced this sort of feeling before, it's completely foreign. But it's exciting too. It invigorates me and makes me feel stronger and braver. Perhaps it's much too soon to say such things, but still ..." He fell silent and leaned forward, stepping so close to her that she had to lift her chin. He gazed into her eyes without blinking and lowered his head until they stood forehead to forehead, hands clasped. The shabby carpet, the Schumann melodies from the gramophone, the worries about the professor—for a moment, all that disappeared.

Emma shivered, just a little. No, she didn't want James to head for the hills. This quiet moment of intimacy was doing her good. She was grateful for his silence, grateful also that he didn't hold her tightly against him. After a few moments, she took a slow step back, but continued to hold James' hand.

He gently stroked her fingers, then asked about the tea. Had he earned a cup after all?

Ten minutes later they were sitting hand in hand on the sofa. The pot of tea and some of Christel's cookies were on the recliner they had pulled up close to the couch. It was still storming outside. Strains of Handel were now drifting from the living room, and Emma couldn't think of more glorious weather or more heavenly music than this. She guessed it was James's company that had transformed the plain cookies into manna and the tea into nectar. She pulled her knees up and leaned half against the back of the couch, half against his shoulder. Then she cleared her throat, "Don't you want to tell me about your trip? Did you find out anything about Papa?"

James sighed. He wasn't comfortable with what he had to tell her. He emptied his cup, set it down awkwardly, and was about to reach for a cookie when she tapped his fingers: report, don't eat! He looked at his watch. Emma acted surprised to see it on his wrist. He poked her on the nose, laughing. "You're cheeky, you know! Give me another fifteen minutes, Emma. I've asked Siegfried to stop by too, so I don't have to repeat everything for him. Ow! Please don't get into the habit of punching me; I have a delicate build." He pulled her to him once more. "I understand that you don't want to wait, but I would like to enjoy these few minutes alone with you."

"Siegfried! So you're now on a first-name basis with Herr Mertens, are you? He came to see me just once, and you know what? He didn't have one single thing to report."

"Well, it still won't hurt to have him around."

"But is what you have to tell me really so bad? And you're making me wait for it? What on earth happened?"

"No, no, stay calm, I'm sure he'll be here in a minute, and the only things I've brought with me are conjecture and suspicion."

"Only? *Only?* What's my father suspected of? No, don't stroke my hands! Stay away from me! I want to hear what you have to say right now!"

"Emma, please, it'll just be a few minutes—ah, see, that'll be Siegfried. I'll let him in."

But when he opened the front door, it wasn't the blond Siegfried who stood before him, but the dark Anton, decked out as usual with presents and flowers. James crossed his arms and was considering how to get rid of him, when Anton, beaming cheerfully, socked him lightly in the shoulder with his free fist. "James, old boy, are you back already? And you came straight here to pay your respects to our dear friend. Now that's what I call being a true gentleman! Has she accepted you back into her good graces? Emma was pretty upset with you, even though I put in more than one good word for you. Well, anyway, how is the lady today?"

Anton didn't wait for James' reply but pushed past him and headed for the stairs. He was already up the first stair when James informed him that Emma was in the study. James wondered a little sourly if Anton had already been up in Emma's bedroom, then he hurried ahead of him into the study.

Anton asked Emma to stay seated, complimented her dazzling appearance and her complete recovery, and presented her with his gifts. He told her not to bother to get up since he knew where the vases were kept and would be right back. James stood puzzled, searching for signs of impatience and exasperation in Emma's face. How could it be that this pushy interloper had been in and out of here, and had won Emma's friendship?

Emma interpreted his facial expression correctly and couldn't help taking a little jab: "After all, Anton visited me every afternoon to keep my spirits up. *You*, on the other hand, couldn't wait to get going."

James would have liked to have said something in reply, but he couldn't think of anything. It didn't matter though since Anton had already rejoined them, carrying his carefully arranged flowers. And it wasn't by chance that he placed his bouquet in such a way that it covered James' bouquet. As soon as Anton sat next to Emma on the sofa, James strolled over to the worktable and pulled his vase forward. Anton grinned, and Emma raised her eyebrows. Immediately James blushed and felt childish, but fate was with him since at that moment the doorbell rang. It wasn't fate, of course, but Siegfried, who apologized for being exactly three minutes late.

There they sat, all four of them, not knowing quite what to do with each other.

James resented the fact that Anton was still making no move to leave. He was also bothered by how Siegfried had made himself comfortable sitting on the other side of Emma.

Anton grinned, because it was so obvious that James was annoyed. He would have liked to give Tommy Boy another smack for his haughtiness, for the way he was either too dignified or too cowardly to confront him directly.

Siegfried, on the other hand, was having trouble concentrating due to his completely soaked shoes and pants. He still wanted to solve a spectacular case, but so far, he hadn't been particularly successful. The only thing he had achieved was exhaustion.

Emma studied the gentlemen, one after the other. Each one seemed more preoccupied with himself than with her or her father. She had waited long enough; it was time for someone to do something. "James, I beg you! Stop fiddling with the flowers! Sit down and finally tell us what you found out!"

The three men flinched, and Emma herself was startled as well. The last time she had shouted so loudly she was still in the cradle. Blushing, she murmured, "Oh, can you please just get started?"

James hesitated, glaring angrily at Anton. Then, as Emma pointedly cleared her throat, he pulled a notebook from his jacket pocket and began his story with his trip to Koblenz, where he had met with Herr Friedhelm, who had declared that Herr Meerbusch was currently away in order to spread the news about the imminent opening of their collection and to acquire more artifacts for the exhibits; he wasn't expected back until October 29th. And yes, they had heard a lot about Professor Schumacher in Koblenz. Nothing good, unfortunately, since complaints were coming in from all over. He was unreliable, unfriendly, impudent, and impertinent. And since the Koblenz Egyptological Collection had organized the itinerary, everyone was contacting them, Herr Friedhelm had declared indignantly. Some people were even considering legal proceedings for breach of contract. Siegfried inquired: "Was there a contract, and if so, what was in it?"

James shrugged; as he had understood it, there had been a verbal agreement, as was usual among men of honor. But be that as it may, he had decided to drive on from Koblenz to Frankfurt, where he had reached Dr. Meinhardt just before he too went away for some time.

"What happened then?" asked Emma.

"Dr. Meinhardt is an extremely obliging gentleman, but unfortunately, he was unable to prevent the owner of the collection—one Samuel Weinstein—from reporting the loss of the Ramses. The gentlemen of the board of directors have heavily incriminated your father. Actually you, Siegfried, should have received notification of this some time ago."

"I'll check with the Königstraße station later, but our colleagues in Frankfurt wouldn't notify our major crimes department unless they'd found some concrete evidence in the case."

"Very well. I left Frankfurt and traveled to Mainz that same day. Here, by the way, the professor wasn't scheduled to give a lecture, but to evaluate the collection of a private citizen."

"That doesn't make sense. Papa always refuses those evaluations."

"Well, not this time. And you'll be pleased about this, for the gentleman with the beautiful name of Sigismund Rafael Piepenbrink couldn't praise your father highly enough. So charming, so amusing and so entertaining! Mr. Piepenbrink kept calling him a great man. Your father stayed at his house for two nights, and he was sorry to see the professor go."

Emma's eyes lit up, but James shook his head. "I hope my feeling of unease is wrong, but the fact is that the professor examined the artifacts and told Herr Piepenbrink that for a more thorough analysis, he needed more time, more rest, and his home environment. And so, he was allowed to take a large number of the artifacts with him. The gentleman is still in good spirits; the professor informed him that this process usually takes two to three months."

"Well, yes, that's how long it typically takes him."

"And you think he's lugging these treasures all around with him until he returns home to Bonn after traveling to who knows where?"

"He may have sent them here or to the university by mail," Siegfried interjected.

"No, I receive all the incoming mail. I would know if anything had arrived," Anton explained.

Siegfried looked at him closely and recognized him as the university porter's errand boy. When he had questioned Anton about the burglary at the Schumacher house, his attitude had seemed rather dismissive and condescending. Siegfried saw him as a lad who lacked discipline and good manners, and who would probably benefit from a few years in the military. "Let's leave that for the moment. James, please continue your account."

In Würzburg, James learned little more than what Emma had already found out on the telephone. Her father had paid only a brief visit to the museum and had acted "like a wild-eyed Rumpelstiltskin" there. However, James had been able to add one further significant detail to the picture; the museum director, one Herr Wellenbrink, had subsequently received an expert evaluation from the professor, which didn't correspond to his usual quality.

"In what way did the evaluation not meet his expectations?" asked Emma.

"Well, your father seems to be either getting sloppy or losing his mind. He dated a bust of Akhenaten to the Old Kingdom and claimed that Hatshepsut was his consort."

Emma gasped; Anton and Siegfried, however, looked perplexed. She explained, "Akhenaten is one of the most famous pharaohs of all, because he exchanged polytheism for the worship of a single god—Aten. He was also the first king whose likenesses weren't significantly embellished but were fairly realistic. In addition, he was the father of Tutankhamun and the husband of Nefertiti. Anyone who knows even a little about Egypt knows these details. Moreover, Akhenaten ruled during the New Kingdom, and he is one of Papa's favorite historical figures. An evaluation that asserts the nonsense James just mentioned is worthless and would likely ruin the author's reputation for good." She turned toward James. "Did Herr Wellenbrink show you the evaluation? Was it in Papa's writing?"

"I don't know your father's handwriting, but I think the director compared it with other appraisals and believes the document to be genuine. He also mentioned that it bore the professor's seal—a cross-legged Egyptian scribe?"

Emma nodded.

"That seal again!" interjected Siegfried. "There is something going on with it!"

"Herr Mertens, we got that far last week but haven't made any progress since."

"Herr Wellenbrink made another remark that bothered me. When he told me about your father's behavior, he mentioned that they had decided not to comply with his wish to present several artifacts during the lecture. All items were to remain behind glass."

What did he mean by that, Emma demanded, sounding irritated. James hemmed and hawed for a moment, since she now struck him as less sweet and gentle than she had just an hour before. Well, a bust of Ramses had disappeared in Frankfurt, as well as several pieces in Mainz, and there had been an incident in Munich too.

"What happened in Munich?"

"Well, I went to Augsburg first—"

"I don't care about Augsburg! What happened in Munich?"

"I'd prefer for James to continue his report chronologically," Siegfried interjected yet again. "I'll get my notes all mixed up otherwise."

"If Emma wants to hear about Munich, you should oblige her, James," Anton declared, glancing at Emma, who wasn't paying even the slightest attention to him.

She sighed. "So, what happened in Augsburg?"

"Here again, they had invited him to give a lecture. Baroness Marie-Luise Elisabeth von Felsenau had asked him to appraise her collection. She's a very determined lady, I can assure you. No sooner had I introduced myself and explained to her butler my request than he pushed me toward her, obviously wishing to lay me at her feet. Before I could even ask a single question, she started to interrogate me. Who was I? How did I know this charlatan? What did I want there? And where were her Hatshepsut and golden scarab? She ended all this by threatening me with a beating. Well, I responded by turning on the charm"—at this, Anton started to chuckle snidely until Emma's elbow brought him to his senses—"and managed to sweet-talk the lady. I answered everything obligingly, let her show me pictures of the pieces and asked if she had already reported the professor to the authorities. Fortunately for us, she hasn't. And do you know why? Because several weeks ago, the police station dared to accept a complaint filed by her personal maid. The good child hadn't been paid for over three months, but regardless, how could the Baroness entrust such a delicate matter to men who obviously lack sound judgment? She has been trying to hire a detective agency, but so far she hasn't found anyone willing to undertake this hunt for the sole sake of fame and glory!"

Despite her tension, Emma smiled, even laughed a little at certain moments during James' description and imitation of the Baroness.

"Go ahead and laugh, Emma. On Tuesday you'll get to see that it's funnier to hear about her than to stand in front of her."

"What do you mean?"

"When the Baroness realized that I was returning to Bonn shortly, she informed me that she was leaving for Hamburg this weekend and had originally planned to spend the night in Cologne en route. But since there is a possibility that your father might return soon to his *miserable hometown,* as she put it, where you, *his sweet and innocent daughter,* might be able to influence him, she demanded to meet you. She will send word to me on Sunday as to when we may call on her at her hotel."

Emma looked at him aghast. Was he truly throwing her to such a dragon? What if the Baroness ended up asking her to compensate her for the losses?! Anton offered to accompany her, but James took a quick step toward him, pulled himself together, and declared that his presence would be unnecessary, since he would go with Emma, of course. Siegfried groaned. His shift was about to start, so could James please finish his report?

Gladly, James replied. He had also gone to the hotel where the professor had reserved a room but hadn't arrived. Emma had already learned that information. However, one evening, an elegant gentleman had come to the reception desk, asked for the professor, and had grown extremely upset when he heard that the guest had never checked in. The gentleman had rushed out of the house with the words, "I'll have something to say about that."

"After that I raced to Munich, and the first thing I did was to go to the museum. There, too, the professor was described as unfriendly and arrogant, and yet another artifact had been reported missing since his visit. This time it was a pendant representing the goddess Hathor. The board of directors was discussing what to do next, but the gentlemen hadn't reached a conclusion by the time I arrived. After all, as they explained, this was a matter of a scholar from their own ranks, who up till now had enjoyed an unimpeachable reputation. In this instance, they have asked that when we find the professor, we please ask him to return the item. They will give us fourteen days, after which they will feel compelled to file a complaint with the police. One final thing: your father left his boarding house there earlier than expected, after having received a message from someone." Parched now after so much talking, James leaned against the professor's desk and asked for a drink of water.

Siegfried rose, snapped shut his notebook, bid Emma goodbye with a kiss on the hand, and nodded briefly at Anton and James. He had a few things to take care of, but he would stop by again the next morning to see Fräulein Schumacher.

"That's quite the string of robberies you just told us about. Is old Schumacher bonkers or what?" asked Anton. Then his hand flew up to his mouth, "Emma, please forgive me, I meant no disrespect. But from what James has told us, your father doesn't seem to have all his marbles. Otherwise, we'd have to assume he has turned to the underworld. Just imagine what the press will make of that: the secret double life of the thieving professor. And even worse, how you'll be portrayed—as his confidante for it all! But whatever happens, I will stand faithfully by your side. You can always count on me." He then glanced at his watch. "Oh, here I'm making grand speeches when I have to say goodbye too. How does that look? But as you know, the weekend is sacred to my father, and as an obedient son I now have to catch the train to Cologne. If it's all right with you, I'll be back on Tuesday afternoon."

Emma nodded and smiled at him. Far too friendly, James thought as he continued to clutch the tabletop as if glued to it there. Grinning broadly, Anton gave him a farewell cuff on the shoulder.

Finally, Emma and James were alone again.

"Will you stay for dinner?"

"If I may, I'd love to."

"Of course. Let's not talk about Papa tonight; I'll tell Tante Tinni all the important stuff in the morning."

He reached out and pulled her close, studying her sorrowful face. She snuggled against him as he spoke, "I'm sorry, darling, about all this today. But we'll find your father and help him, I promise."

Early the next morning, Siegfried rang the bell at Arndtstraße 13a. He had come immediately after finishing his shift. Christel opened the door, but no one else was awake yet.

As Siegfried explained, he only had a few hours to rest up before spending his weekend on duty in Cologne. Before he left, he wished to tell Fräulein Schumacher something.

Christel hurried up the stairs to wake up Emma. She was quite worried since Emma hadn't yet filled her in about the latest developments. Emma threw on her robe and hurried downstairs. She invited Herr Mertens to come into the study, but he refused. He didn't have much to report, he said. He simply wanted her to know that he had explained the case to his superior officer last night (leaving out the part about Johannes Schmitz) and had been able to convince him to put out an all-points bulletin for the renowned Bonn professor. On Monday afternoon, Inspector Wertheim would be coming by the house to speak with Emma.

Emma looked up at him, alarmed.

He patted her hand reassuringly. "On the one hand, there is now the suspicion of theft, and a complaint has already been filed, but on the other hand—and this is the official basis for the search—we're looking for a well-known person who is presumably mentally disturbed and could, thus, put himself and others in danger. Yes, I know that doesn't sound nice, but we want to find your father so that we can get everything cleared up. You know that I suspect a completely different set of connections are in play. Johannes' death and the break-in at your house are connected to everything James told us, assuming he didn't make it all up."

Emma winced and withdrew her hand. What was he getting at?

Nothing, nothing at all. He was just a suspicious person, he declared, and he preferred to err on the side of over-scrutiny. People who appeared in the vicinity of a crime were people to be watched, and several new individuals had recently shown up in Emma's life. Everyone was probably exactly who they claimed to be. She should nonetheless be cautious. With these words, he bowed and left the house, leaving a confused Emma behind.

When James arrived two hours later, he found her transformed: cool and quiet, dismissive almost. She had a headache. Perhaps she was still sick after all, she said. If he wanted to come back for supper, he was welcome. With that, she turned and left him standing in the foyer.

But at dinner Emma didn't laugh or say much either and was reluctant to be alone with him. Even around Alexei, who finally reappeared, she seemed shy. When the Russian suggested that they all go on an excursion to Brühl Castle the next day, she asked James to go without her; she needed to take care of some things. He could call her later that evening to tell her when they would be meeting with the Baroness.

James reluctantly agreed.

On Sunday afternoon, Emma picked up her fountain pen and wrote to Daphne:

> October 24, 1926, Bonn
>
> My dear Daphne,
>
> Last week, I was stuck sick in bed and was a nuisance to everyone. First because I was feverish and miserable, but also because I was in an unbearable mood and certainly very unjust to everyone around me. You cannot imagine how much your letter cheered me up. Your time in London was clearly exciting and amusing, and I await additional reports about all your admirers.
>
> You ask about Papa. It has now been over two months since I showed you his letter, and I can hardly believe that we still don't know where he is. Meanwhile, the police are looking for him and... forgive me, I can't go into it right now.
>
> You also asked about what I am up to and about the Bonn gentlemen. What can I say? May I take advantage of your friendship to write from the heart? I am confused and muddled, and in general, everything is wretched and beautiful and horrible.
>
> I have met a man from Bonn; his name is Anton. I think you would like him. He is frank and direct, very good-looking, and eager to be near me at all times. You can guess that he mustn't be the least bit shy about his feelings, if even I can notice. And indeed he isn't shy at all. I was sick for quite a while, and he came by every day to cheer me up. He brought me reading material and candy and put up with my moodiness.
>
> Still, I'm unsure how I feel about him. He carries my purchases, invites me to cafés, takes care of me, and is trying to improve his relationship with his father because I advised him to. At least, that's what he claims. Can that possibly be true?

Anton is—I don't know how to describe him—very energetic, very attentive. He seems to be constantly reaching for my hand, touching me, looking at me. Don't other women wish for such a man, who pays attention to their every emotion, who keeps telling them how wonderful they are, who would do anything for them, at any time? At first, he infuriated me, and I had no idea how to fend him off. But now I find it very easy to talk to him—he accepts everything with such equanimity and is never offended or in a bad mood.

And I have also learned what an offended man looks like, because quite soon after I met Anton, a young man showed up at our door asking for Papa. Guess who he was? An Englishman, of course! I never would have thought I'd need to go all the way to the Rhineland to meet one. Regardless, I think he's delightful. Does that sound silly? You should know that he is still practically a stranger to me; we only met three weeks ago.

His name is James, and he is tall and always seems to be blushing—maybe that's why I feel a connection with him. He is very sensitive but doesn't think anyone notices. He gets offended very easily, but it never takes long for him to snap out of it again. What do I like about him? I don't know. Then again, shouldn't I, though? Maybe I'm just imagining that I like him, because I've always felt uncomfortable around men like Anton. Is that stupid? I wish I could chat with you in person!

Whenever I say something, James hangs on my every word to the point that he doesn't notice anything else. He takes me seriously, which is new to me, but I think I could swoon half dead in his arms and he would have no idea what was going on or how I felt. I could be completely pale and totally distraught, with everyone else rushing around to take care of me, and he'd just be standing there, happy to see me.

Because yes, that's the beauty of it: he is just happy to see me. This past Friday, he whispered the sweetest things to me after we hadn't seen each other for a week... oh, writing it like that is silly, isn't it? We've only spent a few days together, and already he seems to mean so much to me. But the incomprehensible thing to me is that I can never seem to maintain my composure when he is around. No, that's not quite right. What I mean is: when I'm with him, I end up snapping at him, ordering him to do something, or asking him unpleasant questions. I'm a *completely different person with him, and to be honest, I enjoy that quite a lot. A certain kind of Emma—can you believe that?*

At other times, I feel all small and timid, and don't know what to say. Those are the moments when it's James who shakes off his quiet reserve. He is then the clear-headed one, the safe one, the one I want to lean on. But half an hour later, I want to shake him again for being so incredibly sensitive.

Twice I have had to spend time with Anton and James together. It was horrible! Anton is the one who handles being a rival better. How strange that word sounds—rival! Astonishingly, two men are interested in me. It's exciting but at the same time less pleasant than I used to think such a thing would be.

I guess I'll just have to wait and see what happens. At some point, I should feel certainty about which one might be right for me, shouldn't I? Oh, but that sounds silly again. I'm not thinking of getting married. I can't take anything seriously until I find my father. And there's one more thing standing in my way: the policeman who told me about the search for my father remarked that he considers everyone around me a potential suspect and that I should be careful with anyone I haven't known for a long time. That rattled me because he's right. I was very reserved towards James yesterday, and I think it bothered him. Now that I'm writing about him, I miss his company, and can't believe he had anything to do with Papa's disappearance. Or do I just not want to believe it?

Dear Daphne, look how much I've written about myself and my childish infatuation. I promise to write a grown-up letter next time and tell you all about Papa. The anniversary of my mother's death is in a week, and it's weighing on me. Look, now I'm getting all emotional again, so I'll end this sentimental epistle quickly and hope for your pardon.

*Yours,
Emma*

Without rereading the letter, she sealed the envelope and carried it downstairs. She planned to drop it in the mailbox tomorrow morning.

The telephone rang. It was James, explaining that Baroness Felsenau would be expecting them at the Hotel Königshof on Tuesday at ten o'clock in the morning. She would be leaving by noon that day, so they should be punctual, or she would report them at the closest police precinct.

Emma agreed, then stood up, receiver in hand, without saying a word. She shivered and hoped James would find something to say that would indicate that she could trust him.

But James remained silent. Neither could bring themselves to speak or hang up, but instead waited on the other to make the first move.

Finally, Emma ventured. "Do you have anything else you want to tell me?" she asked softly.

"Do you?"

"I'm a little sad, but I don't know why..."

"You weren't very nice to me yesterday, but you had been the day before. What did I do?"

"Nothing. It's just..."

"What?"

"Nothing. I'm a mess. I'll meet you in the hotel lobby the day after tomorrow. You don't need to pick me up."

"I would love to pick you up."

"Don't. Please."

"Do you want to see me tomorrow?"

"I don't know. Maybe not. I need to think."

"As you wish." James hung up.

Tante Tinni called her for dinner, but Emma had lost her appetite.

MONDAY

"Come along, Mertens!" called Chief Inspector Wertheim to Siegfried. "We're going to look around the university."

Siegfried hurried after the inspector, who was already striding down the City Hall stairs. Four minutes later, they were knocking on the university porter's door.

Anton Wagenknecht opened, gazed in amazement from Wertheim to Siegfried, and nodded at the latter. "You're here about old Schumacher, aren't you?"

"Mertens, you know this gentleman?" asked Wertheim.

"I took the statements in the burglary at Fräulein Schumacher's house, because the Königsstraße station was understaffed at the time due to illness. We met each other then."

This wasn't entirely true, a fact that didn't escape Wertheim's notice. He turned to Anton: "We would like to talk to everyone who had anything to do with Professor Schumacher. You're the porter, right? No? So the porter is where? Sick? All right, then give me a list of all those who work with the professor."

Anton provided the names of the librarian, dean, rector, and of course, Professor Neumann. The latter, he said, was currently traveling. "He is in... wait a minute..." He searched in the porter's desk calendar. "Yes, here, I see that Professor Neumann is in Frankfurt at a meeting of Egyptologists until the end of the week."

Wertheim asked about the students who studied with Schumacher, but Anton couldn't help him with this. He referred them to Neumann's assistant, a Herr Jünger.

Herr Jünger was a tall young man with thinning hair and glasses, and he appeared highly indignant that Professor Neumann was attending the colloquium without him. In addition, he didn't think much of Professor Schumacher; it was about time that the old guard made room for the young. Schumacher was always causing trouble. Sure, when it came to the evaluation of artifacts, he was brilliant, but when it came to the science behind it all, his time had passed.

"Does your supervisor see it the same way?"

The assistant hesitated. "He would certainly express himself more diplomatically."

"Meaning?"

"Professor Schumacher often disrupted the flow of things, and that in turn disturbed Professor Neumann. Friction ensued. Naturally, it irritated Professor Neumann whenever students contradicted him because they had heard something different from Schumacher. You can't teach like that. Don't get me wrong—there were times when Schumacher was right and Neumann was wrong. I should go on record as pointing out that Neumann is an outstanding scientist, but Schumacher has several decades more experience under his belt, as well as an astutely honed intuition."

"Doesn't that seem to indicate, though, that the old guard should stay in their positions a bit longer?"

Jünger pursed his lips and snorted.

"What do you know about Professor Schumacher's lecture tour?"

"Nothing."

"Can you be more specific?"

"Absolutely nothing?" Jünger sounded sarcastic. "I don't know anything about it, nor have I heard anyone talk about it. However, I think Schumacher would have rubbed it in everyone's faces if it had been something major."

"Does Professor Neumann perhaps know something about it?"

"No, I'm sure he doesn't. I told you, old Schumacher would have rubbed his nose in it."

"How well do you get along with your supervisor?"

"Generally speaking, quite well."

"But...?"

"I am of the opinion that I would be more useful to him at the colloquium in Frankfurt than here."

"How many of Neumann's students study with Professor Schumacher too?"

Jünger opened a compartment, took out a black notebook, and copied down several names that were written there in red.

"If they're written in red like that, I guess that means they aren't the teacher's pets, right?"

Jünger slammed the notebook shut. "We just want to know who might prove to be difficult when taking their exams. Are we perhaps done now? I have things to do."

"What do you think, Mertens?"

Siegfried shrugged; he wasn't used to being asked for his opinion.

Inspector Wertheim eyed him with a smile. "Well, it seems to me that the gentlemen don't quite see eye to eye, like playground rivals. What do you think? If Neumann did away with Schumacher, would Jünger keep his mouth shut?"

"Do you think that the professor killed the professor?" Siegfried bit his lip; he couldn't have put it any more inanely.

"Didn't quite mean it like that, but it's a possibility. You see, these closed communities, they don't like to let anything get out, but within their borders, tempers can flare. There's the old chap who knows everything better, who apparently gets all kinds of special treatment and then provides the students with information that the other lad doesn't have or doesn't want to give out. And then there's the young assistant, who already sees himself as the boss. There could be something to find out here. Let's see what the others have to say, shall we?"

The visits to the dean, rector and librarian didn't produce anything new. All three reported on the professor's volatile temperament and his enormous expertise.

However, only the librarian, Dr. Fassbender, seemed to actually feel any affection for the professor. He had spent many a night with dear Heinrich in the reading room, where they had carried on countless conversations over a glass of wine about antiquities, Fontane and their wives. Yes, the librarian considered Schumacher a friend, even though they never socialized outside of the university. However, he knew nothing about the trip and couldn't explain why Heinrich would have concealed such a tour from him of all people.

"How many boys do we have on the tutorial list?"

"Five," Siegfried answered, "including Johannes Schmitz."

"The suicide? That's quite a coincidence!"

"Yes," muttered Siegfried.

"There's just one thing. I don't believe in coincidences until I've eliminated every other possibility. What about you, Mertens?"

"If I may mention it, sir, I pointed out to our colleagues that there might be a connection between these various pieces: the break-in at the professor's house, the daughter who doesn't know where he is, the student who studied with him. Meier wasn't interested and informed me that it was an open-and-shut case."

"Hmmm. You're an ambitious man, aren't you? And not very—how should I put it?—experienced when it comes to human interactions. Why didn't you come to me?"

"I assumed that you would tell me to stay in my place, as you usually do."

"Of course. You have to first see how we detectives do things; everyone starts out small. But I haven't forbidden you to think and speak up. How do you expect to get anywhere if you don't show initiative? Or did you think you'd run off and pull the professor out of a hat single-handedly?" Wertheim chuckled and gave Siegfried a light cuff. "Well, that's all right. The answer is written all over your face."

For the rest of the morning, Wertheim and his assistant hunted down the students on their list. As they might have expected, none of the fellows were taking advantage of the week off from lectures to play sports or get out in the fresh air. The two officers tracked each of them down in his den, mostly still asleep. None of them had heard the professor mention anything about taking a trip.

Kurt Klostermann, however, believed that the old man had seemed distracted during their last tutorial. He had glanced at his watch more often than usual and had also punctually sent them on their way without letting Fräulein Feuerhahn distribute their usual sandwiches. Yes, and Hannes had been the only one who had stayed behind. That happened occasionally because the professor tended to look out for Hannes. But it had all still seemed strange to Kurt. The last meeting? That must have been on August tenth.

Around three o'clock that afternoon, the chief inspector arrived at Arndtstraße with Siegfried in tow. He greeted Fräulein Feuerhahn very politely, asked her to fetch the daughter of the missing professor, and didn't refuse when she offered him some coffee. He also agreed to a piece of freshly-baked cake with a tantalizing aroma.

Beaming, Christel called for her niece and lead the policemen into the living room. When Emma stepped through the door, Wertheim stood up, pressed a polite kiss to her hand, and asked her and her esteemed aunt not to worry.

Emma nodded as she studied him with interest; one didn't meet a chief inspector every day, and this one was going to bring Papa home.

She found him jovial, probably around fifty, rather short yet wiry, with eyes that sparkled warmly and cheerfully, and a Rhenish accent so melodious, that she immediately trusted him. In fact, she liked him rather well. For the first time since receiving Papa's peculiar letter, she felt confident as he sat down to start asking her questions.

He wanted to know everything: Why she was living in England? Why she had returned? Whom she had met? And what she could say about the burglary? He asked about her father's colleagues and his clients, asked to see his letters and maps, notes and drawings, and finally requested a picture of the professor. Emma brought two photographs from the study, of which he chose the full-length photo. Emma tucked the other one into the pocket of her dress.

On their way to the station, Wertheim summed up his conclusions: "No one knew anything about this trip. So we have to ask ourselves if we have been told the truth. Or is someone lying? Or are they all lying? What do you think, Mertens?"

"I didn't get that impression from Dr. Fassbender, but I'm not sure about Jünger. The other interviewees seemed mostly happy to have Professor Schumacher out of their hair."

"If we believe the librarian, we should believe the others. So does that mean that there was no lecture tour at all? Or was it so spontaneous that old Schumacher didn't have time to brag about it? Was he literally there one moment and then gone the next? After all, we have the postcards he sent, and his daughter recognizes his handwriting. We also have the reports of him starting fights all over the place. Nasty arguments, not like the ones he carries on here with his colleagues. He is even said to have developed a taste for theft. Does that seem logical to you? Well, don't be shy, Mertens! I could tell that you already have an opinion and have been to see Fräulein Schumacher more than once. Spit it out, man!"

"Well, we have a Russian, an Englishman, and a Frenchman and we're dealing here with very valuable Egyptian artifacts."

"Mertens, Mertens, Mertens! Now you disappoint me. This is the theory you want to hand me? Our former enemies as the wrongdoers? Which of them do you prefer? Nah, my boy, you won't get far with that kind of thinking."

Siegfried stood stock still and looked stricken.

Wertheim gave him a comforting pat on the shoulder. "My lad, we all make mistakes and trip ourselves up sometimes. You need to forget the whole damn war and all that talk about homeland and honor. None of that is relevant to what we have here. It never is. Look at the person and not at what you think they're supposed to be. Do I look like a 'wandering Jew' to you? Exactly! Now go home, sit down with your little book, and give some real thought as to who could have done what and where. Tell me what you come up with by tomorrow morning." With that, Wertheim shook hands with the abashed Siegfried and disappeared into City Hall.

More than anything else, Chief Officer Messing loved being on patrol at night. Those were the moments he saw himself as the antagonist of evil, the victor over darkness. On the other hand, typing up reports... he preferred to leave that to others.

He fastened his belt and buttoned up his high collar, then reached for the files. What did he have here? A purse snatching. A runaway cat. A beaten-up pimp. He couldn't have cared less about any of these. The bag was gone, the animal had long since returned home, and the pimp had received his just desserts. And that was that.

He turned the next page. Now this sounded more interesting. A professor from Bonn was wanted on two different matters: for theft and for suspected mental derangement. He was hardly surprised. In his opinion, every criminal was deranged. Messing skimmed the description. Medium height, full head of gray hair, dark eyes, mid-seventies, embonpoint. He snorted. Couldn't his colleague have simply written that the wanted man was stout? He disliked embellishment as much as he did the new-fangled question of innocence versus culpability. Messes had to be swept up, without exception! A strong hand was needed! He read on. Why wasn't there a picture with the file? And what was this next sentence supposed to mean? *He looks like Mozart.*

Messing called the young police recruit over. "What does this even mean? The old boy is wandering around the streets in velvet pants and a powdered wig? And if he's missing in Bonn, why am I supposed to be looking for him here?"

The trainee tried to recall what the officer from Bonn had said. It probably wasn't Mozart, just some musician, a famous one from around here.

"Beethoven? Do you mean Beethoven?"

The boy nodded, and Messing rolled his eyes. "What is the world coming to if our German youth don't even know the names of our greatest minds? After all, it's—wait, did you say Beethoven? A stout man with gray curls... I saw someone like that the other day... yes, of course!"

Without a word about where he was going, Messing dashed out the door. This professor couldn't be too far off if he was staying at one of those sleazy motels nearby.

Heinrich August Schumacher continued to wander around the small room, running his hands through his hair until he finally threw himself onto the chair. Here he sat, cut off from everyone, helpless and uncertain about what to do. How could he get out of this? Or was this the end for him? He slaved away, wrote his fingers to the bone, searched for solutions. But could he actually change anything? For his daughter at least? He knew Emma was in Bonn and was worried about him. That was what they had told him. Someone was constantly around her, watching her every move. Something could happen to her at any time, and her safety depended solely on him and his cooperation. He had cautiously explored his possibilities and had tested how far he could go.

He hit the table with the flat of his hand, over and over again, until he could hardly feel the pain anymore. and sank forward wearily. He sat huddled there for an hour, then got up with difficulty and stretched out on the narrow cot. After a while, he raised his head, his eyes riveted on the door.

Someone was coming.

TUESDAY

At promptly ten o'clock, Emma entered the foyer of the Grand Hotel Royal, where James hurried toward her. He smiled, wryly and hesitantly. "Are you feeling all right, my dear? Are things better again between us?"

She gazed at him, cocking her head slightly; her answers to these questions remained unclear, even to herself. She quietly asked that he take her to the Baroness and declared that she had something else to tell him afterward. James led her upstairs, knocked on Room 217, and held the door for Emma when a brittle voice ordered them inside.

An old lady stood at the center of the room, leaning on a walking stick. An impressive mass of blond hair was piled up over her small, pointed face, which was liberally decorated with rouge and powder.

Emma couldn't take her eyes off her.

"Don't stare like that, young lady. It's impertinent and inappropriate for your age! So you are that thief's daughter. Well, you look more respectable than I expected," Frau von Felsenau launched the conversation as she scrutinized Emma, who stood silently before her. "Where is your father, and where is my property? Tell me the truth!"

James interjected, "Madam, as I told you, Miss Schumacher doesn't know where her father is. Of course, we will make every effort to find him, and—"

The Baroness raised her hand. Her question had been directed to the young lady, who surely knew how to speak German.

Emma blinked a few times, blushed, and remained silent. What was she to say to such a fearsome lady?

"It seems to me that this young woman is stupid. Did you fall on your head when you were a child, or why are you just standing there, staring at me with teary eyes? Don't think that that kind of thing will work on me!"

Emma started to seethe.

She straightened up and replied, "And it seems to me that you are a very unpleasant old woman with no manners at all!" As soon as she said this, she clapped her hand over her mouth, but what was said had been said.

The Baroness shook her head indignantly, and a puff of powder trickled off one aged cheek as a single curl came loose and sprung to the floor. Suddenly the old woman started wheezing, grabbed her neck, gasped harder, and leaned even heavier on her cane. Horrified, Emma jumped to her side and wrapped her arms around the old woman, while James pushed a chair under her. The lady who had been so stern only a moment before sat huddled and trembling before them.

"Do you take medicine, Baroness?" asked James.

She nodded and pointed to her old-fashioned reticule, which lay on a dainty table by the window. Emma hurried to hand it to her, helplessly patting the old woman's shoulder. What had she done? She offered a silent prayer that the Baroness would recover.

After a few anxious moments, the old woman started to breathe more evenly, and her trembling subsided as well. Kneeling beside her, Emma pleaded for forgiveness.

"It's all right, my dear. I can be a little irritable at times. Let us think no more of it. I am only interested in my valuables, which your father stole. Does he do this sort of thing regularly?"

Emma swallowed down the anger that threatened to rise once more. No, she said, Papa wasn't a thief. He was one of the most honest and sincere people around.

"That may have been so, but he came into my house, made himself at home, and thought he could sweet-talk me with his insipid compliments. And before I knew it, he was heading for the hills with my Hatshepsut."

"I don't understand it at all, please believe me. The only explanation might lie in some disease of his mind. Did he seem lucid to you?"

"Perfectly clear! He was trying to insinuate himself, no doubt about it. He probably assumed I would marry him if he only persevered long enough, but I can assure you that, in spite of my age, a neat appearance is important to me."

"Papa doesn't dress according to fashion, and neither do you, for that matter. Your dress suits you very well, by the way, absolutely elegant. Papa's habits are very similar to yours; he prefers the tried and true. His suit may be worn out, but he is very particular about cleanliness and personal hygiene. No one can accuse him of being sloppy." Emma realized that she was rambling, but it seemed that this time she hadn't upset the Baroness, who had listened attentively.

The older woman cocked her brows. "The gentleman in my house was clearly not bothered by his dirty fingernails or the egg yolk on his tie!"

Emma couldn't immediately see the rhyme or reason behind any of this; none of it made sense. It sounded nothing like Papa. Oh! But now that made sense, didn't it? It didn't sound like him at all! She looked down at her own clothes. She was wearing the same dress she had on yesterday when she was talking to the inspector. Had she perhaps ...? She reached into her right pocket and pulled out Papa's photograph. "Is this the man who came to see you?"

Frau von Felsenau studied the picture. "There is a certain resemblance, to be sure. But no, this man is not the one who came to see me."

So it wasn't Papa who was out there stealing and lying and cheating! For a moment, Emma was speechless. James stepped in and asked if the Baroness was sure about that. She nodded vehemently.

"But he introduced himself as Professor Schumacher?"

"I wouldn't have let him in otherwise!"

James helped Emma to her feet, guided her over to the desk, and urged her to sit down on the stool. From a drawer, he extracted paper and pencil, and then asked the Baroness to describe her visitor. James questioned her expertly, while Emma drew feverishly. Before them emerged the image of the man who had pretended to be the professor—a man who shared the gray curls, body type, and approximate age of Heinrich August Schumacher, but who was obviously a completely different man. The Baroness checked the drawing, corrected a few details, and then confirmed that this was the person who had gained access to her home.

James took Emma's arm as they strolled down Koblenzer Street toward the royal gardens. A crisp wind was blowing, swirling the leaves of the sycamore and beech trees around their feet and playing with Emma's skirt.

"Let me warm up your hands, darling, you're all pale. What were you going to tell me?"

"I had a visit yesterday from Herr Mertens and his superior, an Inspector Wertheim. I thought he was quite marvelous. Papa is a wanted man now, officially, and I think if anyone can find him, Herr Wertheim can. Oh! But yes, we must go to the station, so we can show him the picture and tell him everything."

James would have gladly strolled on; he thought it felt lovely to have Emma's arm in his, but she was already hurrying ahead. He stumbled after her, but not without first admiring her legs, a glimpse of which a gust of wind afforded him. Pushing down her flying skirt, Emma glanced back at him as she strode on: "James, please hurry!—Oh, excuse me, I... Oh, Alexei, it's you! Please forgive me."

Catching up to them, James greeted Alexei, who was accompanied by a gentleman of similar age whom he immediately introduced. "This is Baron Alexander Zoubkoff, another poor stranger in this beautiful city. Sasha is studying law and is my advisor."

With a cheerful chuckle, Zoubkoff kissed Emma's hand and gave a friendly nod to James, who introduced himself in typical English fashion. Emma realized that Russians must be a particularly attractive group of humans. Like Alexei, Zoubkoff was slender and tall, possessing a natural charm that was irresistible to the opposite sex. "You've found a friend from the good old days here?" she asked, flushing self-consciously under Zoubkoff's unveiled admiration.

"Oh, no, we aren't old friends. Sasha grew up in Moscow, while I'm from St. Petersburg. We don't share any common memories, but we've still spent quite a bit of time exploring whether or not we might have met at court or elsewhere. I'm afraid more vodka has flowed in the process than has been good for me, but you won't betray me to your aunt, will you?"

"Not at all," Emma assured him. Alexei seemed relaxed and especially chipper, clearly delighted to have found a fellow countryman. "What is he advising you about?"

The Russians glanced at each other. Sasha smiled silently, as Alexei stuttered something that made little sense. A surprise, he said, which he wasn't at liberty to reveal yet. When Zoubkoff winked at Emma, James tugged on her arm, reminding her how urgently she wanted to see the chief inspector.

And with that, she hurried off again.

A few minutes later, they were standing in front of City Hall, out of breath from the rush to get there as quickly as possible. The police precinct was located on the second floor, but neither Siegfried

Mertens nor Inspector Wertheim were in to meet them; they were on duty until this afternoon, according to Officer Meier. Could he be of assistance to them?

Emma pulled her drawing out of her coat pocket and presented it to the officer: "This is the man you need to be looking for. He's walking around and claiming to be my father."

"Why would a strange man claim to be your father, honorable Fräulein? Believe me, it is usually the mother who makes such claims regarding strange gentlemen callers."

"What Fräulein Schumacher means," James explained, "is that the gentleman in this drawing has claimed to at least one person to be the Professor Schumacher for whom you are searching. We assumed this would be a matter of significance to you."

"So we should now be looking for this gentleman here?"

"And for my father."

"Which one of the two? Wait a minute..." Officer Meier rummaged through his papers,"... took the Ramses in Frankfurt?"

"This one!"

"So why should we continue to search for your father too?"

"You must find out how this impostor was able to take his place."

"He probably killed the professor, or he would have turned up long ago."

Emma's legs buckled. Killed? They thought her father was dead?

"Have you lost your mind, man?" snapped James at the officer. "Get us someone in here who knows how to act responsibly. Or better yet, call the Chief Inspector and ask him to come to Miss Schumacher's house immediately. Immediately!"

Independent thinking may not have been Officer Meier's strong suit, but he knew how to obey a direct order. He reached for the telephone set, as James guided the sobbing Emma onto the visitor's bench. Slipping an arm around her shoulders, he offered reassurance: "Come, come, darling, this is nonsense. That person doesn't understand half of what's going on around him. I'll take you home now, and the inspector will certainly come as soon as he can. Come on, lean on me. Shall we catch a streetcar, or can you make it on foot?"

Emma didn't answer, so James wrapped his arm around her waist, and she let him pull her limply through the streets until they arrived home. The front door instantly swung open; Tante Tinni had been waiting for them in the hallway. "Sweetheart, come inside. The nice

Herr Wertheim just arrived and said that you asked him to drop by. What's the matter? Why do you look like this? James, what happened to our girl? Emma?"

"Let your niece come inside first," Jean-Baptiste declared. "Go on into the living room. I'll bring Emma."

Without a moment's hesitation, he nudged the exhausted James aside, picked Emma off her feet, and carried her to the sofa. Tante Tinni propped some pillows under her feet while Jean-Baptiste poured a brandy and handed it to Emma. "Drink this."

She obeyed while James thanked the inspector for his quick appearance and explained to him what had happened.

"Oh well, I live right around the corner. Did you bring the drawing with you? No? You left it at the police station? Let's hope the police officer handles it better than the feelings of our young lady here. First of all, you need to know I don't think your father is dead. It's really not all that easy to make a body disappear. What has changed since yesterday? Nothing, except for the fact that we have more information. There is now a chance that your father is completely innocent of the thefts, and that's where you need to focus your attention now, Fräulein Schumacher. Anything else will only drive you unnecessarily crazy." Wertheim deliberately didn't point out that the professor had been missing for eleven weeks by now and that there were no reassuring explanations for why. He stood up. "I'll be on my way then, and you, young lady, don't worry about a thing. Just rest. If my nose doesn't deceive me, there's a very excellent lunch waiting for you. Enjoy it, and I'll let you know when I learn something new."

Christel accompanied him into the hallway and asked quietly, "Do you really think that nothing has happened to my brother?"

"I won't lie to you. Something probably has happened to him, but I'm not thinking the worst yet. You are a woman with common sense. Until three weeks ago, we were in the midst of a hot summer. You cannot hide a body without people noticing it, since it eventually starts to smell. And if he was alive until then, why should that be any different now? It helps to remain very matter-of-fact about things."

Christel nodded.

"That reminds me," Wertheim said, opening the living room door once more, "Fräulein Schumacher, if it's all right with you, I'll send Mertens around later so he can draw up a chronology with you." With that, he made his farewells and strolled leisurely along his patrol route; nothing stimulated his mind more than a walk in the fresh air.

Late that afternoon, Siegfried arrived and said that the drawing Emma had made of the *doppelgänger* would be sent to the police stations in all the cities her father or the double had visited. Then he created a kind of calendar, which he filled in with Emma's help and his previous notes:

Date	Location	Witnesses
8.10	Bonn	Students, James Beresford
8.21	Koblenz	Wilhelm Joseph Meerbusch
8.29–30	Frankfurt	Dr. Alexander Meinhardt
9.5–12	Mainz	Sigismund Rafael Piepenbrink
9.17–10.2	Würzburg	Maria Eggersheim (innkeeper), Dr. Martin Hubertus
10.3.–5	Augsburg	Marie-Luise Elisabeth von Felsenau
10.11–12	Munich	Dr. Franz Josef Brandl, Vinzenz Stadlmeir

Siegfried paced back and forth in front of James and Emma with both index and middle fingers pressed to his temples. He then delivered a summary of their conclusions: "We have several gaps in the chronological sequence here and have no idea where the professor was during those periods. Furthermore, we don't even know if the professor was in any of these places on these dates. We can say only two things with certainty: he was here in Bonn on August tenth, and he wasn't in Augsburg, which makes him innocent of the theft there. Also Koblenz and Würzburg are the only cities in which no thefts occurred. Why was that?"

"In Koblenz, the collection hadn't opened yet, and in Würzburg, everything remained under lock and key—there, the opportunity was simply missing," James replied.

"It doesn't make any sense for us to sit here and ponder where Papa might have been, does it? I suppose your colleagues will now pursue their search with my father's photograph and my sketch. How long will it take to hear anything back?"

"As soon as I get to City Hall, I'll send out the pictures by wire. We might've already heard something back if Comrade Meier was able to send out the photographs himself. In any case, I hope that with a little luck we will get the first useful responses back as early as tomorrow morning."

WEDNESDAY

Shortly after midnight, Chief Officer Messing turned down the narrow alley where the *light-averse riffraff* congregated. For the past two days, he had been doggedly following the other man's trail, and only a few hours had passed since the images of two different men had come through the wire. Obviously, the Bonn officers were poking around in the dark, uncertain of who they were looking for or why. But he didn't mind that; the hunt was all that mattered.

He pushed open the door and stepped into the dining room. The innkeeper glanced up just briefly. The few guests there didn't even bother turning their heads, and instead continued to stare off into space. Messing held out the pictures to the innkeeper and asked whether he had ever seen either one of them.

In the pale light of the oil lamp, they were hardly distinguishable. But the innkeeper nodded, yes; someone who looked like that was staying in one of his rooms. Messing didn't bother with the guest book or waste time on other formalities; he simply asked the innkeeper to take him to his guest. The innkeeper groaned but obeyed. He didn't want to risk trouble with the state over a customer.

The innkeeper knocked. No answer. He knocked louder. No one stirred. "Maybe he's out. Shall I let you in?"

Messing nodded. The innkeeper pulled a bunch of keys from under his filthy apron, searched for the right one, finally found it, and opened the door. A horrific stench met them, a smell even more revolting than the one that already persisted in the hallway. The officer pushed the landlord aside and, with a handkerchief over his nose, entered the dingy chamber.

On the cot lay a man. His gray suit was of good quality, a bit worn and a little tight around the waist. *This man has had his share of food and drink,* thought Messing.

"Is this the man you wanted?" the innkeeper inquired from the hallway.

"Well," the officer tilted his head slightly, "It might be one of the two. The height, stature and hairstyle are about right. The face, however... someone has smashed it in completely. I can't make out a single feature."

Emma, James, Tante Tinni, and Jean-Baptiste kept each other company long into the night. Whenever the women teetered on the verge of their fears, Jean-Baptiste would launch into anecdotes to distract them. Around four o'clock, Christel handed the men pillows and blankets, and for the next few hours, James and Jean-Baptiste found a place to rest on the sofas.

Now, late in the morning, they were sitting at the kitchen table and eating breakfast. No one said anything. Into this depressed mood burst Sybil and Alexei, who rushed into the house, flung open all the doors, and then stumbled into the kitchen, beaming with joy.

"We have something to tell you!" shouted Alexei.

"Guess!" demanded Sybil. They clutched each other's hands and scanned the others' faces expectantly.

Jean-Baptiste stood up. "Are congratulations in order?"

Sybil's eyebrows arched, then she laughed. "No, no! Not a silly marriage, at least not yet. Who knows what might happen next? But no, not that! Keep guessing, please!" She looked at Emma. "Think about it; it should be obvious. Think of Alexei's talent!"

Emma shrugged in confusion. What was her aunt getting at? The others also looked perplexed.

"Goodness me, you're obviously inexperienced in business and wouldn't know a good idea if it came up and bit you. An English lady, a Russian prince, a delightful city, a golden future? Well? Tatatam tatatam, dada dada dadadadaa," warbled Sybil as she curtsied to Alexei, who bowed and drew her into his arms. Light-footed, they swayed around the table in three-four time, then switched to a Charleston, swinging arms and legs so wildly that their audience felt giddy. "Oh, I can't believe you are all so obtuse. Christel, get up and dance with Alexei. Keep your apron on, just dance! James, come here to me. Come closer, don't be silly. Closer!"

Emma watched the joyful hustle and bustle and shook her head with a chuckle. Tante Tinni was dancing the black bottom! Oh. But yes, of course! Hadn't Sybil said she'd find something more suitable for her Russian? "You're going to give dancing lessons!" she exclaimed.

"Oh, there are plenty of dance teachers here. But there is only one dance teacher training academy. We are going to open the second one. It will be quite grand, very distinguished, but not stiff and strict. It will be wonderful! Are you happy? I'll stay in Bonn and become a businesswoman, not a wife!" Sybil laughed and waited expectantly for applause.

Alexei stood beaming beside her, indicating with a wink and a tap on his ring finger that he fully intended to make both of them out of her. Sybil explained how they had been running around the city for the past ten days, meeting with brokers and bankers, florists and hoteliers, and they had just rented a floor at 19 Friedrichstraße. Over the next few weeks, they were going to furnish and decorate the space, as well as advertise and look for customers all over town.

"What does Grandmother have to say about your plans?" asked Emma.

Sybil grumbled that she hadn't told her yet.

"I see..."

"Emma, dear, I'm an adult."

"You are."

"Come on, are you pleased, or do you want me to go back to England and waste my time with Nancy and all the rest of those haughty vipers?"

"Sybil, your language!"

They both laughed, then all at once Emma started sobbing.

"What happened?" Sybil exclaimed, startled.

Tante Tinni and Emma filled her and Alexei in on the latest developments.

"And here you let us prattle on and on about our little escapades and said nothing? But that's—"

Christel interrupted her. "It felt so nice to see how happy you are and to be doing something other than sitting around all sad and worried. I don't even feel like cooking anything. I'm getting hungry though... say, Jean, could you whip us up some of your pancakes?"

The day was stretching on forever. No one could stand to be in the house, yet nobody dared to leave. At any moment, the phone or the doorbell might ring. In the afternoon, they decided to move the living room furniture aside, roll up the rugs, and have Sybil give them a dance lesson. Emma, in particular, marveled at her aunt's talent for dancing and teaching with charm and enthusiasm. But whenever the gramophone made a bell-bright chime, everyone paused to listen, to see if it was the telephone or doorbell calling for them.

Then, at a quarter past four, the doorbell finally did ring. Poor Anton winced as six people welcomed him into the hallway in deepest disappointment. "Am I interrupting something? I'm sorry about that. I just wanted to drop something off. Emma, if you could be so kind, could we talk in private for five minutes? Please, I'll be out of your way quickly."

Emma hesitated, then led him into the study. Only then did she notice the wicker basket Anton was holding. He placed it gently on the table, then took her by the hand and looked at her. And with that, he sank to his knees without taking his eyes off of her. "Dear Emma, what can I say? I'm just a poor sinner and a lad from Cologne at that. And what must come out, must come out. With all your whims and woes, with your—oh, what's the point? I don't even know what I'm saying. I'm head over heels in love with you, and it would be my greatest honor if you wouldn't turn me down flat yet. I know, I know, we haven't known each other very long, but you've stirred something inside of me that's unlike anything I've ever felt before. My parents are tickled pink; I've told them all about you. And, yes, my old man declared that I'd be even dumber than usual if I didn't do everything I could to... No, Emma, this isn't the way it works; I'm babbling like a numbskull! Let me start all over again: Will you marry me?"

This was utterly ridiculous! In novels, men knelt down to confess their love and propose but not in real life! And now, when she should have answered clearly and firmly, all she could think about were two of the silliest marriage proposals that had ever existed between the covers of a book: Mr. Collins and Bendix Grünlich. She giggled, which hardly seemed appropriate, considering the gravity of the situation.

Clearing her throat with a cough, she tried to pull herself together. "Anton, like you said, we hardly know each other. I've never given any thought to marriage, and at the moment, I don't want to. My father is still missing. It's not the right time to think about a future together." She thought she responded thoughtfully and assumed any man of compassion would now rise to his feet, wipe the dust off his knees, and change the subject.

And Anton indeed rose to his feet, although he didn't release her hand. He drew closer to her, put his left arm around her waist, and bent down to her. He held her tightly and whispered in her ear: "And it is precisely because everything is so bleak that I am with you. You won't get through this time alone, and I'm worried that something will happen to you. Rest assured, I'll take care of you and stand by you. We'll finish this thing here, and then I'll ask again and be sure of the answer." He bent down even lower, tightened his grip on her, and kissed her on the neck. Gently, tenderly, and for a long time.

Emma stood helpless in his arms, wanting to leave, and yet... was she possibly enjoying this? Was she thinking about James? When he finally let go of her and turned to the table as if nothing had happened, she was both relieved and confused. He called her over and pointed to the basket, "I used all my charm to convince my neighbor to give her to me. Just look inside."

She lifted off the lid. On a blanket lay a tiny kitten, moving her little paws in her sleep and uttering soft mews. The wee animal was a delicate red tabby. Emma ran her index finger gently over its soft head. The kitten instantly opened her eyes and squeaked at her. A cat! The one wish that Grandmother had refused to fulfill, Anton had made come true. "But—"

"When I saw her, I immediately thought of you: a saucy little red thing just like you."

"I'll take good care of her. Thank you, Anton."

He turned to go, then stopped and asked about the professor. Emma filled him in about the Baroness and the impostor.

He shook his head. He couldn't believe it! How incredible! He would like to stay with her, but he had an appointment with his uncle that he couldn't miss. She was glad to hear that, and feeling relieved, she escorted him to the front door and hurriedly bid him goodbye.

Just as Anton opened the wrought-iron gate to the street, Wertheim and Mertens appeared on the other side and called out to Fräulein Schumacher to wait for them. The chief inspector took the steps in a couple of jumps, while Siegfried followed at a more measured pace.

"Do you have any news?" asked Emma.

"My dear Fräulein Schumacher, we have received a message from Frankfurt. I would prefer for us to go inside."

"Tell me right here and now, please."

"All right, yes. A man has been found who might be your father."

"Why might? Why don't you ask him? Has he lost his memory? But you have the pictures..."

"The gentleman in question is no longer among the living. And he may have had an accident. His face is so distorted we cannot identify him clearly. My dear Fräulein Schumacher, I really shouldn't tell you this here out of doors. Mertens, make yourself useful for once. Fetch a glass of water for the lady and then go inside with her."

Tante Tinni joined them out on the stoop, and Herr Wertheim repeated the news, adding, "Fräulein Feuerhahn, we need your help and that of your niece. Would it be possible for you to pay a visit to our colleagues in Frankfurt, and—it's really not easy for me to ask this of you—to identify the deceased? Please believe me, I don't want to ask this, especially not after I tried to be so encouraging yesterday. But without this trip, we will never be certain about who has been found there. And eternal uncertainty, I can assure you, is the worst."

Emma replied firmly, "Of course, we'll take care of it. Will either you or Herr Mertens be coming with us?"

"I cannot, unfortunately, but I will permit Herr Mertens to accompany you; we have another witness in Frankfurt whose testimony I would like to have. Simply go whenever you are ready. It is entirely your decision, isn't it, Mertens?"

Siegfried nodded. Emma excused herself for a moment, ran into the living room, and asked James if he could chauffeur them to Frankfurt tomorrow.

Wherever she wanted to go, he would take her.

She hurried back into the hallway and declared they could go tomorrow morning at ten o'clock sharp. Then she wished the gentlemen a pleasant night and thanked them for their visit. Tante Tinni listened and marveled at how composed her niece was acting. She asked Emma where she had suddenly found this strength.

"Oh, Tante Tinni, I've cried too much already as it is, haven't I?"

THURSDAY

At the same time that Emma was climbing into James' car in Bonn, Alphonse Meridot was stepping out of the sleeping compartment of the Paris-Frankfurt train. He turned to the official on the platform and requested the address of the police precinct. He then hailed a cab that brought him to Hohenzollernplatz. Once there, he climbed the steps of the impressive building and asked for whomever dealt with international crime syndicates, smuggling, theft, and murder.

The desk officer hesitated; that was a wide range of specialties.

Meridot provided more clarification: "The matter in question concerns the illegal trade in Egyptian mummies. And—let me put it delicately—their *production* in more recent times."

The officer asked the visitor to take a seat for a moment; he would find out who the appropriate contact was.

It took a while, so to kill time, Meridot read the recent issue of the *Frankfurter Zeitung* that was sitting in the waiting area. It wouldn't hurt to improve his German a little by reading it. On page 13, he came across an article about the discovery of a corpse. It was presumably a professor of Egyptology who had been missing for some time. A figure of Queen Hatshepsut found in his belongings supported this theory.

Meridot folded the newspaper carefully and turned back to the officer who was still in the process of phoning various departments: "Excuse me, can you tell me something about the dead man who was found with the Egyptian sculpture?"

"I'll need to refer you to Inspector Schenk for that. Go down the hall, and you'll see the stairway. Third floor, Room 322. Homicide. I'll call ahead to announce you."

Meridot thanked him politely. A few moments later, he knocked on the door of Room 322. Immediately a young officer opened it and led him one room over, before explaining that the detective would be with him shortly and offering him a cup of coffee. While the young man was still preparing the coffee, a man about the size of a bear entered.

The man greeted Meridot with a handshake. "I'm Schenk. What brings you here? Do you know something about our potential professor?"

"I'm afraid I cannot tell you anything about the gentleman, but perhaps you could tell me his name. I am more interested in the connection with Egyptology. May I explain myself?"

Schenk asked him to continue.

In well-chosen words, Meridot described his work for the Louvre: he was, if one wanted to call it that, a kind of museum detective. Originally, his job had been to find new additions for the museum's collection, to maintain contacts with patrons and collectors, and to organize exchanges with other museums, especially the Egyptian Museum in Cairo. But a new wave of Egyptomania had swept in over the past few years, and with it a new cadre of dealers had emerged, ones who were more willing to engage in darker, less ethical practices. The number of mummies being exported to Europe and America was on the rise, and these were being offered not only to museums but also to private individuals. Some of the corpses were remarkably well-preserved... The detective could surely see what he was getting at?

Schenk shook his head before answering: "I haven't encountered such a case before, but I have heard talk about it. What exactly brings you to Frankfurt, Monsieur Meridot?"

"I confess, a vague lead, a faint hunch only. One hears something here, picks up something there, but my intuition rarely deceives me. One of my sources told me about a German gentleman who appears very respectable and unobtrusive. He works for an honorable cultural institution but uses his contacts to conduct his own business without his employer's knowledge. Some of the latest shipments I've seen in Paris are said to have been shipped from your fair city."

"And why are you interested in the dead professor...?"

"Ah! I saw the mention in the newspaper of a Hatshepsut being found with him. Mummies aren't the only artifacts being traded. Every artifact, as long as it is not too huge, is at risk of being stolen or copied. Is the Hatshepsut genuine?"

"I don't know anything about that. And to be honest, we don't know yet who the dead man is. The matter is rather tricky. On the one hand, we have the real professor, who has supposedly been traveling around for weeks, and on the other hand, we have learned that another man may have been posing as this very professor. In addition, there are ambiguities affecting the case, such as mental illness, theft of cultural goods, etc. We are expecting the daughter of the missing man, a Fräulein Schumacher, to arrive later today. After that, I hope we'll have a clearer picture of things."

Meridot's eyes lit up. "Schumacher? You're looking for Professor Heinrich Schumacher?"

Schenk leaned forward. "You know him?"

"Know him would be saying too much; we've corresponded off and on over the years, as happens in our circles when a colleague has an established reputation in dealing with originals and forgeries."

"So this Schumacher was in the business of exposing counterfeiters?"

"Oh no, no. He had nothing to do with that; other people specialize in that. It's more like he has a special sort of intuition, an infallible sense when it comes to ancient Egypt. He grasps—how can I put it?—the human beings behind every object he finds. He senses the person who made the clay pot as well as the person who used it. When he comes across copies, he immediately sends them back to the owner with a note that he couldn't detect any history behind them. He doesn't want to get involved with the shady business of counterfeit trade. I know, I know, it sounds downright fantastic and unbelievable, but the professor is an expert, an admirer, a devotee. It would be a loss for my world if the dead man should truly turn out to be Schumacher. If I may ask you this: would it be too forward were I to ask you to introduce me to his daughter? Could you perhaps notify me by telephone as soon as she arrives? I'm staying at the Frankfurter Hof Hotel."

Schenk thought for a moment, then promised to call and thanked him for the visit. Meridot returned the thanks and made his farewell, then went to his hotel. He would stay put there until the call came.

Over three hours later, the hotel porter put through a call to Meridot's room from police headquarters; the young woman had arrived, and they were waiting on him before making the identification of the dead man.

While James and Jean-Baptiste waited in a nearby pub, Emma sat with Tante Tinni and Herr Mertens in Inspector Schenk's office, answering questions about herself and everything that had happened since her arrival in Bonn. The visitors were startled when there was a knock at the door, and even more so when the inspector answered with a thunderous "Come in!" A gentleman entered the room, bowed politely, and then quietly took a seat behind them.

Herr Schenk gave him a curt nod, set aside his pen, and asked if the ladies were ready to identify the deceased.

Emma swayed a little as she stood up, and Siegfried as well as the strange gentleman instantly jumped up to support her. Meridot took the opportunity to introduce himself; if she would allow it, he would like to speak with her later. With a nod, she accepted Siegfried's proffered arm, before also reaching for her aunt's hand and following the inspector to the elevator.

As the car descended, no one said a single word. Then they found themselves standing in a narrow corridor, half in shadow, half lit by flickering bulbs. Emma clung a little tighter to Siegfried's arm; he patted her hand. He would take care of her. She shouldn't worry, and James would be with her soon.

She nodded.

The corridor seemed endless, with other passages branching off to either side, leading into impenetrable blackness. They passed numerous closed doors until they finally entered a room in which a bright light burned; it smelled sharp and musty at the same time. Inspector Schenk asked them to wait a moment while he stepped into a larger adjoining room. Before he closed the door, Emma caught sight of a row of wheeled tables covered with sheets. She averted her eyes.

The inspector returned with one of the tables a few moments later. Tante Tinni reached for Emma's left hand and squeezed it hard.

"Please don't be frightened, ladies. I told you before that the man who was found was injured. Perhaps you will recognize him by his hands or ears..." Schenk explained sympathetically. With that, he pulled the sheet back from his head and shoulders and down to the chest. He also exposed the man's arms, and all this as gently as if he were tending to a sick person instead of a dead one.

Emma's eyes first registered the full head of gray hair, and she felt tears well up in her eyes. Tante Tinni took a few steps forward and studied the dead man's right hand. She asked her niece to take a look at something. Only hesitantly did Emma step closer, clinging tightly to Siegfried. She hardly dared to look at the hand, but then steeled herself against what she might see there. "Oh! That's not Papa. It's not him!"

"You're sure, Fräulein Schumacher?"

She nodded, leaving Tante Tinni to explain. "My brother has a long scar across the back of his right hand."

"You could have spared yourself this experience if you had included that feature in your personal description, madam."

"I'm too familiar with that scar to think about it anymore. I'm sorry."

"Well, these things happen; I'm just sorry for the anxiety you've endured. An experience like this weighs on you. Please relax for the rest of the day." With that, Schenk shook hands all around before asking if they minded showing themselves back upstairs.

Siegfried took the lead. A few minutes later, they were standing in front of the station, breathing in the fresh air. Emma took an especially deep breath. Papa was alive! She smiled when the Frenchman addressed her. "Mademoiselle, if it's all right with you, I'd like to accompany you for a few more steps."

James leaped up when he saw Emma approaching and ran to meet her. She embraced him, pale but resolute and happy. Jean-Baptiste waved the waiter over to request menus. Everyone made their selections calmly, and Alphonse Meridot offered to cover the bill; they should consider themselves guests of the Louvre.

As they ate, he described his work and his acquaintance with Heinrich Schumacher, which unfortunately only existed via correspondence. Schumacher's daughter was visibly pleased to hear him speak so warmly of her father. They also talked at length about the Bastet figurine, which she had found in the professor's coat, and about James' theory regarding it.

Meridot nodded throughout her explanation. "May I take the liberty of endorsing your theory? You, Fräulein Schumacher, have shown a definite instinct in your comparison of the statue with the drawings. Mr. Beresford, in turn, is on the right track with his assumptions, I think. To understand things properly, I should describe for you the kinds of individuals who are looking to purchase Egyptian art. We have the passionate collector, who has acquired experience and knowledge, and is filled with deep admiration for the skills of our ancestors. He collects with his heart and soul, values authenticity, and is as enthusiastic—perhaps even more, *passionate*, you might say—about seemingly simple everyday objects as he is about the jewelry of a princess. This person, like everyone else, comes in all shapes and sizes. He might be ruthless and willing to sacrifice something or someone in order to gain possession of a piece, or he may strive to act ethically, possibly leaving his collection to a museum. What could I, as a dealer, offer this kind of connoisseur? Only something authentic and genuine. In your case, the figure that Professor Schumacher drew—the Bastet made of alabaster. Like you, I assume that alabaster must have been the original material for this goddess.

"But," Meridot took a sip of his liquor, "the connoisseur is only one possible buyer. Please forgive my arrogance, but the stereotype of the nouveau riche, the less informed, is not a mere cliché; it exists and is spreading. These are the individuals the war and its upheavals have churned to the top. They lust after anything that will entertain them and win them prestige. There are collectors in this group, too, but they lack knowledge and any real interest. They are blind to the elegance of an Isis or the strength of an Anubis. Their primary goal is to show off, and so they order 'some guy with a bull's head holding a spear.' But what does it look like when it stands in their well-appointed foyer. Gray and stony? No, he should be made of basalt and his spear of pure gold. That's how the parvenu imagines Ancient Egypt must have been like, and that's how it must be, thank you very much. He measures the value of an ancient sculpture only according to what he can comprehend. And that would be gold, marble, precious stones. He doesn't want to be cheated, and yet nothing is easier than to sell him a fake. Your marble Bastet is infinitely more valuable in his eyes than the original alabaster one. Often these fakes are replicas of the originals that have already been sold to the real connoisseur. Sometimes they are copied from old drawings by renowned scholars. And so the dealer earns his cut twice. Threefold in fact: he didn't have to pay a single centime for the original, the copy costs him a pittance, and he usually fails to attract unwanted police attention. Once the dust settles, the original rests securely inside a safe, while the counterfeit is accepted as genuine by the ignorant."

"But if one of the buyers happens to find out about the fraud, isn't that dangerous for the dealer? The kind of person you're talking about isn't likely to take being cheated lightly, is he?" asked James.

"As a rule, official complaints are rarely filed, but I have certainly heard of cases in which one swindler or another has met an untimely demise. I'm afraid that's one of the risks of that profession."

"Which brings us to the unknown…"

"Ah, yes, the unknown gentleman in the basement morgue with his Hatshepsut. You see, I'm here in Frankfurt because I'm searching for a criminal of the highest order. He has taken up a particularly unsavory variation of the Egypt business: he smuggles mummies. For the most part, these are mummies that have been specially made—pardon the expression—for this purpose. I see you are shocked, of course. Such perfidy must shock any decent person. I'm no longer concerned solely with the reputation of the Louvre or of the field of antiquities in general. No, I feel the need to disrupt the craft being pursued by these criminals."

The longer Meridot spoke, the more eagerly Mertens listened; this was shaping up to be a case that spoke to his imagination. "How are you going to uncover this person? Where do you start?"

"Ah, good question. The major museums and universities have been aware of the problem for a long time, and so the only mummies that find their way into our halls are those whose provenance is fully documented. Anyway, our efforts are now leaning towards leaving more and more archaeological discoveries in the countries of origin. But as far as private collectors are concerned, they are clearly more interested in embalmed priests and princes. Nothing attracts people more than a hint of the macabre. A dead princess in her golden coffin..."

"So you plan to visit Dr. Meinhardt?" asked Emma.

"Do you know the gentleman?"

"Monsieur Barbier and I met him three weeks ago. I can't imagine he would be involved in such underhanded activities."

"Oh, but I didn't say that. I'm asking around, poking in the dark. Please, don't jump to conclusions!"

James thought of something: "Monsieur Meridot, I'm afraid you can save yourself a trip to see Dr. Meinhardt. He left on a trip about two weeks ago and probably hasn't returned yet."

"That's unwelcome news. I shall probably have to change my plans, which is rather irksome. I was really hoping that he would have some valuable information for me, so now I'm left with only the university and the historical museum. Unfortunately, institutions like these are rarely offered dubious mummies. By 'unfortunately,' I only mean in regard to my investigation; please, don't get me wrong. The smaller the market, the fewer corpses there will be."

When Meridot asked the waiter for the bill, Siegfried asked if he could accompany him to the university; he had a witness to question there about the case in Bonn. Meridot agreed.

"Is there a chance that you might learn something about my father there? Something that might lead us to him?"

Meridot pondered this. That's certainly possible. Should he contact them in the next day or so?

Emma didn't want to have to wait that long and asked if the gentlemen would notify her immediately if they found any clues about her father.

The Frenchman suggested they meet for tea at his hotel around five o'clock. It wasn't too chilly, after all, so perhaps his companions would like to take a stroll later on?

Emma nodded, and reached for James' hand and squeezed it. He slipped his arm around her, pulled her close, and asked anxiously if she might be ready to go home after all that she'd been through?

She declared that she had recovered from her fright and that if he didn't insist on going home, she would prefer to stay here.

Christel watched Emma and James for a moment before leaning over to her Jean. She whispered to him that she wanted to give the young people some time alone. Would he be willing to take the train back to Bonn with her? Jean nodded, and she winked at him mischievously before catching her niece's attention. "My dear, I don't feel so great, and I'm much too tired to walk around Frankfurt right now. If James could take us to the station, then we'll just head on home."

Emma found this suggestion ridiculous. Even if Tante Tinni just waited for them in a bakery, she could still get home faster by car than by train. But her aunt insisted, explaining that she found train rides with her fiancé romantic. So they agreed: Emma and James would return alone later that evening.

From the church steeple, the bells struck five o'clock. Under the warm glow of the hanging wicker lamp, the image of two figures were reflected in the dark panes: Elisabeth and Mareike peacefully playing a game of dice, laughing, and nibbling on freshly baked waffles.

"If only it were always like this, Mama."

The mother looked at the girl, asking herself: Why couldn't it always be this way? Just the two of them? But such a thing was impossible. Her husband made it possible for them to live in this very house, to eat waffles and play. Without him, they would be living on charity, sharing a barren shelter, possibly starving. Plus, even if she were willing to endure such conditions, leaving wasn't an option. He would never let her go. He needed her. Not that she thought that he loved her in some strange, sick way. No, she merely served as a front, she knew that. For a long time, she had convinced herself that she recognized something like desperation and longing in his blows, falsely believing that she might somehow save him, if only she were to remain silent and forgive him. But he had never asked for forgiveness, not even during the first year of their marriage. And she had never understood what was happening to her. The only time he had ever left her alone or had cared even a little about her well-being was when she was expecting Mareike, their only child. Because he had wanted a child to round out the perfect image. Elisabeth wished to be strong and brave, but in the sixteen years of her marriage she hadn't even confided to her sister.

She gathered up the dice and asked Mareike to clear away the dishes; they should start getting the house ready. Not a crumb visible, not a piece of furniture out of place.

Mareike did as her mother said right away. She understood far too much already about the situation and her father. The fact that her father didn't love her was just part of her normal life, as was the reality that she had to avoid other people. Still, she managed to be a happy child most of the time, at least when her father wasn't at home. He was, unfortunately, returning tomorrow after a two-week absence. While he was gone, he had telephoned frequently, at different times: once, four times, ten times a day. He had even left a timetable with them, indicating when Elisabeth could go shopping, when she had to be home, and what she should cook. She didn't always stick to it, like today with the waffles. She had almost expected him to magically materialize in the kitchen as she was mixing the batter but nothing had happened.

Mother and daughter worked in silence, washing dishes and wiping, cleaning, arranging, and moving furniture around. "Could you endure poverty?" asked Elisabeth so quietly that Mareike barely understood her. "But no, it's not right to ask you that. You have no idea what it would be like."

Mareike looked at her mother squarely and took heart; they didn't usually talk about her father. "Yes, Mama, I think I could."

Elisabeth nodded. If only she could find the strength! Why hadn't she used the days without him to find a way out? Surely there would have been someone she could have confided in, someone who would have protected her? She immediately banished such thoughts, beginning to return to her diminished state. Before leaving, he had locked up all of her jewelry in his safe and instead of leaving so much as a single mark, he had set up a strictly established line of credit at stores that could provide only the most basic provisions. With such measures in place, he ensured that the crippling fear of poverty would hold her prisoner.

In the hotel's tearoom, Emma jumped up out of her chair as Alphonse Meridot and Siegfried Mertens entered. "Well?"

The gentlemen took their seats. Siegfried began, "I have spoken with Professor Neumann. He insists he knew nothing about your father's trip."

"But is that plausible? All of a sudden, people are claiming that they didn't know anything about this trip, when until recently it was big news?"

"We haven't found anyone who knew about it. And Professor Neumann also doubts that your father would have undertaken such a lecture tour at all, because he wouldn't have had the time. Did you know that shortly before your father's departure, the department had inherited a collection of Egyptian rarities? Your father had offered to catalog them and to situate them in their proper place amongst the pieces that they already possess. Professor Neumann thinks it would have been quite unlikely that he would leave so suddenly, breaking his promise to assist with the new acquisitions."

"Papa didn't write to me about that. When did he agree to do this?"

"He must have promised it a few days before he disappeared."

"Then Professor Neumann is quite right; Papa is true to his word. Always. Is that the only reason you went to see him? To ask him that?"

"Inspector Wertheim wanted to make sure that this wasn't perhaps part of some plan hatched by some of your father's competitive colleagues. These professors don't seem to get along particularly well with each other."

"That's true, they never shy away from a potential conflict, but they are nonetheless united by their love of the subject. Does knowing this put your mind at ease?"

"Well, from the very start, I felt that there was something more significant behind your father's disappearance than a mere fight among colleagues. And from all that Monsieur Meridot has described today, it does indeed look like a widespread conspiracy!"

Meridot threw up his hands in mock horror. "Ah, a conspiracy! Doesn't that sound like dark forces and magic circles and world domination? Naturally any criminal enterprise on a larger scale is a matter of cooperation, secrecy, and silence, so to that extent Herr Mertens is right. Like him, I believe Professor Neumann is innocent, and I'm certain that the other gentlemen I spoke to today think the same. It is, however, as I suspected. They are all aware of the mummy trade and are trying to keep themselves clear of it."

"So was your trip to Frankfurt fruitless?" asked James.

"Oh no, I wouldn't say that. After all, I was privileged to make your acquaintance, and"—he bowed his head slightly to Emma—"an opportunity to meet such a charming young lady is worth any trip. But I will make one more attempt: even if Dr. Meinhardt is away, I will visit his collection."

"But it is rarely open to the public, and at this hour..."

"I happen to know Herr Weinstein. He is among the many people I know who share a fascination with Antiquity. While Herr Mertens was on the phone with his supervisor, I called the bank and got lucky. Herr Weinstein is expecting me at seven o'clock."

"That late!" Siegfried exclaimed.

"Pardon?"

"Forgive me, I would have very gladly accompanied you, but Inspector Wertheim is expecting me at the station tomorrow morning, and I must return to Bonn today. If we hadn't met you, we would have been on our way back a while ago."

Emma pondered: Would it be impolite to let Herr Mertens take the train? As had happened to her during her trip with Jean-Baptiste, she suddenly felt seized by curiosity. Then something occurred to her. "Herr Mertens, when you spoke with Inspector Wertheim, did he tell you if any new information had come in? Papa's picture should have reached all the other police stations a while ago, and surely those officers have made inquiries by now about whether it was my father or the unknown man who had visited all the collections?"

Siegfried jumped up, excused himself hastily, and dashed out of the salon. The three others gazed at each other in astonishment.

He returned about fifteen minutes later. "I must apologize. I just called the Inspector again; this afternoon we only had time for a brief chat," he explained.

"Well?" Emma urged him on.

Siegfried opened his green notebook. "The innkeepers in Munich and Würzburg couldn't make a clear identification. Herr Stadlmeir and Herr Brandl in Munich named the unknown gentleman in your drawing as their visitor, as did a Herr Wellenbrink from Würzburg. We know nothing yet from the Frankfurt contacts. Although the corpse of the presumed double was found here, we can't draw any conclusions yet. The dead man had only been staying here for a few days. This means that Herr Friedhelm from Koblenz was the only witness who has clearly identified your father."

Professor Schumacher was famished to the point of feeling dizzy. He couldn't recall when he had last eaten. In this windowless room, he had long since lost his sense of time, which had once been so precise. They had left him with nothing: neither his suit nor his watch, nor his papers, nor his wallet. At first, he had tried to count the days, but they had kept interrupting him. Sometimes an hour might pass, sometimes three or four; but regardless, they never left him alone for long. They brought him jewelry, statues, and stone tablets, which he sketched and examined. Originals, copies, ordinary fakes, and for all of them he issued certificates confirming their value and authenticity with his name.

They told him how they had ruined his reputation in the eyes of his fellow scholars and that no one was concerned about his absence. They dictated letters to his daughter and postcards to his sister. He didn't explain to them how jarringly wrong these dictations would seem to Emma, hoping that something good might come from this oversight. But then they informed him that Emma had returned to Bonn. They described to him how she looked, what she wore, what she said and did. And now he was afraid. Up to then, he had thought that they would come to an agreement, that someone would miss him and start searching for him. But nothing had happened.

In his desperation, he began to insert errors and falsehoods into his evaluations. They skimmed his reports and said nothing. He grew bolder, writing nonsense and fantastic claims in them, but they still didn't notice. They knew next to nothing about Egypt. They weren't interested in the art; they only cared about the money. There were three of them, but he hadn't seen the third man, who had been traveling around in his place and discrediting him.

And now they had stopped coming. Since when? He couldn't say. This hunger—at least twenty-four hours must have passed since his last meal. Had they forgotten him, or was he supposed to starve in here? The longer he waited to do something, the more powerless he would become. He had to seize the opportunity!

He was stuck in a simple cellar. They had installed a coal stove so that he could work in this cold dungeon. The smoke traveled through a pipe that vanished into the wall, which meant that this cellar couldn't possibly be several stories underground. The wooden door didn't seem thick; it looked old and brittle to him. However, it wasn't this door that held him here, but his guards, the ones who were no longer showing themselves...

He would risk it! The professor grabbed his chair and smashed it against the door with all the strength he could muster. There was a loud crash. He quickly threw the chair to the floor and lay down beside it. If they came, he would claim he had tripped and fallen against the door. They wouldn't believe him, but that was all he could come up with. He waited, listened. Nothing. He got up and walked to the door, straining to listen. No one came. Excellent.

He banged the chair against the door, again and again, no longer caring whether someone came or not. He simply had to get out. But was he even making a difference? Yes, the wood suddenly began to splinter. He continued to slam the chair against it as sweat ran down his forehead and back. His heart was pounding so hard he thought he was losing his mind. He refused to give up, but then the chair broke. Furious, he flung the backrest away and examined the door. He had knocked a small hole in it. He ran to the cot, wrapped his right hand in the blanket, and started punching and kicking against the opening. In one final moment of desperation, he threw his whole body against the door, and it broke apart with a loud crack. He fell out of the room, crashing to the floor. Every bone ached. He could hardly breathe from where he lay amid the shards of broken wood.

For a few minutes, he couldn't move as he struggled for breath, but then finally the pain and dizziness subsided. With difficulty, he picked himself up as blood trickled from his shoulder and right hand and his head throbbed. He leaned against the wall, just for a moment, before dragging himself along it down the narrow corridor until he reached the stairs. He paused but heard nothing. He hauled himself up the steps, gripping the banister tightly, and reached for the handle on the door at the top of the stairs. At first, he was scared that the door might be locked, but it swung open, quietly and without resistance.

Two wall lights illuminated the foyer. Why were the lights on? He staggered to the entrance. Locked. He looked around. The corridor that ran past the basement door continued to the back of the building. Panting, he shuffled down it, found an unlocked room, and staggered toward the patio door at the other end of it. He opened the door and stepped out into the darkness. Carefully he set one foot on the soft grass, taking one step after the other and expecting to meet an obstacle at any moment. And then he reached a wall. He scanned it and groaned with relief when he realized it only reached his shoulders. He had to do it. He felt around until he found a ledge. He put one foot on it, pushed off with the other, and in a last-ditch effort, pulled himself over the wall. He fell heavily to the ground on the other side and closed his eyes in exhaustion, lying motionless in the wet grass.

At just before seven o'clock in the evening, Emma, James, and Alphonse Meridot were waiting for Herr Weinstein in front of the dark bank building. A car pulled up punctually on the hour. A chauffeur stepped out, opened the back door, and extended his hand to a petite elderly man.

Emma had imagined Herr Weinstein as a red-faced, cowardly man who ruthlessly seized art treasures but was otherwise miserly. Yet in front of her stood a tiny, very old man who blinked kindly at her and kissed her hand. He warmly embraced Alphonse Meridot, then offered his hand to James and thanked his driver, who helped him up the grand staircase in an exceedingly respectful manner. The latter unlocked the front gate and disappeared.

Meridot took the elderly gentleman's arm, and inquired about his health and recent acquisitions, about his family and a dachshund named Friedolin. Meanwhile, the chauffeur returned, effortlessly picked up his employer, and carried him up to the second floor. There he set him down and escorted him into a brightly lit office, lavishly decorated with paintings and sculptures. Emma recognized a Boucher and a Watteau, and instantly felt thrilled by the full bookcases, where she spotted some of her favorite novels. She felt ashamed of the prejudice she had formed solely based on Weinstein's wealth.

"My dear Alphonse, what brings you here today?"

Meridot provided a detailed explanation of the trail he was following, how Dr. Meinhardt's name had come up, and how he had hoped for his assistance.

The old man looked dismayed. His wonderful director, the subtle and cultivated connoisseur, would certainly never be involved in crimes such as art theft and smuggling, and even less did he consider him capable of murder or of ever approving of such a thing.

Meridot again tried to put his mind at ease, reassuring him that he only wanted to ask him about a man he had possibly encountered whose criminal activity was causing a lot of headaches.

Upon hearing Meridot's explanation, Herr Weinstein seemed even more unsettled. Should he be worried about Meinhardt?

Then Meridot asked, "How long would Dr. Meinhardt be traveling? When he was expected back?"

He would be back in Frankfurt around noon the next day, and would report here immediately, because they were open on Sundays and Meinhardt's help would be urgently needed.

Meridot asked, dear Samuel, if he could possibly come back again tomorrow? Would he be interfering too greatly with his schedule?

"Alphonse, I beg you, the clarification of such misdeeds takes precedence over our little tasks. Will you also honor me with another visit?" he asked, turning to his young guests.

With a quick glance at Emma, James nodded. "We've changed our plans so much already, another half-day's delay shouldn't matter, should it?"

"But if we stay, we'll need to look for a place to sleep tonight. Are you sure you would be comfortable with that? Wouldn't you rather be in your own bed?" Emma wanted to know before promptly blushing.

"Oh, I sleep in other people's beds all the time," James replied, at which he turned red as well. "Well, in boarding houses, I mean, and hotels and inns. Not in... you know..."

Meridot and Weinstein were amused, silently marveling at the fact that Britain was still populated; it seemed that contact between the sexes remained a poorly practiced art there.

Samuel Weinstein had pity on the two young people: "If you would like to lodge here overnight, you are welcome to do so. The upper floor has some comfortable guest rooms." He continued, noticing Emma's uncertainty, "Also I don't think I will go home again today but will stay here as well."

"If we wouldn't be a burden to you, we would be delighted to accept your invitation. James, would you be kind enough to get my bag from the car?"

"You didn't bring your toothbrush and night things, did you?"

"Why yes, I did. I don't go anywhere without being prepared."

FRIDAY

The phone rang, and the porter suddenly longed for the time when such a machine wasn't around, disturbing him. Hardly anyone bothered to drop by in person anymore, he thought. There was a sign on his door with his office hours, which everyone observed unless a pipe broke or deliveries arrived. However, more and more people were now thoughtlessly calling at the most inopportune moments. Even his wife was talking about wanting to install a telephone in their home. This would suit her just fine, since then she could gossip with her friends all day without having to step outside the door, but he wouldn't like it at all!

Annoyed, he picked up the phone and barked into it, "Porter, Rhineland Friedrich Wilhelm's University!", and listened to hear who had dared to disturb him. Then he stepped out into the hallway and looked around. Where had that boy disappeared to again? "Anton? Anton!!! Come here! Snap to it!"

And as requested, Anton sprinted down the hall.

"Your uncle is on the line! Don't let this happen again! Not while you're on duty! Hurry up, will you?"

His assistant promised and hurried to pick up the phone. "Good morning, Uncle.—Yes, of course.—This is a surprise!—Yes, sure, I'll do that.—Today? I—All right.—I'm on my way.—Yes, right away, of course!"

The porter looked at him suspiciously and snapped, "What do you mean you're on your way? You've only been at work for an hour!"

"Something's happened. My aunt, you know? She needs my help right away. You would help your aunt if she needed you, wouldn't you? I promise to come in early on Monday and put the boxes away but right now I have to go." Anton was already untying his apron and slipping on his jacket. After grabbing his hat and umbrella, he offered a hasty good-bye and hurried toward the station.

"Well, Mertens, what have you brought me?" The inspector nodded encouragingly.

Siegfried plunged right into his report. He explained about Meridot, the fake professor and his disfigured face, the mummies and smuggled antiquities, and Neumann's statement that Professor Schumacher's hasty departure seemed highly unlike him.

Simon Wertheim listened, "Well, what do you think?"

"I don't know, Inspector. I keep reading through all these statements and thinking I should've understood everything a long time ago, yet I'm still staring at the facts and don't see how it all fits."

"It, Mertens?"

"I don't get it. I don't see how it all adds up. Maybe I'm not cut out to be a detective?"

"A detective isn't a magician, don't forget that. He is, or at least should be, human. Let's give this some thought. What's bothering us? Making us uncomfortable? It might just be a trifle, some small detail."

Together they jotted down on slips of paper the names of everyone involved in the case, and grouped and regrouped them by event. Wertheim eventually leaned back and called out to Sergeant Meier to fetch him some coffee and pastries, and to bring something for Mertens too. Siegfried straightened up proudly, feeling honored, while Meier left city hall cursing.

"You know, Mertens, we shouldn't lose sight of young Schmitz. I've crossed off the professors, since I don't think they had anything to do with Schumacher's disappearance. They enjoy bickering with each other far too much. But we still know too little about Johannes Schmitz. That's one thing. The other is the one major question we have yet to answer: Where did the rumor that the professor was heading off on a trip actually start? The only solid clue we have is his letter to his daughter. What was the date on that?"

Siegfried leafed through his papers as he sipped on the coffee Meier had forced on him. "It's dated August fifteenth."

"So on the tenth, Schumacher's students and this Mr. Beresford were the last people to see him in person. And yet he supposedly wrote five days later about his plans to leave quite soon on a major trip. That's possible, but it strikes me as strange. And the only reason his daughter came to Bonn when she did was that letter. Well, now let's imagine that Schumacher was grabbed by someone, but no one was supposed to notice. What would the kidnappers do? They'd need to spread the word that he was heading off on a trip in order to explain his disappearance, but his daughter lives in England.

So why this letter? Was he forced to write it? She said that it's his writing but not his tone. Could he have been drugged? But then we get off onto another track. Let's stick to your lead with the old stuff that's getting stolen and counterfeited." Wertheim walked around the table; sitting for a long time tired him out.

He made a snap decision to pull on his coat, grabbed their pastries, and asked Mertens to accompany him. A stroll down to the Old Customs Building and back would get their juices flowing again.

The inspector set a brisk pace, so that even the much taller Siegfried had trouble keeping up. They didn't say a single word until they stood at the Rhine. "Goodness gracious, Mertens, what amazing luck we've had! It's beautiful here, truly beautiful, and the human race isn't doing too bad right now, either. This is what I call home: connected to the Rhine and the wider world from there. Here, wrap that scarf tighter around you. We'll sit on the bench and put our heads together."

Wertheim bit into a cinnamon raisin roll, its familiar sweetness an immediate source of comfort. "Where were we? All right, well, let's come up with a theory and think it through to the end. The professor has been kidnapped. We don't know the motive, but that doesn't matter right now. He was forced to write to his daughter, so we have to wonder, why? That part's important. She wasn't here, but then she came. Did they want her to do that? Why would they? Wouldn't she be something of a nuisance to them? I make the whole world think that the professor is away, and then his child starts looking for him. It makes no sense. Why did she get that letter in the first place?"

Siegfried mused, "If I didn't want her to come, I would have explained that I wasn't available to see her. Not me, of course, but if I were a kidnapper or even her father, if I wanted her to stay away. That could've worked too."

"Mertens, don't make this complicated."

"We can assume that Professor Schumacher would have liked to have seen his daughter. In our theory, he was abducted. As his kidnapper, I'd force him to write a letter so his daughter stayed put where she was."

"All right, but it didn't work. Why?"

Siegfried considered what he knew about Emma, recalling her insistence that the letter hadn't felt *right*. "The only reason I'd allow him to write this letter is because I know the two of them write to each other quite a bit. If he doesn't contact her, his disappearance will be noticed. And if his daughter keeps writing to him and doesn't receive any response, my crime will be exposed as well. I dictate his every word, because otherwise I suspect the professor might tell his daughter something between the lines. But I've never read any of his letters, so I don't know what the tone is like between father and daughter. I will have him write letters that correspond with my idea of the kinds of things fathers write to their children."

"Very good, Mertens, well done. If that's the rationale behind all this, then we've learned one thing: the kidnapper knows Schumacher's habits. At least he knows when he writes and receives mail. Who would have this kind of information?"

"The sister and her French gallant."

"Careful, Mertens. That still sounds to me like cheap prejudice. What reason would the sister have to kidnap her brother, and how would she get him to write that letter? Does she threaten never to bake him a plum *prummetaat* ever again? Did Barbier torture him by singing the Marseillaise? Nah, nah, they're both in the clear."

"Well, the porter receives and posts the professors' correspondence, and at least the invitation from Koblenz was sent to the university, not to Professor Schumacher's residence."

"Tell me, when we were on Arndstraße last Wednesday evening, didn't we run into a young man coming out of the house? Did you recognize him? I had a fleeting impression that I had met him before. Wasn't that the fellow who works for the porter?"

Siegfried groaned loudly, "Yes, that was Anton Wagenknecht. He's been making eyes at Fräulein Schumacher, always fawning over her."

"Jealous?"

Siegfried snorted. "Certainly not."

"I didn't think so. Too bad actually. She's a pretty young thing and would've suited you nicely, but we all have our preferences."

"Heavens, I'm an idiot!"

"What—"

"Anton Wagenknecht, of course! Fräulein Schumacher was the one who told us that everyone at the university supposedly knew about the professor's trip. And she, in turn, got that information from Anton!"

Herr Weinstein sent his chauffeur upstairs to Emma and James with a sumptuous breakfast and the key to the exhibition space; they were welcome to look around at their leisure, since Herr Weinstein knew how interested they were in the beautiful objects on display.

This was how they came to be strolling through the collection, which contained not only Egyptian, but also Phoenician, Greek, and Roman finds. Each artifact was accompanied by a text explaining where it had been found, its age and its purpose, and there were also lovingly designed dioramas depicting everyday scenes from past empires. Everything in these halls showed the dedication and passion of both the collector and the curator. James and Emma dragged each other from one display case to the next, reveling in the opportunity to share what they each knew. They gazed in silence before the beauty of a sphinx, compared each other to the gods and goddesses, and glanced aside sheepishly whenever their hands happened to touch.

"And with that, the bird takes flight. Mertens, go back to the station and show me what you can do. I want you to find out everything you can about Wagenknecht. I'd really like to know who this uncle of his is. Don't assume that the boy is the villain. It might all be quite harmless. While you do that, I'll go and see Fräulein Schumacher to ask about the boy."

Despite his best intentions, Inspector Wertheim could only speak with Fräulein Feuerhahn, who was sweeping leaves in the narrow front garden. "Yes, well, that's too bad. Anyway, how are you feeling? Was it awful yesterday?"

"Well, I won't lie. It wasn't nice at all, but if it had been my brother, then it would have been worse. You have to be grateful for small blessings."

"Let me have your broom for a while; I could use a little exercise. And you can tell me how the mail works here. Your brother and his daughter, do they write to each other often?"

"Since Emma moved to England, full time Heinrich began writing her every few weeks, and Emma would answer right away. It was very important to Heinrich that his daughter know about everything and that she not forget him. And once a year she came for a visit, always around October 31. That's Emma's birthday…"

"Who knows all about these things? About the writing and the visit."

"The whole street knows. It's not just Emma's birthday; her mother didn't come home on that day. That was in 1918, the day the British dropped their bombs. I'm sure you remember that."

He nodded. "And Fräulein Schumacher always came home a few

days before that date? That was the annual tradition?"

"Heinrich worked that out with her and her grandmother. Sometimes she arrived two weeks before the day, sometimes just a few days."

"What did the planning look like for this year?"

"That hadn't been settled yet, but my brother probably meant to arrange things so that Emma could stay until Advent."

"And when your niece didn't find any mention of the trip in her letters, she got worried?"

"She wasn't the only one! My brother would never forget that day. I was concerned that our mother's illness might have started to develop in him—she died in an insane asylum. I think that's why I tried to ignore his absence as long as I did: I didn't want to find out that he, of all people, might be losing his mind!"

"I see..." muttered Wertheim before handing the broom back to Christel. "Well, it looks neat now, doesn't it? But you know, there's one last thing I haven't asked you yet. Johannes Schmitz? Did you know him?"

"Hannes, yes, of course. He was a dear boy."

"Can you think of anything else about him?"

Christel paused, then answered: "When my brother suddenly disappeared, Hannes showed up at the door every day, asking for him. He was very upset. After two weeks, he gave up, but I ran into him sometimes. He would just be standing at the same corner, over there. I thought he might have been watching the house to see when Heinrich came back. I mean, my brother helped the boy a lot, but Hannes seemed really desperate."

"You see, you have helped me again. That must mean something. Have a nice day and give my regards to Fräulein Schumacher. I'll be in touch when we've made further progress with our search."

"Dearest Aunt, aren't you delighted to welcome the best nephew in the world to your charming home? And I'm so hungry I can hardly stand it!" With that, Anton Wagenknecht embraced his aunt, kissed her left and right on the cheek, and then swept past her into the hallway. After hanging his hat and coat on the rack, he picked up the newspaper lying on the dresser and stepped into the kitchen. "Well, Mareike Mousetail, what is my favorite cousin up to these days? Are you practicing cooking so you can be a good little housewife someday?"

Mareike smiled but remained silent. Although she didn't see her cousin all that often, she admired him from the depths of her young girl's heart. She secretly enjoyed the way that he teased her good-humoredly and how he remained unruffled no matter what the circumstance, and he was also, in her young eyes, the smartest man in the world.

Elisabeth quickly cut in, "Is something wrong with your mother?"

"Why no, what would make you think that? Didn't your dear husband, Herr Gemahl, tell you that I was coming? He called me this morning and summoned me, so here I am. What's cooking on the stove? Did I mention how hungry I am? Mareike Princess, could you slice me some bread, please, if that's all there is?"

Mareike immediately jumped up, cut a piece from the loaf, buttered, and salted it, and added an apple to the plate. Elisabeth handed Anton a bowl of soup to go along with it, and with great relish, he took a seat at the kitchen table and opened the newspaper with a satisfied flourish. He absentmindedly flipped through the pages until he caught sight of a drawing and skimmed the article underneath.

Elisabeth looked over his shoulder. "What an unpleasant man! Why are they looking for him?"

No one of importance, just a petty thief, Anton said. Then he folded up the paper, rubbing his forehead thoughtfully.

"Are you sure you should be here and not at his office? You see, he's not here."

"Yes, of course. I'm supposed to go to his cultural temple, but I was early, and I wanted to see you and the little princess too. Mother will be so glad to hear about how you're doing. By the way, your sandwich is excellent, Mareike. You'll make some man very happy when you grow up."

"Please don't tell the child things like that."

"Well... I'll be on my way. If I find him, I'll ask Uncle to invite me to dinner, then the princess can sit next to me. Deal?"

Mareike beamed and giggled as he kissed her on both cheeks.

Elisabeth accompanied her nephew into the foyer. Anton eyed his aunt critically. "Tell me, aren't you even a little glad to see me and your husband again? He's been away for two weeks, surely you missed him? When I have a wife, I want to be greeted jubilantly, even if I've only been gone an hour."

Elisabeth smiled. She was just a little tired, but yes, she was glad.

"There's a man sleeping in the garden! Mommy! Mommy!!! Come quick, I have found an old man! *Mommy!!!*"

Sighing, young Frau Müller wiped her hands on her apron. Hans was her pride and joy, and she was looking forward to her second child, who had been kicking more and more vigorously in her belly the past few days. But occasionally she wished Hans could content himself more with picture books and teddy bears. Regardless of the weather, he always wanted to run and romp through the garden. And he never stopped calling for her, demanding her undivided attention and an endless supply of sodas, chocolates, and other treats.

She stepped out into the garden, and Hans immediately grabbed her by the hand before dragging her across the lawn right through the flower beds, past the bushes. She wanted to scold him because stepping on the borders was something Papa had expressly forbidden. But then she found herself in front of an old man lying against the wall. She instantly sent Hans into the house and knelt beside the stranger. He was dressed in a simple shirt and coarse pants, which were much too thin for the season. He looked like he'd been mistreated. With practiced hands, she felt for his pulse in the crook of his neck and located a faint throbbing underneath the ice-cold skin. She reached for his shoulder; the clothes were damp. He had probably been there all night.

She hurried into the house, grabbed two woolen blankets, and instructed Hans to run to the neighbor and ask her to call for a doctor. Obediently, the child dashed off while the mother ran back into the garden. She carefully wrapped the old man in the blankets and rubbed his hands and cheeks. Hopefully they hadn't discovered him too late.

It was not long before Dr. Wagner arrived, guided by Hans. He examined the man with care, noting the effects of hypothermia and inadequate nutrition over a longer period of time. He was concerned about the stranger's age and suspected that he might have suffered a heart attack. This man needed to get to a hospital right away. Once again, Hans dashed to the neighbor and asked her to call the hospital.

Shortly after two o'clock, Emma and James returned from their simple lunch to the bank building, where they once more passed the elegant receptionists. Emma watched her companion closely: how would he react to these beautiful women?

He didn't seem to notice them at all, but instead crossed the foyer holding Emma by the hand and strode down the hallway that led to the annex. Through the glass door, they caught sight of Meridot, Weinstein, and Dr. Meinhardt chatting in the garden between the bank and the exhibition building.

When Herr Weinstein noticed them, he waved them over as Dr. Meinhardt stepped toward them: "How lovely to see you again! Have you made any progress since we last spoke?"

James informed him about his trip, and then Emma asked Dr. Meinhardt to look at her father's picture: Was this the same man he had spoken to?

The curator pressed a pince-nez to his nose and studied the photograph closely, then handed it back, "The gentleman I spoke to was definitely not the man in this picture. If this gentleman is your father, I must say I'm greatly relieved."

Herr Weinstein invited his guests to move indoors; he felt it was getting a little chilly out here. They took their seats in the curator's office, and once again Meridot described the nature of his research. Dr. Meinhardt sat speechless during this explanation, his gaze wandering from Meridot to Weinstein and back. How could he help, considering that he had no knowledge of any abominations like this?

"You see, my dear Dr. Meinhardt, there is a great deal of money at stake. An unscrupulous collector will pay a small fortune for a royal mummy, whether it's genuine or not. He may buy it illegally, but he wants to feel like everything is above board. He likes knowing that the sarcophagus comes to him through honorable channels. But the same does not hold true for the mummy. He doesn't care how it got there. He merely wants someone to confirm that what he now has is the real thing. This is why this shadowy organization has tried to involve various well-known museums in their endeavors by using their good names. Surreptitiously, of course, without the owners' knowledge. It's enough to find an employee willing to unlock a side entrance and look the other way. A little extra money for a harmless little favor. What's the big deal? Nothing is stolen, nothing is destroyed. Maybe this person wants to give their girlfriend a special evening out, tell their young son a scary tale in front of strange gods, or work on a painting in peace and quiet. Some sob story, a handful of bills, and the place is yours for a few hours. And it was in this context that your name came up, Doctor."

Meinhardt sprang to his feet. "Do you mean to say that I took a bribe to let who knows whom into our collection and drag our reputation through the mud?"

"Did you?"

The curator was momentarily speechless, as he glared furiously at the Frenchman. "Of course not!"

"Who else has access to the keys?"

"Herr Weinstein, of course, and I also have a spare key at home in my safe. Another key is kept at the bank desk in case of fire. However, it's kept in a safe, and it takes three very trustworthy bank employees to put in the combination."

"By that point, your exhibits would probably go up in smoke. Be that as it may, could you please find out if both of those keys are where they are supposed to be?"

Without another word, Dr. Meinhardt stormed out of his office. Meridot and James rose, ready to follow him, but Herr Weinstein assured them that Meinhardt wouldn't attempt to flee. Meridot smiled and took a seat, though James seemed unconvinced.

As it turned out, the old gentleman was right, and the curator returned with a key in his hand.

"I spoke to my wife on the phone. My duplicate is at home. And this is the one I just took out of the bank safe. It took me a while to gather the three gentlemen together, I'm afraid. In fact, I think we should simplify this arrangement for the sake of our artifacts, Herr Weinstein." With that, Dr. Meinhardt walked over to his desk, pulled another key from his vest pocket, and unlocked his rolltop desk, thus revealing three drawers. He pulled open the middle drawer, reached in and then froze for a heartbeat before opening the other two drawers. Then he rushed out of the office again, calling over his shoulder for them to follow him. Except for old Herr Weinstein, the others complied with this request. Meinhardt hurried ahead into the exhibition hall, where he switched on all the lights and inspected every display case and vitrine.

"Nothing is missing. Fortunately. But there is no way I misplaced my key; I'm very particular about security."

"Dr. Meinhardt, may I ask you if this key only works on the locks to these rooms?"

Meinhardt turned to Meridot. "No, no, it is a master key for the entire annex. You can open any room with it: my office, the washroom, the gallery, the storeroom."

"Where is the storeroom located?"

"In the basement, where we store our new acquisitions until they're catalogued and ready for display."

"If it isn't too much trouble, I'd like to take a look around there. It's probably a larger space?"

"Well, as a matter of fact, yes, it occupies the entire area and is roughly divided up by partitions and cabinets. If you'll follow me, I'll take you down there." Once again, the curator dashed ahead.

When he reached the basement, he cried out softly. The iron door to the storeroom was open—only a crack—but someone must have unlocked it. He was about to yank it open and rush into the storage area when Meridot pulled him back.

"Stay here, all of you. Quietly, I beg you," the Frenchman whispered, moving back onto the stairs and waving for the others to join him. "Didn't you notice? The storeroom is lit up. Don't you think that suggests that someone might be in there?"

"But at this hour?" Meinhardt whispered back. "That would be dangerous. The bank is open for business, customers are coming in and out, and—"

"Nothing could be safer. You wait for a suitable moment and voilà! There you go. In broad daylight, among all those people, hardly anyone would pay attention to you. Now tell me, is this the only entrance?"

"Yes. No... I mean this is the only way to bring larger objects in or out of the storeroom. There are two other narrower shafts that lead into the garden. They're basically just for fresh air, but a slender person could probably get through them if they had to."

Meridot looked at Emma. "Mademoiselle, I would prefer not to have you here. I think it's safer for you to keep Herr Weinstein company, if just for his own sake. Please go up to him and lock the door behind you. Please."

Emma hesitated only briefly, then climbed the stairs, moving faster with each step. She felt like she had whenever Mama had asked her to fetch potatoes or preserves from the cellar: she would descend the stairs bravely, marching resolutely to the shelf and grabbing what she wanted before turning around. And once she had done that, fear of what might be lurking in the cellar would wash over her, and she would stumble up the stairs, panic-stricken. She hadn't felt safe again until she had locked the door behind her. And that same feeling of anxiety was returning to her now.

Herr Weinstein was quite startled when she rushed into the office, slammed the door, and turned the key. "We're supposed to lock ourselves in!"

"My dear Fräulein, what on earth has happened?" The old gentleman looked very pale sitting there in his chair. Emma immediately apologized for giving him such a fright and tersely filled him in on what little she knew. She pulled an armchair up quite close to his, and they huddled together next to each other, listening and staring steadily out into the garden. Time slowed to a near standstill.

Then suddenly they heard shouts. Emma jumped up and ran to the window. Herr Weinstein called out to her not to get any closer, but she didn't heed him. Voices again! She thought she heard James yelling something unintelligible. Then there was a bang, once, twice. More shouts. She pressed herself against the window. Why couldn't she see anyone? She searched the entire space outside the window, but suddenly, just below her, a tightly woven grating slid upward, blocking her view.

Weinstein insisted that she back away from the wall, and this time she hastily obeyed. The old man tugged her back down next to him, clutching her arm. She pressed herself deeper into the armchair and stared at the window, in which a man now appeared. The setting sun was blazing right into Meinhardt's office, and for the first time in her life, Emma cursed her red curls. She could feel how her hair was being illuminated by the last twilight glow, how it flamed up against the gray dimness of the study. She threw herself on the floor and tried to curl up into a tight ball but didn't dare move any further. Yet, she still managed to attract the stranger's attention. He seemed to be hardly more than a shadow, but Emma had the vague feeling that she had met him somewhere.

Standing stock still and slightly crouched, the man looked all around him. He glanced into the office. He had obviously seen her, for he moved a little closer to the window and hesitated, possibly considering whether to break it.

The voices returned again; Emma heard footsteps in the hallway, running toward the garden. A metallic thud sounded from outside. "That must be the grate on the other shaft," Weinstein whispered.

The intruder took off! He ran to the left toward the wall, away from the sun's dwindling rays, and that's when Emma recognized him. Friedhelm! Herr Meerbusch's secretary! The man who had told them that her father had come to visit them in Koblenz. The one who had laughed at her when she had stumbled. Emma jumped up and ran to the window. Meridot and Meinhardt were now in the garden, and to her right, James was climbing out of the second hatch. Meanwhile, Friedhelm had reached the bushes which were out of the three men's field of vision. Now that he was at the wall, Emma knew he was about to escape.

She tugged at the latch, yanked open the window, and shouted, "Over to the left! The left! In the bushes! It's Friedhelm!"

James shouted for her to close the window. The man had a gun with him and had already fired it twice. She did as he asked, but stayed at the window and watched what was happening, as if to make sure that no harm would come to the men. Just as Meridot and James reached the place where she had lost sight of Friedhelm, she saw the latter scaling the wall. He swung himself over the top of it and disappeared. Meridot was the first to reach the same spot. He pulled himself up in one powerful motion and looked in all directions, but with a regretful shake of his head, he told James and Meinhardt that there was no one in sight.

A few moments later, the men entered the office and explained how they had startled the burglar in one of the storeroom aisles. He had vanished into the tangle of shelves, cabinets, and boxes, so the three men split up to block every possible exit. Dr. Meinhardt had positioned himself at the stairway exit, and the fleeing man had run straight at him and fired, though only into the air. However, when the curator didn't immediately jump aside, the other man had aimed at his heart and threatened to pull the trigger if he wouldn't let him pass. Quick-witted, Meinhardt slammed the door and threw himself to the ground as the second shot went off.

The stranger fled back into the storeroom, knocking Meridot down and climbing out one of the narrow hatches. James was guarding the other shaft, so he heaved himself up into the garden at the Frenchman's shout, while Meridot, along with Meinhardt, exited the storeroom via the stairwell.

"But he's not a stranger. It was Friedhelm! Didn't you recognize him, James?"

He shook his head. With all the running around, he had hardly been able to recognize anything. Was Emma sure? After all, she had only met him once.

"I'm absolutely sure. While I was talking to Herr Meerbusch, he was standing behind him, just staring at Jean-Baptiste and me. An unpleasant person! But what was he doing here? Was he trying to steal something?"

"Mademoiselle, that's what we are going to figure out now. He wasn't carrying anything, and he couldn't have had anything hidden in his suit pockets. Gentlemen, we need to thoroughly search the storage area. Dear Samuel, I beg you to stay here. You need to rest."

This time Emma refused to stay behind but insisted on coming along for the search. They carefully examined every aisle, every shelf, every compartment. Dr. Meinhardt then called out for them to join him. Between two ceiling-high cabinets, someone had piled up several boxes, thus partitioning off a kind of room. During their first hurried search through the cellar, they hadn't noticed this area. Together they now removed the barrier, crate by crate.

In front of them stood a sarcophagus. A plain coffin, once brightly painted and probably from the New Kingdom. "Dr. Meinhardt, does this piece belong in your collection?" asked Meridot.

"No. No, not at all."

The two men stepped closer and lifted the lid, leaning it carefully against the shelf as James and Emma drew nearer. A mummy lay inside, its head and shoulders covered with a plaster mask that bore a depiction in bright colors of the dead man and his jewelry.

Dr. Meinhardt bent over and touched the mask gently, running his index finger along it gingerly. "These colors and the material's solidity…"

"Yes. And look at the bandages."

"You mean…?"

"What do you think?"

"I think, Monsieur Meridot, you can remove the mask without worrying about its value."

"What does that mean?" asked Emma.

No one answered. Meridot lifted off the mask and handed it to James, before pulling a narrow knife from his jacket and slitting the linen bandages from shoulder to temple. "These bandages are very soft, aren't they?"

"Too soft."

Emma pressed against James, who held her close but didn't take his eyes off the corpse.

Meridot pulled aside the cut strips of linen. A man's sunken and leathery face peered out. "Imagine if you knew nothing about what an embalmed Egyptian corpse looked like after thousands of years.

How it would react to the oxygen, how the bandages would bond with the resin and skin, how it would smell. Imagine a lavish feast with champagne and caviar and flickering candles. And now this mummy; the exhilaration, the shudders."

Meinhardt nodded, visibly shaken. "Why is he here? How did he get in here?"

Meridot shrugged with a shake of his head. "If we find this Herr Friedhelm, we will ask him, but I suspect he knew about your vacation and brought interested customers down here in your absence. He probably told them how strict the laws are and how he works for this respected collection that has more treasures than it can display. He likely explained that this mummy would never be exhibited, that people weren't interested in plain artifacts like this, but the collection couldn't sell it officially. What he told them was nothing more than what they wanted to hear. So they came to an agreement, and they were supposed to take this coffin out of this space just as it had been brought in. You weren't meant to ever notice anything, and yet your good name would have vouched for the authenticity of this poor creature."

"Yes..." replied Meinhardt slowly, deep in thought, "but I don't understand—why was my key missing? This can't be the first time that this Friedhelm was here, could it? And it would have been impossible for him to get the sarcophagus down here along with its sad contents without help. I mean, why didn't he have a duplicate key made? We would never have come down here if I hadn't missed my own key."

"I don't know, but let's assume that even criminals are human beings. This means we can further assume that even the smartest villains can lose their keys. Yes, maybe someone even stole it from him. You don't usually lock your office, do you?"

"No, I don't, you're right. But—"

"Forgive me, but the more important question now is should we inform the police?"

"Of course, why wouldn't we?"

"Naturally, why wouldn't you..."

"You don't want to?"

Meridot explained himself: "Friedhelm will be scared that the police are on his trail and will go underground, don't you think? You know the saying about too many cooks spoiling the broth? I'm afraid that my trail will be trampled if too many run roughshod over it. So would any of you mind granting me a few days before we notify the authorities?"

"Herr Weinstein will be the one to decide that, but I think you will find him amenable to your suggestion."

"I think so, too, Dr. Meinhardt. Thank you."

Later that evening, James and Emma sat across from each other at a table. They were enjoying dinner at an elegant restaurant not far from the bank. Herr Weinstein had extended his invitation to them, and Emma, after talking to Tante Tinni on the phone, had accepted his offer for them to stay a little longer as his guests. Monsieur Meridot had bid them goodbye but had promised to return to Bonn if his inquiries were successful. When Emma had asked him what he would do next, his answer had been somewhat vague.

James patted Emma's hand. "Darling, how are you feeling? I'm so sorry. These two days must have been horrible for you. Are you terribly upset?"

She considered how she felt, then slowly shook her head. No, she was feeling surprisingly well. Not that she found looking at dead bodies particularly pleasant, and she didn't intend to make a habit of it. But James shouldn't imagine that simply because she was a slender creature that she lacked brains, stamina, and whatever else it took to face life.

"But I'm not saying that at all. I'm just worried."

"Well, then let me ask you... How are *you*? Are *you* feeling well? You ran after a man who could've shot you today. Aren't you feeling the least bit upset and frightened?"

"I don't know what you're getting at, but if it doesn't shock you too much, then yes, I am upset and frightened. And the fact that that mummy was a person who was cheerfully walking around just a couple of months ago, until someone killed him just for the sake of money, bothers me greatly. Only a complete drunkard would lack all feeling in such a situation!"

Emma blushed. "I'm sorry. I thought you believed... Oh, I was just being silly."

"Would you like to explain a little more?"

"I can't. Or maybe I can. Do you think women are especially delicate and timid and cautious and need to be shielded from everything?"

THE MISSING PROFESSOR 223

"I'm afraid I've never given that much thought. But I do think that men should be particularly careful with women, just as fathers are careful with their children."

"So you equate women with children? Do you think we're incapable of thinking and taking care of ourselves?" Emma's voice might have grown a little louder because the guests at the next table flinched.

"Pardon me? Don't be silly. What's going on here? A debate on women's suffrage? Before you accuse me of anything, rest assured, I'm all for giving you the vote."

"Well, here in Germany we've been able to vote for a long time, and it's simply laughable that you're sitting here thinking you can graciously give me that right."

James stared at her open-mouthed. What on earth was going on? Here she was, accusing him of beliefs in all sorts of things that were completely foreign to him or that he was rather indifferent about. It annoyed him, and yet he found that he rather liked this agitated Emma. The way she glared at him, the way she held her head, the way her neck arched delicately...

"Are you listening to me at all?"

"No."

"Excuse me?"

"Oh, I'm... I'm sorry, of course I'm listening to you, but I don't understand what you mean. Look, I've never thought women were mentally weak, not in the slightest. Believe me, if you knew my mother... but that's irrelevant right now. What I meant is that the physically stronger—if you'll grant me that—always have a responsibility to use their strength to protect the weaker but not to oppress them. Is that so wrong?"

Emma was silent.

"Darling, please... If you insist, I will never fight on your behalf. I'll leave all the fighting to you. I'll stand behind you and offer good advice on whether you need to watch your guard or aim for the stomach. Oh, don't look away, I already saw that you were laughing. There, just a little bit. Please don't be mad at me anymore; I'm not terribly good with conversations like this. You will always be able to push me into a corner, so very easily. Because, my darling, I have long known how clever you are, and I'm afraid you will now know how little I can say that about myself. There, you're laughing again! Just admit it: good ol' James might not be either smart or handsome but you like him anyway."

Emma laughed. She couldn't help it, though she hadn't quite settled down yet. This might have simply been a misunderstanding but wasn't that because he was strolling blind and deaf through the countryside? Shouldn't it be obvious to everyone how unfairly women were treated by the world? Shouldn't a man in love recognize this fact and want to change it? On the other hand, the matter-of-factness with which James and Jean-Baptiste, even Anton, stood protectively in front of her whenever they had to pass through crowds of people, how they carried heavy things for her, adjusted her chair, and helped her into her coat. Did they do all this to emphasize her gender's weakness? Or was it rather a reflection that her well-being was something precious to these men? On the other hand, these might just be learned manners without any actual meaning.

Gazing into James' honest face, she recognized his confusion and smiled at him. All these questions could wait until they found Papa.

SATURDAY

Shortly after midnight, Emma awoke, crying out for help and thrashing about. For hours she was unable to fall back asleep again, tossing and turning, walking around her room, sitting on the windowsill, gazing out into the night. When she finally nodded off, the clock was striking four o'clock.

The following morning, James knocked on her door. When no one answered, he peeked inside. Emma was sleeping soundly in her rumpled sheets, so he withdrew quietly and had his breakfast with Herr Weinstein. The two men avoided any mention of the previous day's events; the old gentleman was more interested in Mr. Beresford's plans for the future.

They chatted for about an hour, at which point James decided it was time to head back to Bonn. However, Emma was still asleep and now he was standing in front of her door, feeling uncertain as how he should proceed. How do you go about waking a young lady without arousing unwarranted suspicion?

He took a deep breath, then marched straight toward her bed before shouting "Good morning!" in her ear, nearly knocking her off the mattress. Feigning indifference, he dropped into a chair and began to inspect his fingernails. When Emma still didn't get out of bed, he bellowed a jaunty, "Up and at 'em, comrade!" Surely that would convince her that his motives for sitting in her bedroom were upstanding and not the result of his desire to catch sight of her in her nightgown.

Rubbing her eyes, Emma winced and covered her ears. Why was he yelling at her as if they were fellow soldiers? Was he trying to prove to her that women were no different than men in his eyes? This thought irritated her despite the speech she had given yesterday. "What time is it?"

"It's after nine o'clock, and—"

"What the devil! Why didn't you wake me earlier?" She swung out of bed. "Turn around, please."

James dutifully obeyed and stared at the wall.

Still exhausted, Emma reached for the blanket to modestly wrap around herself, but knocked the bedside lamp to the floor as she did so. James wheeled around, ready to drive off any attacker with his fists. Whatever he might have said yesterday, he wasn't about to trust her fighting skills. Nonetheless, there was no one in the room to beat up, only Emma with tousled hair and a nightgown that was clearly unsuitable for chilly winter nights. What a delightful surprise! James would never have suspected that she would wear such a gauzy, sheer, really quite enchanting, even breathtaking... ahem—sort of garment. He gulped.

Emma didn't notice the way James was watching her as she continued to struggle with the stubborn blanket. Just as she was about to pick up the fallen lamp, James abruptly wrapped his arms around her and kissed her. He held her tightly against him, kissing her cheeks and her eyes, then devoting himself at length to her neck and then her lips. Confused, she let it happen, even caught herself thinking that her neck was finally receiving adequate attention after so many years of neglect. She also fleetingly wondered if she found Anton's or James' more skillful. Then all at once she became fully aware of the situation and pushed James away.

"Oh, my goodness, darling, please forgive me! That was unforgivable, I... just... that nightgown and you... I'm so sorry, that shouldn't have happened. I'll wait for you downstairs, please take your time. I'm sorry, please believe me."

As he was leaving the room, Emma wanted to tell him to come back. In a slight state of confusion, she got dressed. Shouldn't she feel more indignant and upset, and less cheerful and excited?

Like Emma, Anton had spent a restless night. Unable to sleep, he had gotten up just past dawn to wander the streets of Bonn. What was he going to do? He'd always known that his uncle's business wasn't entirely on the up and up, and that was precisely what had drawn him to it. 'The world is a rotten place," his uncle had said, "It's just begging for someone to take it by the horns and bend it to his will. Because only the strong survive, Anton. Remember that. If we don't seize opportunity when it strikes, someone else will." Words that had once had power over him now rang hollow and trite. What a fool he had been! For the sake of little money and a few cheap thrills, he was now in a real fix.

Everything was going fine until the incident with Hannes at the bridge. Anton should have confided in the police when his uncle had waved off the mishap by remarking that they had no idea what good might come from it; weak people were a threat to great plans. Hannes! Anton had been standing in front of Hannes one moment and the next he had disappeared, just disappeared! Only now was Anton finally beginning to truly feel the loss of his friend. If only he hadn't let his uncle talk him into this whole messy affair! If only he hadn't fallen for his persuasive arguments! Even the story about the professor. He hadn't fully grasped the gravity of the plan. His uncle had couched it all in very different terms. He had spoken of a common cause, of a slight diversionary maneuver, of a trifling that would make them both some money. And then what?

Then the old bastard had escaped. Escaped! The news caught Anton off guard, but he had kept that thought to himself. When his uncle found out, though, he had flown into a rage, revealing more to Anton about his character than he had meant to. Anton had noticed something in the way he looked at him, something sinister that he had not seen before, and suddenly he had realized what kind of person he had gotten involved with and had admired so much. The affable façade, the charm, and the polite demeanor vanished; nothing but greed remained. And he had caught sight of something else too. This was a man who actually took pleasure in inflicting pain on others.

Done with his walk, Anton was now at the breakfast table at his aunt's house, observing in silence the family in front of him. He reflected on how the introverted Mareike sat huddled in her seat; how his aunt stared into the distance and how she fulfilled his uncle's every whim, her face rigidly impassive despite her husband's studied politeness and words of endearment. Why had he never noticed this before? But then again, he was rarely at home with them all together. Normally, he met up with his uncle alone at the museum or somewhere else, hardly ever at his house.

"Elisabeth, dearest, Anton and I have to leave in a few minutes. And Mareike must hurry to make it to school on time. Enjoy your day, my darling. Come along, Anton, we have things to do."

Anton's uncle bent over Elisabeth and kissed the top of her head, but Anton noticed how he gripped the back of her neck so tightly that the collar of her dress choked her. He gazed into his aunt's eyes, wishing there was something he could do, but she only shook her head slightly and formed a silent, "No."

Reluctantly, he left her before taking the first opportunity to get away from his uncle by pretending to remember some errand or another that he had forgotten to run for him. Once alone, he wandered the streets, wrestling with his conscience.

Siegfried Mertens had spent the previous day trying to learn more about Johannes Schmitz and Anton Wagenknecht. He had walked great distances across Bonn and Cologne, and the results of his effort were impressive. But he hadn't been able to reach Wertheim at the police station, and so he now found himself standing in front of Wertheim's apartment on Saturday afternoon.

The inspector looked a bit rumpled when he opened the door to his assistant and motioned him inside. "Well, Mertens, where's the fire? Are you hungry? Good! Then head to the right, into the kitchen. I'll whip us up something good."

Siegfried sat rather stiffly on the kitchen bench and watched as Wertheim cut and fried onions, sliced mushrooms, whisked eggs, grated cheese, diced boiled potatoes, transforming it all into a lighter-than-air omelet.

With the ease of a professional, he slid it out of the pan, divided it in half, poured two glasses of Kölsch beer, and placed both plates on the table. "Come on, my lad, lighten up. You're not sitting at the table with the King of England. Eat up!"

Wertheim dug in with gusto and Siegfried followed suit. Then, as they stood side by side at the sink washing dishes, the junior officer reported on what he had found out. "My first task was to learn more about Johannes Schmitz. Good student, orphan, rower, no money, worked under Neumann and Schumacher, quiet. We already knew all that. I was surprised that no one mentioned any friends. So I asked the landlady—and you would've been proud of me; I agreed to a drink at a pretty early hour. If the old lady drinks that stuff regularly, she'll live to be a jolly hundred. I had to eat dry cake too. And two pieces at that. But once I did that, she talked. She must have snooped around since she knew how many pairs of socks he owned and the frequency of his nocturnal excursions. She could tell me everything. He didn't have friends over all that much. He found them embarrassing." Siegfried pulled out his green booklet. "Her exact words were, 'A rowdy bunch they were, loud and foul-mouthed, sloppy drunk even before lunch.' But one member of the group was a childhood friend, and he didn't like to see poor Johannes stuck all by himself.'"

Wertheim put the plates back up in the cupboard and poured them a second beer. "Go ahead, my boy, I'm hanging on your every word."

"She couldn't recall the boy's name, and it's not possible to identify this particular crew of rowdy young men, when there are so many of them running around Bonn. But the mention of a childhood friend was a good clue, so I went back to the station and took another look at Schmitz's file. His family moved to Bonn when he was nine years old, so was the childhood friend from Bonn or from Cologne, where he had lived previously? I made a note of the addresses where the family had resided and then went to Cologne. Actually, I had wanted to make my inquiries by phone, but would you believe that no one in the Cologne offices picked up their phone?" Siegfried took a deep sip of his beer, leafed through his book, and continued. "And while working on all this, I noticed that Schmitz and Wagenknecht were both from Nippes, the same neighborhood in Cologne. That didn't have to mean anything, but nevertheless, I had all the records of their families pulled up for me at the registry office. And guess what I discovered?"

"The two boys lived down the street from each other?"

"It's better than that: their parents were next-door neighbors. The boys were born in the same year and attended the same school until the Schmitzes moved to Bonn. And because I didn't want to rely on that alone, I decided to drop by their old school. The school secretary has been sitting in the same chair for thirty years and was bored. She poured me a shot of schnapps right off the bat."

"Mertens, what sacrifices you are making! But what does a damaged liver matter in the face of justice?"

"She handed me the key to the archive. Schmitz and Wagenknecht were in the same cohort, and more than once, the two of them cooked up something together. Wagenknecht was the clever one, and Schmitz was the artist. Oh yes, the landlady had also mentioned that he could paint beautifully."

"Mertens, stay on track!"

"I didn't discover anything about an uncle at the registry office, but at the same time, the official there was anything but helpful. So I went to see Anton's parents. The father is making overtures to go into politics and was out making nice speeches somewhere, but the mother was at home. A very pleasant person, genteel even. She was curious about my questions regarding the uncle, who could only have been her sister's husband, but she has lost practically all contact with them. What she couldn't say was whether or not her son was in touch with her brother-in-law. I pressed her on this, but she remained quite cool and cautious. She believes her sister is dependent on her husband and is convinced that her sister broke off relations with her because of him."

"And this uncle? Do we know him?"

"Well," Siegfried beamed, "we have him in our records as a witness in the Schumacher case."

Heinrich August Schumacher lay pale and gaunt against the immaculately white pillows. He was still unconscious, his pulse fluttering weakly. As before, no one knew his name. The physician, Dr. Wagner, feared the worst and regretted not being able to notify his relatives. He asked the nurse to wash and comb the old man's hair, to tidy up his appearance for his fellow patients.

During Wagner's later rounds, he looked more closely at the unconscious man. Now that the old man made a respectable impression, he noticed that his skin had been well taken care of and his teeth were healthy. He examined the hands: there were no calluses, no sun damage, just some scratches and faded ink stains. He studied the stranger's face and pondered why this man seemed familiar to him.

The nurse stepped up beside him. "Doesn't he look like Ludwig van Beethoven? Just a little less grim, I think."

The doctor glanced back at the professor's face and agreed with her. But there was something else...

Lost in thought, he strode out of the room and down the hall to his examination room, where he reached for a stack of newspapers on his desk and flipped through them. There it was: a professor from Bonn had been reported missing and, in the physical description, there was a comparison to Beethoven. The photograph next to it showed a handsome gentleman with an impressively full head of hair. The doctor involuntarily ran his fingers through his few paltry strands and sighed. The man in the hospital bed was considerably thinner, and he looked older, but Wagner recognized him despite his sunken cheeks. And with that, he folded up the newspaper and dialed the police.

The police officer in the Düsseldorf City Hall gazed at the woman in front of him. She looked elderly and shriveled up, and had clearly had a rough life. However, along with her threadbare coat, she wore a mink collar, gloves of the finest leather, and new shoes. She once more tapped the newspaper clipping she had presented to him. "That's my Karl, that's definitely Karl. What on earth has happened to him? Why are you looking for him?"

Her hand trembled as well as her voice, and he could already see the first tear trickling down her pale cheek. He stepped toward her, offered his arm, and led her into a guard room.

"Have a seat here, please." He sat down opposite her and asked her for the picture. "Who is this Karl?" he asked kindly.

"Well, that's my husband, Karl Klepper. I'm Frau Klepper, and the butcher's wife just gave me this. I don't read the newspaper myself. I'm always too busy. I'm just a cleaning lady, you know... but what about Karl? Who drew this picture of him? I'm all mixed up..."

The officer didn't know the answer and asked his assistant for help. Did he know why Herr Klepper was in the newspaper?

"Something came in the other day. They are searching for a professor from Bonn, as well as another man who looks like him."

"Then call Bonn right away and ask about it! Now, Frau Klepper, take a deep breath; we'll find out what's going on. Why didn't you know your husband was missing before now?"

"Karl is a traveling salesman, that's how we met. He tried to sell me garters. Garters, me!" she laughed sheepishly, and the sergeant smiled back. "We've had a few bad years now. But in the summer, he found a new job. He has to drive all over Germany for it, but the pay's pretty good. He often wrote to me and sent me presents, because he said I was going to have a good life now. This collar and my shoes, all that. Like some fine lady. When I get on the train these days, fine gentlemen sometimes even give up their seats for me, because I look so distinguished."

"You look quite elegant, Frau Klepper. Your husband has excellent taste. When did you last hear from him?"

"It must have been two weeks ago, I think. He said he'd be home for St. Martin's Day and that I should order a fat goose. Is Karl coming back home now?"

"Well, we have to find your Karl first, don't we? Don't worry about it, we—if you'll excuse me for a moment?" The officer broke off his commentary as he caught sight of his assistant waving to him from the next room. He rose, walked over, and listened intently, then he glanced over at the woman nervously opening and shutting her purse repeatedly. In his role as a police officer, it was moments like this he hated the most. He took a deep breath and straightened his shoulders before returning to Frau Klepper.

Samuel Weinstein gave Emma and James a particularly gracious farewell, asked them to keep him informed of their progress, and invited them both to visit him again. He especially hoped that Fräulein Schumacher's Papa returned home soon. Overwhelmed by his kindness, Emma embraced him and thanked him from the bottom of her heart for the hospitality he had shown them. She also bid Dr. Meinhardt a warm farewell.

Dr. Meinhardt took James aside one last time and suggested that he remain in touch about his job search; if it was all right with Mr. Beresford, he would keep his ears open for him and would be glad to offer him a personal recommendation. James thanked him with a broad smile, then took Emma's arm. It was finally time to go home. He helped her into the automobile, and then with one last wave, they set off.

Although the sun was shining from a bright blue sky, the approaching winter was already making itself felt. Emma wrapped herself in the travel blanket. She was holding James' notebook and leafing through it. "I'm sorry to say it, my dear Mr. Beresford, but your handwriting is pure chicken scratch. Can you even read it yourself?"

"You might find this hard to believe, but I won prizes for the best penmanship three years running. I was an exemplary student, and I can assure you that I earned stellar marks in all my other subjects too. But what are you looking for anyway?"

"For a date. Look, I just remembered that the only person who hasn't been shown Papa's photograph is Herr Meerbusch. It wouldn't be much of a detour if we stopped by and questioned him."

"Do you think that's necessary? After all, Herr Friedhelm identified him."

"James! You want to take that criminal as a serious witness? Please remember what Monsieur Meridot said: he has been using his position to hide his activities. Herr Meerbusch may be in danger if Friedhelm is trying to take cover in Koblenz. We should warn him, and that's why I'd like to know if he is back from his trip. You had mentioned a date, I remember that."

"Turn back a bit more, another page. Yes, look, there on the right. Wonderfully legible, clearly a twenty-nine."

"So he's been back in Koblenz since yesterday. Please, let's stop there."

"But we don't even know where to find him. He might not be spending his Saturday at the museum."

"We can try. Please, James."

Anton dashed down the stairs and was already running through the streets again; he had to think. Seriously and urgently. His uncle had ordered him to find the professor and bring him back. The very same man that Anton had been hiding: Professor Schumacher. The man whose daughter, Emma, had been entrusted to Anton's care. He'd been responsible for observing her comings and goings and most of all for preventing her from looking for her father. Nothing his uncle had told him had been true; that much was clear now.

Anton could no longer mask his horror from his uncle. But when he expressed his shock his uncle had responded derisively, laughing, calling him a fool, a dreamer, and a hypocrite. There was no way, he said, that Anton had ever honestly believed that it was mere petty theft. A prank? If it were all a harmless game then he never would have brought his nephew in on it. Just one look at Anton and you knew that he was a selfish good-for-nothing, callous, and determined. All traits that his uncle admired. "As you very well know," his uncle had added, "sometimes you have to be ruthless in order to achieve great things."

Anton had merely nodded in response, even though he was suddenly overcome with nausea, barely able to stand. Where should he start looking? How should he go about finding the professor? Shouldn't they hit the road before Schumacher went to the police?

The uncle waved him off. If the old man had done that, someone would have shown up here a while ago. How should Anton go about finding him? Hadn't he seen the blood on the ground and on the garden wall? Anton needed to pull his wits together.

At this point, Anton wanted to refuse his uncle's orders, longed to tell him to get himself out of this mess on his own. But his uncle beat him to the punch: Wasn't Mareike growing up to be a delightful young lady? If the girl were properly guided, they could use her for one plot or the other...

"You would use your own daughter like that? Your child?"

"If she were a boy, she'd know the drill by now. But she's just a girl, so why should that bother me? Haven't I always told you women were meant for pleasure, nothing more? If you'd had a firmer hand with that Schumacher girl, she wouldn't have caused such a ruckus."

Anton had remained silent, simply nodding to everything his uncle said. And now he was running through the streets from one hospital to the next. Old Schumacher must have sought help somewhere.

Siegfried and Wertheim were standing by the south-bound railroad track, when Siegfried swore to himself that he was finally going to learn how to drive.

"Mertens, do you have the gentleman's private address? Without it, there's really no point in driving into town. Have you notified our local colleagues?"

Siegfried froze. No, in his rush to get ready to leave, he'd forgotten.

Wertheim groaned. "Boy, you really need to learn to work with other people. We're defenseless on our own, but we can't change anything now. The train is coming, and at least there are two of us. Did you at least remember to bring your gun along? Be prepared for anything. That's something else you need to remember."

The younger officer tapped himself on the chest and nodded. He always carried his gun with him; that was one thing he never forgot.

At two o'clock, Emma and James pulled up in front of the Private Egyptological Collection in Koblenz.

"No one's around. See, we've made this trip for nothing." James glanced around, eager to keep going.

But Emma couldn't hear him, since she had already jumped out of the car and was hurrying up the steps. He ran after her. "You're close to my idea of perfection, Fräulein Schumacher, but I'm afraid you're much too impatient."

"Mr. Beresford, I should point out that even if I were patient, I'd still be less than perfect. Now ring, knock, or do whatever it takes to call attention to us."

James bowed and rang the bell. No one appeared, and he was about to drag Emma away when she leaned forward and put her ear to the door. "I heard something. Be quiet for once, please. There! Those are footsteps!"

She straightened up and knocked. Once more, James tried to pull her away; he found her incessant knocking in poor taste. But all of a sudden, the door opened, and Herr Meerbusch stood before them, in his shirt sleeves, a napkin in his hand. Surprised, he looked at Emma, then at James. "Fräulein Schumacher, if I am not mistaken. What an unexpected pleasure! What brings you to me?" he asked, stepping aside to let them inside. "Please excuse my casual appearance. I was just treating myself to a bite to eat. You can probably guess how busy I am at the moment. We open next week, after all."

He led them into his study and took a seat behind the desk. With care, he rolled down his shirt sleeves, buttoned his cuffs, lit a cigarette, and held out the case to James.

James declined, saying he didn't smoke.

What could possibly have brought Fräulein Schumacher and her companion to him, the director repeated.

Emma introduced James, pulled her father's picture out of her purse, and handed it to Herr Meerbusch: "I don't want to keep you long, and I'm very sorry to bother you again, but it turns out that it wasn't my father who went on that lecture tour, but a man posing as him."

Meerbusch took the photograph, and with furrowed brow, he studied it. After a moment, he replied, "This is all rather puzzling. It would never have occurred to me that someone other than your father would respond to my invitation. The gentleman who came to see me was not this man."

James cut in, "Your answer is astonishing, seeing as your associate Herr Friedhelm was questioned by the police a few days ago, and he identified the real Professor Schumacher as your visitor. How do you explain that?"

The director stared in bewilderment at James.

The latter continued, "However, we have reason to treat Herr Friedhelm's word with caution, considering that he shot at me yesterday."

"He did what?"

"He fired at me and two other gentlemen. Because we surprised him with a mummy that could hardly be more than a few months old."

Emma watched the director closely, as his puzzled eyes darted back and forth between James and herself. They gave a detailed accounting of yesterday's events, while Meerbusch listened in silence.

Then suddenly, he brought his fist down on the table. "Herr Friedhelm left me a message saying a relative of his had fallen ill, and he was taking a few days' off. So, you're telling me that you think he's involved in some kind of corpse smuggling and is using my collection as a cover? I think I would have noticed something like that. We work very closely together... it's simply not possible..." Meerbush's voice shifted from its usual pleasant tenor to nearly a murmur. "On the other hand, I've certainly noticed that Friedhelm isn't the exactly the warmest person, and that, as my right-hand man, he has a great deal of latitude to handle business matters when I'm away. I trusted him."

Meerbusch rose and walked to the window. "You said this happened in Frankfurt? In Weinstein's collection? Dr. Meinhardt is the curator there, a very capable man who knows how to captivate an audience. Did you know that he was the one who suggested your father's lecture tour to me? He said that organizing this trip would help us spread the word about our collection and open some doors."

Back in the car, James and Emma pondered what to do next.

"We can't just head home, can we? Should we go to the police? Or drive back to Frankfurt?" asked Emma.

"There's no way I'm driving you back to Frankfurt! You saw how shocked Meerbusch was; he'll notify the police. We're going to Bonn now! Just think how worried your aunts must be. From there, we can tell Siegfried and Herr Wertheim what we've discovered, and they will know better than us to whom we should turn. Besides, we promised Monsieur Meridot we wouldn't do anything yet. I mean, what has actually changed? Friedhelm lied, but that can't really surprise you."

"I don't know, something is bothering me. Something doesn't fit. As Monsieur Meridot said, I need to trust my instincts!"

"That may be true, but my gut is trustworthy too, and it's telling me to take you back to Bonn." Without waiting for her agreement, he hit the gas.

Emma wrapped herself in her blanket and stared out the window; he was right, and though she didn't like to admit it, she longed for her family and her own bed. She sighed. Tomorrow was October 31st, and she had hoped to celebrate this day together with Papa. But maybe a miracle could still happen. Perhaps he was unlocking the front door at this very moment. Once inside, he would slip into his old robe and retire to his study for his nightcap of gin, just for half an hour, which always turned into one or two. He would spend that time reading, sketching, and writing. In the morning, he would read to her the best excerpts of what he had written the night before. Then he would intercept the mailman and give him the most urgent letters, whether the letter carrier wanted them or not.

Emma saw it play out before her eyes, as if it were happening right now. The way her father stood on the steps, reached for the mail bag, and slid the letters into it... "Yes! Of course! Of course!" she cried out, not long after James had crossed the city limit and was driving along the Rhine.

He hit the brakes hard and scolded her. Didn't she know that driving a car required concentration and that the driver shouldn't be distracted? What in the world had made her shout like that?

"We have to go back, immediately! Turn around! Right now!"

James demanded clarification.

"Papa's seal box! I saw it in the cabinet but didn't register it. In the director's office! We've got to go back! He has to tell us more about Friedhelm. He's got Papa. I know it! Meerbusch must be able to help us!"

"That's a job for the police."

"They don't know anything for sure. We'll ask Meerbusch, and then go to Bonn and tell Wertheim, all right? Just think: what if Dr. Meinhardt is in cahoots with Friedhelm? Everything with that key is very suspicious. Please turn back!"

Tante Tinni hurried down the hall and yanked open the front door. It wasn't Emma, however, but a police officer who stood on the stoop. "Hello. How may I help you?"

"Fräulein Feuerhahn?"

"Yes. What's happened? Is my niece—".

"I have good news, my good lady. May I come in?"

Christel invited him inside.

"We just received word from Koblenz that they've found your brother. At least it's most likely your brother, I should say. He's in a hospital. The doctor there has asked you to contact him. I have written down the telephone number for you. Here."

Tinni sank down on the stairs and couldn't stop laughing and crying. If Emma came home right away, her joy would be complete! They could all go to Koblenz together tomorrow to visit Heinrich or to take him home right away.

238

Anton was already on his fourth hospital. He once again told the nurse at the reception desk the story he had invented about his missing grandfather, who was confused and for whom he was desperately searching. He gazed imploringly at the young woman, his tone so persuasive that it didn't occur to her to ask him for his papers. "Yesterday around noon, they brought in an old gentleman who might be your grandfather. He has curly gray hair and is quite haggard. He's unfortunately not responsive right now. It's quite possible that he wandered around for a long time and then collapsed from exhaustion. Why don't you go to the ward on the third floor and ask there?"

If she had been on duty an hour earlier, she would have known that the stranger was no longer a stranger, but Heinrich August Schumacher. She would have also known that a policeman had been stationed by his side to keep an eye on him.

Desperate, Anton dragged himself up the stairs. What else could he do? If he told his uncle that he hadn't found the professor perhaps he would truly drag Mareike into his shady dealings? He had only a vague idea of what that might look like. Should he risk it? Betraying the professor, on the other hand, was a game with a clear outcome.

He stepped into the hallway and asked a nurse about his supposed grandfather; she sent him to the last room on the right. Unsuspecting, he opened the door. He instantly recognized the professor, and only then caught sight of the policeman, who glanced up with interest.

"Excuse me, I'm looking for my grandfather, and the nurse at reception said it might be this gentleman here. But unfortunately, it's not. I've been looking all day, hopefully nothing has happened to him." With a bow, he pulled the door shut behind him and hurried out of the hospital. He would tell his uncle that he had done as he asked but hadn't been able to do anything else.

Alphonse Meridot was waiting. He watched Emma and James depart, retreating deeper into the entry of a building just down the street from the Egyptological collection. It took over an hour before Meerbusch also left. Meridot then strode down the street as if he were looking for an unknown address. He hesitantly climbed the steps to the gallery building's entrance, studied the door and the address sign, and seemingly compared them with a note in his hand before ringing the bell, looking all around, and miming the actions of an impatient man. Nobody watching him would have noticed how he opened the lock with a lockpick. He pushed his spectacles up his nose with a shake of his head and called out loudly, "That took you long enough, my good man," and disappeared inside.

Hesitating for a moment, he got his bearings and listened. The first thing he did was examine the exhibits in the display cases in the foyer area: original artifacts, albeit of moderate value. He pulled out his lockpick once more and then looked around the exhibition hall. He didn't recognize any obvious forgeries, nor did he discover anything of interest on the second floor. All the artifacts seemed to have been selected to suit the tastes of a public that was more interested in beauty and exoticism than in art, everyday life, and history. The visitor to this collection would experience an Egypt like the filmmakers and novelists imagined it. This gallery was guaranteed to be a great success, he thought.

Meridot then opened the rooms along the corridor on which Meerbusch's office was also located. Most of the rooms were empty, though two contained desks and worktables, and another looked like a functioning pottery workshop. Meridot clicked his tongue; things were starting to get interesting. In Meerbusch's correspondence, however, he found nothing of importance, only the usual communiques with banks, offices, and suppliers.

He then made his way to the basement, a gloomy and damp vault with numerous partitioned spaces, most of them unused. Wooden boxes were stacked in some of the chambers. He searched each one but continued to find no evidence of the mummy trade. There were statues and busts, smaller trinkets. Disappointed, he looked around. This wasn't the building Friedhelm had used for his business. How annoying! It would have fit everything so nicely.

Meridot only superficially inspected the remaining partitioned spaces; two of them held worktables scattered with receipts. In one separate room, he found a couch and a small stove. He examined this space more closely and found reddish-brown stains on the floor. Blood, he thought. Convinced that he had found Professor Schumacher's cell, he left the building, bid his invisible host farewell, and leisurely strolled down the street.

It wasn't until supper time that Anton ventured back to his uncle's house. He thought that the longer he was out, the more it would prove how eagerly he had been searching. Mareike opened the door, her eyes teary and puffy. He wrapped his arms around her in a warm hug and asked what was wrong, hoping she would tell him that her mother hadn't allowed her to have chocolate or some other treat. But Mareike said nothing; she broke free from him and dashed upstairs to her room.

He walked through the living room and the dining room, before entering the kitchen. He called out for his aunt and was met with a whimper. "Tante Lissi, where are you? Please tell me!"

He again heard the slight whimperings in the direction of the living room. Then he found her, curled up behind the sofa, her arms crossed over her face. With a jerk, Anton pulled the furniture away and knelt beside her. He spoke to her gently and asked her to look at him. When she did, he felt sick. "What...?"

She mumbled something unintelligible. He picked her up, set her on the sofa, and fetched a damp towel with which he gently dabbed her face. Then he poured her a glass of brandy and asked her to drink it.

"He was furious, so very angry."

"Does he do this a lot?"

"Not like this."

"What do you mean?"

"Not so people can see anything."

Anton's thoughts were churning as he strode into the hallway. "Mareike, come down here, right now! Mousekins, get a bag or a suitcase and pack some things for yourself. Quickly, be a good girl! Tante Lissi, I'll be right back. If my uncle comes back, promise me you won't tell him anything."

Dr. Meinhardt unlocked the front door. In the foyer, he called out to his wife that he had brought dear Herr Weinstein home with him. "Darling, I hope it won't cause you too much trouble. Do you think you can put a simple supper on the table for us?"

She replied from upstairs, "Well, you'll have to make do with mashed potatoes and vegetables." Laughing, she hurried down the stairs.

With his usual amiability, Herr Weinstein beamed at his hostess, kissed her hand, and begged her pardon for just showing up; her husband had kidnapped him.

"But no, I am delighted to have you with us again. No apologies, please."

"My dear Magda, as always, I am so pleased to be here, and I cannot think of anything more delicious than your mashed potatoes."

Monsieur Meridot wasn't the only person who wished to enter the Koblenz gallery unobserved. Friedhelm appeared soon after the Frenchman left, but he chose to go through the gardens, not willing to take even the slightest risk of being seen. He unlocked the terrace door, barricaded it from the inside with a filing cabinet, ran down the hall to the entrance, and locked the door.

Now he was lying in the basement on a cot next to the gurgling furnace. What a mess! For a long time, neither Meerbusch nor anyone else had suspected how he was using them for his own purposes. He could forget about his little business, at least in this area. And who was to blame for that? He recalled the image of Emma, standing in the window and recognizing him. He had sensed that this red witch was trouble the moment she had showed up with that portly Frenchman. She had pretended to be innocent and doe-eyed, but she was a damned hussy. Twenty or even ten years ago, that fake letter from her father, instructing her to stay in England would have been enough to make a woman fall in line and obey. Her father was going on a trip, and that was all she needed to know. But these days, young women like her thought they were entitled to have an opinion and run all over the planet. And that was the only reason why he was squatting here in this shabby hiding place, fearing for his life. He had a dark suspicion about why Karl had stopped contacting him. Karl had developed rather sticky fingers of late and believed that he could get away with everything that he'd stolen. But Karl wasn't the problem. It was Emma. All Friedhelm's troubles stemmed from that little red-headed bitch.

Then the doorbell rang and someone started banging on the door. Friedhelm started up with a jolt. He silently sprinted upstairs, crept to the second floor, and peered down cautiously out of the window. The witch herself! Standing there, asking to be let in.

James doubted the logic of what they were doing. By now it was dark, and he looked around with unease. What did Emma imagine would happen? That she could prance in and Meerbusch would suddenly know where Friedhelm was hiding, guess the professor's whereabouts, and lead them to him? He couldn't say why, but he felt like they should leave. Immediately. "Emma, this is a very stupid idea. I beg you, let's get in the car and go to the nearest police station. I must've been out of my mind to agree to this. Come on now, please!"

But Emma shook him off. She felt she was close to finding Papa. She pounded on the door one more time. Then a voice rang out, "I'm coming, just a minute!"

"Was that Meerbusch?"

"Probably. Emma, I beg you, don't ask him about that box. Say you forgot something. If it's really your father's box, let's politely apologize and notify the police."

She nodded, but her thoughts were racing. If Herr Meerbusch was still in the building, why hadn't he switched on the lights? The door opened a crack, but she couldn't see anyone. "Herr Meerbusch?"

"Fräulein Schumacher, once again!"

Emma and James wheeled around. Standing on the bottom step below them was Meerbusch. "What else can I do for you?" he asked, approaching.

"I... I lost an earring, I think... maybe in your office..." Emma stammered.

"Did you now?"

James stepped in front of Emma. "It's not all that important; we didn't mean to disturb you again. If you happen to find it, could you please send it to the Schumachers' Bonn address? Emma, come now, your aunts are expecting you." He wanted to lead her away and put her in the car. The way Meerbusch stood before them, smiling smugly, worried him.

"But now that you're here, we should look for it, don't you think?" Meerbusch took the steps in two leaps, grabbed Emma's upper arm, and pulled her with him. That was when he noticed the door, which was slightly ajar. "Did you open the door?"

"No," Emma whispered.

James tried to pull Emma free, but Meerbusch wouldn't let go. Without taking his eyes off the crack in the door, the director pulled a firearm from his coat. Small, dainty, and strangely elegant, it took Emma a moment to realize it was something other than an elegant little trinket. She tried to jerk her arm away from Meerbusch but couldn't break his grip. James sprang forward, rushing at Meerbusch, who deftly pushed him aside and pressed the gun to Emma's temple. "Quiet now!" he commanded. With the tip of his foot, he nudged the door open and, at the same time, yanked Emma in front of him.

Thinking of that moment later, she couldn't tell what happened first. The door burst open, a shot rang out, and a flash blinded her. She closed her eyes as the fingers on her arm released her. A jolt threw her to the floor, and someone stumbled over her. Then more gunshots, shouts, footsteps, silence. She opened her eyes and brushed her loosened hair from her face. The foyer was engulfed in darkness, and she seemed to be alone. Carefully she sat up, peering around hard until she got used to the darkness and could dimly make out stairs, doors, and tables. Where was James? She didn't dare to call out, but slowly crept to the entrance and pulled open the door.

Then she screamed. James was lying on the steps, his head on the sidewalk, bloodied. Rushing to him, she took his hand and patted his cheeks. His eyes fluttered, opened briefly. Then he drifted away again, unable to respond to her.

Emma tugged at his coat. Where was he injured? What was she supposed to do? She glanced up and down the street, searching all the facades. No lights, no passersby, no voices, no one to turn to. "You need a doctor! I'll be right back, okay?" She stood up and, at that same moment, felt someone grab her by the hair and yank her backwards. Crying out in pain, she struggled, trying to see who had her, but the strange hand had buried itself in her hair, causing the rest of her curls to come loose. This helped the invisible hand get a better hold on her and drag her back up the steps. With the other hand, he seized her shoulder and forced her forward, down into the basement, where he shoved her into a low chamber and locked it. No window, no crack to let light in; she could see nothing. Nor could she straighten up; the ceiling was barely shoulder height. She cautiously pushed herself forward, sliding her hands across the floor. She touched something and gasped. In front of her lay a human being. Trembling, she searched for his wrist but couldn't find a pulse. She felt for the crook of his neck and gasped. Blood! What she had just touched had to be blood! She wiped her hand frantically on the dead man's arm and slid away from him as far as she could.

Out of breath and blind with fury, Anton sprinted down the street. How different it looked now! The recently constructed houses to the left and right—square, bright, and friendly. Before today, they'd seemed like such a desirable destination for his future. They'd lost all their charm. He now suspected that there were no happy families behind the windows, only people who were oblivious to the suffering of others. Had no one ever noticed how his aunt and Mousekins were wasting away?

He turned into the neat front garden and called for Mareike to open the door for him. When she let him in, he asked her about the luggage and if she had everything she needed.

She didn't have their papers; Father kept those in the safe along with Mama's jewelry.

"Where is your Mama?"

"Still in the living room. I helped her into her coat and shoes. You want to take us with you, don't you?"

"Yes, Mousekins, I do. A cab is going to get here any minute, so get a move on. Take everything outside, and I'll get your Mama."

Mareike dragged the two packed bags through the front door while Anton carried the still half-stunned Elisabeth out of the living room. A vehicle squealed to a stop out on the street, and a car door slammed. But it wasn't the cab Anton had arranged.

It was Wilhelm Joseph Meerbusch, who took the luggage out of his daughter's hands and wrapped his fingers tightly around her wrists. "What do you think you're doing? Have we planned a family trip, dear nephew? And forgotten to invite the fair damsel's father?"

"If you let us go right now, we won't say a word. You can count on it. If only for my father's sake, I don't want a scandal. You can calmly think about where you'll go next, settle up your affairs. I don't care. Just get out of my way!"

There was real amusement in Meerbusch's face; he seemed to savor this moment. He squeezed Mareike's hands harder until she cried out. "Anton, do you think you can give me orders and advice? You're dumber than I thought. It would be better for you if you would accept your role in life as someone who takes orders. That's all you're good for, nothing else. I shouldn't be surprised that you're so sentimental and weak. Your whole generation has gone soft, just look at your friend!"

"Don't you dare say anything about Hannes!"

Meerbusch laughed. "I'll do whatever I like! He always let me call the shots for him."

"He wouldn't have stopped working for you if that had been true. But it wasn't. You didn't have power over him, like you thought you had!"

"Have you given any thought, my dear nephew, as to why he jumped? There you were, standing right in front of him, trying to help him. You probably begged him not to jump, didn't you? Just like an old granny."

Anton was silent.

"I'd be happy to explain. The simple fact is: He believed me more than he believed you. It was easy, far too easy. I offered to help him and warned him about you, told him about your anger problems, your insatiable greed, and your disappointment that he had betrayed your friendship. I would have loved to have been there when he jumped away from you, driven by nothing but fear. With every word you threw at him, with every step you took toward him, his fear of you—of you and only you, Anton!—must have grown. You didn't understand any of it, and so you became his murderer. And let me tell you something else: It will be easy for me to find witnesses for what happened and to hand you over to the police. What can you do about that? Not a single thing. It'll be your word against mine. And now this game is up. Elisabeth, into the kitchen! Now!" He didn't doubt her obedience for even a second, and instantly Elisabeth asked her nephew to carry her back inside.

Anton studied his uncle soberly and set his aunt down on a bench in the foyer. "Let go of Mareike," he said quietly.

Meerbusch laughed. Then he strode past him without haste, dragging Mareike and Elisabeth along with him. Anton let him pass.

Satisfied, Meerbusch stood with Mareike and Elisabeth in the kitchen. He wasn't surprised that Anton had backed down after his brave little show of force. Meerbusch had judged him correctly, taken control of the situation and put him in place, just as he always did. Very few people could claim that they had such powers of judgement and persuasion. Well, he had had one lapse in judgement. He had underestimated Friedhelm. But all's well that ends well, as the saying goes. And he certainly didn't need to worry that Anton would step out of line again. He pushed his Mareike and Elisabeth away from him; Mareike stumbled and crept underneath the kitchen bench, while Elisabeth sat huddled on top of it. Watching them cower, Meerbusch laughed.

Anton didn't feel much of anything as he watched Meerbusch sink to his knees. It was as if he had merely swatted a fly. He might feel differently later, but for right now, he stood over his uncle and knew he had done what needed to be done. He had saved his aunt and his niece and had put an end to a monster. A quick, merciful end. He wouldn't run, he wouldn't make excuses. He would tell it like it was.

This man had abused his wife, kidnapped people, and might even have been responsible for a death or two. He wrapped the cast-iron skillet up carefully in a kitchen towel; the police would need it. He shook out his cramped right hand. The two blows had taken all his strength.

"Please, don't look over there. I'm profoundly sorry. So very, very sorry. All these years... you shouldn't have had to go through all that. Not what happened before, and not what just happened either. Please come out of here. Go into the living room, please. I'll call the police. Everything will be all right. Mousekins, please, come out of there; it's all over now. Yes, that's it, go into the living room. Tante, keep yourself together for just a moment longer. Someone will come to help you very soon."

Still calm, he picked up the phone in the hallway and asked to be connected to the police station. It was urgent. Nothing happened; the line remained silent. Then the operator explained that she couldn't reach anyone, and that he should try again in a few minutes. As he hung up the phone, he wavered. He ran back to the kitchen and threw up. Trembling, he hung over the sink, tears streaming down his face.

At twelve past seven that evening, the train pulled to a stop at the Koblenz station.

"Do you want me to call our fellow officers now?" asked Siegfried.

"Go ahead and do that. I'll wait for you outside and see if we can get a taxi."

But Siegfried didn't reach anyone at the precinct; it was probably due to the approaching thunderstorm, the operator explained. He asked her to keep trying and to pass on a request to send officers to come to the address he gave. A potential suspect in a kidnapping and murder case might be staying there. Then he hurried to Wertheim, who was waiting in the cab.

Twenty minutes later, they found themselves driving along the new street that had seemed so strange to Anton just one hour ago. When they climbed out of the car, it was raining.

"Herr Wertheim, the garden gate and door are open. And there's luggage sitting out here..."

Wertheim drew his gun, before slipping slowly across the lawn and up the front steps. He then motioned for Siegfried to join him. "I'm going inside. I don't care about the rules right now. You stay here until I call you, understand?"

"No, sir. You wait here with me, or I'll go in with you. You told me to not go it alone, so you shouldn't do that either."

"Mertens, it's your career you're jeopardizing."

"Exactly."

As they stepped into the hallway, they both heard Anton's choking gasps. Siegfried pushed his way forward and entered the kitchen. At first, he saw only Anton, whom they had hoped to find, though not in this condition. It took a moment for Siegfried to notice that someone was lying next to the kitchen table. Pointing the gun at Anton, he bent over the man on the floor. Wertheim stepped into the room and covered the three steps to Anton, who was now slumped over on the floor. "Mertens, what happened to that man?"

"Dead. Beaten to death, I think."

"Keep looking around."

Siegfried left the kitchen, and Wertheim held a sliced onion under Anton's nose; this had worked wonders for some of his female acquaintances.

Rousing, Anton clutched at the inspector. "The bastard... the miserable bastard... my cousin, my aunt... I couldn't help it, I didn't want to do it. He should've let them go. He laughed and laughed, he always just laughed." He sobbed harder than he had sobbed in the past two decades. Still crying, he continued: "And Hannes, my good, good Hannes! He tortured him too, and I didn't do anything to help him! I just pretended that everything was all right... much earlier... I should've done this earlier... but it's just as well, isn't it, Inspector? You came just for me, didn't you?"

Wertheim sat down beside him on the kitchen floor and put an arm around his shoulder. "My boy, just calm down. Can you do that? Take a deep breath, and we'll get to the bottom of all this. Do you think you can help me? Can you focus on my questions?"

Anton looked at the inspector, and over their heads the thunderstorm hit. As lightning momentarily illuminated Wertheim's face, Anton nodded in awe. Yes, he would help him, of course; there was nothing else for him to do.

"That man over there, is that the uncle who called you yesterday?"

"Yes, that's him: my aunt's husband."

"Wilhelm Joseph Meerbusch, right?"

Anton nodded.

"And do you know who killed him?"

"I did." He pointed at the wrapped pan on the kitchen table. "With that. It wasn't hard. It was the right thing to do, wasn't it?"

"I don't know, my boy. Why did you do it?"

"He was beating my aunt, and he kidnapped Emma's father. He's a thief and a cheat. It had to be done."

"You wanted to protect your aunt. I can understand that."

James awoke in a dark room, bewildered and confused. His shoulder ached, as did the back of his head. Where could he be? Had he been tied up? With much effort, he managed to raise his arms. No rope bound him; someone had wrapped him in several blankets. But who? Why? Where? And Emma? "Emma? Emma, are you here?... Is anyone here?... Hello?"

"Shh, not so loud, or you'll wake my son. It's all right, just lie still."

"Yes, but—who are you? What am I doing here? What happened?"

"You should know that better than we do, shouldn't you? We've been taking care of you, so just be still. Your shoulder needs rest. I've called a doctor, but he probably can't get here before tomorrow morning. Don't worry, I was a hospital nurse and can handle these kinds of injuries on my own. But I'm certainly talking out of turn, aren't I? I suppose whatever's happened to you doesn't really involve me. Are you comfortable? Would you like something to drink?— Wait, I'll help you, one little sip at a time, that's it. You see, I'm Frau Müller, and we—that is, my husband and I—went out for a short evening walk, once around the block. And there you were, lying in front of the Egyptological Museum, and you had obviously been shot. At least, it was clear to me, though my husband thought you were drunk and had passed out. But I found the bullet; a shot grazed your upper arm, but it will heal. The bruise on the back of your head will hurt a bit longer. We carried you here together. Obviously, otherwise you wouldn't be here." She laughed quietly. "You should rest, and we'll see how things are in the morning. I'm going to bed now, all right? Go back to sleep."

She spoke softer and slower with each sentence, and James let her voice and the rushing rain guide him back to sleep. Tomorrow morning, yes...

The kitchen was sparkling, as was the bathroom. The living room was meticulously tidy, and Emma's bedroom looked alluringly cozy. Wearily, Christel leaned back in her brother's wing chair.

Nonetheless, all that work had done little to lessen her excitement and worry.

Jean-Baptiste came in and gave a regretful shrug; he hadn't been able to reach the nice inspector. The other officers at the station had tried to assuage his concerns. Couples in love occasionally lost track of both decency and time. Sybil snorted; her niece would never forget either.

"But maybe James' car has broken down?" suggested Alexei. "They could have stopped somewhere along the Rhine for lunch, and then the Opel wouldn't start?"

Emma was freezing. She held her knees pulled tightly up to her chin, but the cold penetrated her to the core. She wanted to move, but she feared touching the dead man again. Earlier, she had tried crawling over to the door, but she had been unable to do anything. The room was completely empty; it was just her and the dead man. Was that Meerbusch? Who had shot at them through the doorway? Why wasn't anyone coming? Even if she was scared of that person, his coming would be better than this.

She felt so cold. She rubbed her hands over her shins and shoulders, rocked back and forth, and buried her head as deeply as she could into the collar of her coat. At some point, she noticed the ongoing hissing and pattering. It must be raining, and this observation seemed strangely comforting to her. Her favorite hours were the ones she spent in her room during a downpour, snuggled up with her books and knitting. She concentrated on that memory, dreaming herself into her down bed and imagining the rumbling coal stove. It almost helped. Then there was a crash, and something hit the ground with a roar, outside of her prison. She listened. The water splashed and rushed, gurgling and turbulent, as if someone were running a bath. Suddenly she felt wetness seeping through her shoes. Reaching to the floor, her fingers made a little splash. She felt all around her; the water was at least a good half inch high, and it seemed to be rising. She scrambled to the door and kicked it, but it didn't budge. More and more water flowed through the crack under the door. Not much, but steadily. The splashing sounds grew louder and louder. And once again, she heard a rattling noise, and she suspected that it must be the gutter, which hadn't withstood the onslaught of water and was now somehow directing the rain into this cellar. She put her ear to the wall, and the adjacent room really did seem to be flooding from the outside. Starting to feel panicked, she kicked the door as water continued to pour inside.

Mertens and Wertheim left the Koblenz precinct; their colleagues had recommended an inn that offered good food and decent rooms. Anton Wagenknecht was in custody and would be transferred to Bonn sometime next week. The interference by the Bonn officers had been settled to mutual satisfaction, and they had also been informed of the finding of the professor. Tired and hungry, the inspector and his assistant retired to the inn and sat down at a table, both eager to end the long day in a peaceful manner. Tomorrow morning they would accompany their Koblenz colleagues when they searched the museum; it was too late and too damp for that today, and besides, there was nothing at the museum that could run away from them, now was there?

"Ah, what a pleasant surprise on this soggy evening! Do you mind, Herr Mertens, if I join you? Or do the two of you good sirs have something to discuss that I would interrupt?"

Siegfried and Wertheim glanced up. "You would be most welcome! Please, do take a seat. Herr Wertheim, surely you don't mind? May I introduce Monsieur Meridot from the Louvre in Paris? I have told you about him."

Wertheim stood up and shook the Frenchman's hand, explaining that Mertens hadn't merely told him about him. No, his assistant had spoken of him with marked enthusiasm. Meridot smiled and defended himself, saying that he was very seldom the object of any enthusiasm, but that Herr Mertens possessed a high degree of adventurousness and zeal, as befitted a young man.

Wertheim chuckled; Monsieur Meridot was uttering the truth there, but unfortunately it was his task as Mertens' superior officer to channel these abilities into solid police work. "Mertens, don't look so offended; we'll get there! Let Monsieur Meridot and I have a little fun teasing you a bit. If I thought you were nothing more than a dreamer, you wouldn't be sitting here right now."

As they enjoyed their suppers, Meridot and Wertheim recounted the dicey situations, dangerous moments, and funny incidents they had encountered over the years. The three of them philosophized about good and evil, and it wasn't until late in the evening that they got around to what had brought them together. Meridot was relieved to hear the story of Professor Schumacher's escape, while he shook his head regretfully over the death of Meerbusch, who could no longer serve him as a source of further information. After some hesitation, he confessed to the two civil servants of breaking into Meerbusch's museum earlier that evening and asked that he be allowed to join them on their visit tomorrow.

OCTOBER 31, 1926

At three o'clock in the morning, Alphonse Meridot woke with a start. Still bleary, he wondered what he had been dreaming about when the knock at his door had interrupted his sleep. He got up quietly and pulled a dainty revolver out from under his pillow.

"Yes?" he asked, without opening the door.

"Pardon me, Monsieur Meridot, may I come in? Something important has occurred to me."

"Herr Mertens? One moment, please." Meridot stowed his weapon and opened the door.

Siegfried stood before him in his coat, his pajama pants peeking out beneath it. "I couldn't sleep, and when the rain let up, I thought it would be a good idea to take a short walk. When I passed by this hotel and remembered you were staying here, I took that as a sign. I'm sorry. Did I wake you up?"

"Well, yes, you did, but I'm accustomed to such things. I rarely get my information during normal business hours. But how can I help you?"

"You see, Wertheim always tells me to trust my instincts without blindly holding on to them. What I can't get out of my head now is just one little thing. I was at the hospital earlier, after the local officers told us that the professor had been found. Unfortunately, he is still unconscious, but the doctor said that he's optimistic. And then he explained his diagnosis in some detail, but while he was doing that, my attention must have wandered. Only a little while ago did I remember something he'd said. He called Schumacher's sister about half past eight, and she said she would come as soon as her niece returned home. I'm sure it's just my imagination that is making a big deal about this, but I just keep asking myself, shouldn't James and Fräulein Schumacher be home by now? It takes less than two hours to get to Bonn by car. You told us that they left Meerbusch's gallery around half past three. But they still hadn't arrived back in Bonn by half past eight? If something had come up, Fräulein Schumacher would have contacted her aunt. I mean, I don't know what they decided to do. Maybe they wanted to be alone and were planning to tell a little lie when they got home. I apologize, Monsieur Meridot, I shouldn't have woken you up." Siegfried was about to leave, but Meridot held him back. Mertens' concern didn't seem all that silly. "You are worried about your friends. That's understandable and quite decent of you. And you're right, they should have gotten home a long time ago. From what I know of your friends, I'd be surprised if they let others worry for the sake of a brief moment of pleasure."

"Friends? I—but no, it's just this case. I wasn't even sure for a long time if Mr. Beresford might not be—but that doesn't matter."

"What do you suspect?"

"I don't want to call it a hunch, but are you sure that James and Fräulein Schumacher actually left the gallery?"

"Yes, absolutely sure."

Siegfried sighed, then said goodbye before apologizing yet one more time. But Meridot called him back once more. "I have a suggestion: our only clue is the gallery itself, so that's where you and I are going to take a look around."

Emma kept nodding off, but she startled awake whenever she slid all the way down to the floor. She was crouched with her back against the door and her knees pressed against her chest, trying to stay as far away from the cold water as possible. She had her coat wrapped tightly around her with the collar turned up. For a long time, she had been scared the cellar would fill up and she would drown. When the rain finally tapered off, she sobbed with relief.

But there she still squatted, frozen through, wet and exhausted, with a dead man next to her. She wouldn't last much longer. Her body ached, burned, trembled; breathing was difficult, and she realized that if she fell asleep just then, she might never wake up. Yet why should she keep fighting to stay awake? If the door opened, then it was bound to be the man who had locked her in there. Whatever he intended to do with her, he wouldn't be bringing her flowers. Drowning almost seemed merciful in comparison. But then...

She thought of Tante Tinni and Aunt Sybil, of Papa and Grandmother. And of James. And of Anton a little, too. She would have liked to believe she could will them to her location through the power of her own thoughts. But could James even still come? Was he alive? She leaned out of her crouching position onto her knees and considered sliding down further onto the floor just to stretch her arms and legs out for a moment. She longed to stand upright and straighten her back. With difficulty, she resisted the temptation and lowered her head back down to her bent knees, which she hugged tightly.

"Herr Mertens, you should look away. You shouldn't watch me open a lock without authorization."

"Nonsense. We should compare techniques sometime."

"You can...? You know, you should probably reevaluate your attitude toward law and order. But for now, let's go in."

"Show me the pottery workshop. Did you take a closer look in there?" Meridot answered to the negative and led Siegfried to the room. "What do you think Meerbusch set up this workshop for?"

"His reasoning might have sounded innocent enough. Perhaps for making copies of smaller items to be sold to interested visitors. However, I don't believe that. Forgeries were more likely to be made in here than replicas."

After pulling on his gloves, Siegfried rummaged through the drawers and shelves. In the bottom drawer of a narrow chest, he found several drawings, specifically of a cat that he recognized immediately. These had to be the professor's originals, he thought. The sketches stolen from his house had just been found in the museum of the man who, according to Anton, had arranged for Schumacher's abduction. He showed them to Meridot.

"I think we should take another look around Meerbusch's office. I was only interested in his correspondence and calendar before, but I remember there were some sculptures in there, too. Forgive my carelessness; I was only focused on my search for the mummies."

In Meerbusch's office, Meridot left the search to Siegfried while he took a seat on the sofa. After a few minutes, the latter called out joyfully, "Meridot, look—the cat! In the flesh, so to speak. Which one do you think it is?"

Meridot took the figurine from him. "It's the fake one made of marble, so it was also taken from the professor's house."

Still searching the room, Siegfried uttered another cheer. "It just keeps getting better! Do you know what this is? This is Schumacher's seal set. From everything Anton has told us so far, Meerbusch was convinced he had planned everything down to the last detail. That's where he made his mistake—in his exaggerated planning and in his ignorance of human nature. He felt he just had to seal the letters he sent in Schumacher's name. If he had made sure the professor took along pants, underwear, and shirts instead of this set, who knows? His daughter might have accepted the story she was told. But she was perfectly right: who leaves on an impromptu trip and takes nothing with him but this unwieldy little box?"

"There, you see once again how we all have to be careful not to follow only one train of thought. This isn't just true for Meerbusch, but also for you and me. I didn't give a single thought to that cat yesterday afternoon, despite the fact I had spoken to Fräulein Schumacher about it. Draw your own conclusions from that, Mr. Mertens."

"I still have a lot to learn; that's what I've learned so far."

"Would you like to look around some more?"

"Yes. Want to help?"

Emma lifted her head. It seemed to be getting colder and darker. Was she already losing her senses, or had she heard something? Footsteps? Should she call out? She had nothing to lose. Then, she heard voices.

"Let's check the basement tomorrow. It looks like it's underwater."

"Whatever you like."

Mertens and Meridot were turning around when they suddenly heard loud thuds below them.

"Hello? Is someone down here? Identify yourself!"

Emma yelled, "Here, I'm here! Please, get me out, please, please!" Siegfried took the last three steps in one leap and hurried through the icy water, ripping open all the doors until he finally came to the locked coal shaft where Emma had lost hope that anyone would find her.

At his heels, Meridot asked Siegfried to step aside and set about unlocking the door with his tools. When it burst open, Emma tumbled out. Siegfried caught her and picked her up off her feet.

Meridot wrapped his coat around her blue-tinged, half-frozen form, shivering in Siegfried's arms. "Mademoiselle, we're taking you straight to the hospital."

They carried her to Meerbusch's office, where she finally fainted. Meridot called for a cab, and half an hour later, Emma was lying among several warming pans in a bed just two floors above her father's. Until late Sunday afternoon, she slept so soundly that not even the hourly changing of hot water bottles could wake her.

James, on the other hand, woke up with the sun. And with an aching skull that wouldn't let him hold a clear thought. In bewilderment, he stared into the eyes of the doctor who had finally found the time to check up on him. This visit wasn't absolutely necessary: Dr. Wagner had worked with Frau Müller during the war and was aware that she would have made an excellent doctor had German society been less intolerant of female doctors or intelligent women in general. In any case, Wagner informed James that thanks to her skill, he would be left with little more than a romantic scar once all was said and done. Now the police would have to be notified and the culprit punished, and then the young man could put this episode behind him.

Suddenly, James came back to life: the police. Siegfried. Meerbusch. Emma. Where was she? With both hands, he reached for the doctor, pulled himself upright, and asked about everything he could think of. Confused and muddled questions. Dr. Wagner had trouble making sense of them, but then he caught the name Schumacher.

"Schumacher? We admitted to the hospital a Professor Schumacher yesterday morning, and last night, we were joined by a Fräulein Schumacher. What an amazing coincidence! Within the span of twenty-four hours, our clinic admitted first the father, then the daughter, both severely hypothermic and unresponsive. Please calm down, young man! I can't make sense of your babbling. Slow down, please, just one sentence at a time. Both are doing moderately well, but I believe I will be able to hand the girl back to you in very good condition. So, stay here for the time being. No excitement and no contradictions! You are in the best possible hands with Frau Müller, and you will be going home tomorrow morning."

The aunts and Alexei were already on the train to Koblenz by seven-thirty in the morning; Herr Mertens had put through a call to them shortly after six to inform them about Emma. With some trepidation, he had then made his way to the inn to confess his nocturnal adventure to Inspector Wertheim. Nor did he omit the fact that he had illegally broken into the Egyptological Museum.

"Siegfried, the trouble you get into when I'm not around! What do you expect from me now? Should I read you the riot act or grant you a pardon? There is a reason why even the police are not allowed to do whatever they like. Do not think that you are above these rules, just because your transgression has led to something positive. On the other hand, I do not want you to blindly obey every rule out there. Once you do that, your personal sense of self-responsibility ends. That's why I'm going to simply walk away from this matter. I have no idea about what's been going on, and you can sort all this out by yourself. That's what it's like sometimes, though sometimes it isn't. How is Fräulein Schumacher doing?"

"She's quite weak, but it doesn't seem to be serious."

"Good, I'm glad to hear that. I suggest you and I have breakfast now, and then we'll explain your latest offense to our Koblenz colleagues."

Around eleven o'clock, Christel, Sybil, and Alexei arrived at the hospital. While Sybil and her Russian went upstairs to Emma, Christel marched to her brother's bedside. There he lay before her, gaunter than he had been in the prior thirty years and more silent than she had ever seen him. The nurse pushed a chair to the bedside and told her that Herr Schumacher had opened his eyes once briefly that morning and his pulse had been gaining strength. With a little time and attentive nursing, he would soon be walking around again. With that, the nurse left the brother and sister alone.

Christel took Heinrich's hand and squeezed it. "What an awful, stupid boy you are—what have you gotten yourself into again? But just wait and see, I'll get you back on your feet again."

She patted his hand, and he mumbled, barely audible: "Christel, be a dear and make me some Rievekooche."

"Heinrich, are you awake now? Say something!" But he hadn't moved even a little in his pillows.

"Nurse, please come quick! My brother just spoke to me! He wants some potato pancakes!"

The nurse hurried over, looked at the patient, and felt his pulse. "Don't worry, he'll be fine. He's asleep now. What was that about potato pancakes? It'll be a while before he's allowed to dine like usual."

Entering quietly, Sybil leaned down to Christel and told her that Emma would have to stay in the hospital for the week. She had pneumonia.

Christel nodded. "Oh, I'm not too worried about Emma; she's a tough one. During the war, she even survived the Spanish flu. Is the girl awake? Can I see her?"

"We'd like to come back this afternoon. The doctor said she should be awake by then for sure. How is my brother-in-law?"

"He wants potato pancakes! He'll be just fine. And as for the three of us, let's go have a delicious lunch somewhere, shall we?"

James ate lunch too. The Müllers were treating him as if he were an old family friend. Afterwards, however, he couldn't hold out any longer. He asked for a taxi to take him to the clinic, thanked the couple from the bottom of his heart for their generous hospitality, and promised to contact them about repaying them for what he owed them.

"You don't owe us anything," the couple objected.

"I'm afraid I will... My wallet must have fallen out of my pocket, and I won't be able to pay for the cab without your help." James blushed. He had never asked anyone other than his father for money before.

Herr Müller laughed good naturedly, pulled his wallet out of his vest pocket, handed James some bills, then called the cab James had requested. Before doing so, however, he made James promise to call them back if he started to feel unwell again or was unable to return home that day for any reason.

James had just stepped out of the car and was paying the driver when Siegfried and Wertheim approached him from the other side of the street. "Mr. Beresford, it's nice to see you, and now we're all back together again. However, you look rather the worse for wear. What happened to you?"

James kept his explanation brief, eager to see Emma.

"Well, the best thing for you is to find another bed as quickly as possible. Mertens and I, we wanted to check on a few things here in Frankfurt before we left. Let us help you up the steps. You still look fairly wobbly on your feet. Well, look at the three of us, arm in arm—shouldn't we sing a little song or something?"

"You're in high spirits, Inspector."

"It's just a façade, believe me. I wish we could have reached Herr Wagenknecht before he killed Meerbusch. It's weighing on me, that's all."

James didn't understand what the inspector was talking about, but he wasn't really listening either.

Siegfried, on the other hand, drew his brows together. "It seems to me that that bastard doesn't deserve much pity, Inspector!"

"Oh, my boy, think about it. What about the Wagenknecht boy? How do you think he'll feel for the rest of his life? And just think what we have to put together now—your bastard could have told us all sorts of things. And, oh! I can think of one other thing that will annoy you. The Koblenz officers just informed me that they found a dead man in the coal bin. Did Fräulein Schumacher say anything to you about that?"

Siegfried stopped so abruptly that James stumbled, but Wertheim kept him from falling. "In that little cubbyhole? No, she didn't say anything about that, but she hardly said anything when we found her. Who do you think we're talking about?"

"Apparently one Maximilian Friedhelm. Shot. Probably by Meerbusch, whom we can't question anymore."

"So he came back to Koblenz after all! I wish I'd stuck with Meridot. We could have nabbed that crook!"

By then they had reached the fourth floor. After depositing James in a chair outside Emma's room, the officers knocked on her door. A nurse opened it and explained that the patient was asleep. James scrambled to his feet.

"I'm her fiancé, so please let me see her. As you can imagine, I'm going out of my mind with worry."

She sighed and let him in. "But only for a moment!"

Supported by Siegfried, he stepped through the doorway. Emma looked small and delicate to him. Her face was whiter than the sheets, and her red curls, caught in two tight braids, seemed to draw all color to themselves. Her breath rattled.

"Is she going to be all right? Dr. Wagner said she has pneumonia. Is she stable? When will she wake up?"

"We're taking care of her, so don't worry."

"May I sit here? Please."

The nurse replied in the negative. If they let that start, she muttered, crowds of young men would start hanging around the women's ward.

Mertens and Wertheim helped James downstairs to the reception area. "What are we going to do with you, Mr. Beresford? We can't leave you sitting here. How are you going to get back to Bonn? Do you think you're up for taking the train? If so, you can ride back with us."

"My car's here. It's parked in front of the museum."

"There aren't any cars along there. What kind is it?"

"An Opel, four-seater, red."

"There was one like that in front of Meerbusch's house. The Koblenz police are having a look at it as we speak. But are you fit to drive?"

Once again, chance intervened in a way that neither Siegfried nor Wertheim found easy to believe. At that moment, Alexei led the Misses Feuerhahn and Mallaby up the hospital stairs and discovered their friend in the lobby. "James! We were wondering where you were. How are you doing? What happened?"

All three bombarded James with questions, hardly any of which he could answer satisfactorily. Wertheim interrupted the barrage and asked if the good Russian knew how to drive a car. Alexei nodded.

"Wait a minute. Siegfried, order us a cab, and I'll make a quick call to the precinct. Maybe they'll release James' car to us."

A few minutes later, he walked back up to the small group, beaming, and addressed Alexei: "Come with me to the station. We can pick up James' car, and then you can drive it back to Bonn today."

NOVEMBER

Christel decided to stay in Koblenz for the time being, which resulted in the household at 13a Arndtstraße going through a considerable transformation. Sybil approached Frau Vianden first thing Monday morning and asked about the rooms on the third floor, which were dusty and had been consigned to oblivion.

"Yes, those were the servants' quarters. Musta been twenty years since someone lived up there."

"Let's go take a look at them now. Alexei, Jean, up you go. James, you stay down here and take care of the kitten. It needs love and warmth, which you've got in spades!"

Under the sloping roofline, six minuscule rooms with tiny windows faced each other across a narrow passageway. Nonetheless, Alexei could stand upright in the little rooms, so Sybil decided they were usable. The trio cleared out one chamber after the other, dragging dilapidated beds, moth-eaten curtains, rusty coat hooks, broken chairs, and ramshackle lampshades down the stairs. Frau Vianden met the challenge with glee, scrubbing the floors and cleaning the windowpanes with such aplomb that the others could only gaze at her in awe.

In one of the little rooms, Sybil discovered two wardrobes and three chests in which Heinrich had stored Charlotte's old clothes. She found herself unexpectedly caught up in memories of her own: the ball gown she had admired on her nineteen-year-old sister, Charlotte's wedding dress, maternity skirts, embroidered blouses, and even Emma's baby dress. They all evoked the life of Sybil's lost sister and a time that felt strange and long ago. For an hour, Sybil brushed out the dresses, placed cedar and lavender in the compartments, and then closed the door behind her, wondering if Emma even knew about the room.

When Frau Vianden left the house after a long day of work, the three others sat down wearily at the table with James, who was curious about what all the cleaning meant. Alexei didn't know the answer either: "Say, kitten, we've been helping out nicely, but what for?"

"Well, we're moving in here until our dance academy earns enough money for us to find a place of our own. Jean is also going to give notice on his lodgings; this game of hide-and-seek is simply ridiculous at your age, you know. And we're not shipping James off to the boarding house every night anymore, where he's all by himself."

Jean-Baptiste was about to protest, but Sybil cut him off. "Christel will be glad if she doesn't have to make all the decisions anymore. When you move to France, it will relieve her to know that Emma isn't living here alone with her father. For all I know, they're both complete nincompoops when it comes to running a household. And what will happen then? Christel will refuse to leave."

"That's all well and good for you, you're family. But I can't just move in here!" interjected James.

"Fiddlesticks! First of all, Alexei isn't family either, and secondly, I don't have the energy to argue with your nonsense. For the next few days, Jean will sleep in Christel's room, James in Emma's, and Alexei with me. Tomorrow morning we'll buy some beds and whatever else it takes to get the chambers ready, and then you can take up residence there, like civilized and proper gentlemen," Sybil declared with a wink at Alexei.

"You'll stay with me, of course. It's not like I give one whit about what the Privy Council widows think of me. Jean, you take care of the craftsmen. One of the chambers must be turned into a bathroom. Surely that's doable, and perhaps pairs of rooms can be combined to create larger spaces. Money opens a lot of doors, doesn't it? But please negotiate decent prices. If I'm not going to marry a wealthy man, I need to start living on a budget!"

Sybil's money truly worked wonders; the very next afternoon, a master carpenter set about knocking down the attic walls. When Christel called, she could hardly make out a single word over the loud knocks and thuds that traveled down the telephone wires. However, Sybil deftly ignored her suspicious questions about what was going on there, a skill she had acquired from her previous marriages. Although she felt sorry for Emma and her father, she was not displeased to learn that both of them would have to stay in Koblenz until the following week. Their conditions were improving steadily, but Heinrich in particular was quite ill and Emma was recovering slower than they had hoped. The doctors were satisfied with her physical condition; she no longer had a fever and could breathe more freely. But she was withdrawn, frequently broke down in tears, and reacted to others with sensitivity and fear. Christel hoped that this would fade once the father and daughter were finally allowed to see each other but both had been ordered to strict bed rest. This meant that Christel was constantly running up and down the hospital stairs to deliver messages between Heinrich and Emma. If this continued, she would demand her own bed on the fourth floor!

Over the next few days, paperhangers, carpet installers, and carpenters came and went, transforming the forgotten attic into a cozy suite of rooms with a bathroom. Jean-Baptiste proved to be a hard negotiator, and Sybil marveled at how little the renovation was costing her compared to one of her Parisian designer dresses.

After the furniture and curtains were in place and Sybil had finished decorating the space with her light touch, Frau Vianden offered her highest praise: "Oh, Mrs. Mallaby, you've done yourself proud up here. I would be willing to clean up here for free!"

Finally, the Schumachers were released to return home on Tuesday, and although James objected, Alexei drove to Koblenz before sunrise in his place to fetch them. Jean-Baptiste consoled James with a stroll through town, where he purchased more books, flowers, and candies than Emma could reasonably read, admire, and consume. In addition, Sybil procured a housecoat for her brother-in-law, a very non-transparent flannel nightgown for Emma, and an embroidered apron for Christel.

At four o'clock in the afternoon, Alexei drove up with the trio, safe and sound. Unusually self-conscious, Sybil greeted her sister's widower, who gave her a friendly hug and complimented her appearance. But she waved him off, saying that there were truly more important things in life, and that she was grateful from the bottom of her heart to see him hale and healthy and to have her niece with her again.

"Children, we're just standing around here in the hallway. Emma and Heinrich need to get back to bed now, and I want to finally see my kitchen again." Christel shooed everyone away.

When the convalescents were in their rooms, Sybil took Christel aside. "I have a confession to make. Will you please follow me?"

She nervously showed her handiwork to the other woman.

Dispassionately, Christel looked at one room after another, then exclaimed, "So this is what you've been up to? All that beautiful money! But, oh, how nice it is up here. Just right for James and Alexei!"

"Well, I was actually thinking of James and Jean..."

James hurried to Emma, who was lying obediently in her bed and cuddling with the kitten. He hugged her and sat on the edge of the bed. "Darling, you have no idea how worried I've been about you. I'm so glad to have you with me again! But what's wrong? You look so downcast."

Emma sighed. "I'm not melancholy; I'm just wrestling with myself. I've been thinking a lot these past few days, and something keeps bothering me. Would you be so kind as to hand me that red box on the shelf?"

James brought it to her, wondering what might be inside. She plucked it impatiently from his hands, lifted the lid, and rummaged around inside until she triumphantly pulled out a pair of scissors. Before James could even guess at what she was planning, Emma had grabbed her long red braid and was slicing the shears into it. One strand after another plopped onto her pillow.

"Emma! Your beautiful hair, I beg you! Emma!"

"Look in the table drawer—no, the other one—yes, pass me that ribbon and the little blue box in there. Thank you."

Speechless, he settled down beside her and watched as she calmly and serenely tied up the cut hair and placed it on her nightstand. Then she opened the etui and removed the necklace Grandmother had given her. She handed it to him and turned a little to the side.

"Will you put it on me, please? Look" —she opened the locket— "this is Mama. With her red curls. I used to think they were the only thing I had of hers, but now this long hair only reminds me of the way that man grabbed me and dragged me away. Can you at least try to understand what that feels like to me?"

To James' astonishment, tears sprang to his eyes. He lightly touched her newly exposed neck, kissed her gently on the cheek, and held her tightly, as if by doing so he could protect her from everything, from the future as well as the past.

When Sybil looked in on Emma an hour later, she was shocked. "Emma dear, what have you done?"

Emma explained her decision one more time. Sybil studied her critically, picked up Emma's brush, and worked with the remaining curls, pushing them here and there, pinning the sides, parting them in the middle. She finally shook her head. "I'm going to schedule an appointment for you at Salon Mirabelle with Madame Mirabeau herself. You can't stay looking like this. And we'll have a wig made from this braid."

"Gladly. Before you go, could you please pass me my writing materials?"

Emma felt like she needed to write down what she had experienced in order to wrap everything up. A letter to Daphne certainly lent itself to that. She began with the Bastet she had found, and with Papa's letters and postcards dictated to him by Meerbusch to keep her away. She wrote about the mummies and about Weinstein and Meridot, Siegfried and Wertheim. She also set down on paper the terrible hours she had spent in the garden shed and the horrible night in the flooded cellar. Tears smeared the ink in many of the lines. Then she continued:

> *Since all this happened, Siegfried Mertens has informed me about how everything is connected—as far as they can know, at least, since both men (that is, Friedhelm and Meerbusch) are now dead. Siegfried came all the way to Koblenz just to tell me the final story. No, no, he isn't in love with me, not in the slightest, but I suspect we might become good friends. Well then, let me see if I can get the facts all pulled together.*
>
> *Meerbusch had a long history of shady business dealings, and we don't know how, when and why, but for some reason, he decided to try to make a profit from Egyptomania. He had dealt with Friedhelm in the past and believed he could trust him. Friedhelm, in turn, thought he would never find a better cover than that supplied by another crook, especially one whose primary goal was to maintain a respectable façade. This meant that Friedhelm could offer his customers mummies, but henceforth as an employee of a museum. If someone figured out the scam, he could have just blamed everything on Meerbusch.*
>
> *Meerbusch had no clue when it came to Egyptian history, which was why he needed someone who could produce the fakes. He probably got a lot of them from Egypt directly—you*

wouldn't believe how vibrant the counterfeit trade is there! But that wasn't enough for him; he wanted something special, as I already explained in quoting Meridot. And that's where Anton came in. Anton had a friend who not only knew Egyptian history—because he had studied with Papa and Neumann!—but who was also quite talented when it came to painting, modeling and carving.

His name was Johannes, and at some point in the spring, the two of them dreamed up a joke: they wanted to find out who was the better connoisseur, Neumann or Papa. Johannes copied one of the statuettes from the Bonn collection and presented it to both of them. He had practically convinced Papa, but he was too nervous. Papa took a shot in the dark and claimed the figurine was a copy. He asked Johannes what he was going to do with it. Papa believed Johannes' claim that he wanted to transfer to art school and to present this as his application project. If Papa agreed to write up an evaluation on the figure, then Johannes was bound to be admitted. Papa took this all in good faith, so he went along with it.

Anton didn't realize all that his uncle was capable of, and he told him about what had happened. That's when Meerbusch's plan was born. Johannes would make the forgeries, and Papa would write the evaluations for them. Meerbusch approached Johannes first, who as a penniless student was open to suggestions. Hannes was to produce a few forgeries, and if they sold, he was to continue. Meerbusch wanted to increase his business and truly believed that Papa was also interested in making some money. He came to Bonn and asked him, but Papa refused, of course. I imagine this must have presented a tricky problem for Meerbusch, which explains why he sent Friedhelm to kidnap Papa.

Now he had Papa and thought Johannes would produce the forgeries and Papa would write the evaluations. But Johannes unexpectedly got cold feet. Meerbusch played on his fears, told him he couldn't get out of their arrangement, and made him afraid of Anton, of all people. So the poor boy killed himself, even though Anton wanted to help him.

Anton, by the way, was supposed to keep an eye on me, and that was how Meerbusch knew that I had found the marble cat. So he sent Anton to steal it. To think that he was always around me, and I had no idea what danger I was in… Siegfried said he will probably go to jail, but not for manslaughter or murder. I feel sorry for him and am rather glad for the sake of his aunt and niece that he killed that man. I know I shouldn't think that, but they are now free, thanks to him.

I just wonder why he brought me that letter from his uncle, which put me on his track in the first place. And why do you think he asked me to marry him? Did his uncle want that, or did he really like me? Siegfried says I could visit him in prison after the trial and ask him, but I don't think that's necessary. After all, I am very much in love with James. I think. I've never been in love before, but that's what it must be. I'll tell you more about that some other time. My fingers hurt now from writing so much.

But I still have to tell you about Papa's double. It may surprise you, yet I almost feel sorry for him. He was a poor fellow who simply had the bad luck of showing up at Meerbusch's house one day in the hope of selling something. Meerbusch was trying to come up with a way to proceed so that Papa wouldn't betray him. Then, there was this man: younger than Papa, but with the same gray shaggy hair, the same paunch, and an extensive knowledge about all sorts of things. That's when he made the man a business proposition. His name was Klepper. For the first few weeks, he had to read up as much as he could about Egypt, so as not to be discovered immediately, then he sent him off.

It's ironic, isn't it, that there is no honor among thieves. Friedhelm was marketing corpses right under Meerbusch's nose, and Klepper thought nobody would notice him filching things from the galleries. He just wanted to make his wife's life easier. But when Meerbusch heard about it, he killed him with his bare hands! After that, Friedhelm must have grown careless as a result of being scared that Meerbusch would find out about his secret activities too. In the end, Meerbusch shot him. And I was caught in the middle of it all! Horrible, isn't it?

Emma wrote a little more about the motives of the crooks and ended the letter with the hope that Daphne might send her a cheerful note in response. When she had written the last word, she heaved a sigh of relief. She had shut the door on what had happened and finally felt at peace.

On Friday, Emma, cheerful and fully recovered, headed to the Mirabelle Beauty Salon for her transformation. More than anything, she wanted to appear modern, chic, and confident.

As she entered, her eyes fell on the shop window. A notice announced that the salon was looking for a secretary—young, hardworking, and with excellent knowledge of English and French. Could it possibly be a sign of things to come?

THE MEDITERRANEAN SEA

Heinrich August Schumacher sat on the deck, wrapped head to toe in a woolly blanket as he gazed out over the glittering waves. He had only a few more days at sea until Alexandria, where Zahi Saddik would meet him and take him on to Cairo. His eyes followed the flying fish leaping over the waves. He was enjoying every moment of the journey; with each passing day, he drew closer to the warmth that the doctors had recommended for him.

All the ghastliness of the last few months have finally paid off, he thought. If it hadn't been for all that, he wouldn't have been invited to Egypt for a six-month stay. He wouldn't be looking forward to working in the museum at Cairo or to meeting Howard Carter in person. Even if he hadn't personally done a thing, his case had resulted in putting a gang of smugglers out of business. Monsieur Meridot, whom he only knew from a few letters, had arranged for all this by providing the necessary introductions. And indeed, the invitation from the museum had arrived in Bonn quickly, along with the boat tickets. He didn't have to pay for any of it. His arrival was being impatiently awaited, and his hosts wanted him to have a marvelous time and hoped for his cooperation in their work.

He had grinned and laughed so much in recent days that his jaw ached. His only regret was for Emma, whom he had left behind after only two weeks together. She had surprised him with her stubborn determination: she would remain in Bonn and travel to England once a year. She had said, "And that's that!" and forbade any further discussion. She had accepted a job in town, which meant that there would be someone to take care of him once Christel moved to Toulouse.

The professor had made one request, however. Christel could marry in his absence, but he asked her to not move until he was back home. She had promised him that, and he had to admit that he rather liked Monsieur Barbier: down-to-earth, honorable, highly competent, and a charming conversationalist. And what a cook!

What would happen next? Who could possibly know? They would simply have to wait and see. For here and now, he was content, floating across the sea, his lifelong dream just beyond the horizon.

Printed in the USA
CPSIA information can be obtained
at www.ICGtesting.com
CBHW011515060724
11156CB00012B/138

9 781685 770136